BEING ALIVE IS WONDERFUL.

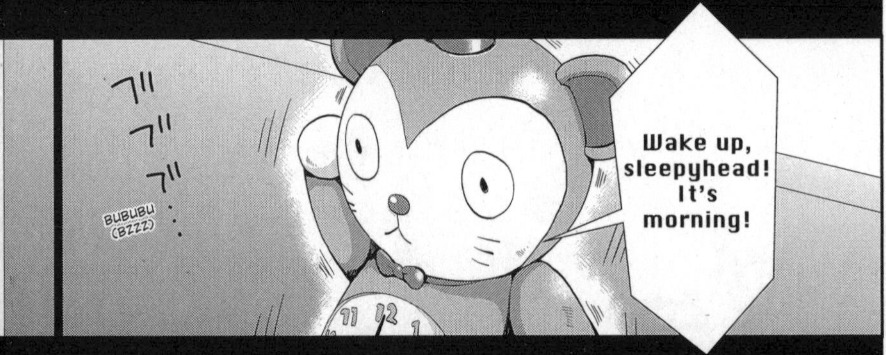
Wake up, sleepyhead! It's morning!
ブブブ・・・
BUBUBU (BZZZ)

I...

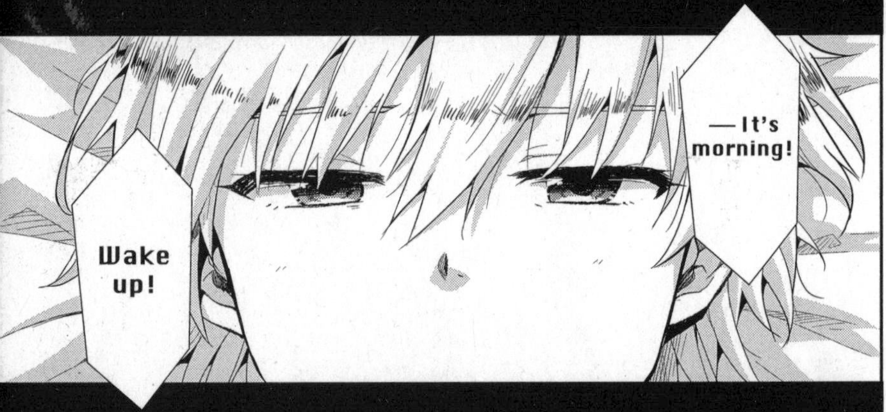
—It's morning!
Wake up!

...WON'T GIVE IN.

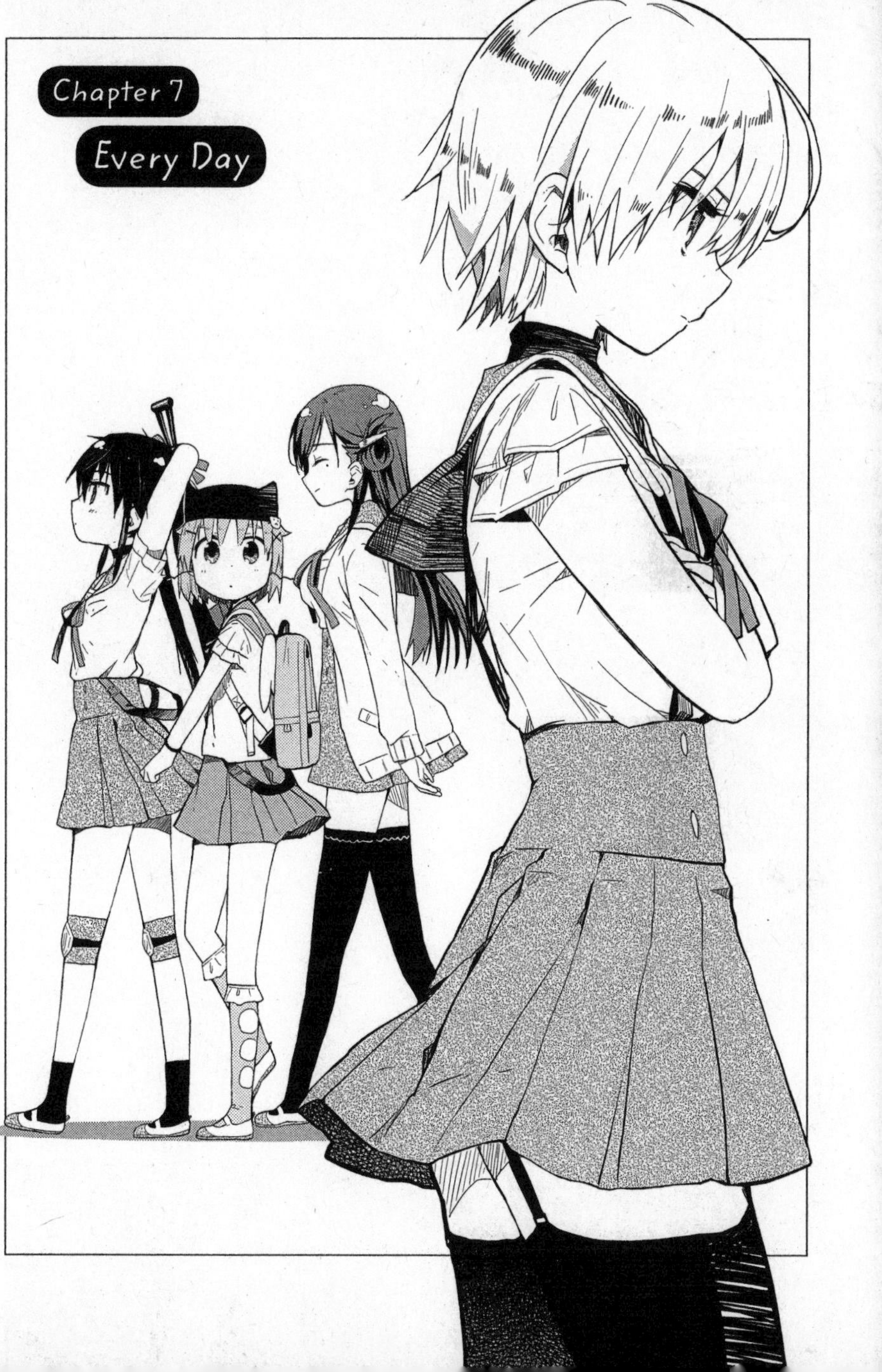
Chapter 7
Every Day

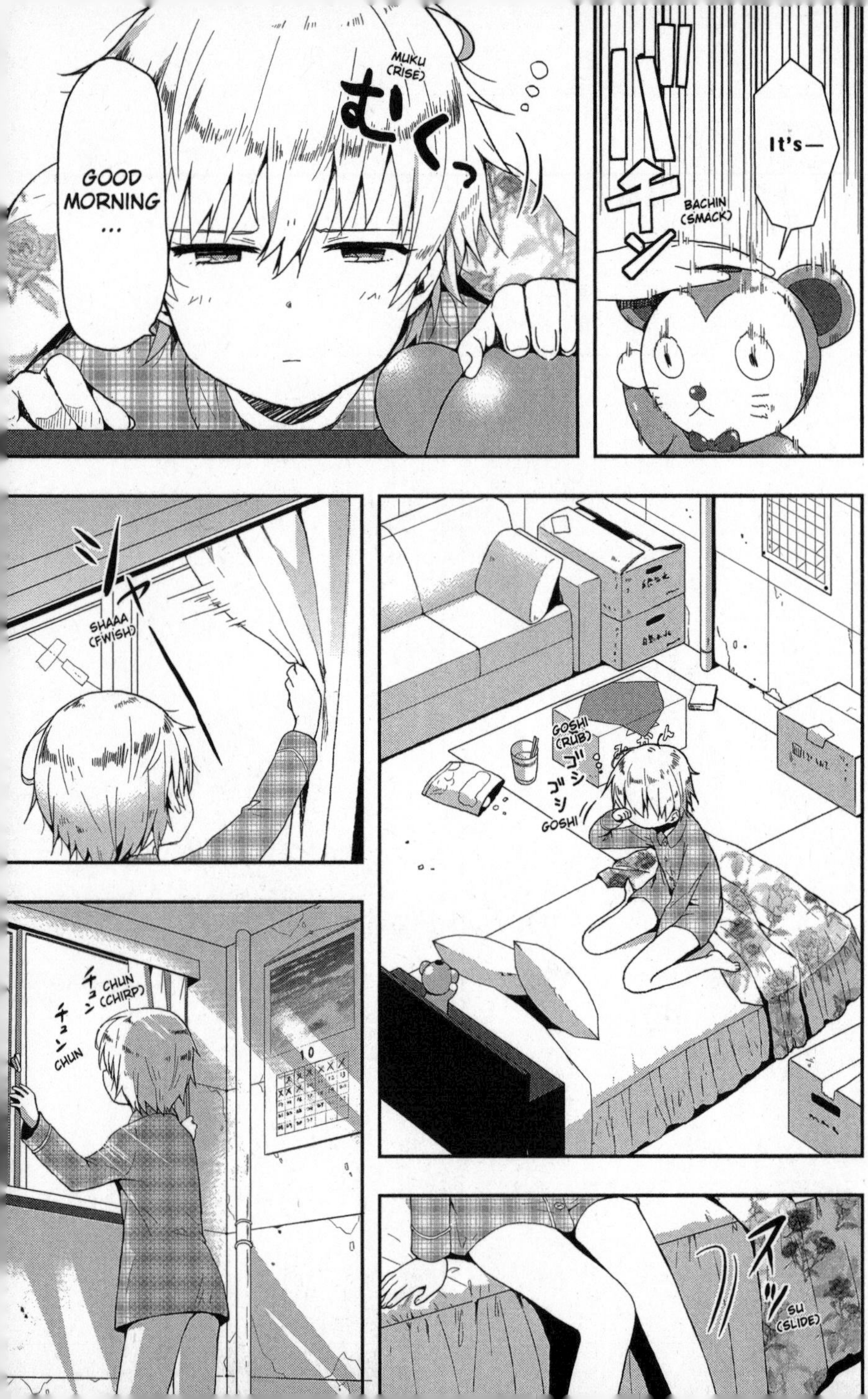

It's—
BACHIN (SMACK)
MUKU (RISE)
GOOD MORNING ...
GOSHI (RUB)
GOSHI
SU (SLIDE)
SHAAA (FWISH)
CHUN (CHIRP)
CHUN

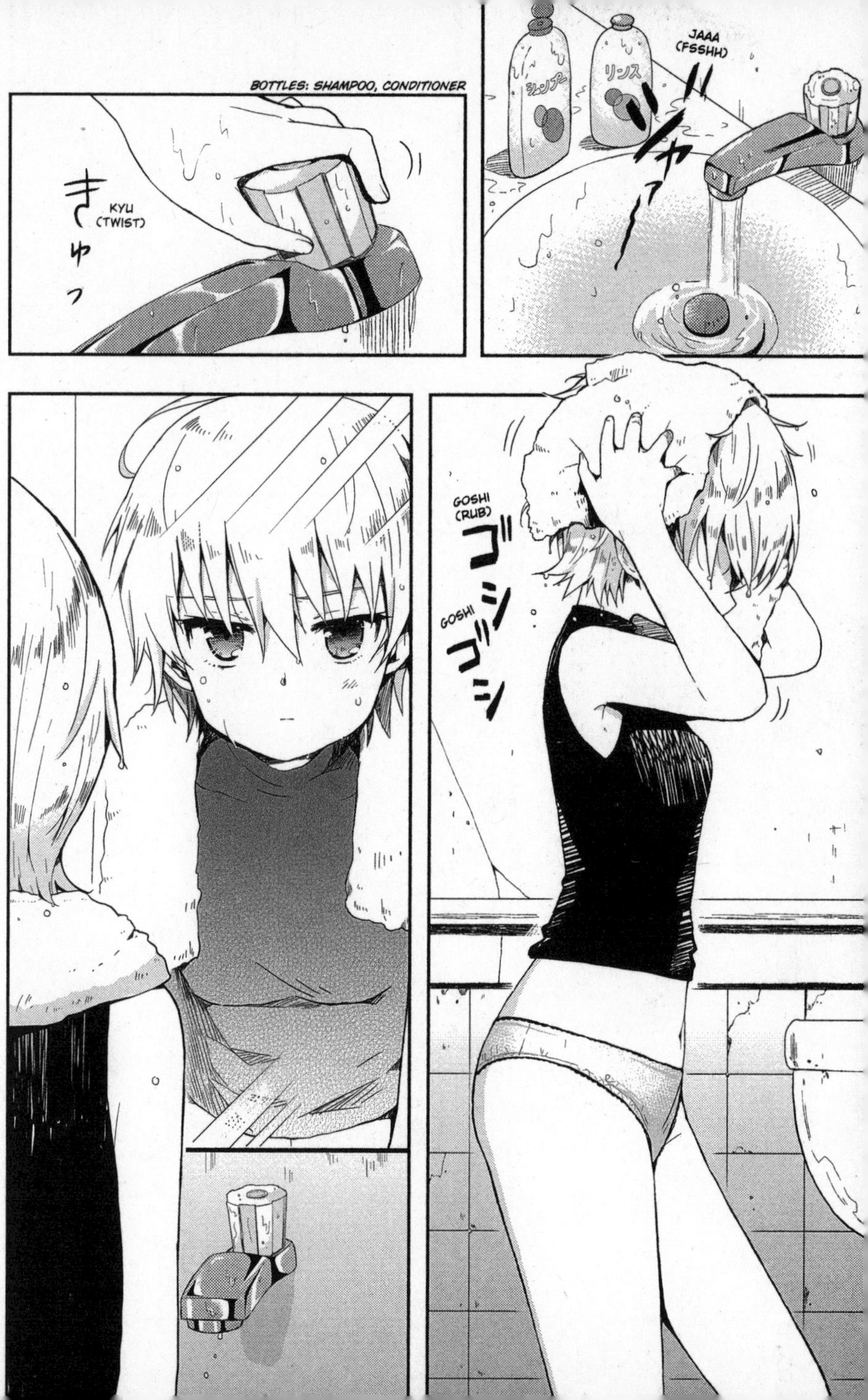
BOTTLES: SHAMPOO, CONDITIONER
シャンプー
リンス
JAAA (FSSHH)
ジャアー
KYU (TWIST)
きゅっ
GOSHI (RUB)
ゴシ
GOSHI
ゴシ

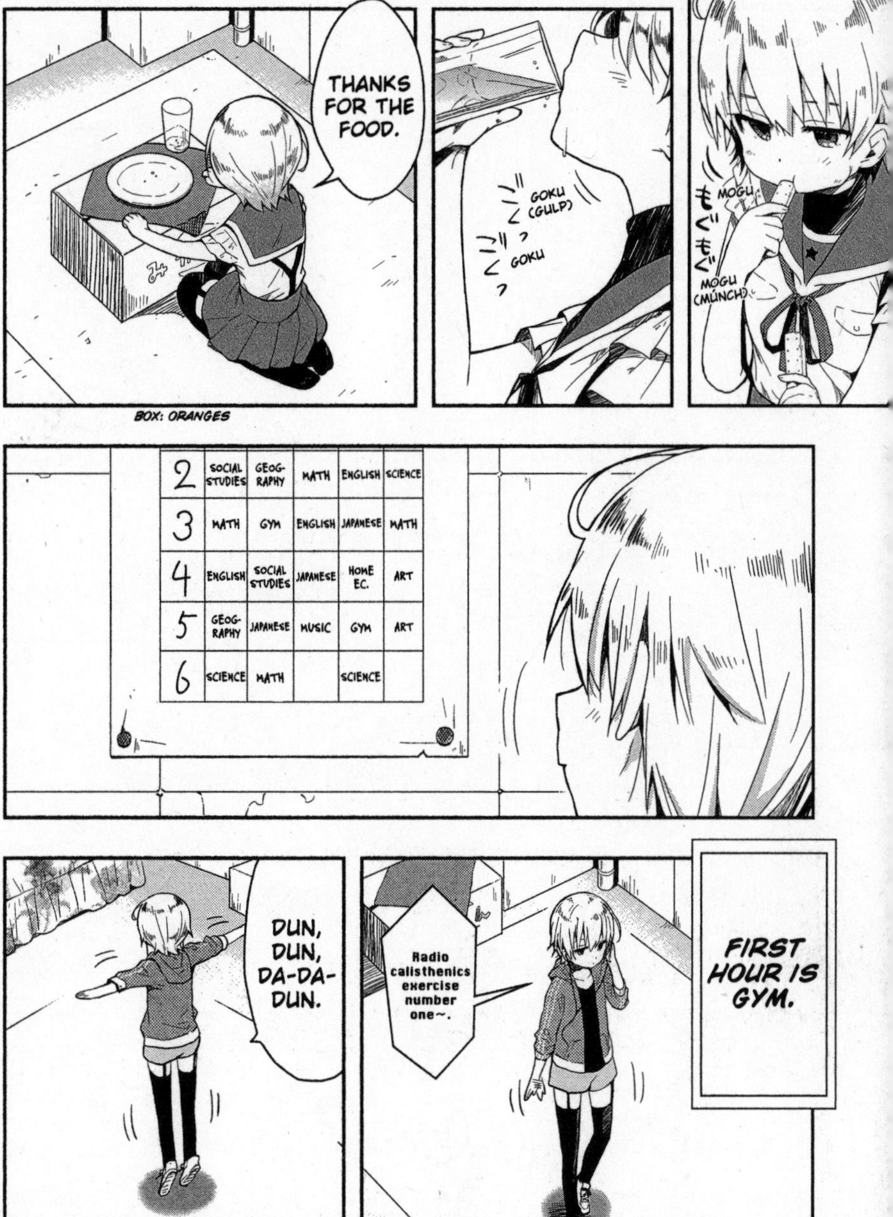
MOGU
もぐもぐ
MOGU (MUNCH)
GOKU (GULP)
GOKU
THANKS FOR THE FOOD.
BOX: ORANGES
2 SOCIAL STUDIES GEOGRAPHY MATH ENGLISH SCIENCE
3 MATH GYM ENGLISH JAPANESE MATH
4 ENGLISH SOCIAL STUDIES JAPANESE HOME EC. ART
5 GEOGRAPHY JAPANESE MUSIC GYM ART
6 SCIENCE MATH SCIENCE
FIRST HOUR IS GYM.
Radio calisthenics exercise number one~.
DUN, DUN, DA-DA-DUN.

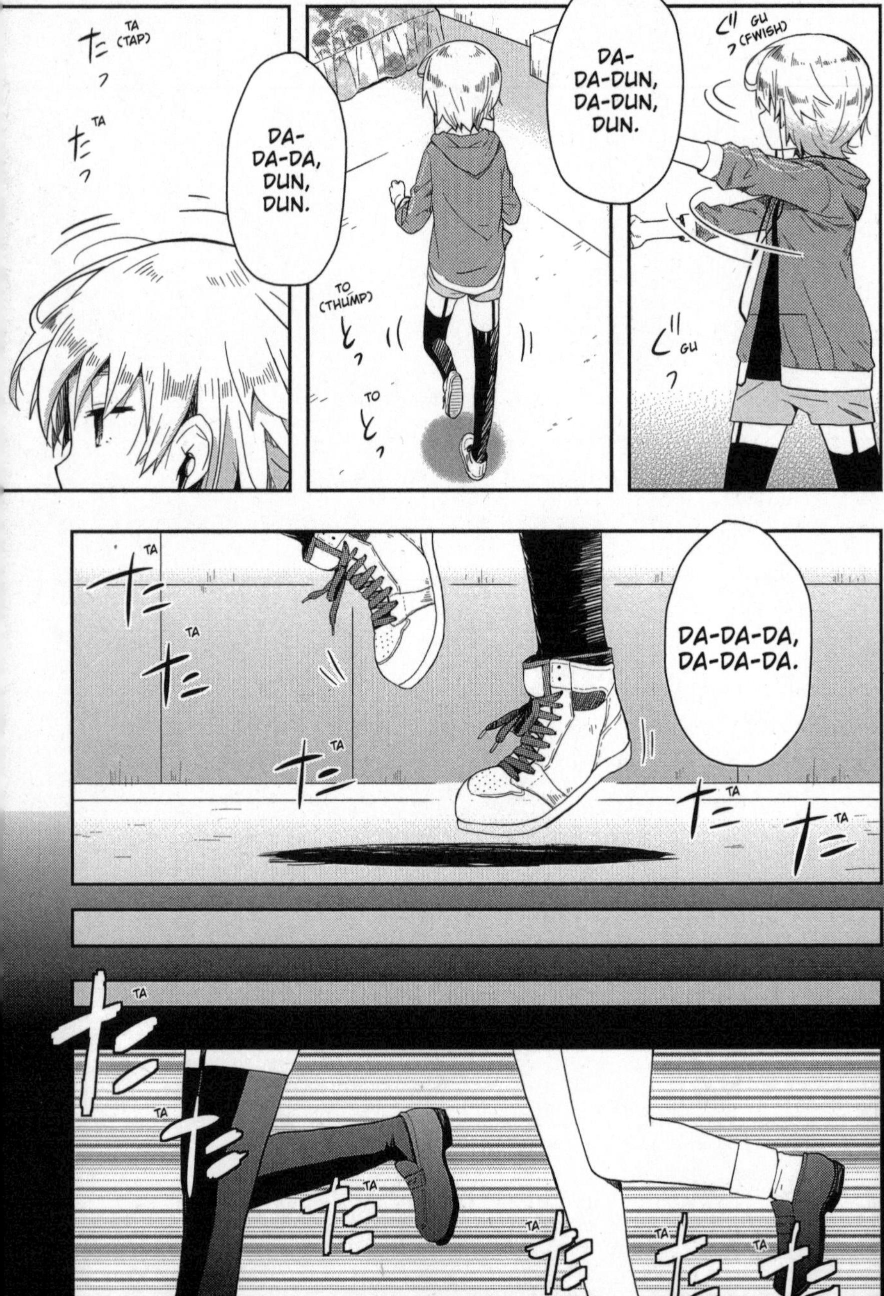
GU (FWISH)
GU
DA-DA-DUN, DA-DUN, DUN.
TO (THUMP)
TO
DA-DA-DA, DUN, DUN.
TA (TAP)
TA
DA-DA-DA, DA-DA-DA.
TA
TA
TA
TA
TA
TA
TA
TA
TA
TA
TA
TA

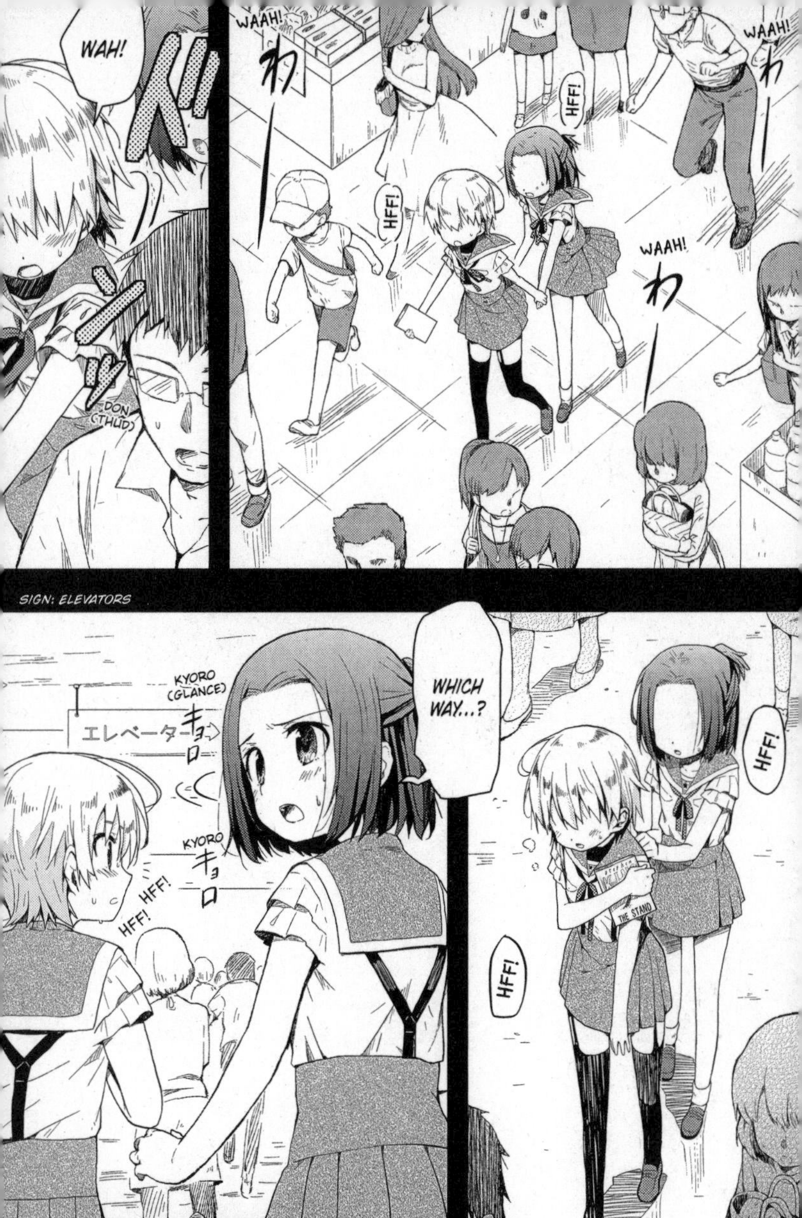
WAAH!
わ
HFF!
WAAH!
わ
WAAH!
わ
HFF!
WAH!
DON (THUD)
HFF!
HFF!
SIGN: ELEVATORS
WHICH WAY...?
KYORO (GLANCE)
キョロ
エレベーター
KYORO
キョロ
HFF!
HFF!

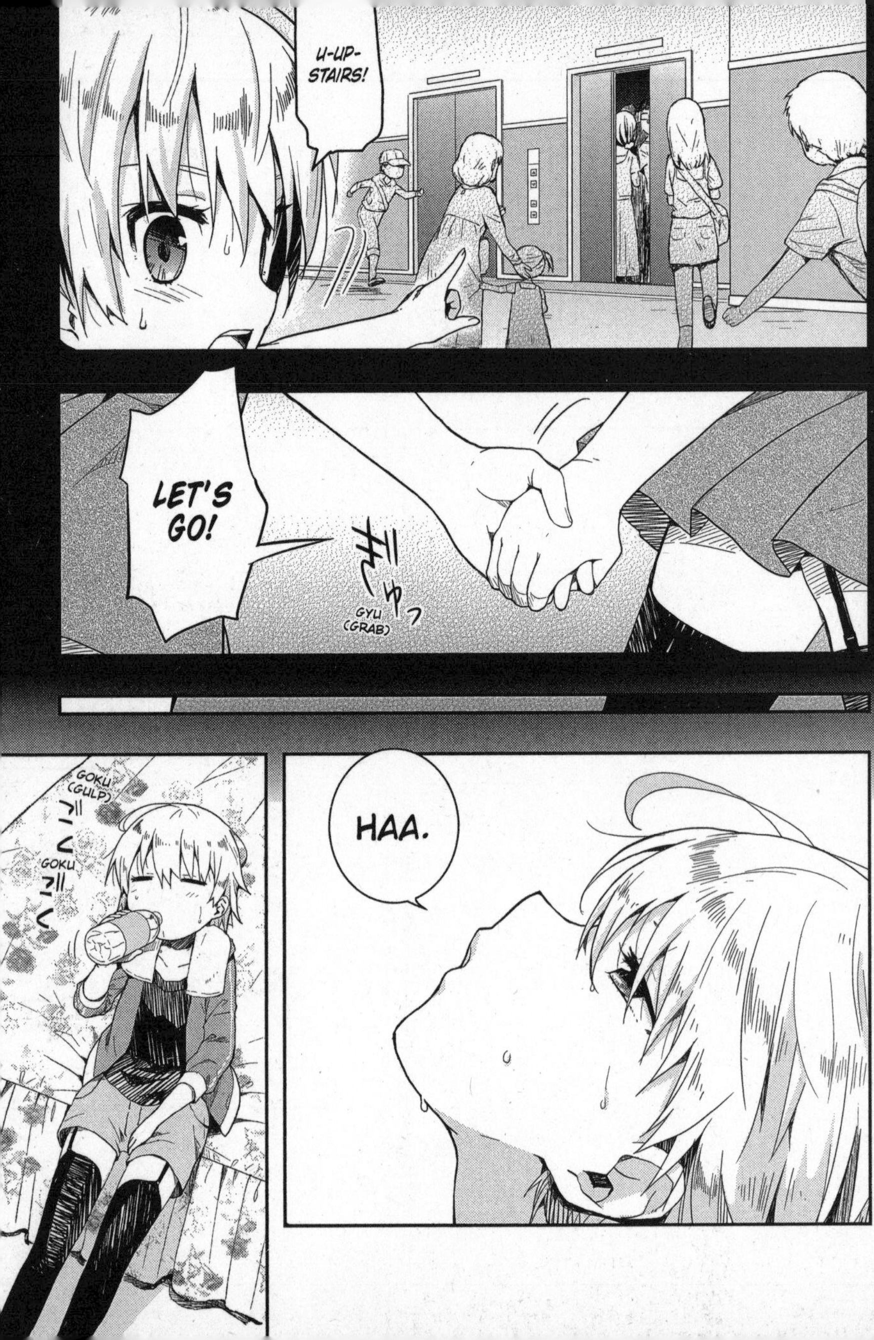
U-UP-STAIRS!
LET'S GO!
ぎゅっ
GYU (GRAB)
HAA.
ごく
GOKU (GULP)
ごく
GOKU

SECOND HOUR IS MATH.

HMMM...

KARI
(SCRITCH)

KARI

GOSHI
(RUB)
GOSHI

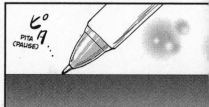

PITA
(PAUSE)

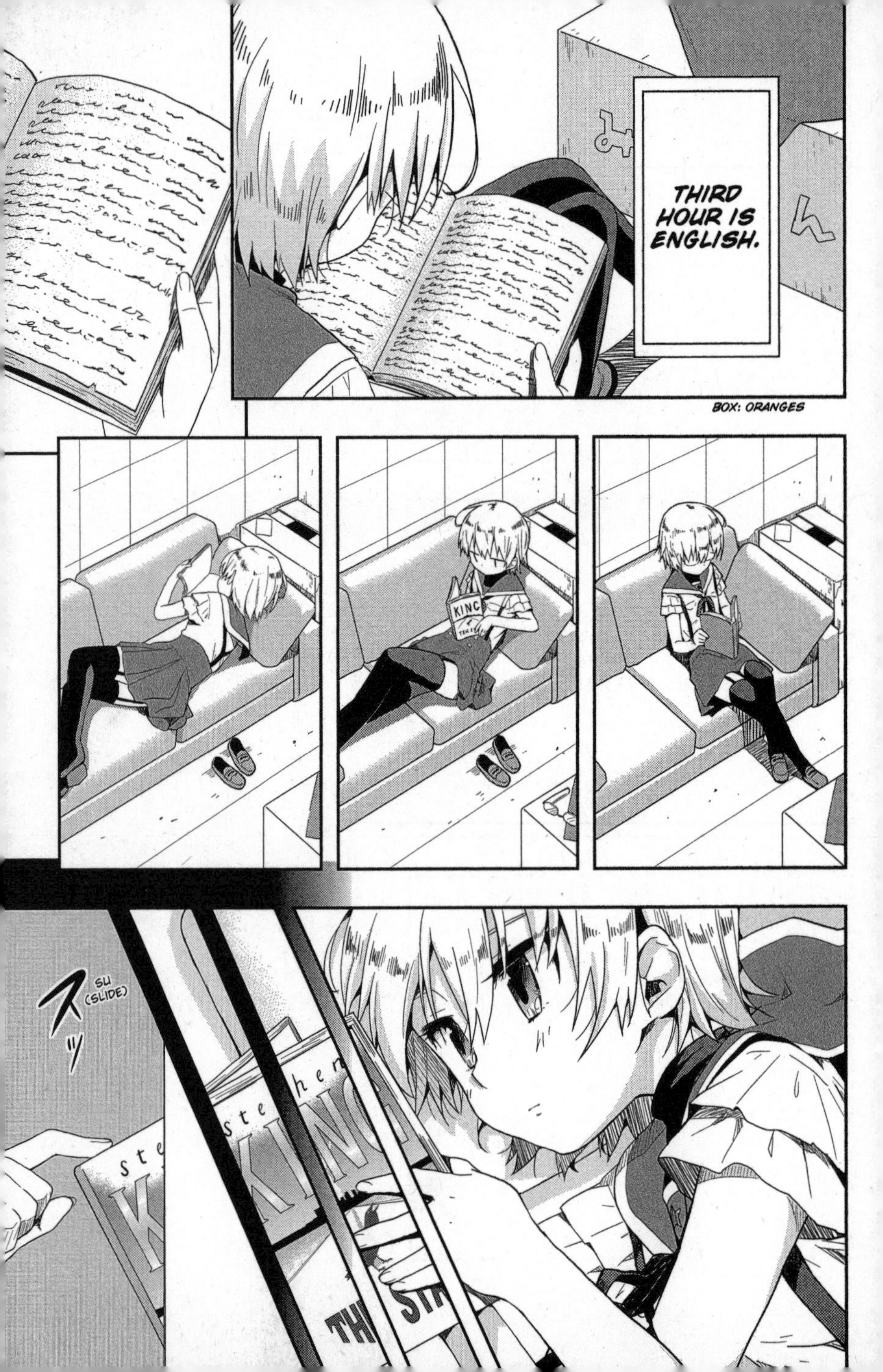
THIRD HOUR IS ENGLISH.
BOX: ORANGES
KING
SU (SLIDE)
stephen KING
THE ST

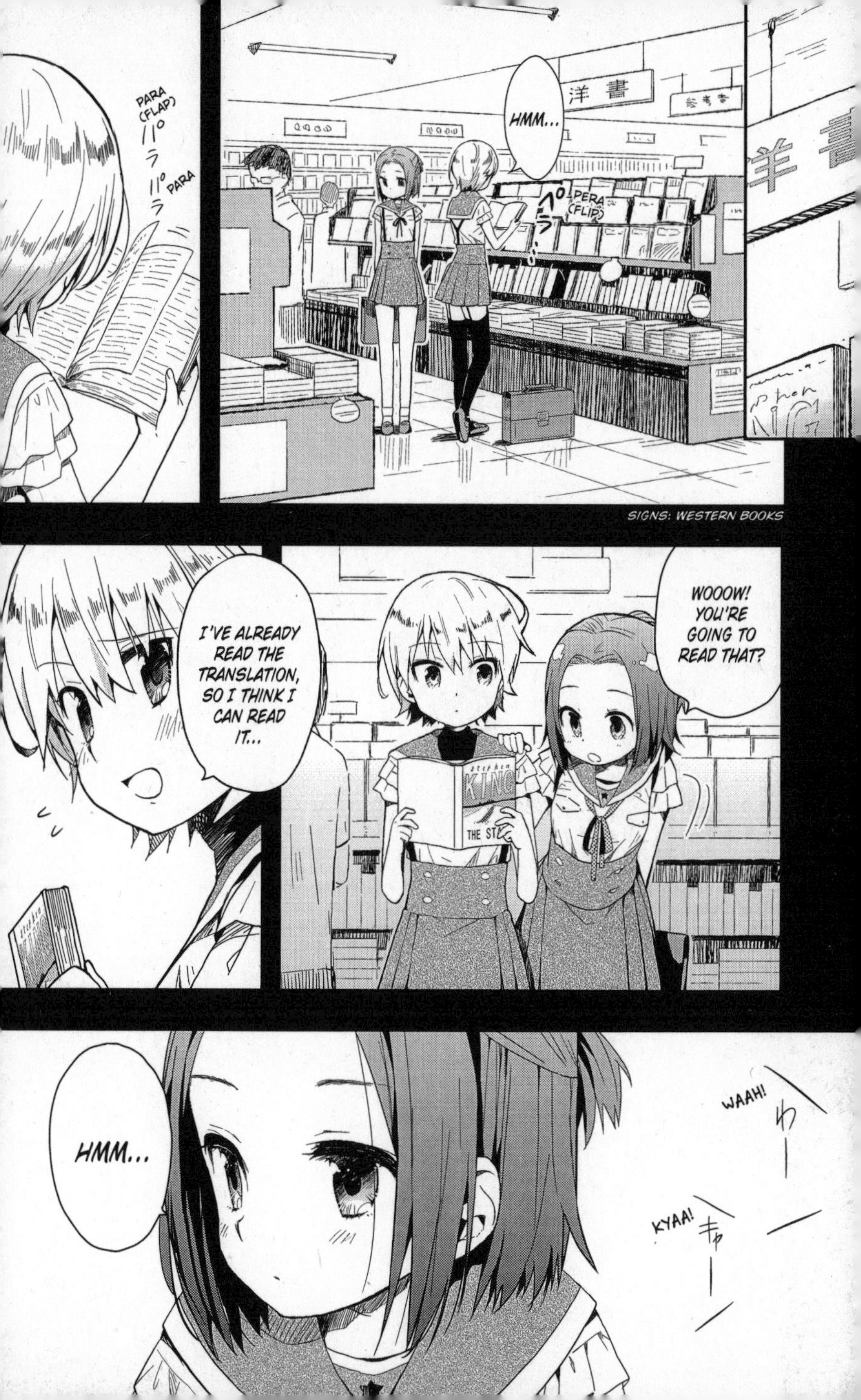
洋書
参考書
HMM...
PERA (FLIP)
ペラ
PARA (FLAP)
パラパラ
PARA
SIGNS: WESTERN BOOKS
WOOOW! YOU'RE GOING TO READ THAT?
stephen KING
THE ST
I'VE ALREADY READ THE TRANSLATION, SO I THINK I CAN READ IT...
WAAH!
わー
KYAA!
キャー
HMM...

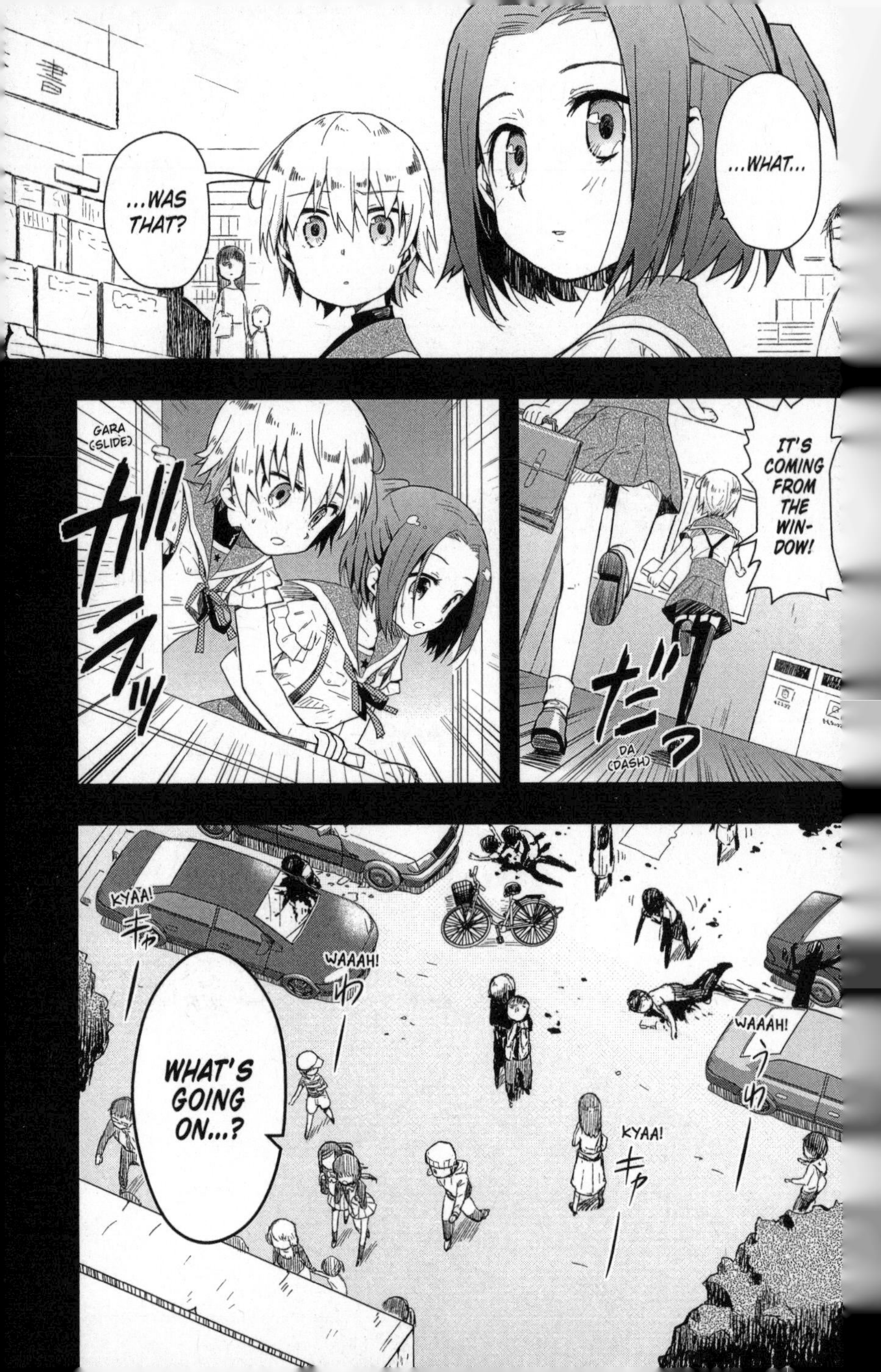
...WHAT...
...WAS THAT?
IT'S COMING FROM THE WIN-DOW!
DA (DASH)
GARA (SLIDE)
WAAAH!
KYAA!
WAAAH!
WHAT'S GOING ON...?
KYAA!

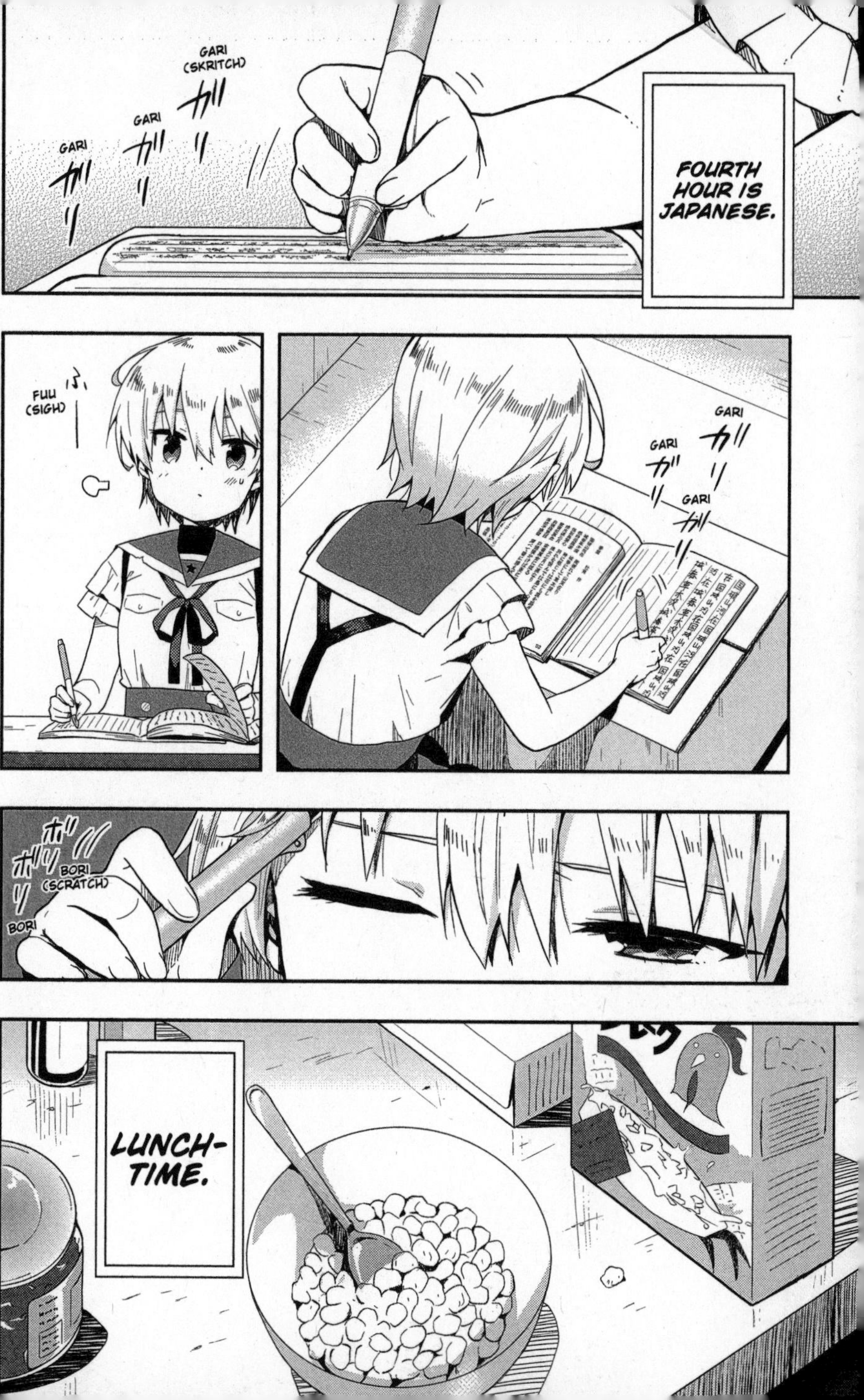
FOURTH HOUR IS JAPANESE.
GARI (SKRITCH)
ガリ
GARI
ガリ
GARI
ガリ
GARI
ガリ
GARI
ガリ
GARI
ガリ
FUU (SIGH)
ふぅ
BORI (SCRATCH)
ボリ
BORI
ボリ
LUNCH-TIME.

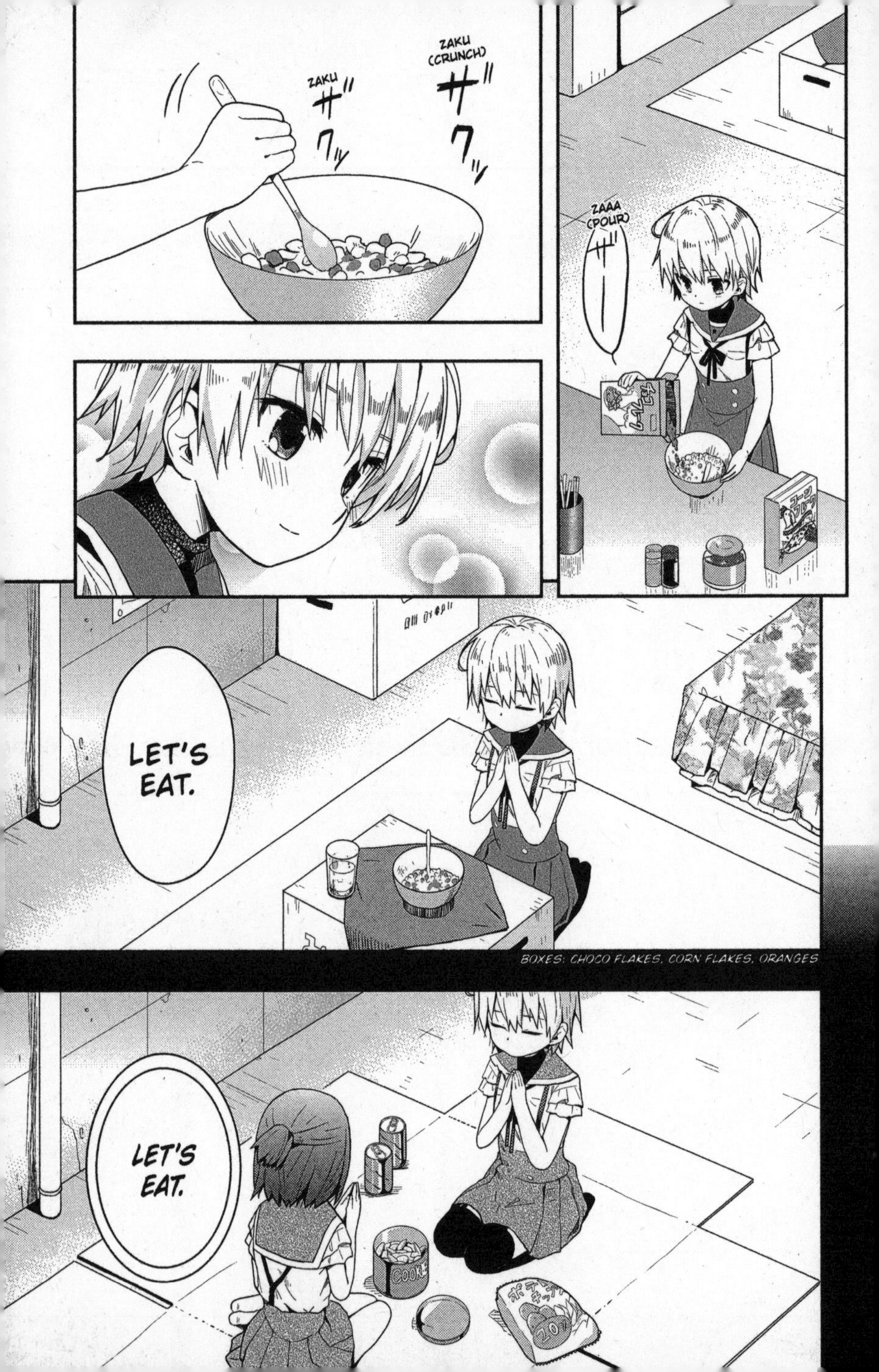
ZAAA (POUR)
ZAKU
ZAKU (CRUNCH)
LET'S EAT.
BOXES: CHOCO FLAKES, CORN FLAKES, ORANGES
LET'S EAT.

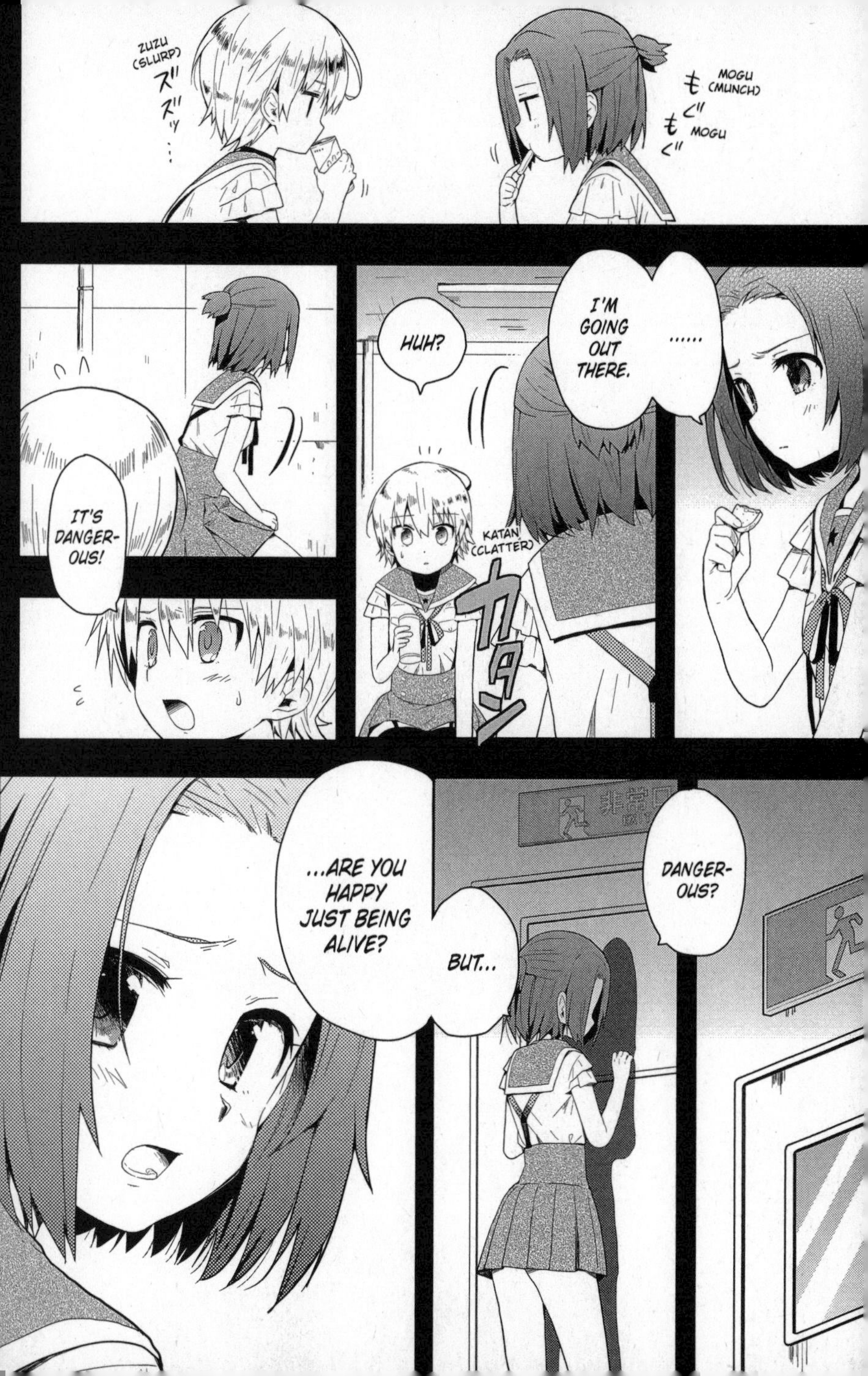
もぐもぐ
MOGU (MUNCH) MOGU
ズズッ…
ZUZU (SLURP)
......
I'M GOING OUT THERE.
HUH?
カタン
KATAN (CLATTER)
IT'S DANGER-OUS!
非常口
EXIT
DANGER-OUS?
BUT...
...ARE YOU HAPPY JUST BEING ALIVE?

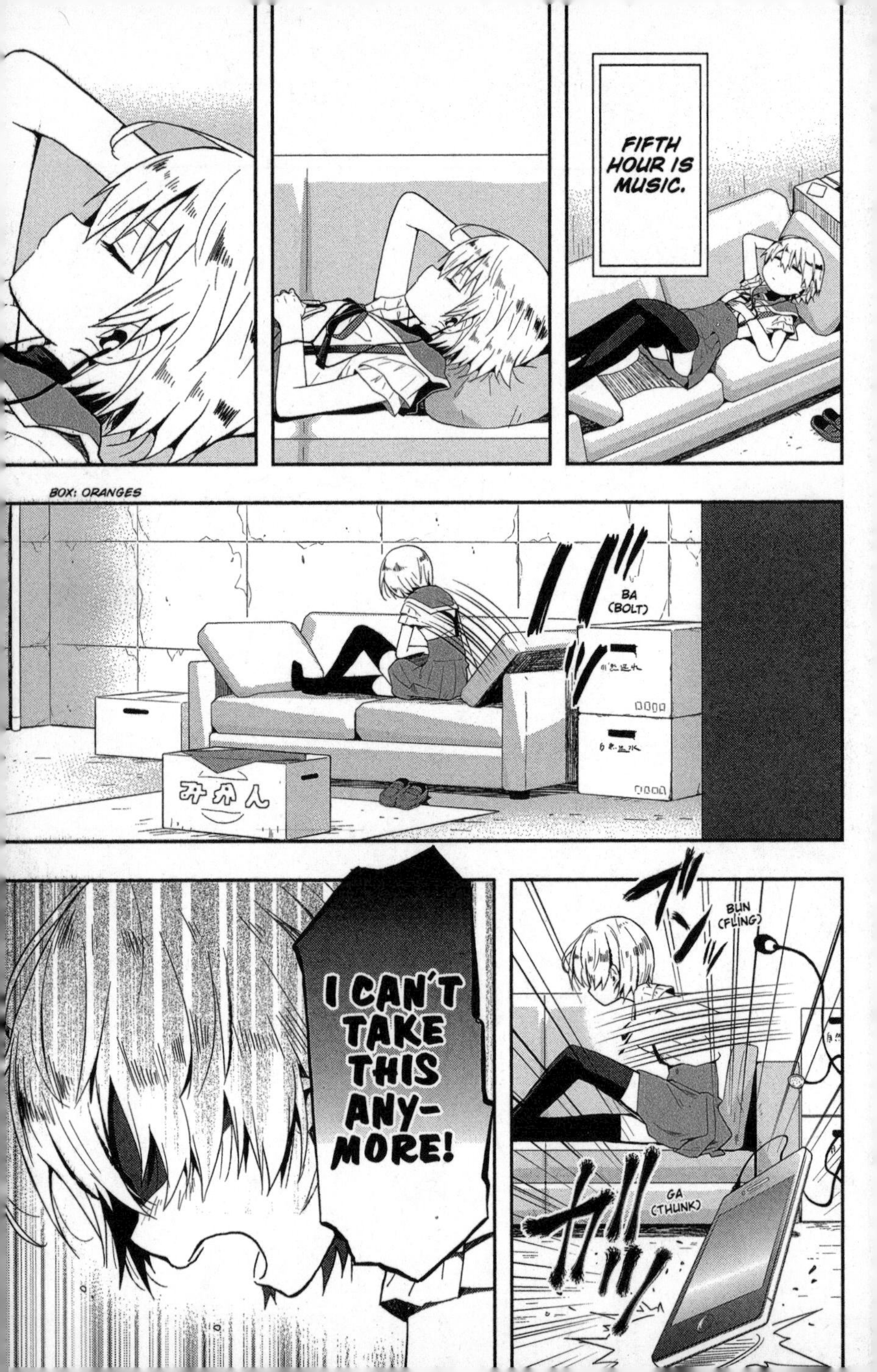
FIFTH HOUR IS MUSIC.
BOX: ORANGES
BA (BOLT)
みかん
BUN (FLING)
GA (THUNK)
I CAN'T TAKE THIS ANYMORE!

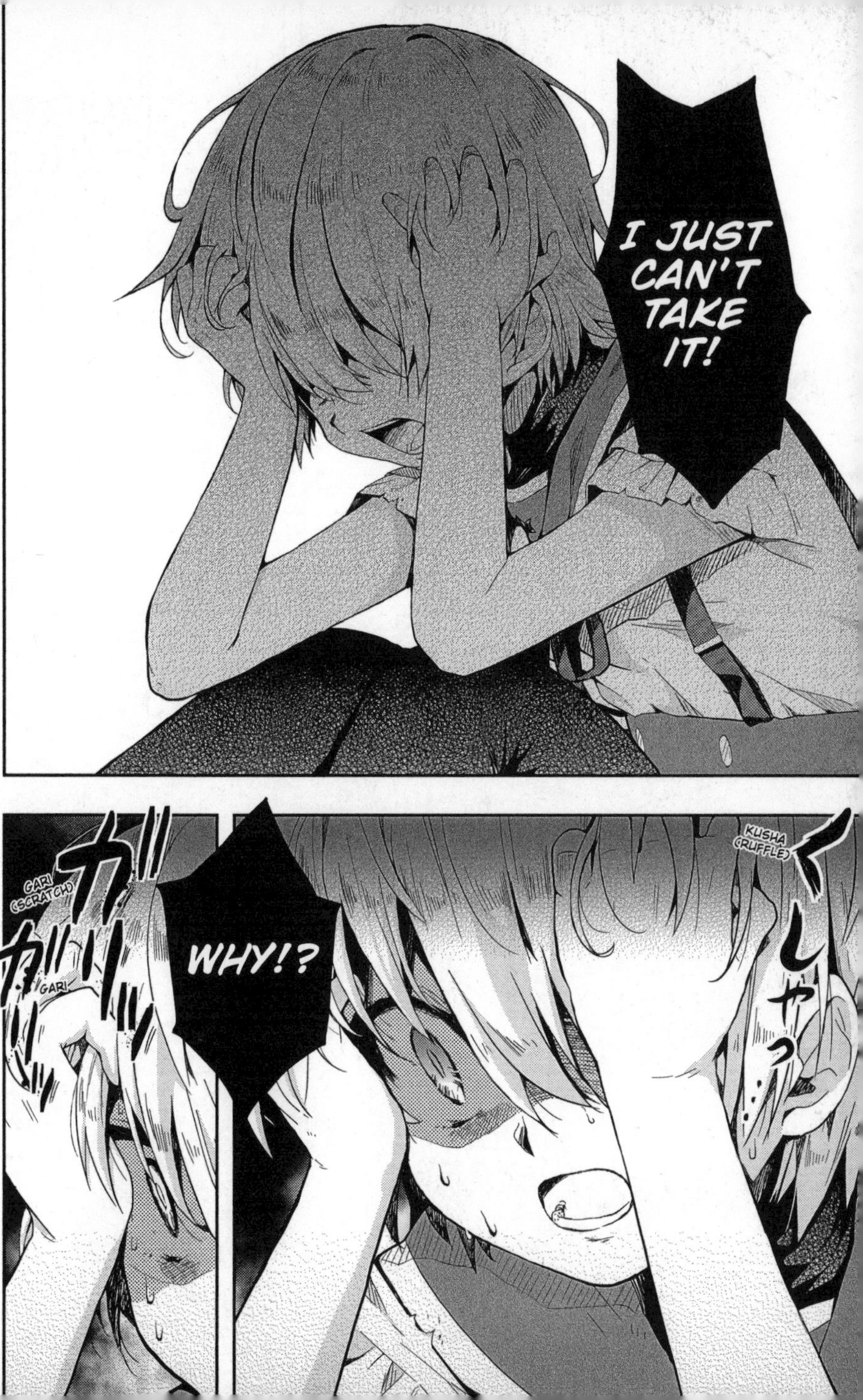
I JUST CAN'T TAKE IT!
KUSHA (RUFFLE)
くしゃっ
WHY!?
GARI (SCRATCH)
GARI

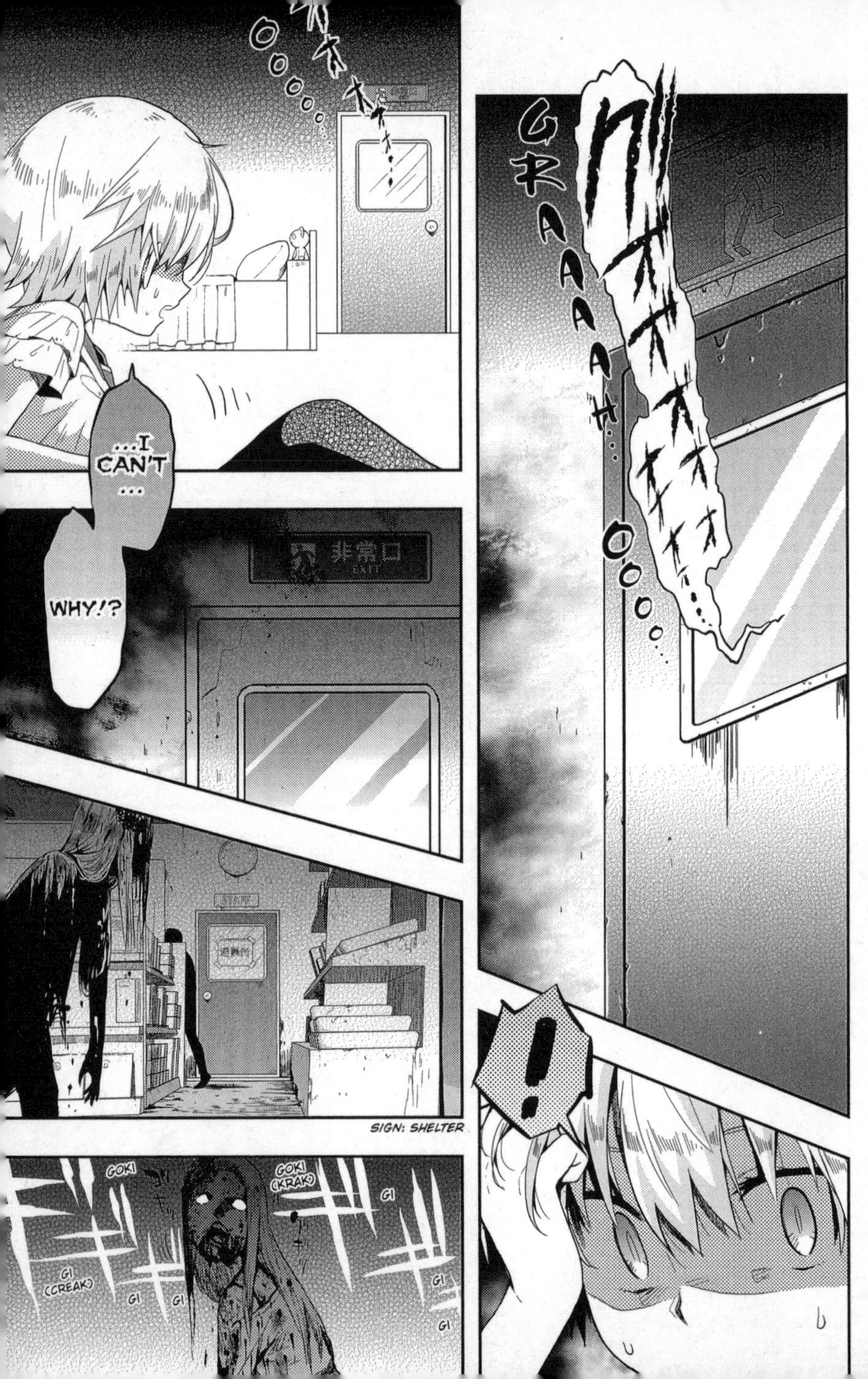
GRAAAAAAH...
OOOO...
OOOOO...
...I CAN'T ...
WHY!?
非常口
EXIT
STAFF
SIGN: SHELTER
!
GOKI
GOKI (KRAK)
GI
GI (CREAK)
GI
GI
GI
GI

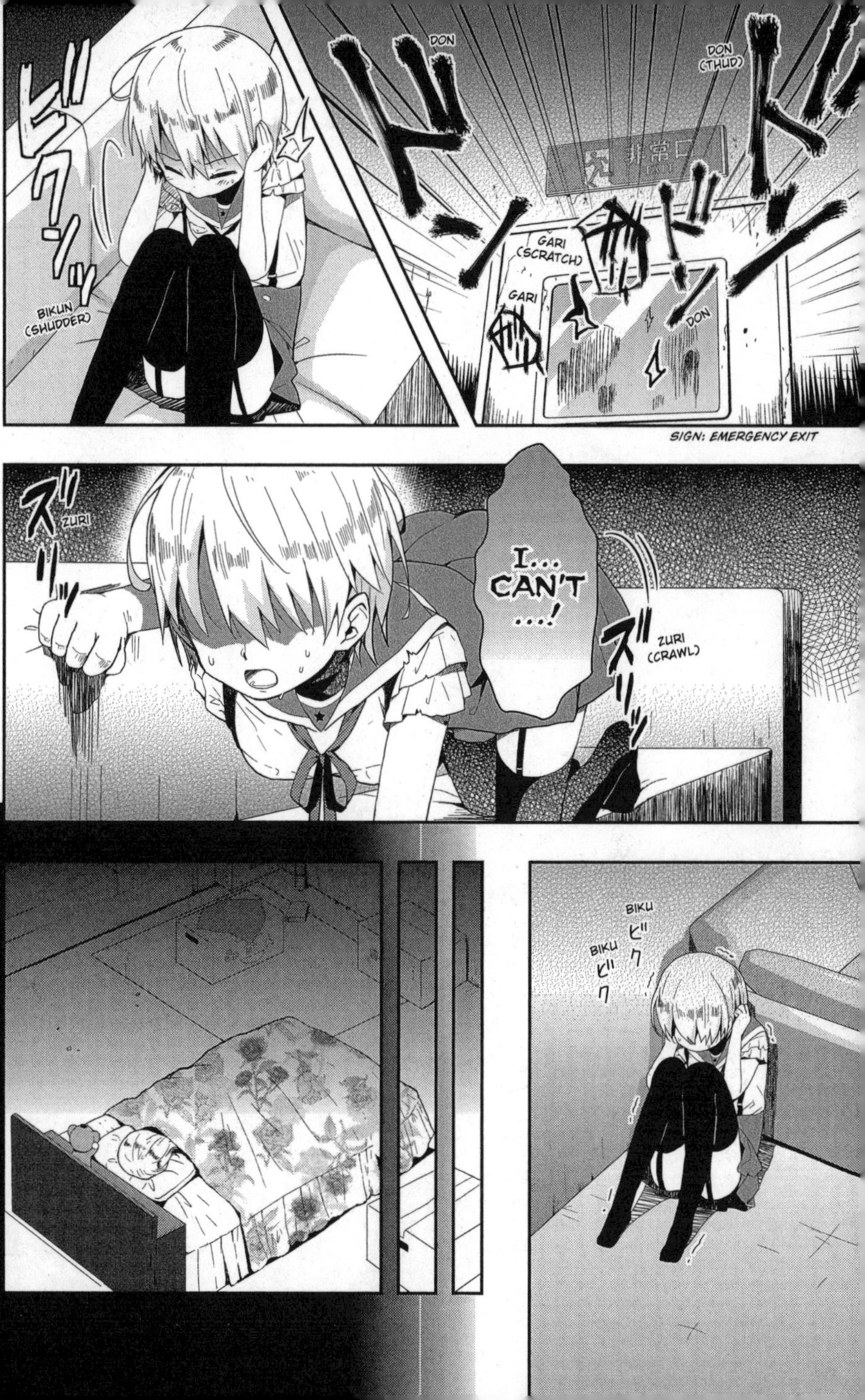

DON
DON (THUD)
GARI (SCRATCH)
GARI
DON
SIGN: EMERGENCY EXIT
BIKUN (SHUDDER)
ZURI
I... CAN'T ...!
ZURI (CRAWL)
BIKU
BIKU

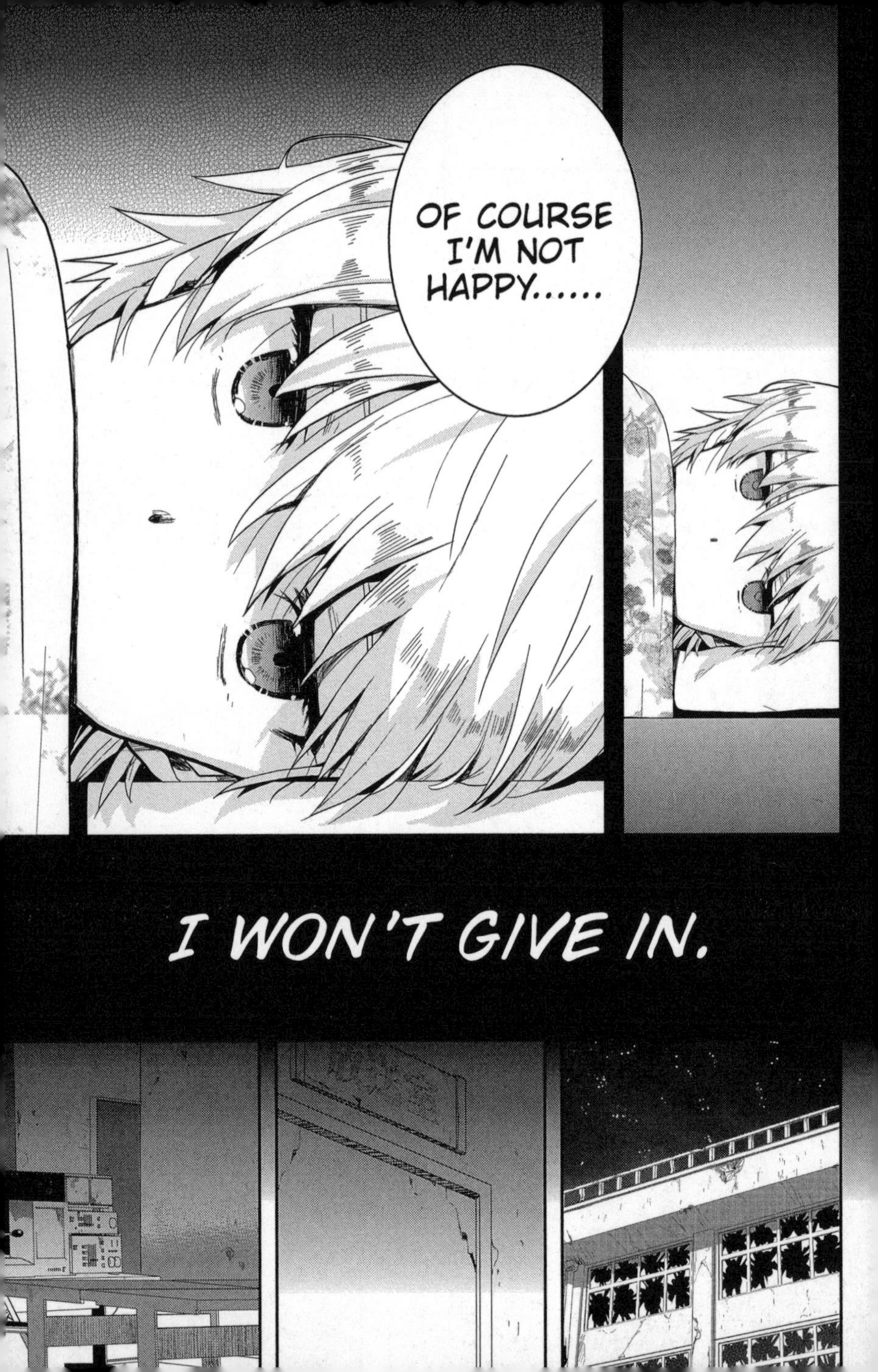
OF COURSE I'M NOT HAPPY......
I WON'T GIVE IN.

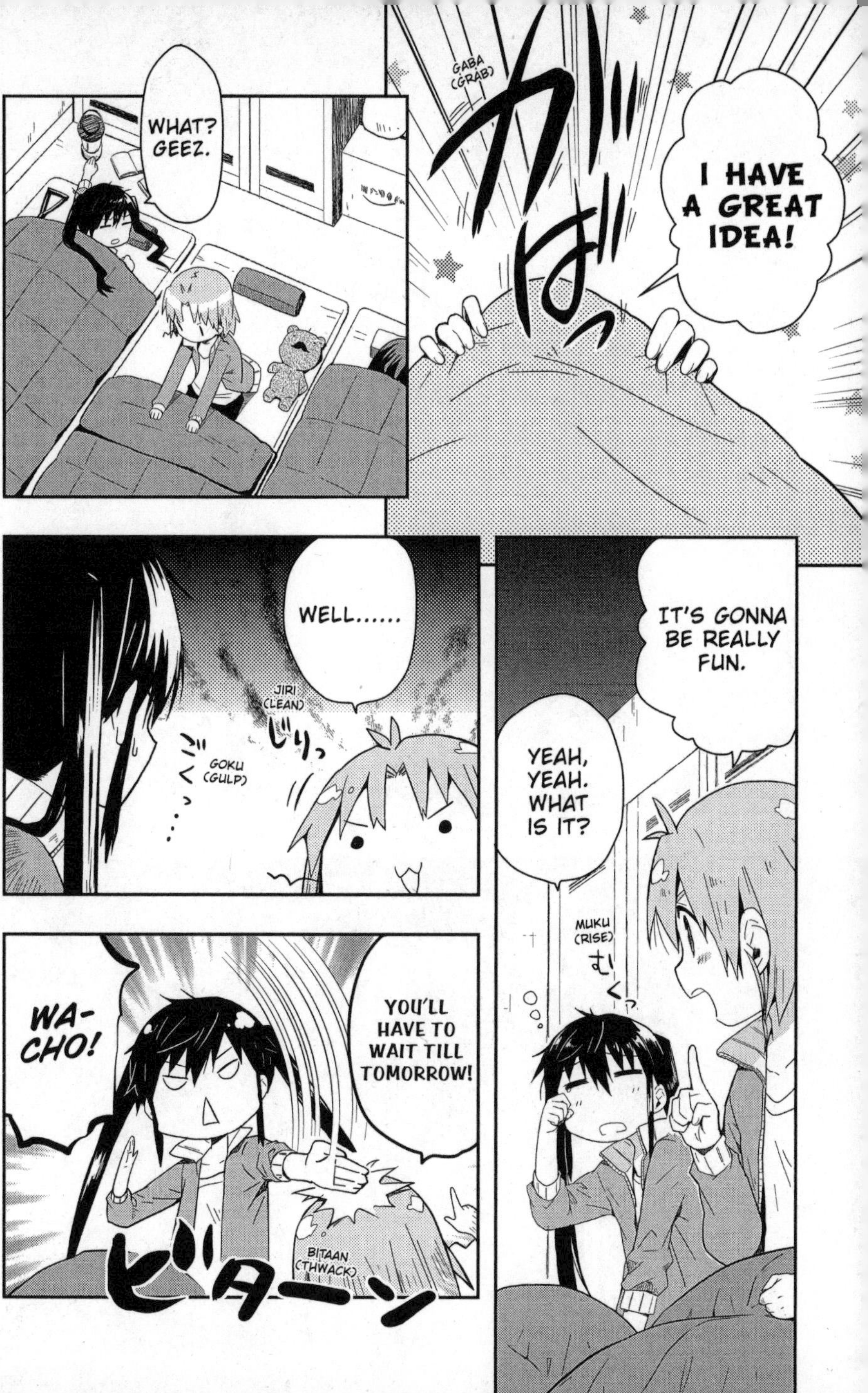
GABA (GRAB)
I HAVE A GREAT IDEA!
WHAT? GEEZ.
IT'S GONNA BE REALLY FUN.
YEAH, YEAH. WHAT IS IT?
MUKU (RISE)
WELL......
JIRI (CLEAN)
GOKU (GULP)
YOU'LL HAVE TO WAIT TILL TOMORROW!
WA-CHO!
BITAAN (THWACK)

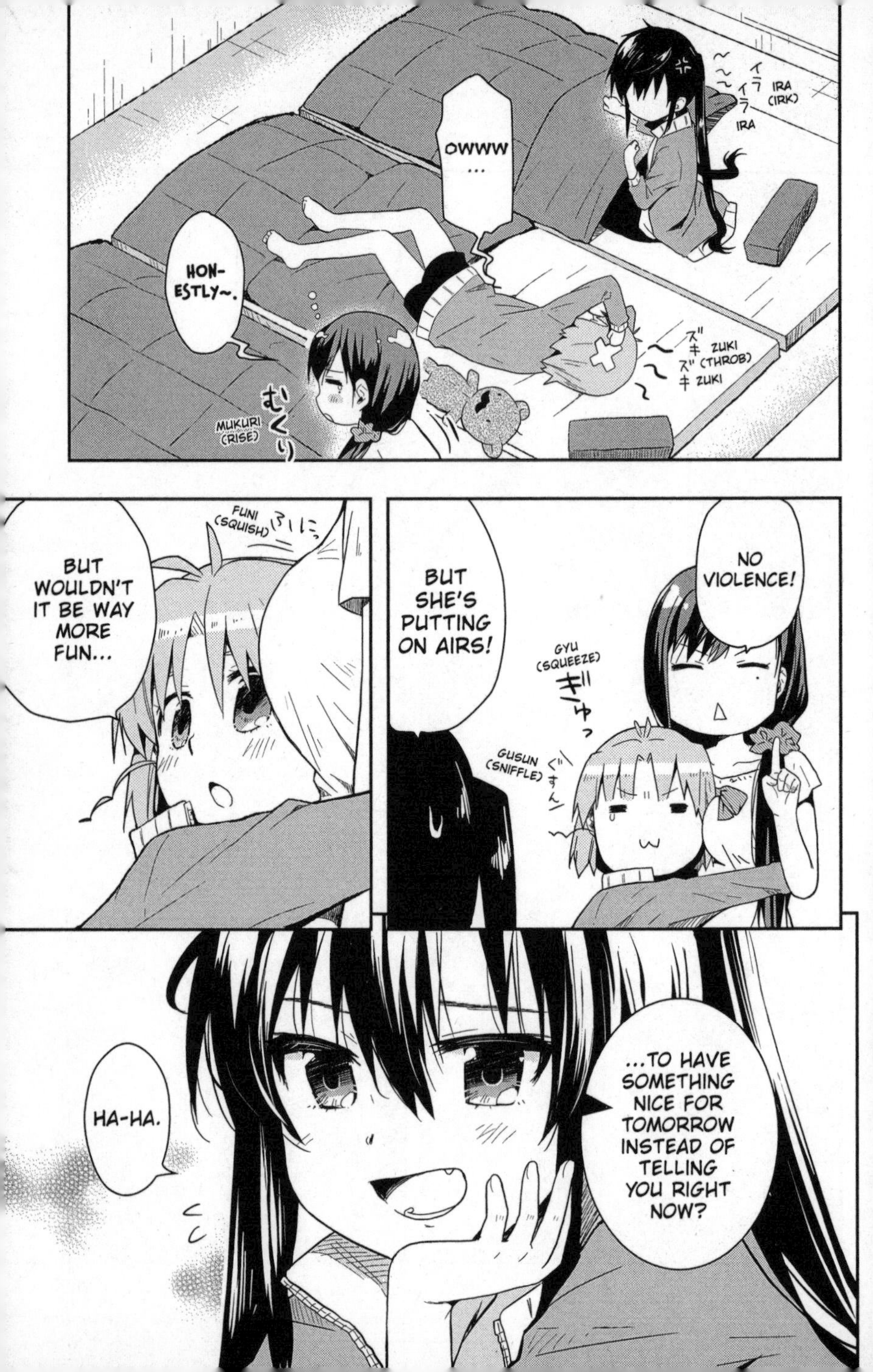
イライラ
IRA IRA (IRK)
OWWW...
ズキズキ
ZUKI ZUKI (THROB)
HON-ESTLY~.
むくり
MUKURI (RISE)
NO VIOLENCE!
ぎゅっ
GYU (SQUEEZE)
ぐすん
GUSUN (SNIFFLE)
BUT SHE'S PUTTING ON AIRS!
ふにっ
FUNI (SQUISH)
BUT WOULDN'T IT BE WAY MORE FUN...
...TO HAVE SOMETHING NICE FOR TOMORROW INSTEAD OF TELLING YOU RIGHT NOW?
HA-HA.

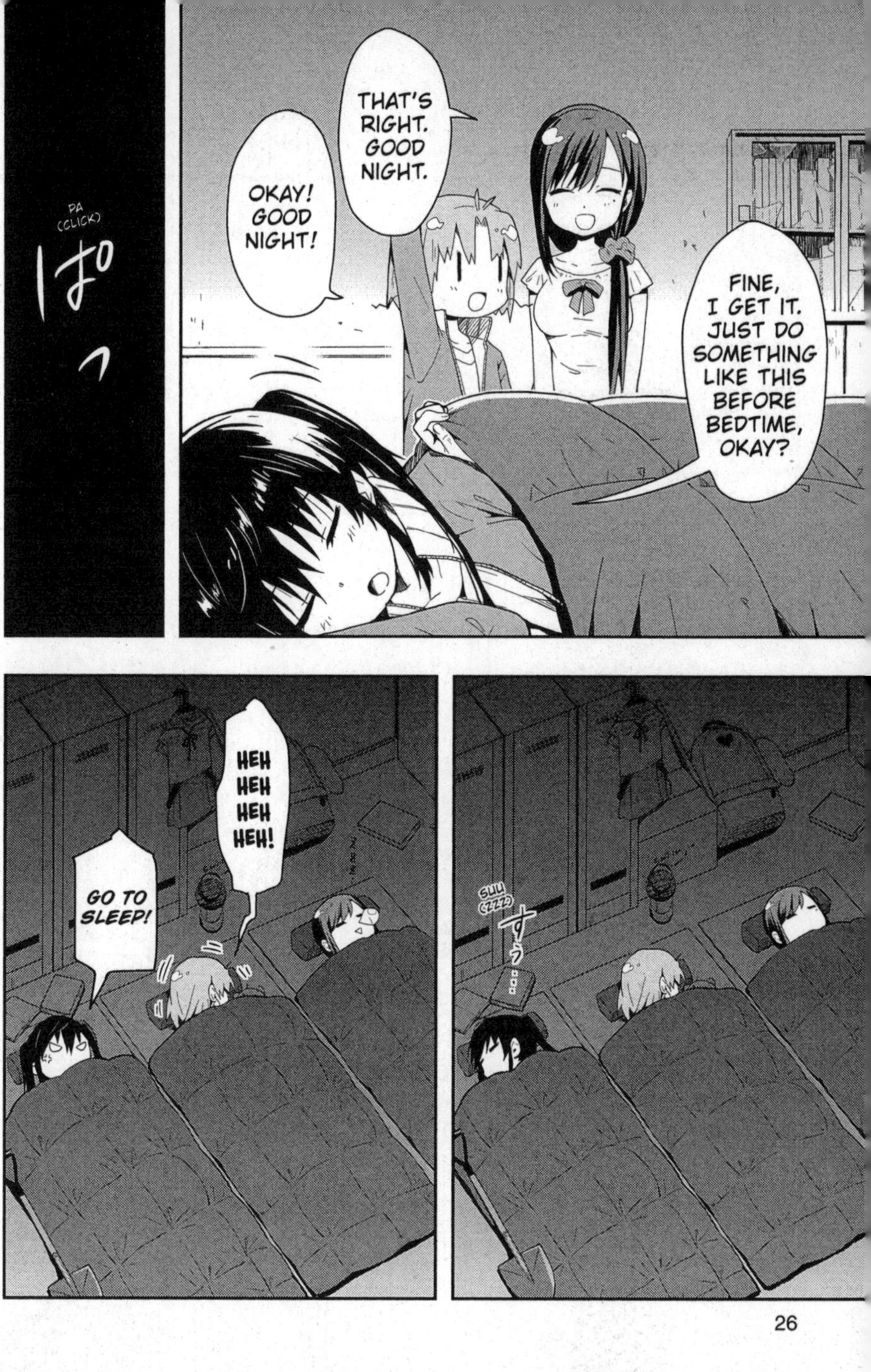
FINE, I GET IT. JUST DO SOMETHING LIKE THIS BEFORE BEDTIME, OKAY?
THAT'S RIGHT. GOOD NIGHT.
OKAY! GOOD NIGHT!
PA (CLICK)
ぱっ
SUU (ZZZZ)
すぅ…
HEH HEH HEH HEH!
GO TO SLEEP!

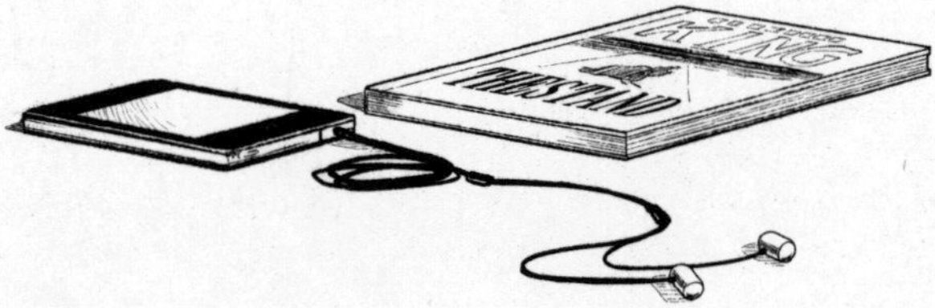
KING
THE STAND

SCHOOL-LIVE!

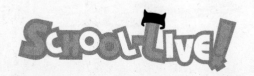

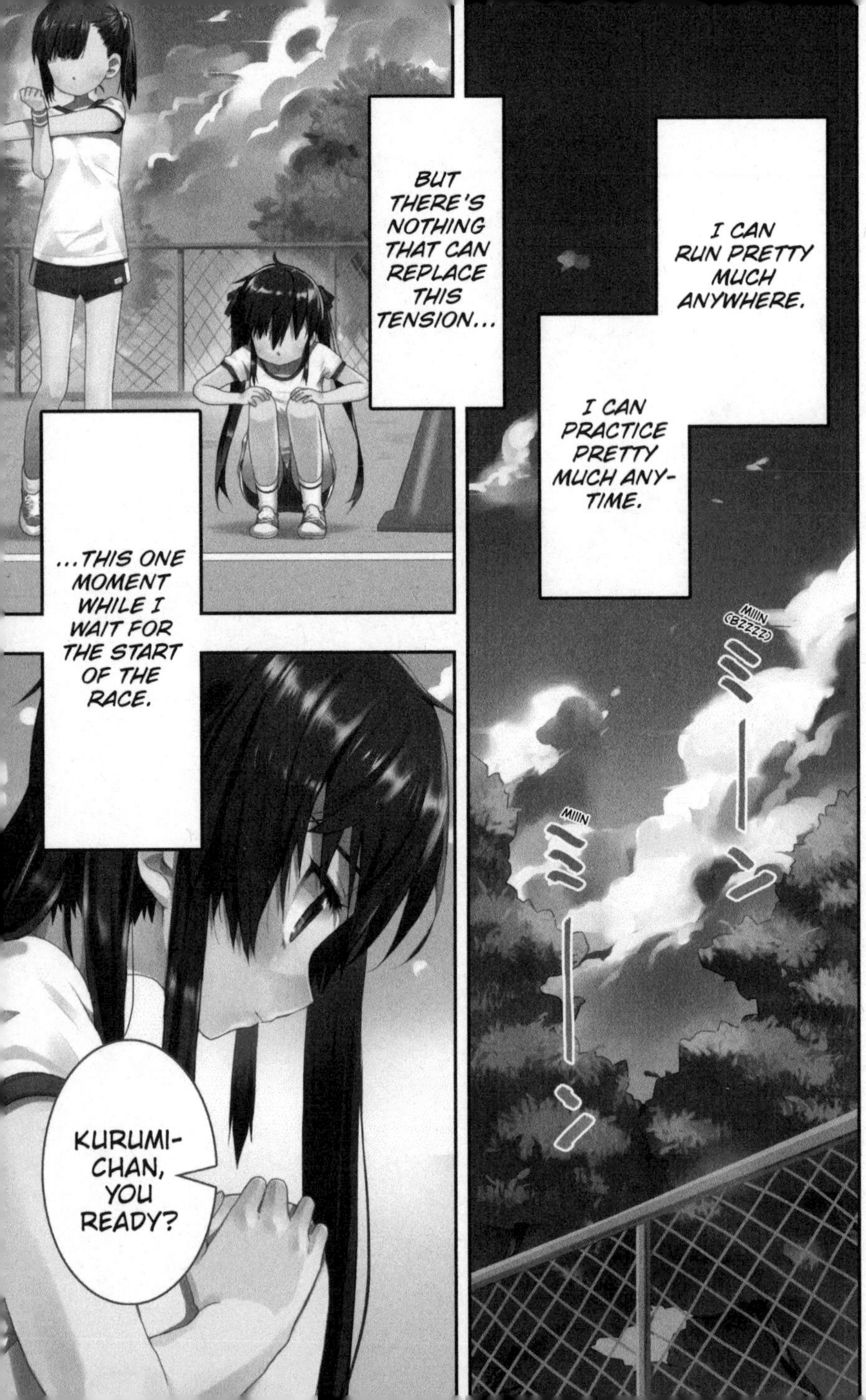
I CAN RUN PRETTY MUCH ANYWHERE.
I CAN PRACTICE PRETTY MUCH ANY-TIME.
MIIIN (BZZZZ)
MIIIN
BUT THERE'S NOTHING THAT CAN REPLACE THIS TENSION...
...THIS ONE MOMENT WHILE I WAIT FOR THE START OF THE RACE.
KURUMI-CHAN, YOU READY?

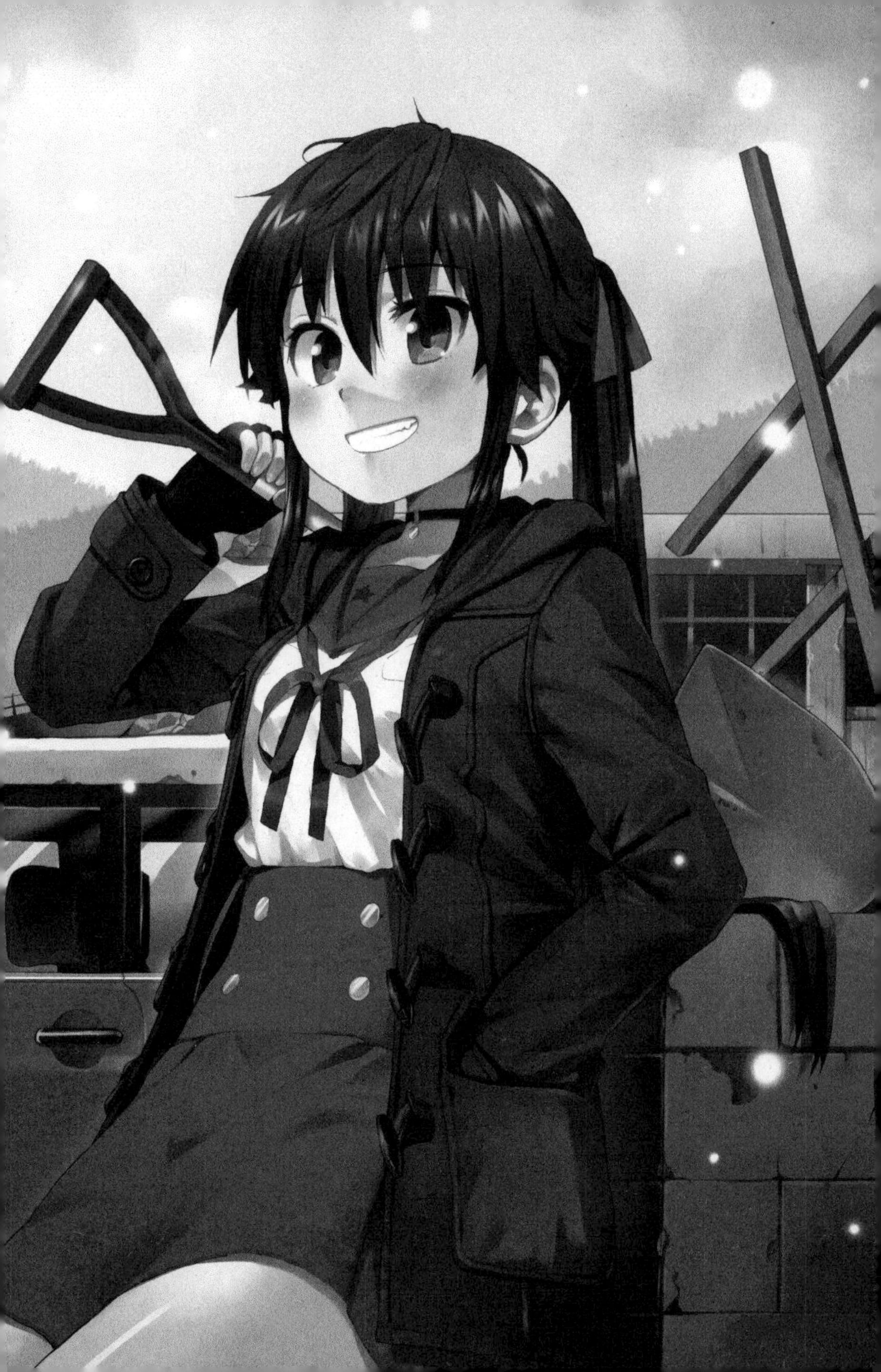

Chapter 8
Field Trip

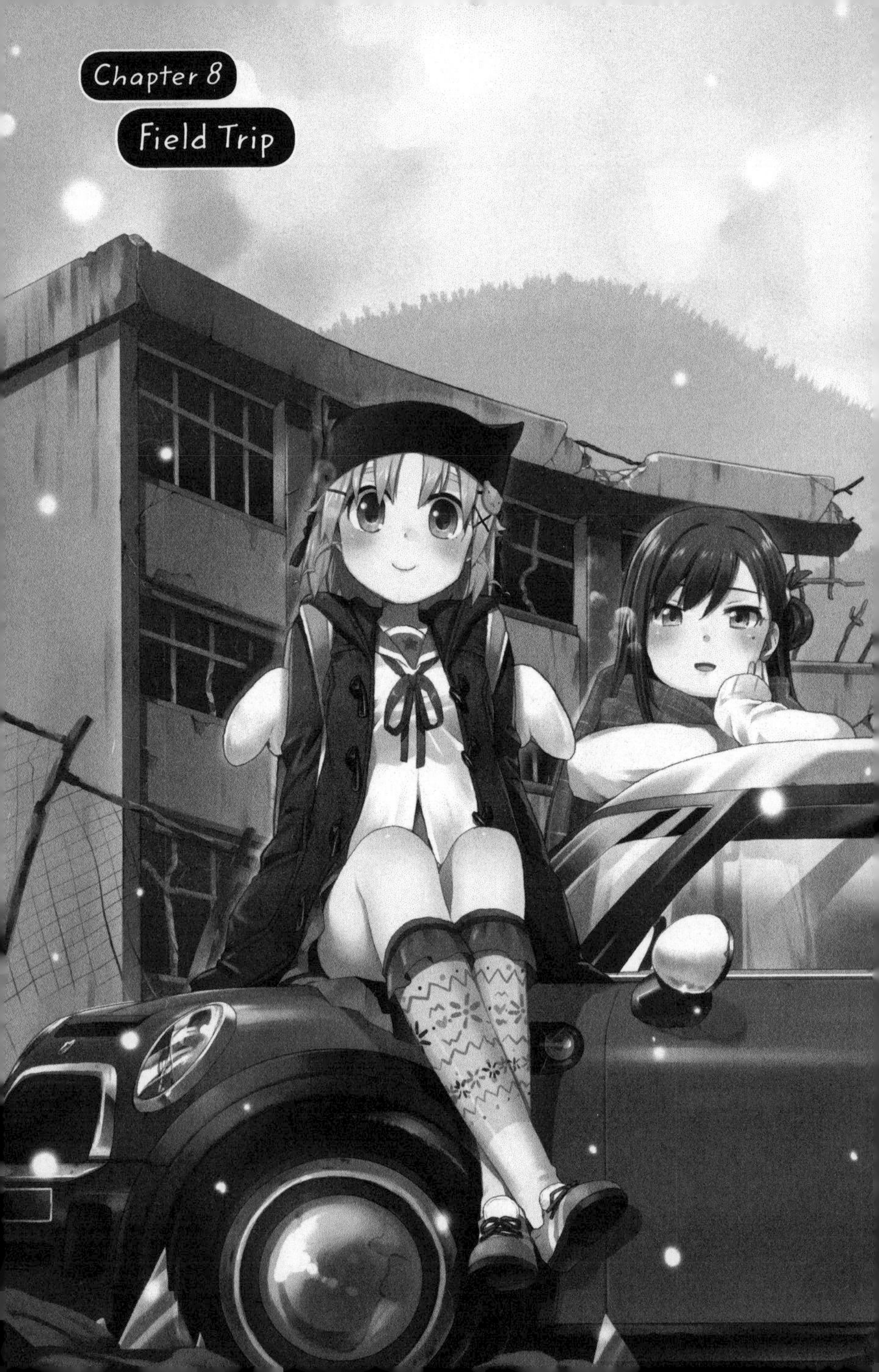

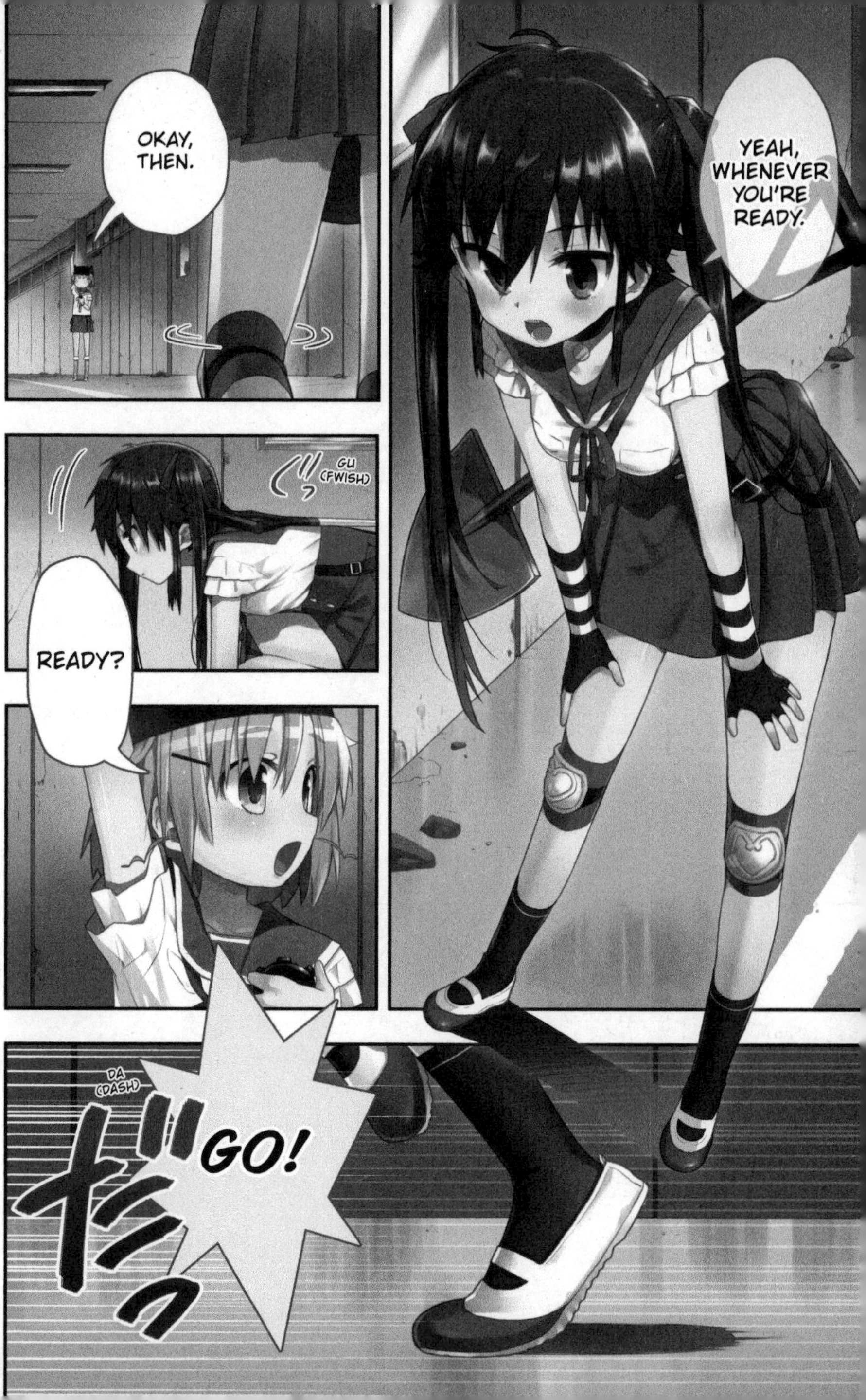
YEAH, WHENEVER YOU'RE READY.
OKAY, THEN.
GU (FWISH)
READY?
DA (DASH)
GO!

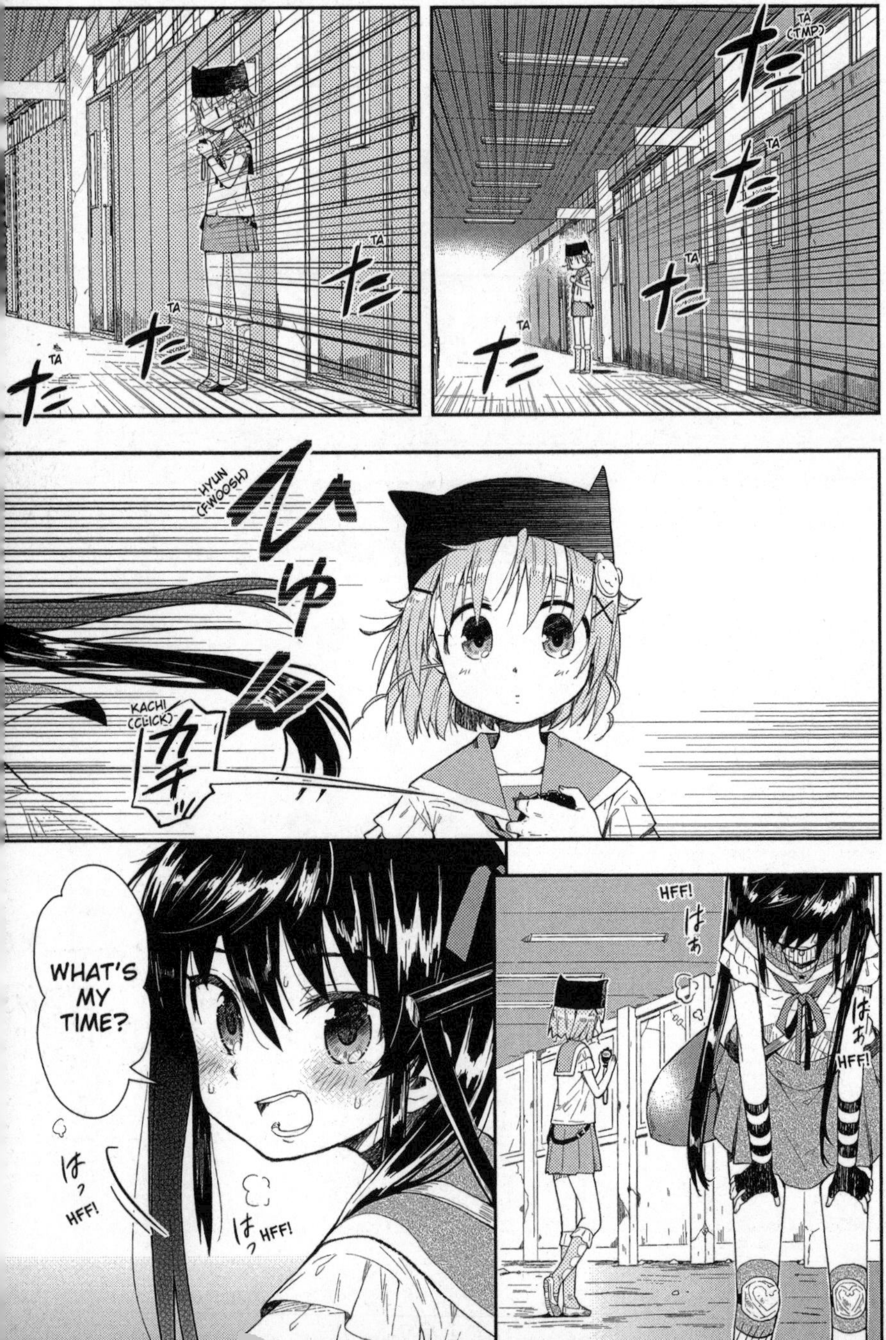
TA (TMP)
TA
TA
TA
TA
TA
TA
HYUN (F:WOOSH)
KACHI (CLICK)
HFF! はぁ
はぁ HFF!
WHAT'S MY TIME?
はっ HFF!
はっ HFF!

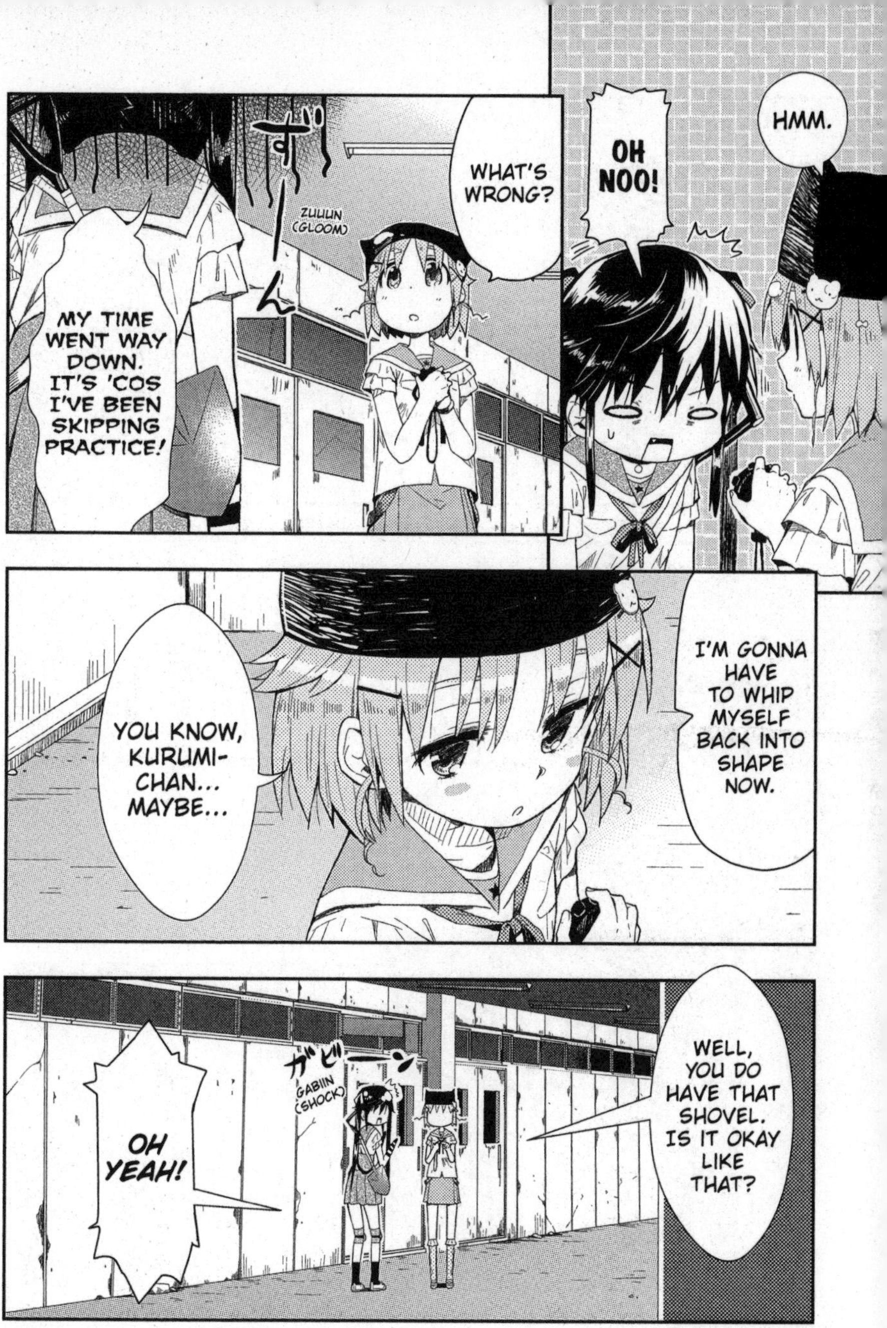
HMM.
OH NOO!
WHAT'S WRONG?
ずーん
ZUUUN (GLOOM)
MY TIME WENT WAY DOWN. IT'S 'COS I'VE BEEN SKIPPING PRACTICE!
I'M GONNA HAVE TO WHIP MYSELF BACK INTO SHAPE NOW.
YOU KNOW, KURUMI-CHAN... MAYBE...
WELL, YOU DO HAVE THAT SHOVEL. IS IT OKAY LIKE THAT?
ガビーン
GABIIN (SHOCK)
OH YEAH!

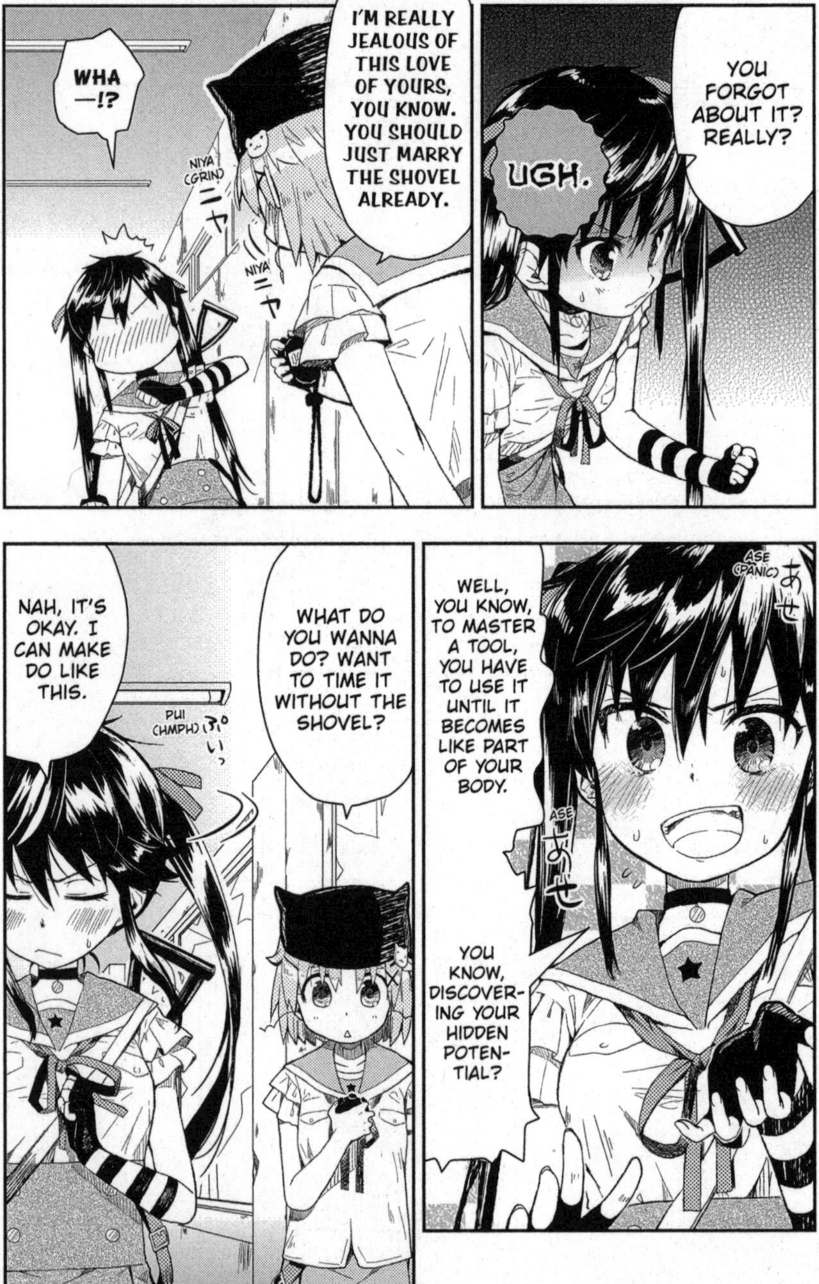
YOU FORGOT ABOUT IT? REALLY?
UGH.
I'M REALLY JEALOUS OF THIS LOVE OF YOURS, YOU KNOW. YOU SHOULD JUST MARRY THE SHOVEL ALREADY.
WHA—!?
NIYA (GRIN) ニヤ
NIYA ニヤ
ASE (PANIC) あせ
WELL, YOU KNOW, TO MASTER A TOOL, YOU HAVE TO USE IT UNTIL IT BECOMES LIKE PART OF YOUR BODY.
ASE あせ
YOU KNOW, DISCOVERING YOUR HIDDEN POTENTIAL?
WHAT DO YOU WANNA DO? WANT TO TIME IT WITHOUT THE SHOVEL?
NAH, IT'S OKAY. I CAN MAKE DO LIKE THIS.
PUI (HMPH) ぷいっ

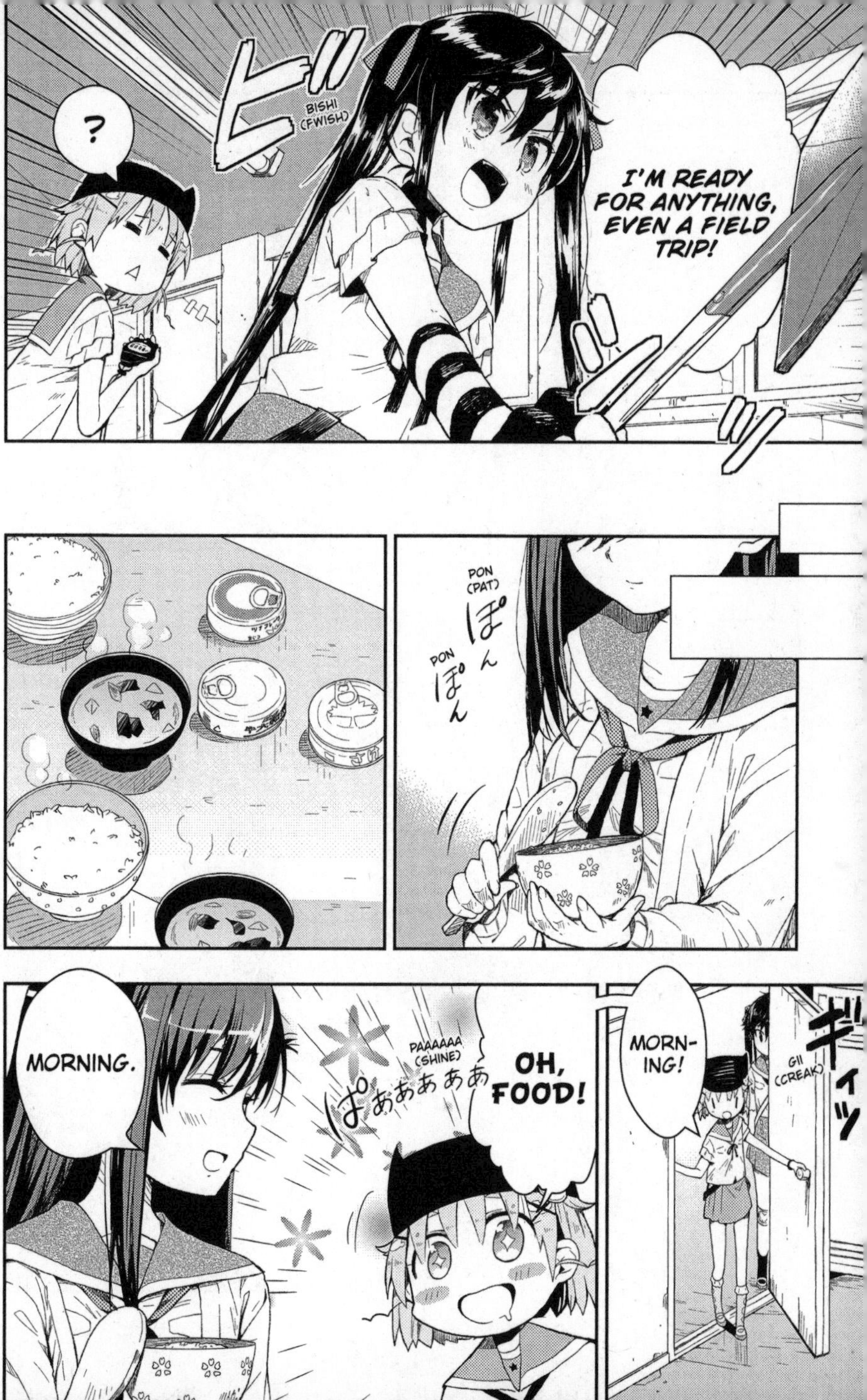
I'M READY FOR ANYTHING, EVEN A FIELD TRIP!
ビッ
BISHI (FWISH)
?
PON (PAT)
ぽん
PON
ぽん
ギィッ
GII (CREAK)
MORN-ING!
OH, FOOD!
ぱあああああ
PAAAAAA (SHINE)
MORNING.

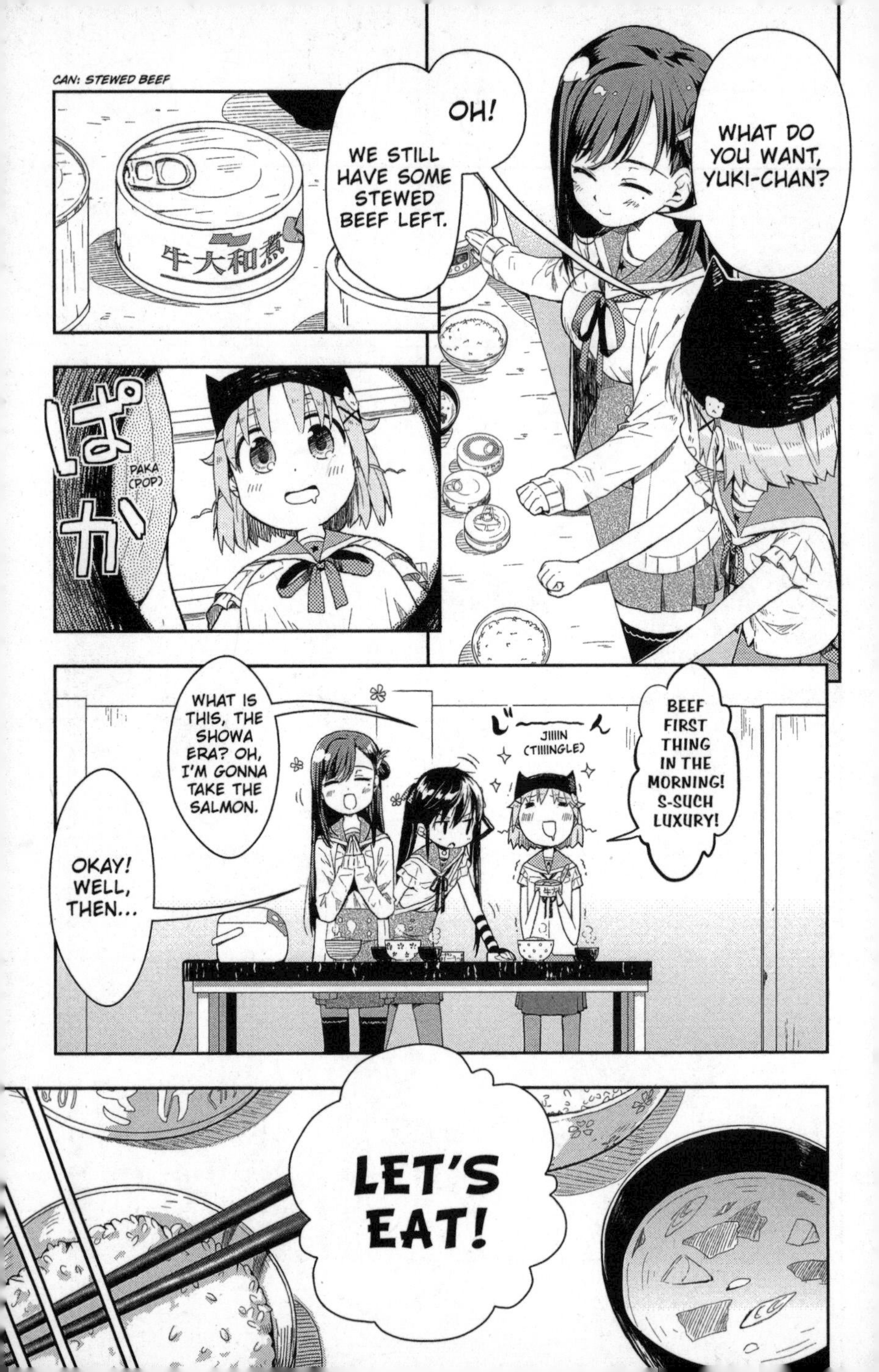
WHAT DO YOU WANT, YUKI-CHAN?
CAN: STEWED BEEF
牛大和煮
OH! WE STILL HAVE SOME STEWED BEEF LEFT.
ぱかっ
PAKA (POP)
BEEF FIRST THING IN THE MORNING! S-SUCH LUXURY!
じーーーん
JIIIIN (TIIIINGLE)
WHAT IS THIS, THE SHOWA ERA? OH, I'M GONNA TAKE THE SALMON.
OKAY! WELL, THEN...
LET'S EAT!

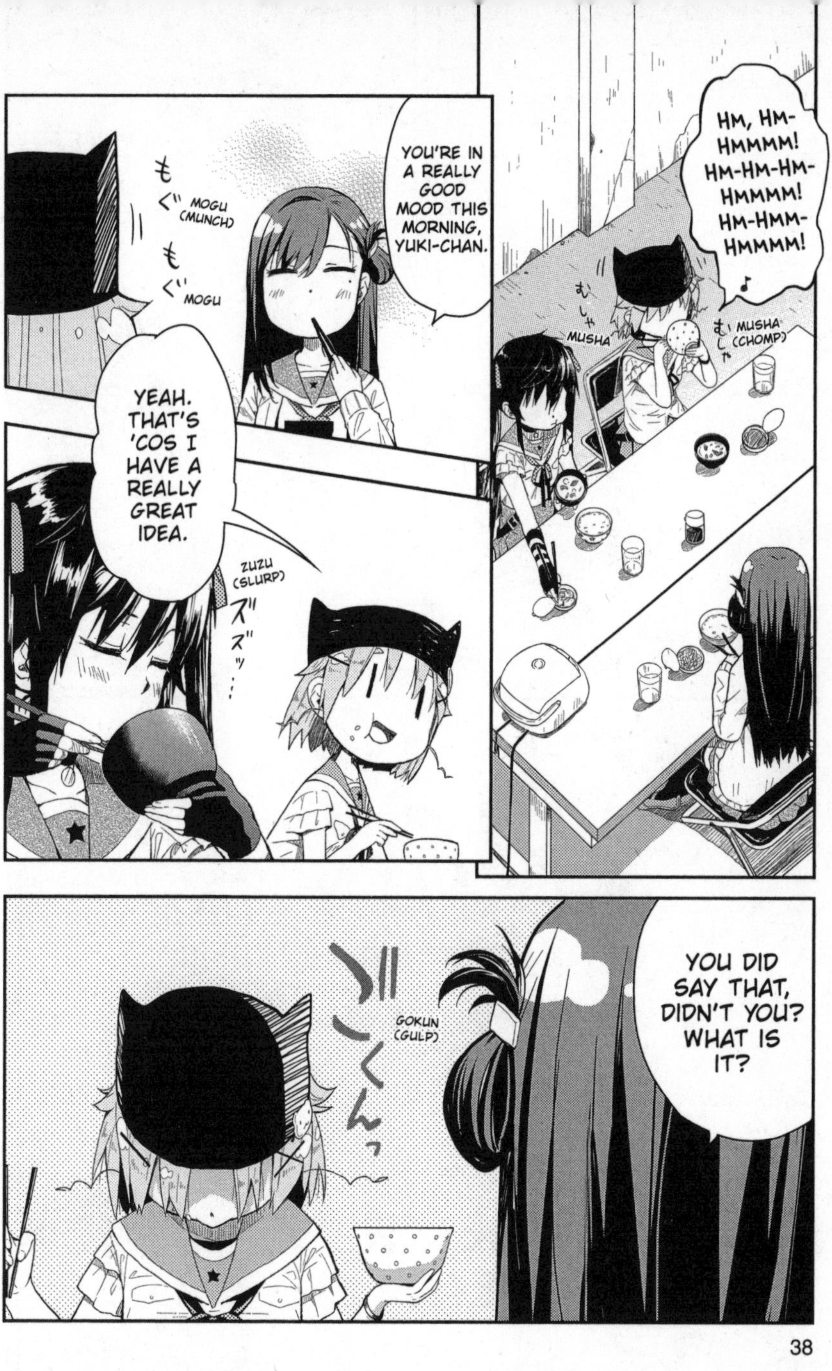
HM, HM-HMMMM! HM-HM-HM-HMMMM! HM-HMM-HMMMM! ♪
むしゃ
MUSHA
むしゃ
MUSHA (CHOMP)
YOU'RE IN A REALLY GOOD MOOD THIS MORNING, YUKI-CHAN.
もぐ
MOGU (MUNCH)
もぐ
MOGU
YEAH. THAT'S 'COS I HAVE A REALLY GREAT IDEA.
ZUZU (SLURP)
ズズッ…
YOU DID SAY THAT, DIDN'T YOU? WHAT IS IT?
ごくんっ
GOKUN (GULP)

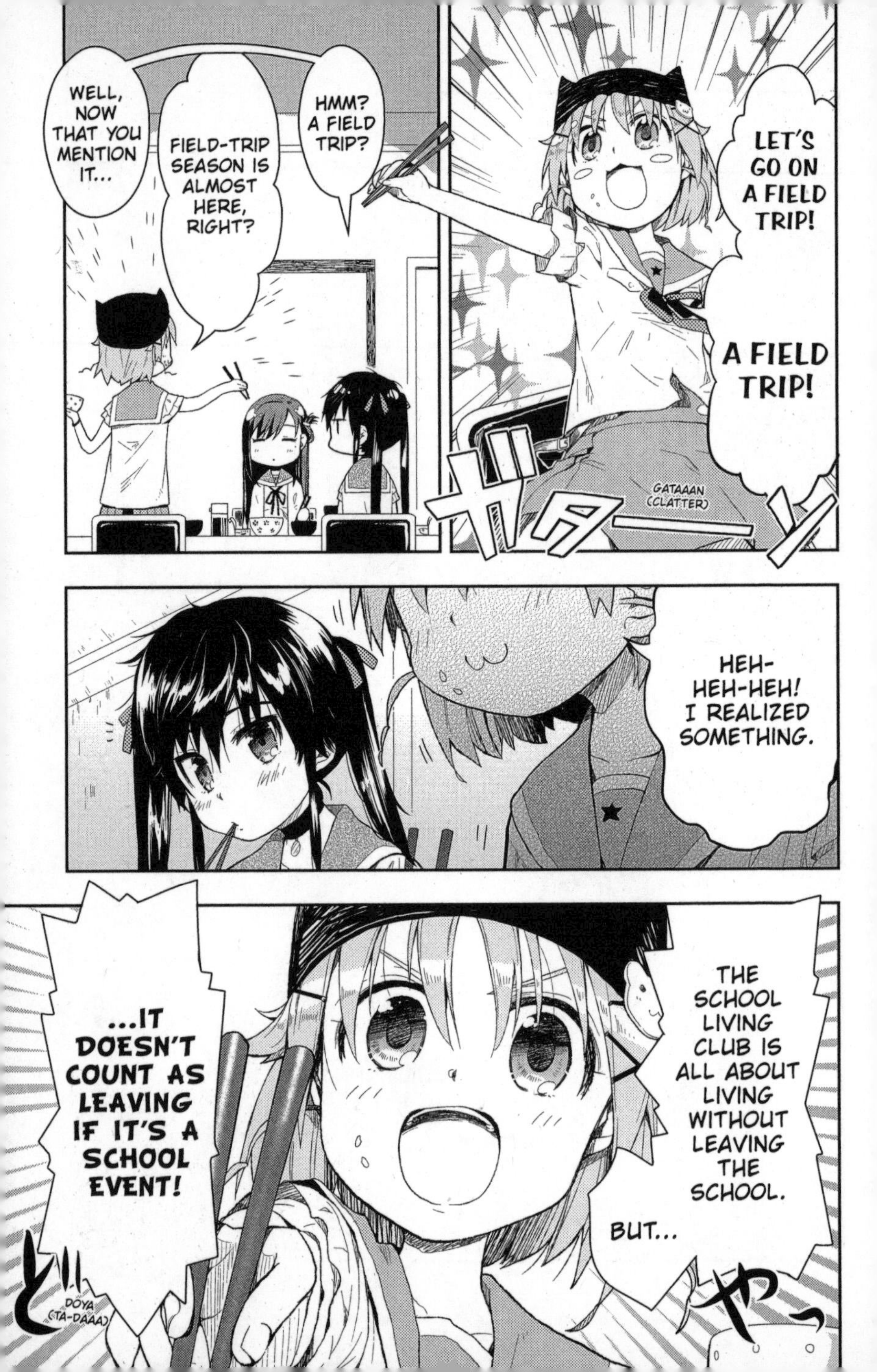
LET'S GO ON A FIELD TRIP!
A FIELD TRIP!
GATAAAN (CLATTER)
HMM? A FIELD TRIP?
FIELD-TRIP SEASON IS ALMOST HERE, RIGHT?
WELL, NOW THAT YOU MENTION IT...
HEH-HEH-HEH! I REALIZED SOMETHING.
THE SCHOOL LIVING CLUB IS ALL ABOUT LIVING WITHOUT LEAVING THE SCHOOL.
BUT...
...IT DOESN'T COUNT AS LEAVING IF IT'S A SCHOOL EVENT!
DOYA (TA-DAAA)

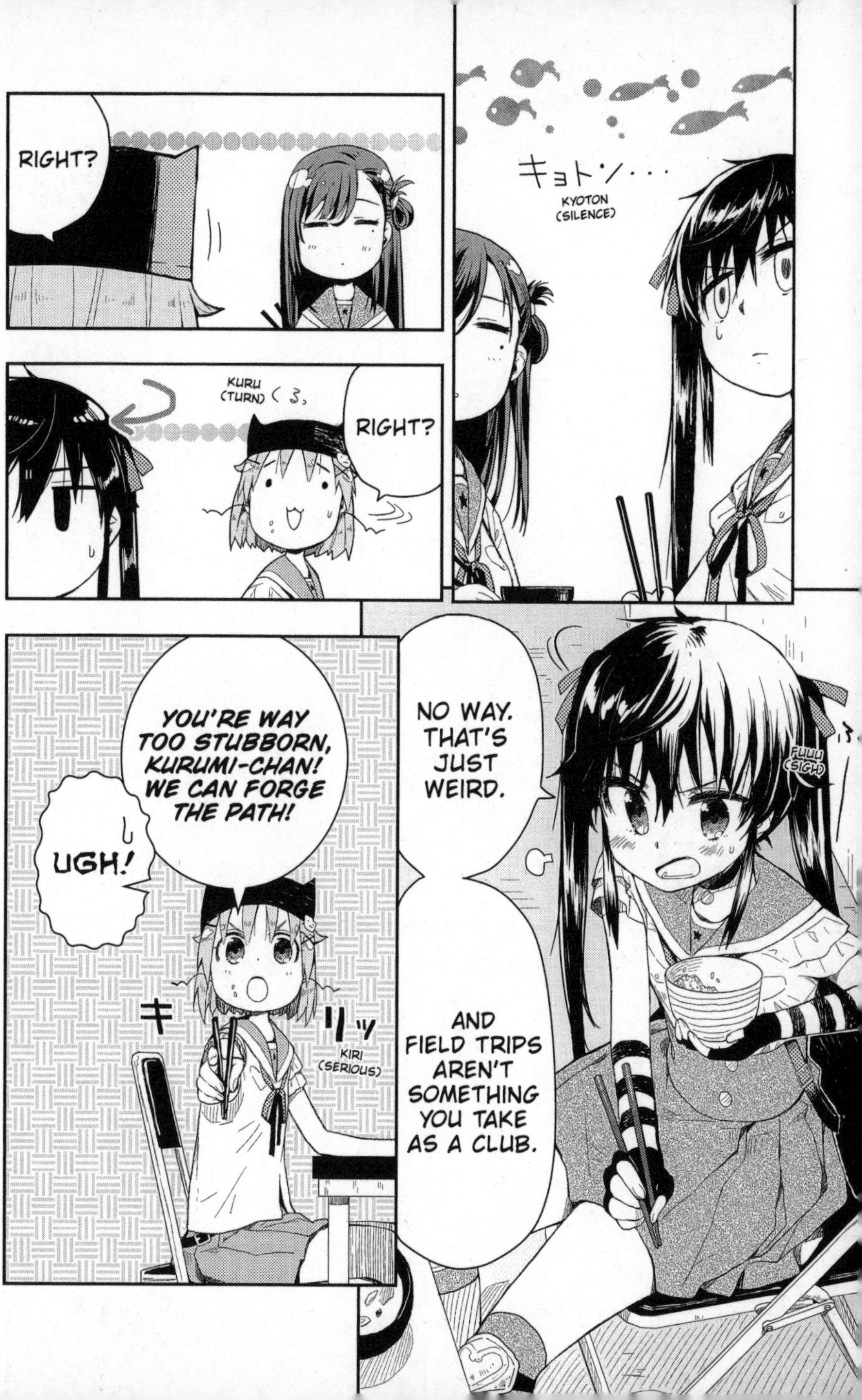
キョトン…
KYOTON (SILENCE)
RIGHT?
KURU (TURN) くる
RIGHT?
NO WAY. THAT'S JUST WEIRD.
AND FIELD TRIPS AREN'T SOMETHING YOU TAKE AS A CLUB.
FUUU (SIGH)
YOU'RE WAY TOO STUBBORN, KURUMI-CHAN! WE CAN FORGE THE PATH!
UGH!
キリッ
KIRI (SERIOUS)

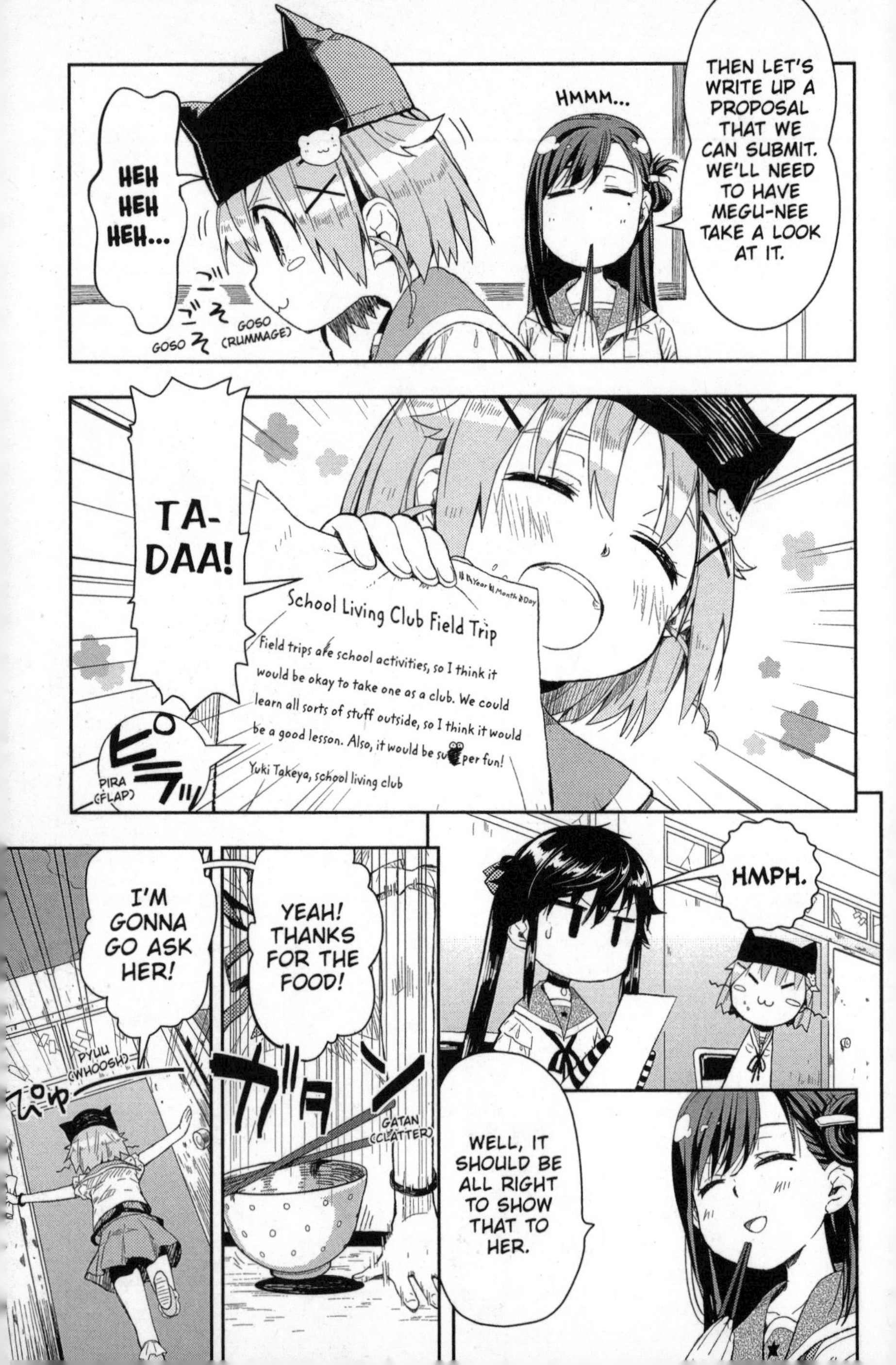
THEN LET'S WRITE UP A PROPOSAL THAT WE CAN SUBMIT. WE'LL NEED TO HAVE MEGU-NEE TAKE A LOOK AT IT.
HMMM...
HEH HEH HEH...
GOSO GOSO (RUMMAGE)
TA-DAA!
School Living Club Field Trip
Field trips are school activities, so I think it would be okay to take one as a club. We could learn all sorts of stuff outside, so I think it would be a good lesson. Also, it would be super fun!
Yuki Takeya, school living club
PIRA (FLAP)
HMPH.
WELL, IT SHOULD BE ALL RIGHT TO SHOW THAT TO HER.
YEAH! THANKS FOR THE FOOD!
GATAN (CLATTER)
I'M GONNA GO ASK HER!
PYUU (WHOOSH)

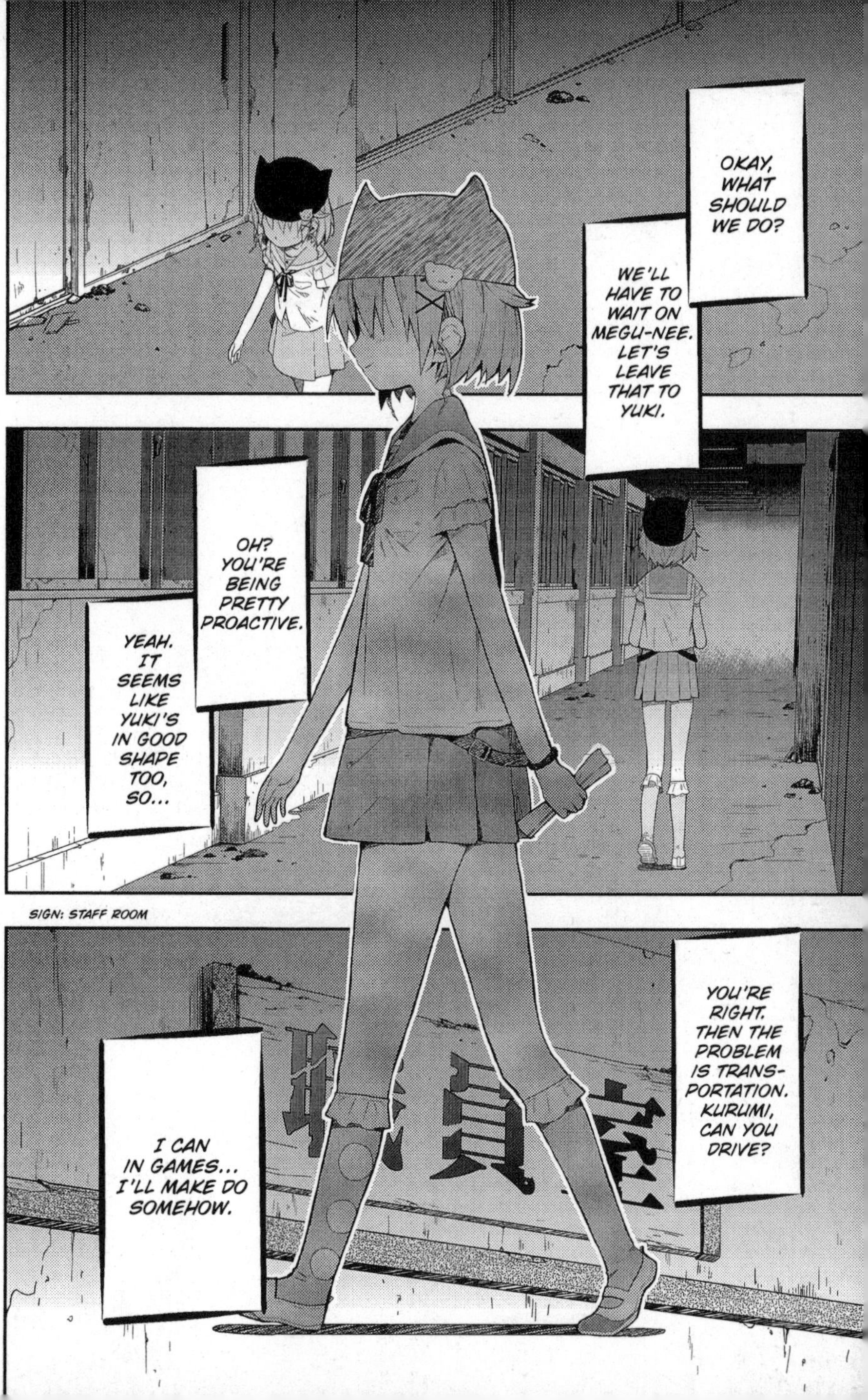
OKAY, WHAT SHOULD WE DO?
WE'LL HAVE TO WAIT ON MEGU-NEE. LET'S LEAVE THAT TO YUKI.
OH? YOU'RE BEING PRETTY PROACTIVE.
YEAH. IT SEEMS LIKE YUKI'S IN GOOD SHAPE TOO, SO...
SIGN: STAFF ROOM
YOU'RE RIGHT. THEN THE PROBLEM IS TRANS-PORTATION. KURUMI, CAN YOU DRIVE?
I CAN IN GAMES... I'LL MAKE DO SOMEHOW.

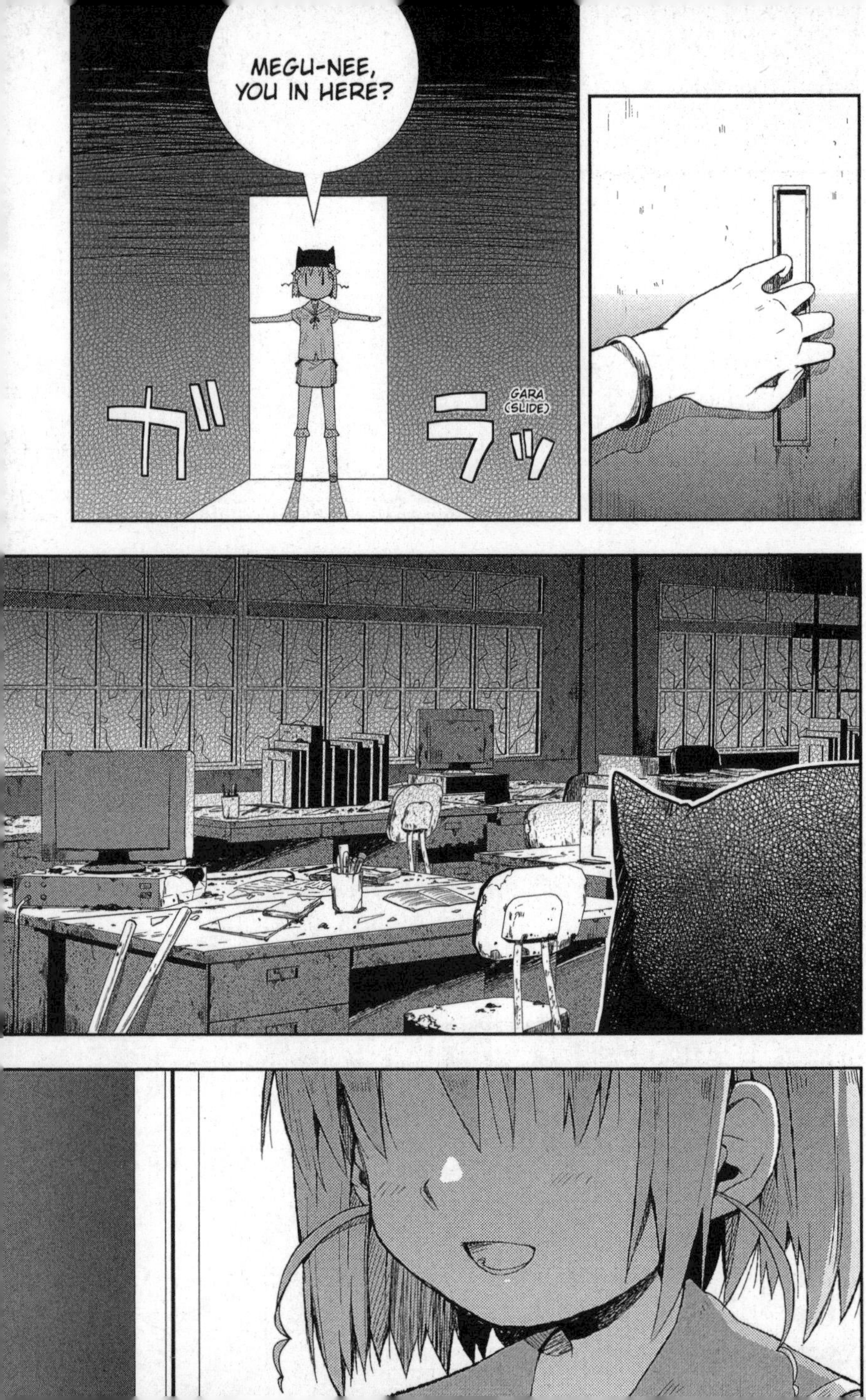
MEGU-NEE, YOU IN HERE?
ガラッ
GARA (SLIDE)

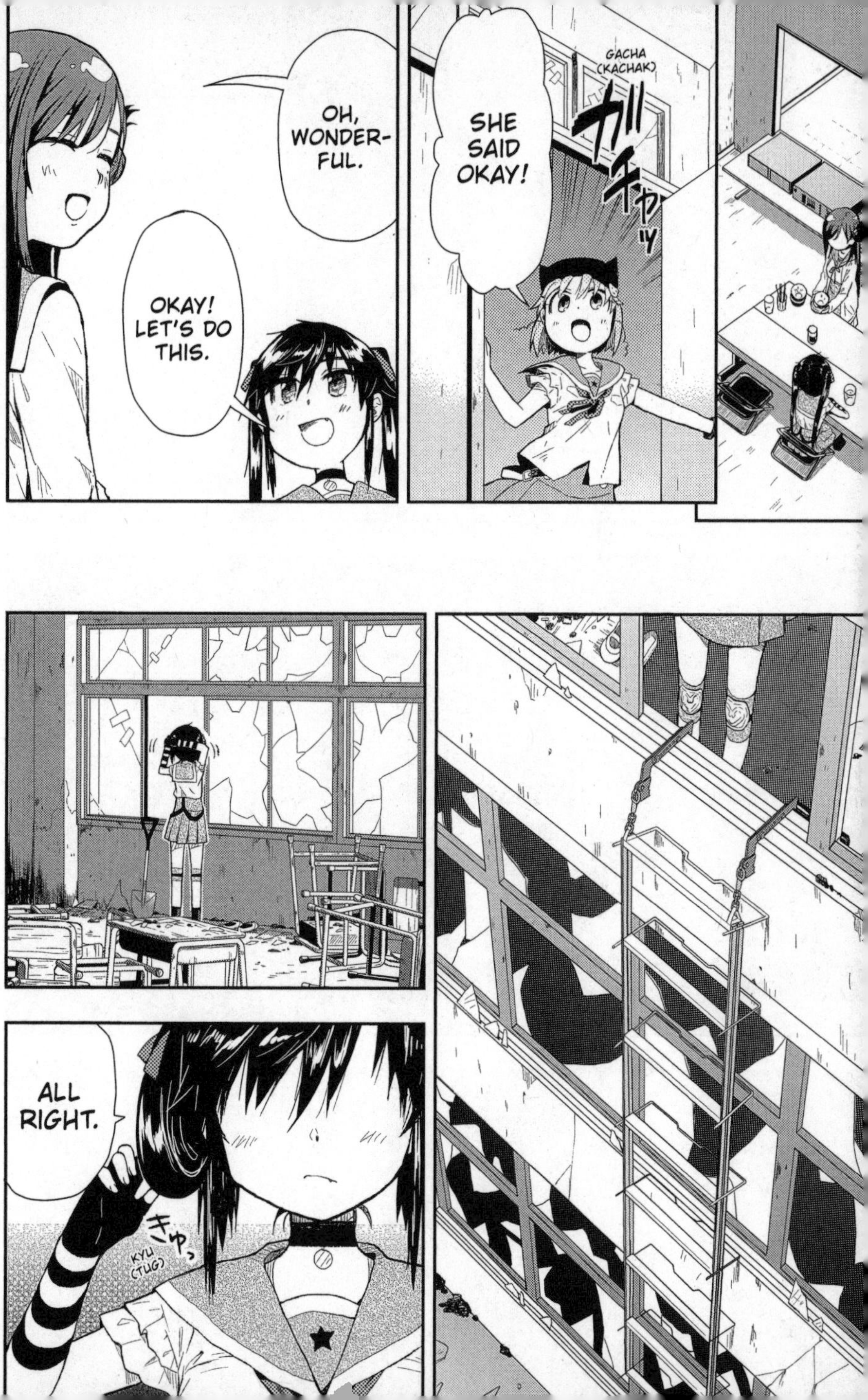
GACHA (KACHAK)
ガチャッ
SHE SAID OKAY!
OH, WONDERFUL.
OKAY! LET'S DO THIS.
ALL RIGHT.
きゅっ
KYU (TUG)

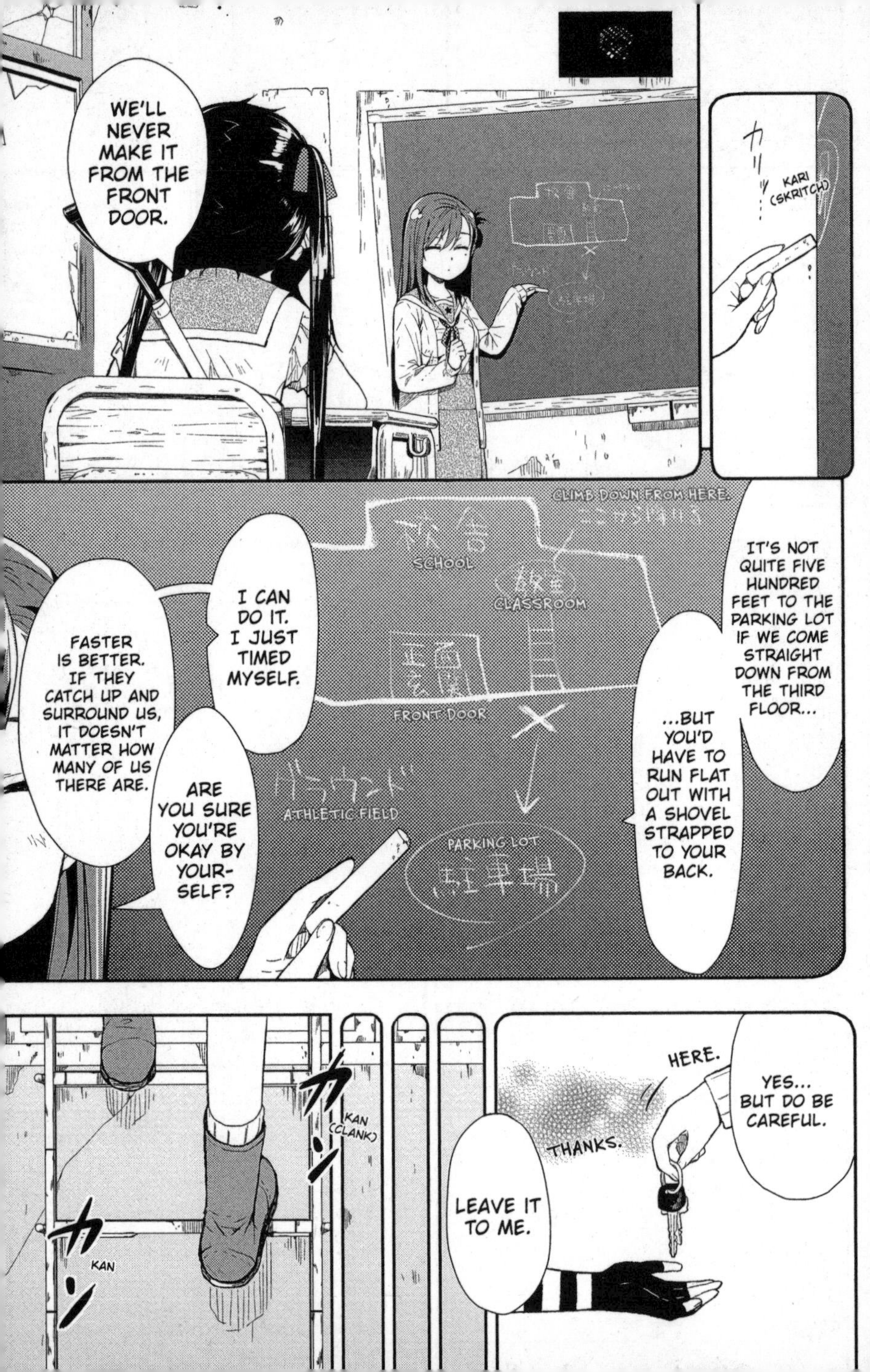
カリッ
KARI (SKRITCH)
WE'LL NEVER MAKE IT FROM THE FRONT DOOR.
CLIMB DOWN FROM HERE.
SCHOOL
CLASSROOM
FRONT DOOR
ATHLETIC FIELD
PARKING LOT
IT'S NOT QUITE FIVE HUNDRED FEET TO THE PARKING LOT IF WE COME STRAIGHT DOWN FROM THE THIRD FLOOR...
...BUT YOU'D HAVE TO RUN FLAT OUT WITH A SHOVEL STRAPPED TO YOUR BACK.
ARE YOU SURE YOU'RE OKAY BY YOUR-SELF?
I CAN DO IT. I JUST TIMED MYSELF.
FASTER IS BETTER. IF THEY CATCH UP AND SURROUND US, IT DOESN'T MATTER HOW MANY OF US THERE ARE.
YES... BUT DO BE CAREFUL.
HERE.
THANKS.
LEAVE IT TO ME.
カン
KAN (CLANK)
カン
KAN

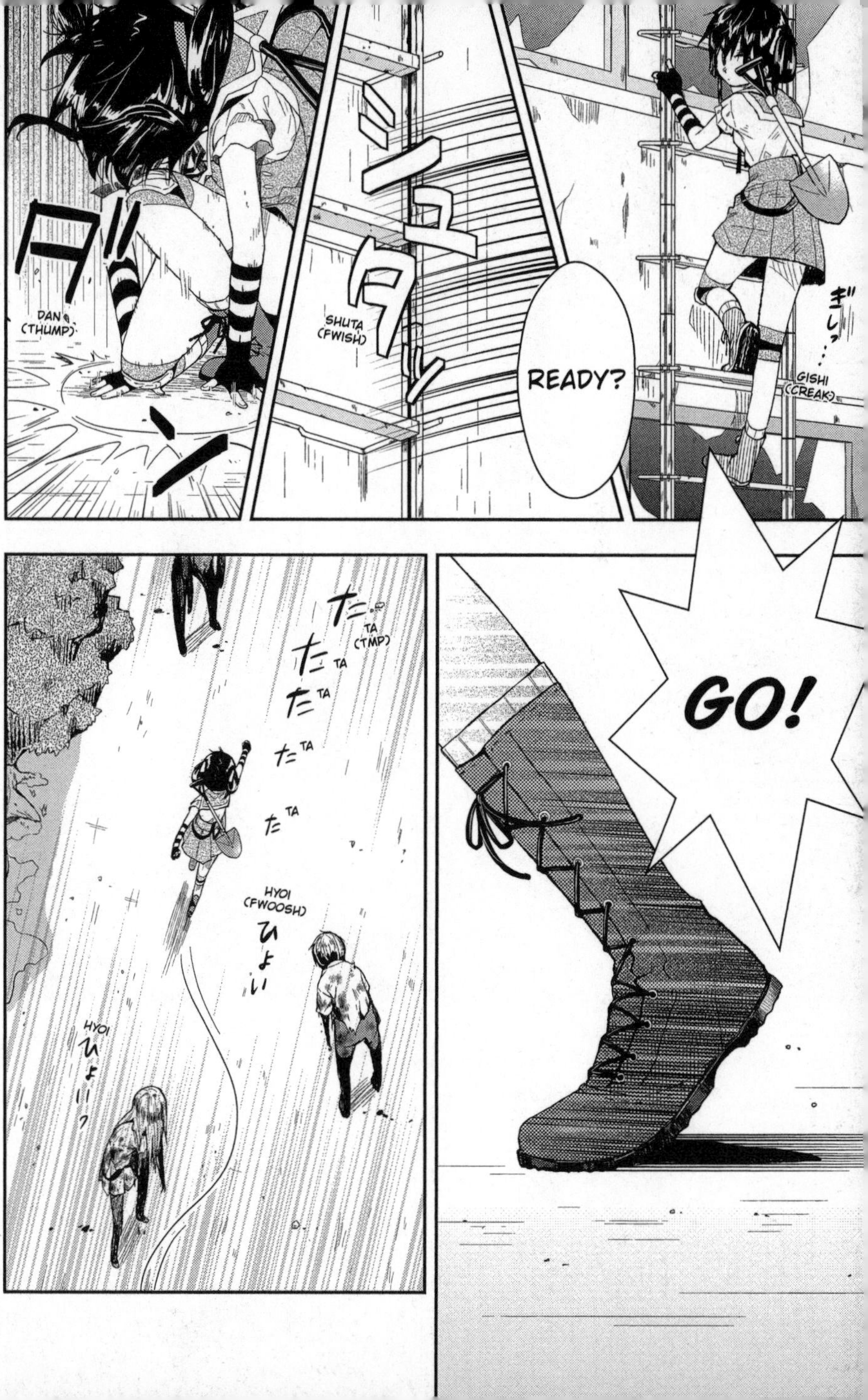
ぎしっ…
GISHI (CREAK)
READY?
シュタッ
SHUTA (FWISH)
ダンッ
DAN (THUMP)
GO!
た
TA (TMP)
た TA
た TA
た TA
た TA
HYOI (FWOOSH)
ひょい
HYOI
ひょいっ

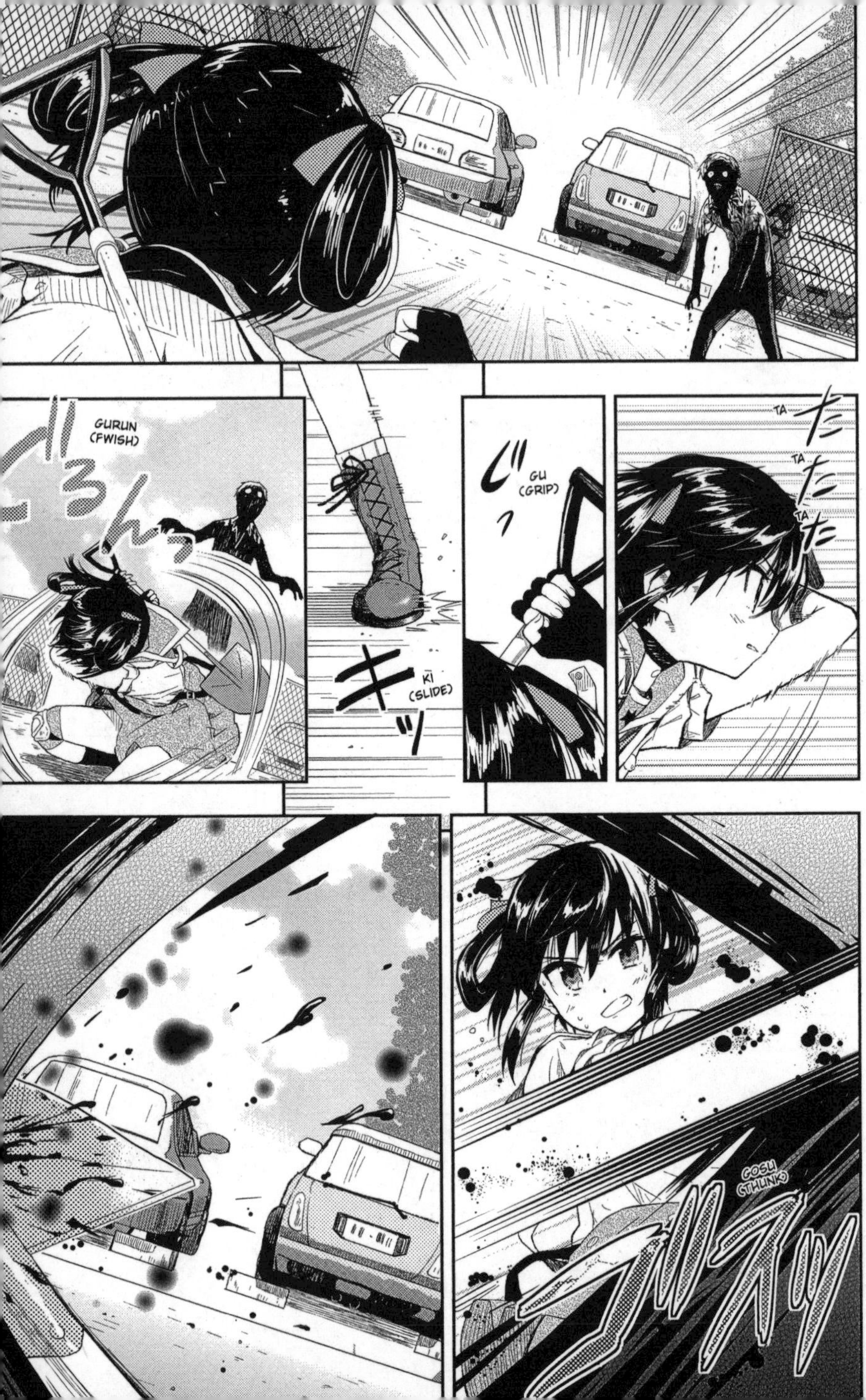

TA
TA
TA
GU (GRIP)
KI (SLIDE)
GURUN (FWISH)
GOSU (THUNK)

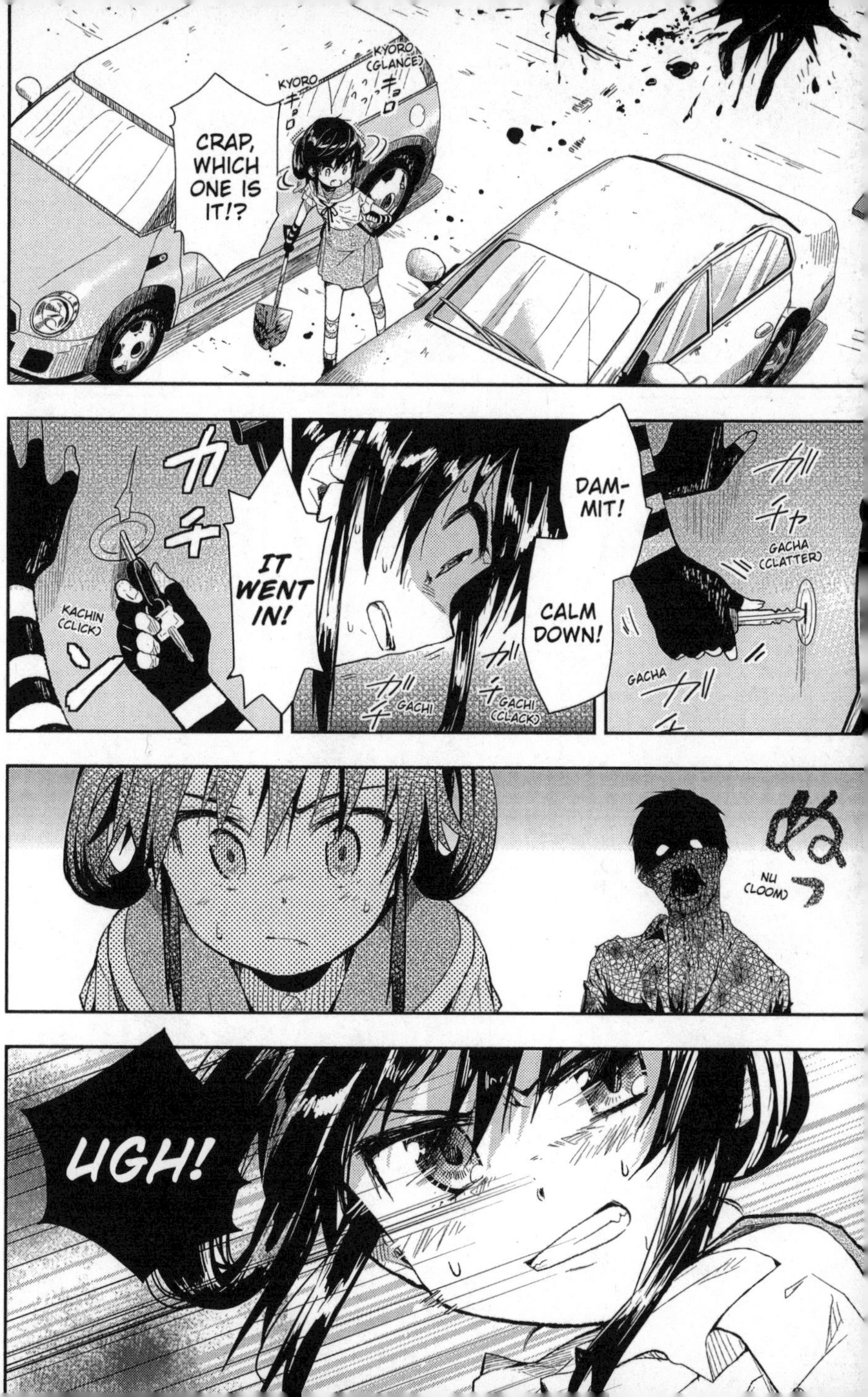
KYORO (GLANCE)
KYORO
CRAP, WHICH ONE IS IT!?
GACHA (CLATTER)
GACHA
DAM-MIT!
CALM DOWN!
GACHI (CLACK)
GACHI
IT WENT IN!
KACHIN (CLICK)
NU (LOOM)
UGH!

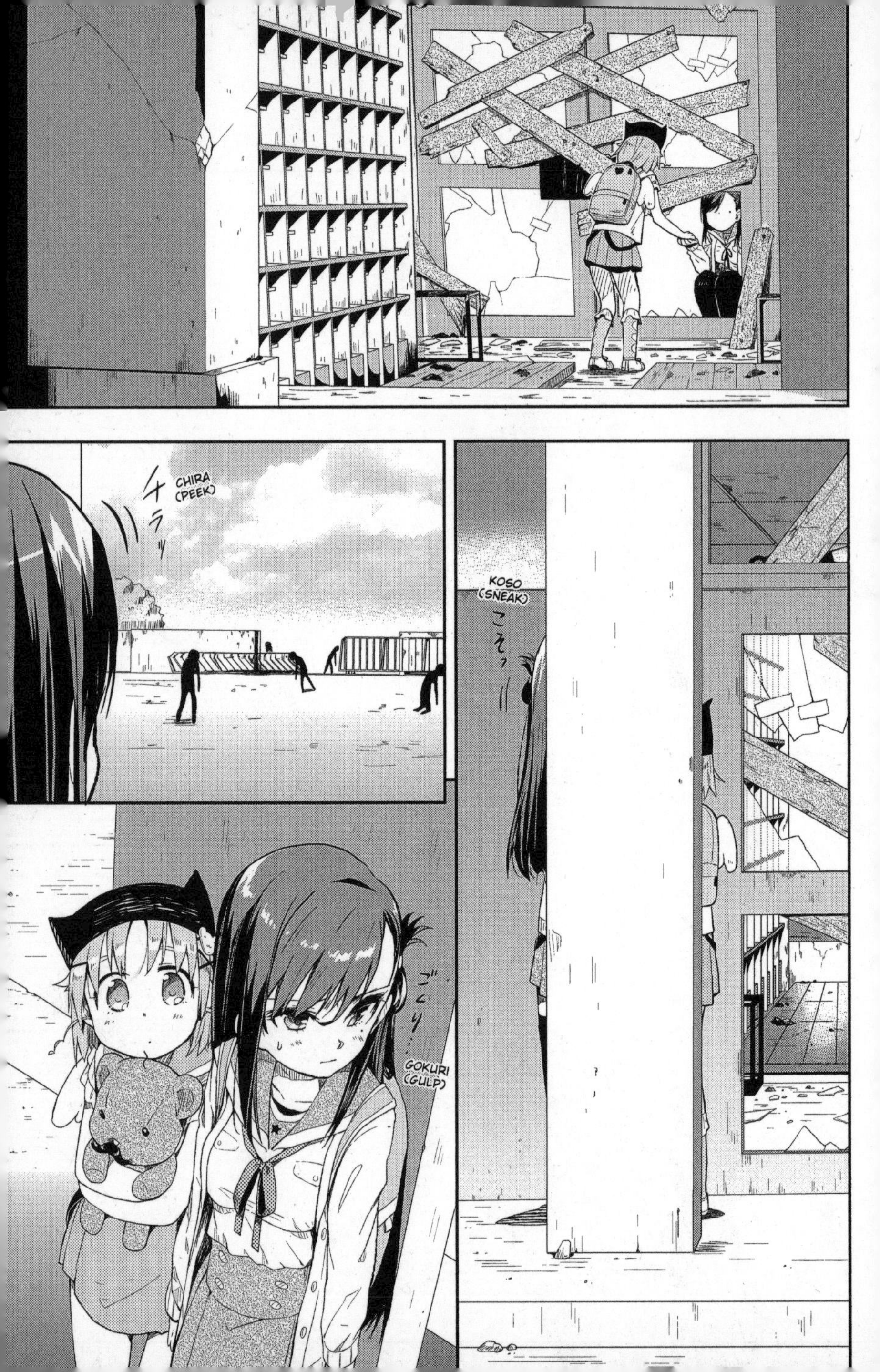
KOSO (SNEAK)
こそっ
チラッ
CHIRA (PEEK)
ごくり…
GOKURI (GULP)

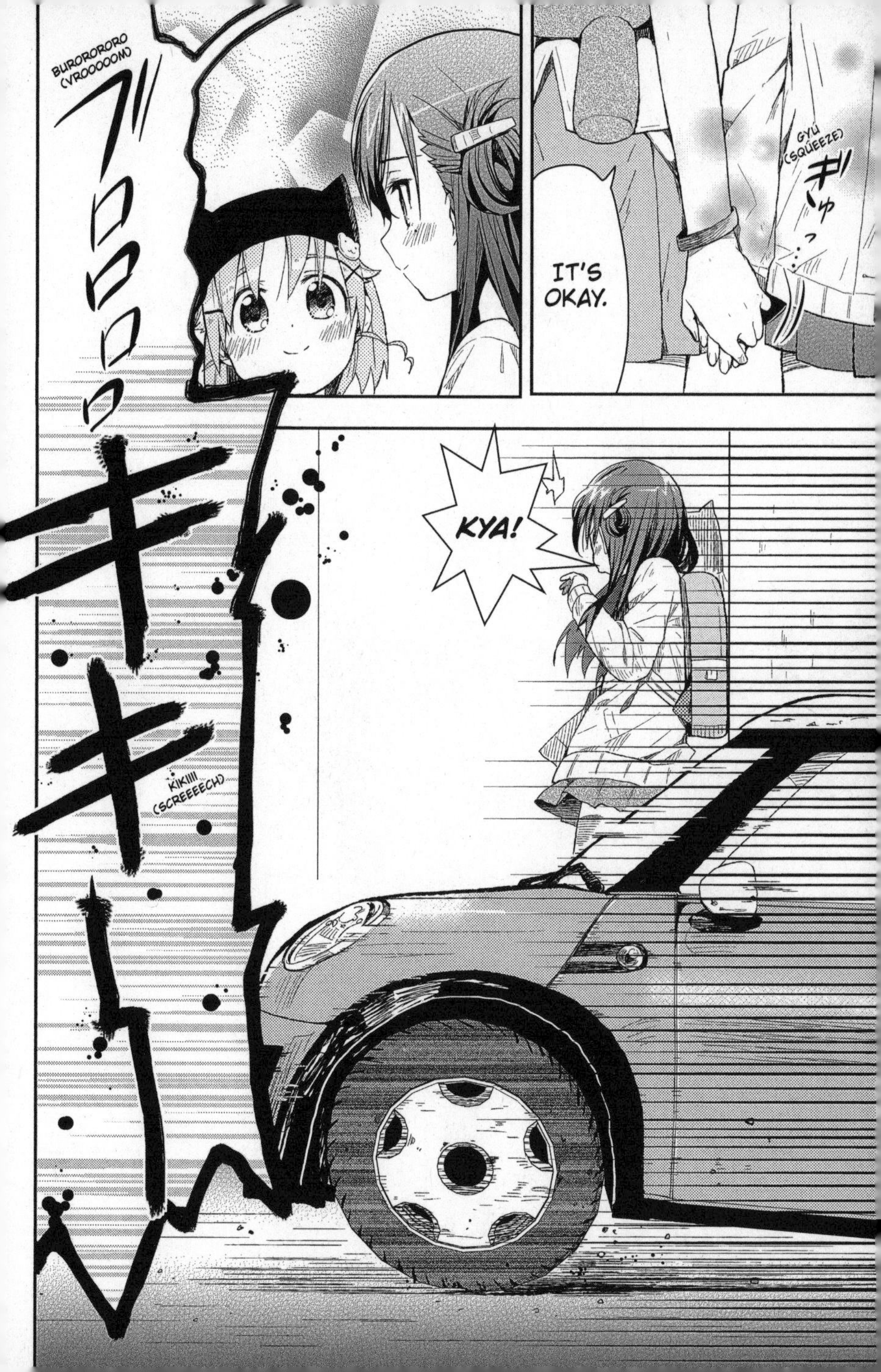
GYŪ (SQUEEZE)
IT'S OKAY.
BURORORORO (VROOOOOM)
KYA!
KIKIIII (SCREEEEECH)

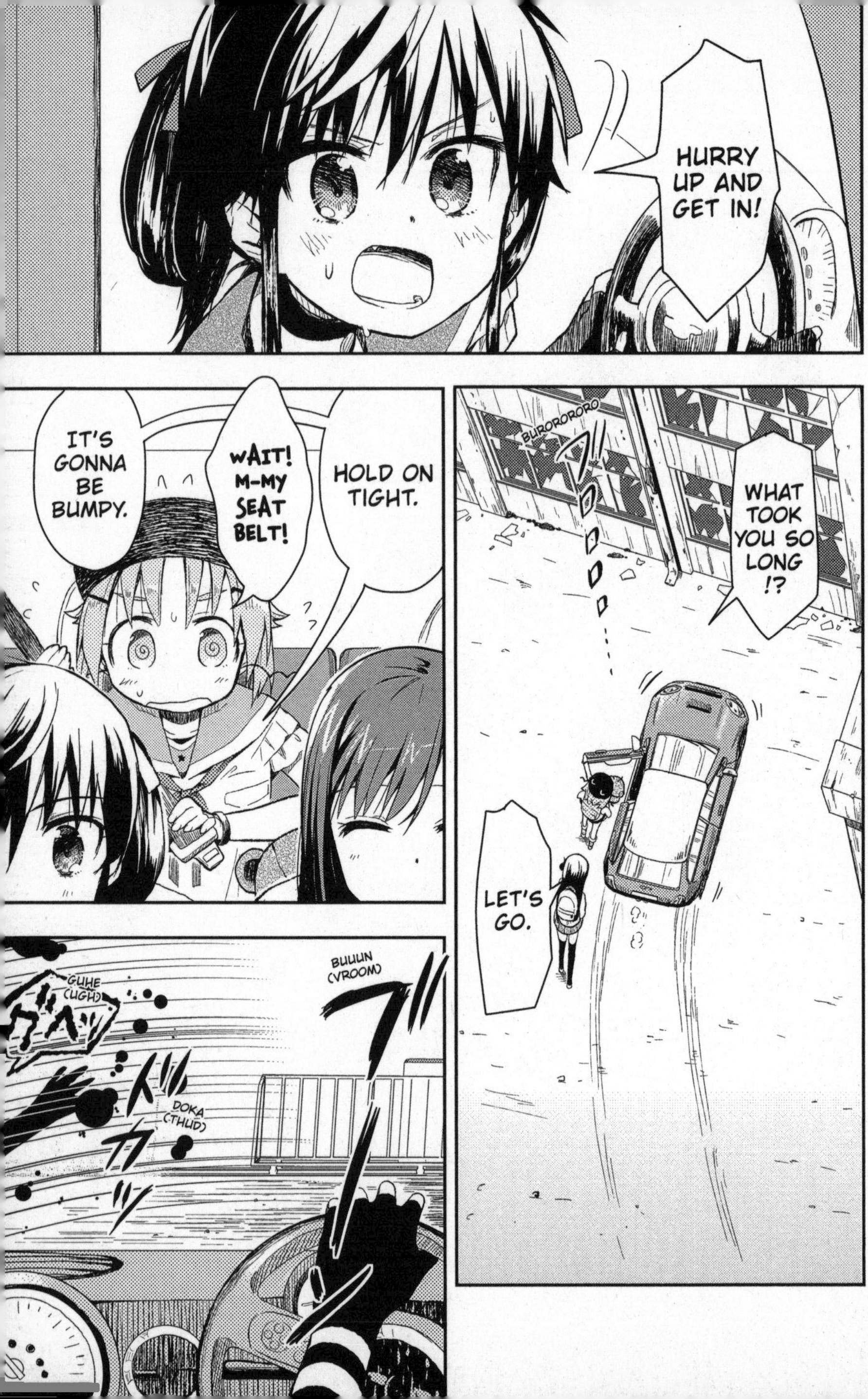
HURRY UP AND GET IN!
BURORORORO
WHAT TOOK YOU SO LONG!?
LET'S GO.
HOLD ON TIGHT.
WAIT! M-MY SEAT BELT!
IT'S GONNA BE BUMPY.
BUUUN (VROOM)
DOKA (THUD)
GUHE (UGH)

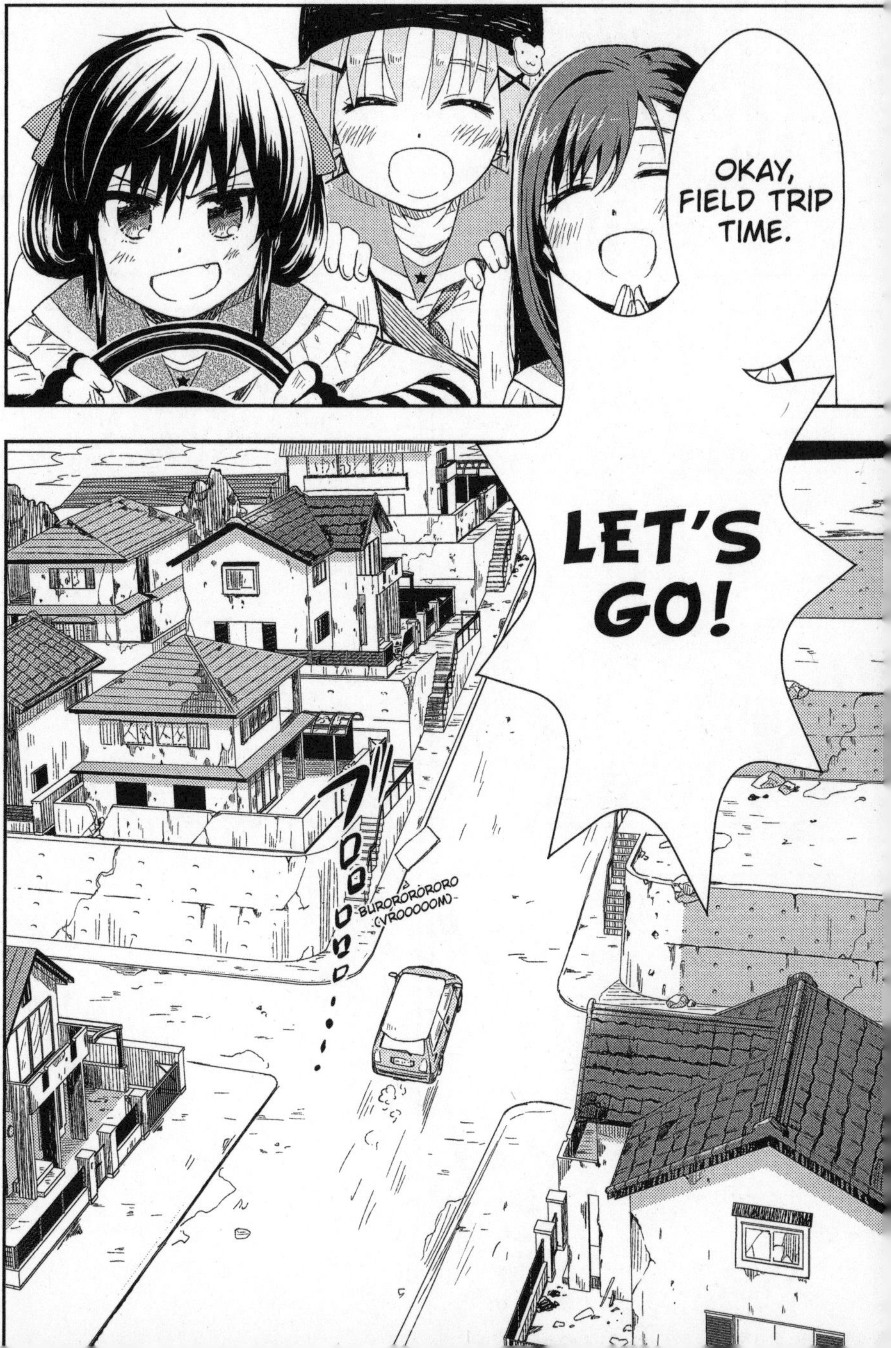
OKAY, FIELD TRIP TIME.
LET'S GO!
BUROROROROROROR
(VROOOOOM)

SCHOOL-LIVE!

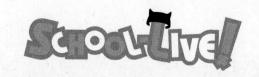

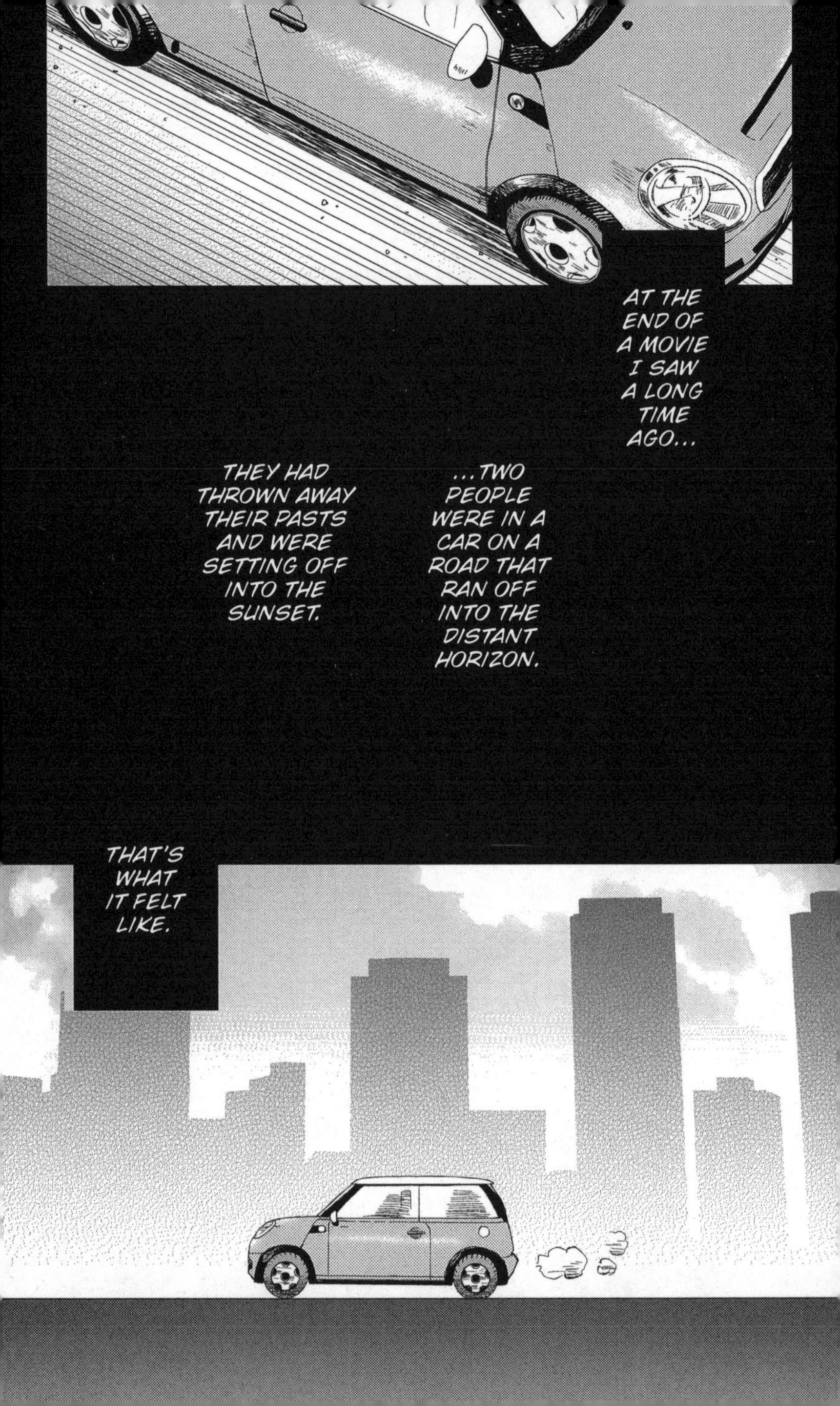
AT THE END OF A MOVIE I SAW A LONG TIME AGO...
...TWO PEOPLE WERE IN A CAR ON A ROAD THAT RAN OFF INTO THE DISTANT HORIZON.
THEY HAD THROWN AWAY THEIR PASTS AND WERE SETTING OFF INTO THE SUNSET.
THAT'S WHAT IT FELT LIKE.

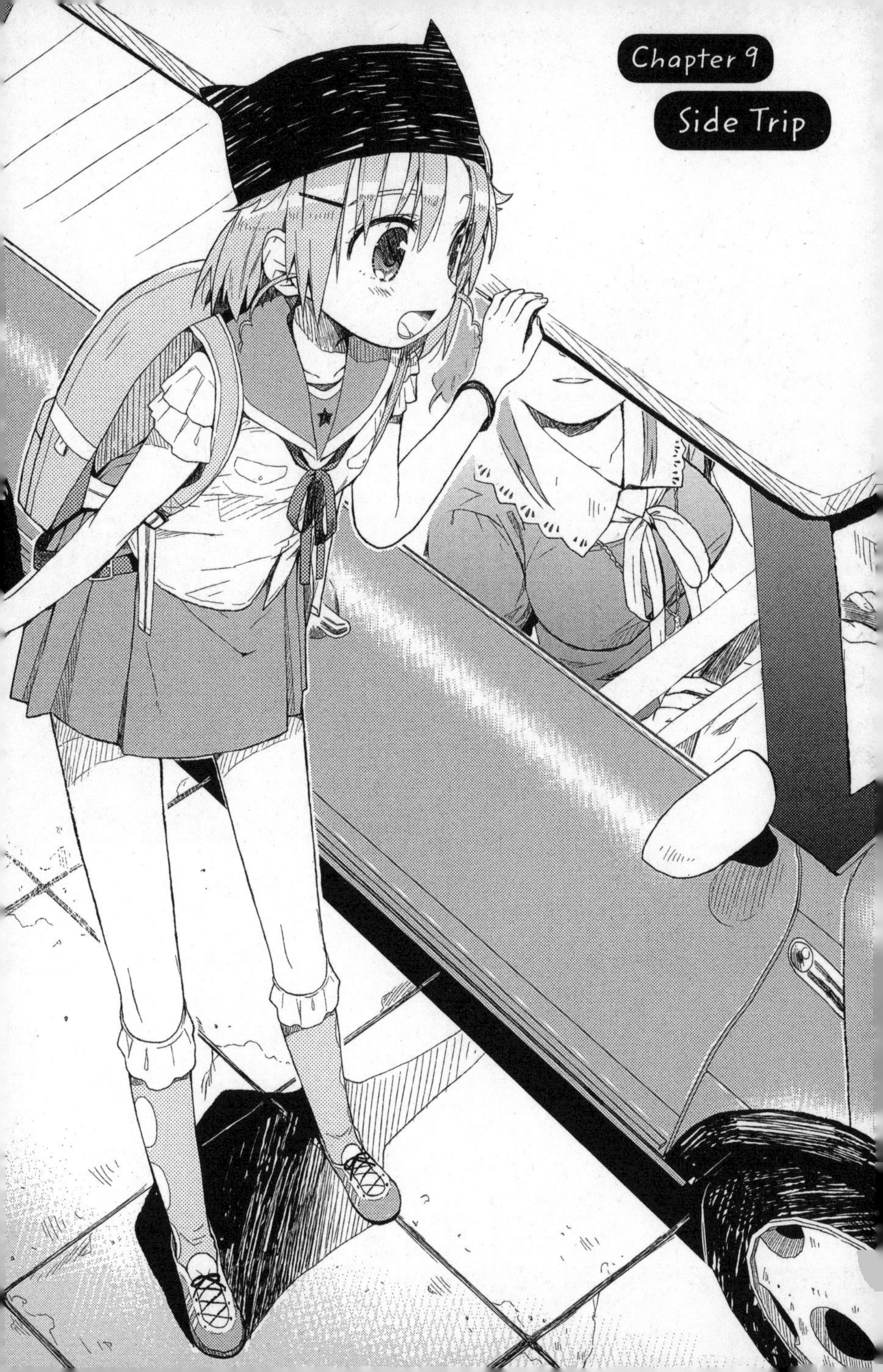
Chapter 9
Side Trip

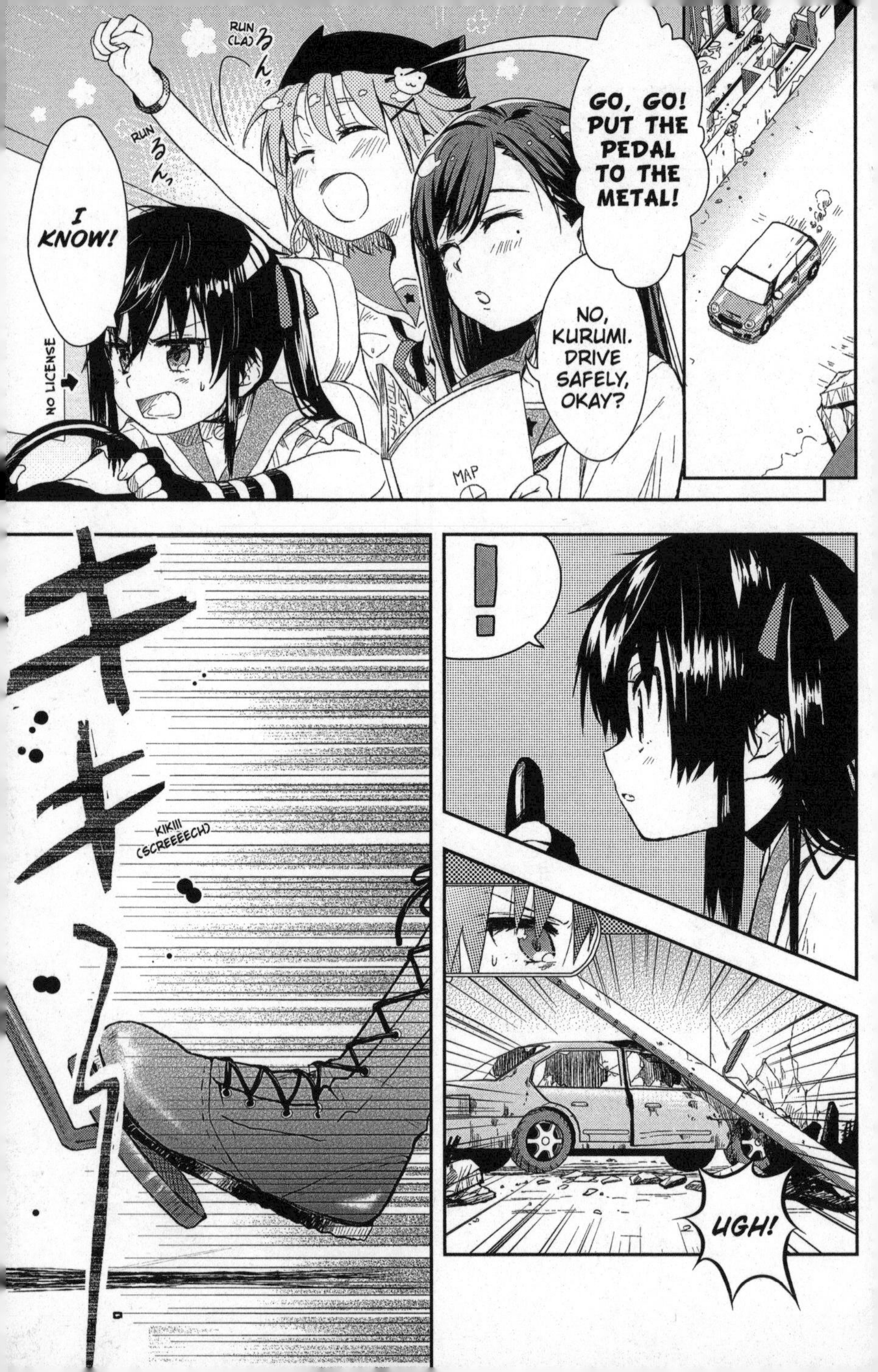
GO, GO! PUT THE PEDAL TO THE METAL!
RUN (LA) るん
NO, KURUMI. DRIVE SAFELY, OKAY?
RUN るん
I KNOW!
NO LICENSE
MAP
!
UGH!
キキ
KIKIII (SCREEEECH)

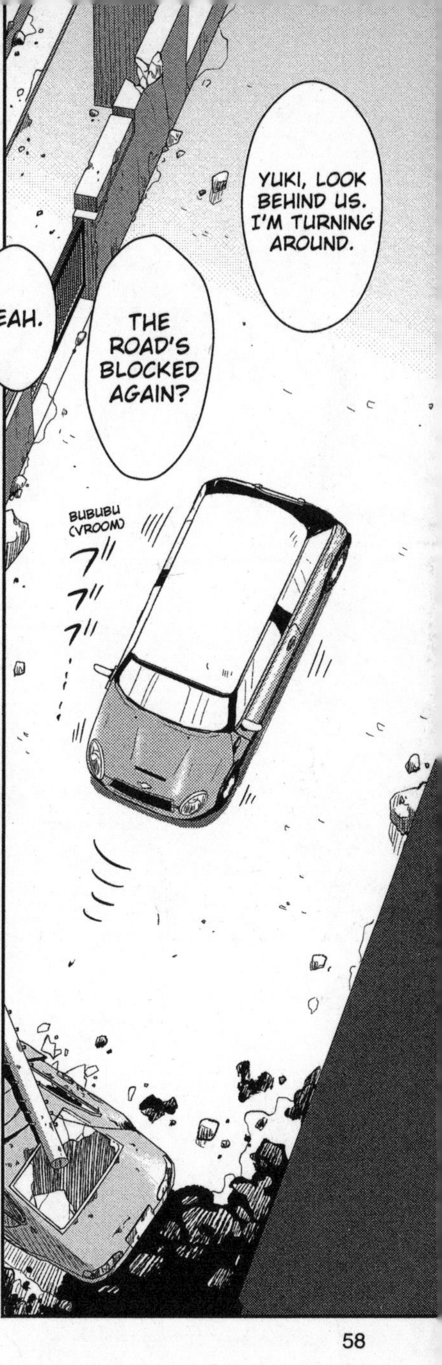
YUKI, LOOK BEHIND US. I'M TURNING AROUND.
THE ROAD'S BLOCKED AGAIN?
YEAH.
BUBUBU (VROOM)
ブブブ

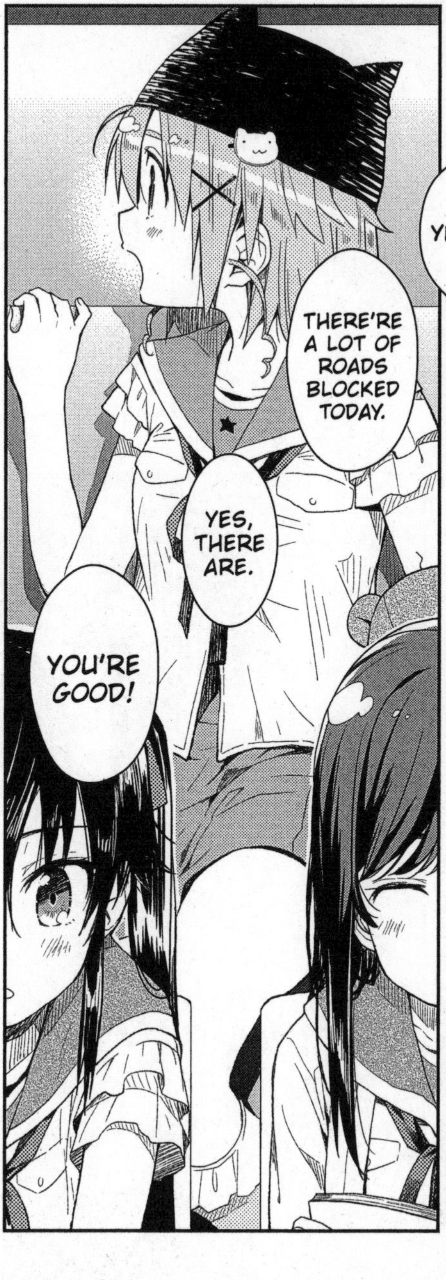
THERE'RE A LOT OF ROADS BLOCKED TODAY.
YES, THERE ARE.
YOU'RE GOOD!

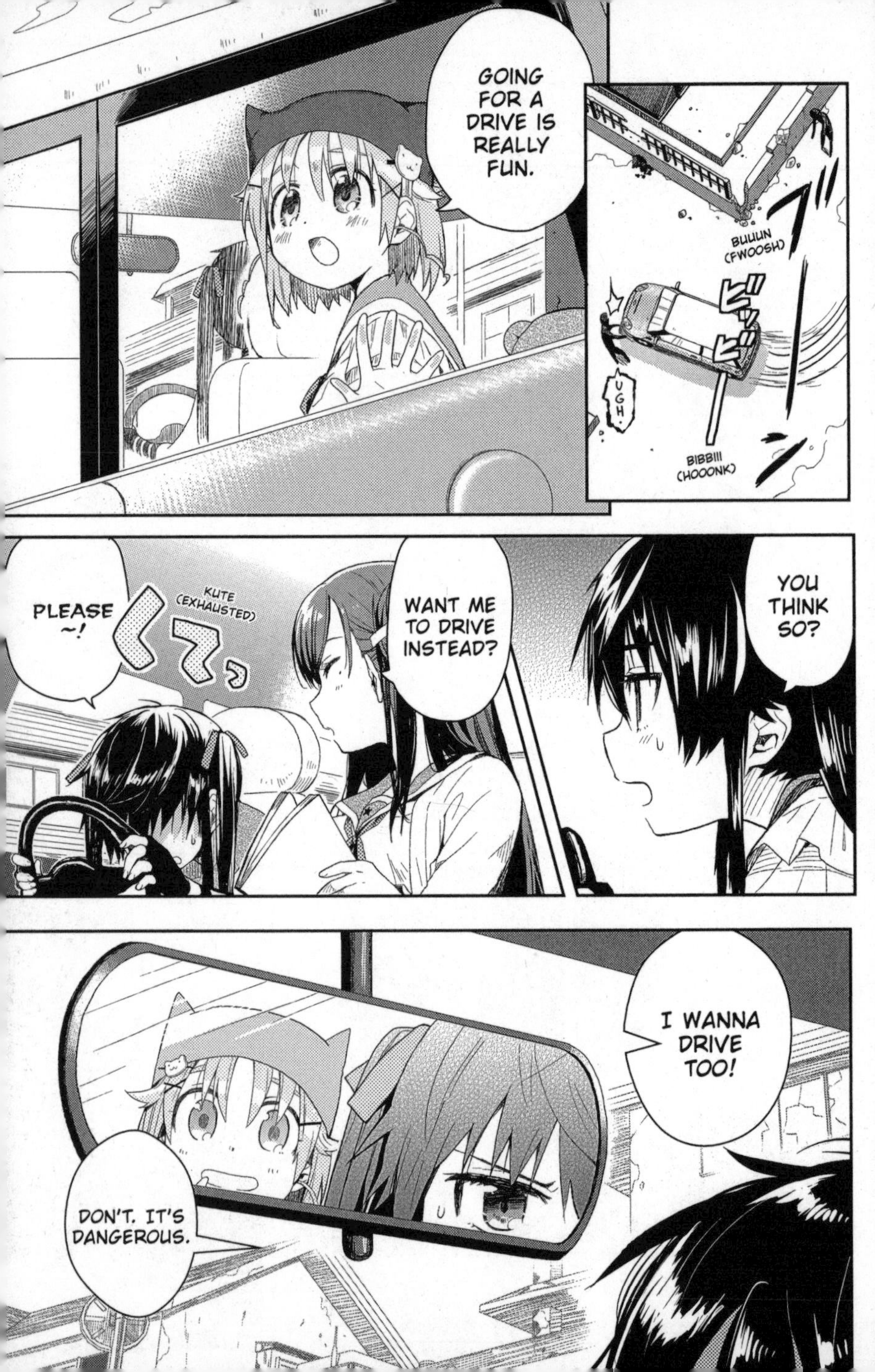
BUUUN (FWOOSH)
UGH.
BIBBIII (HOOONK)
GOING FOR A DRIVE IS REALLY FUN.
YOU THINK SO?
WANT ME TO DRIVE INSTEAD?
KUTE (EXHAUSTED)
PLEASE ~!
I WANNA DRIVE TOO!
DON'T. IT'S DANGEROUS.

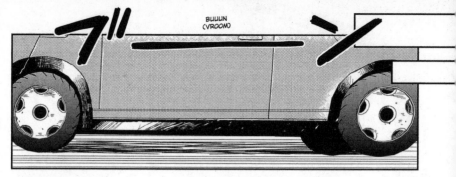

BUUUN
(VROOM)

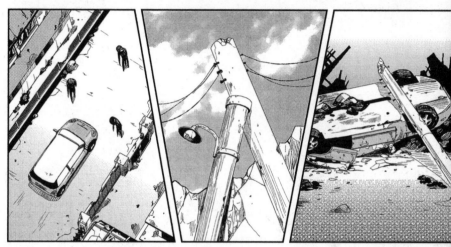

I'M LOST
......

OH, UMMM ...

MAP

KURU

KURU
(TURN)

WHICH WAY NOW?

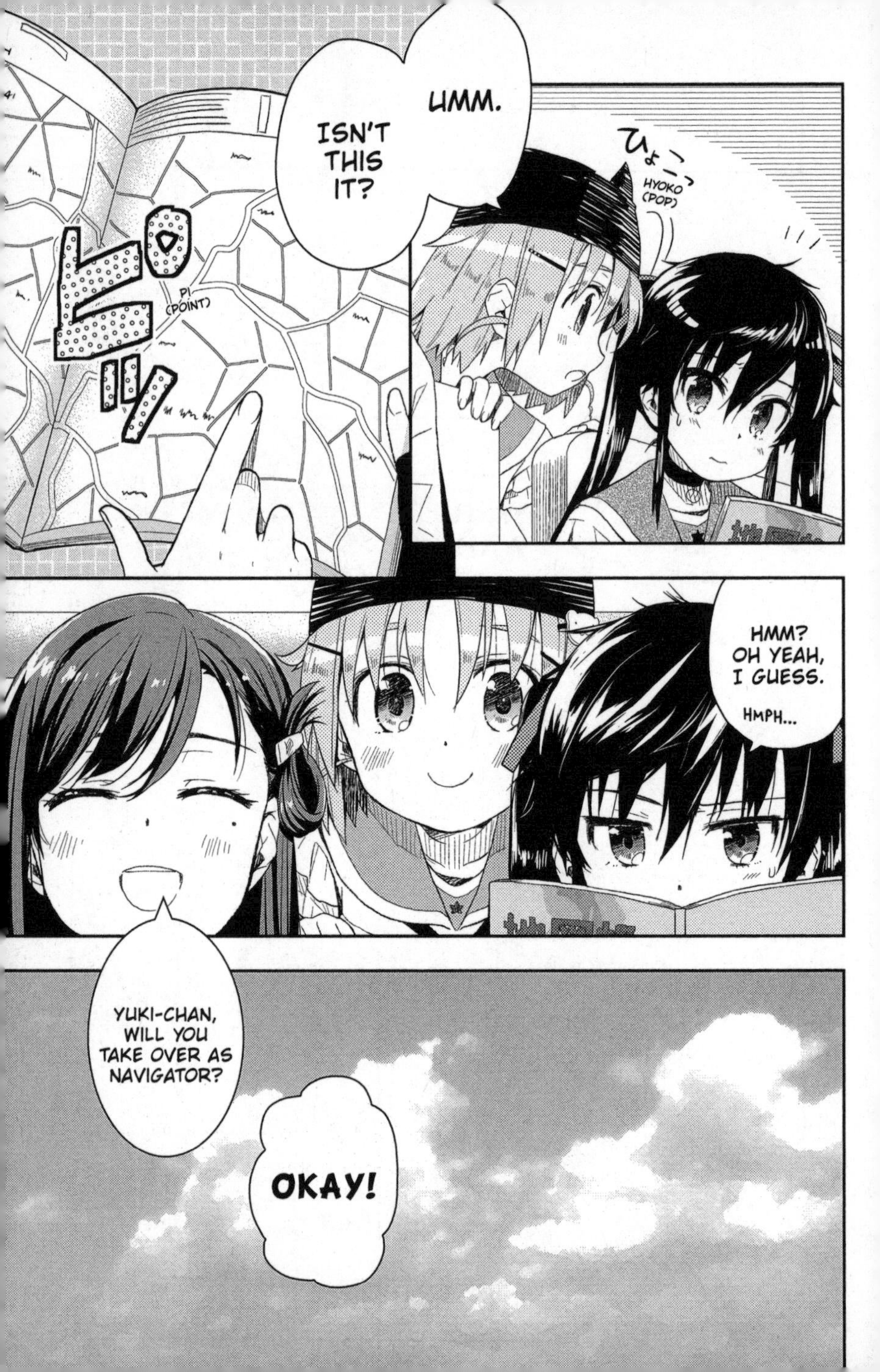
UMM.
ISN'T THIS IT?
ひょこっ
HYOKO (POP)
ピッ
PI (POINT)
HMM? OH YEAH, I GUESS.
HMPH...
YUKI-CHAN, WILL YOU TAKE OVER AS NAVIGATOR?
OKAY!

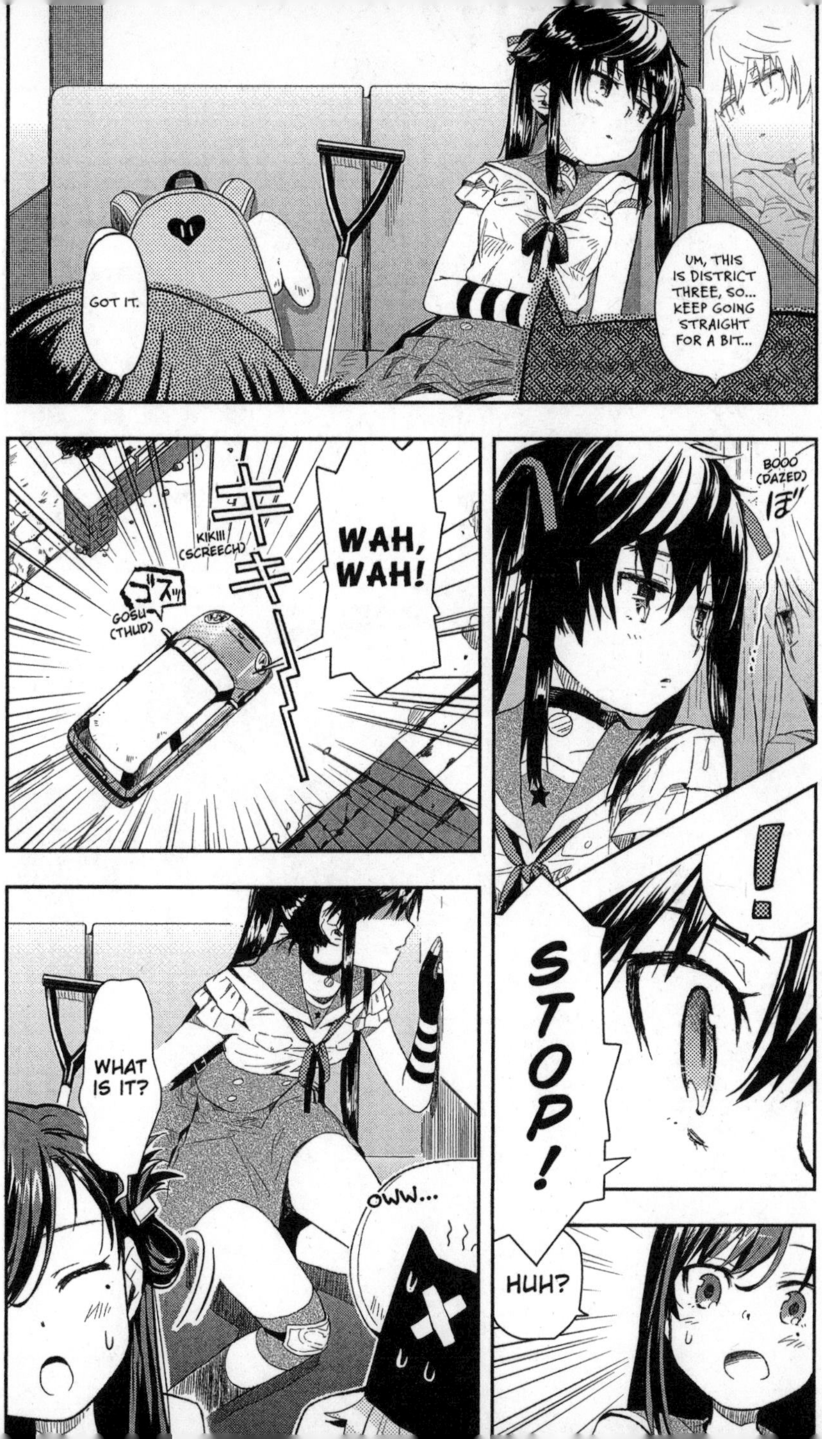
UM, THIS IS DISTRICT THREE, SO... KEEP GOING STRAIGHT FOR A BIT...
GOT IT.
BOOO (DAZED)
ぼ
キキー
KIKIII (SCREECH)
WAH, WAH!
ゴスッ
GOSU (THUD)
!
STOP!
HUH?
WHAT IS IT?
OWW...

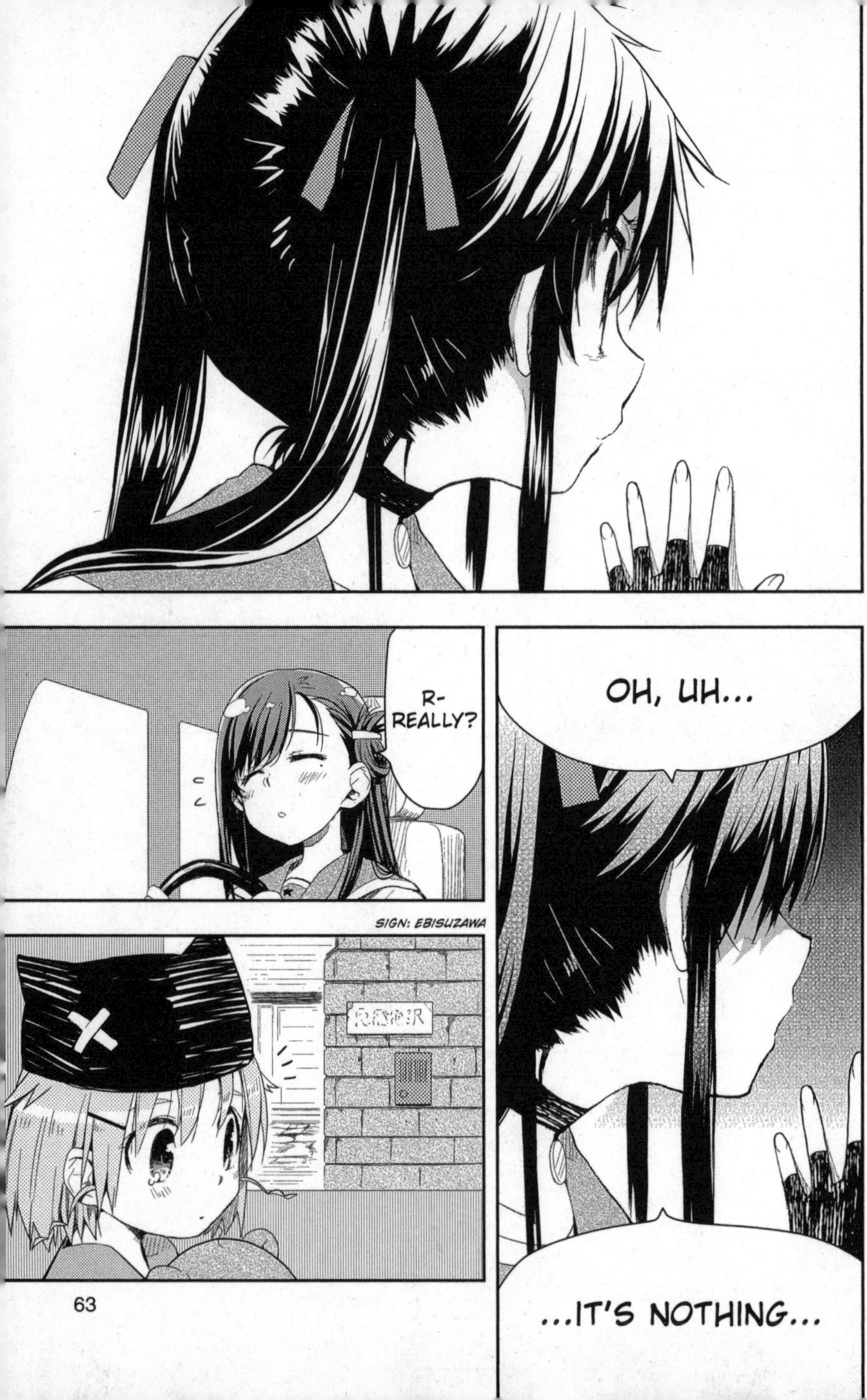
OH, UH...
...IT'S NOTHING...
R- REALLY?
SIGN: EBISUZAWA

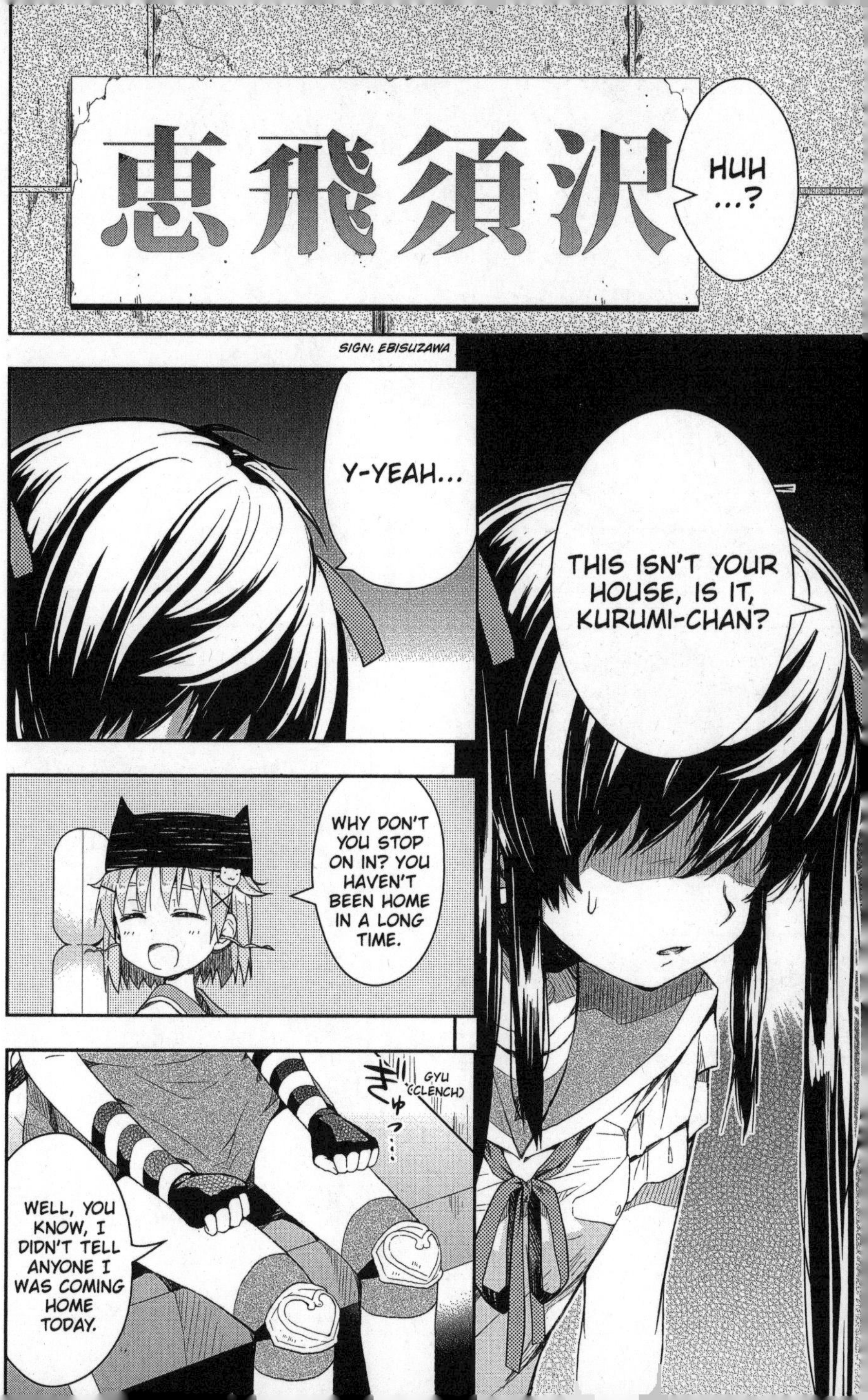
恵飛須沢
HUH ...?
SIGN: EBISUZAWA
THIS ISN'T YOUR HOUSE, IS IT, KURUMI-CHAN?
Y-YEAH...
WHY DON'T YOU STOP ON IN? YOU HAVEN'T BEEN HOME IN A LONG TIME.
ぎゅっ…
GYU (CLENCH)
WELL, YOU KNOW, I DIDN'T TELL ANYONE I WAS COMING HOME TODAY.

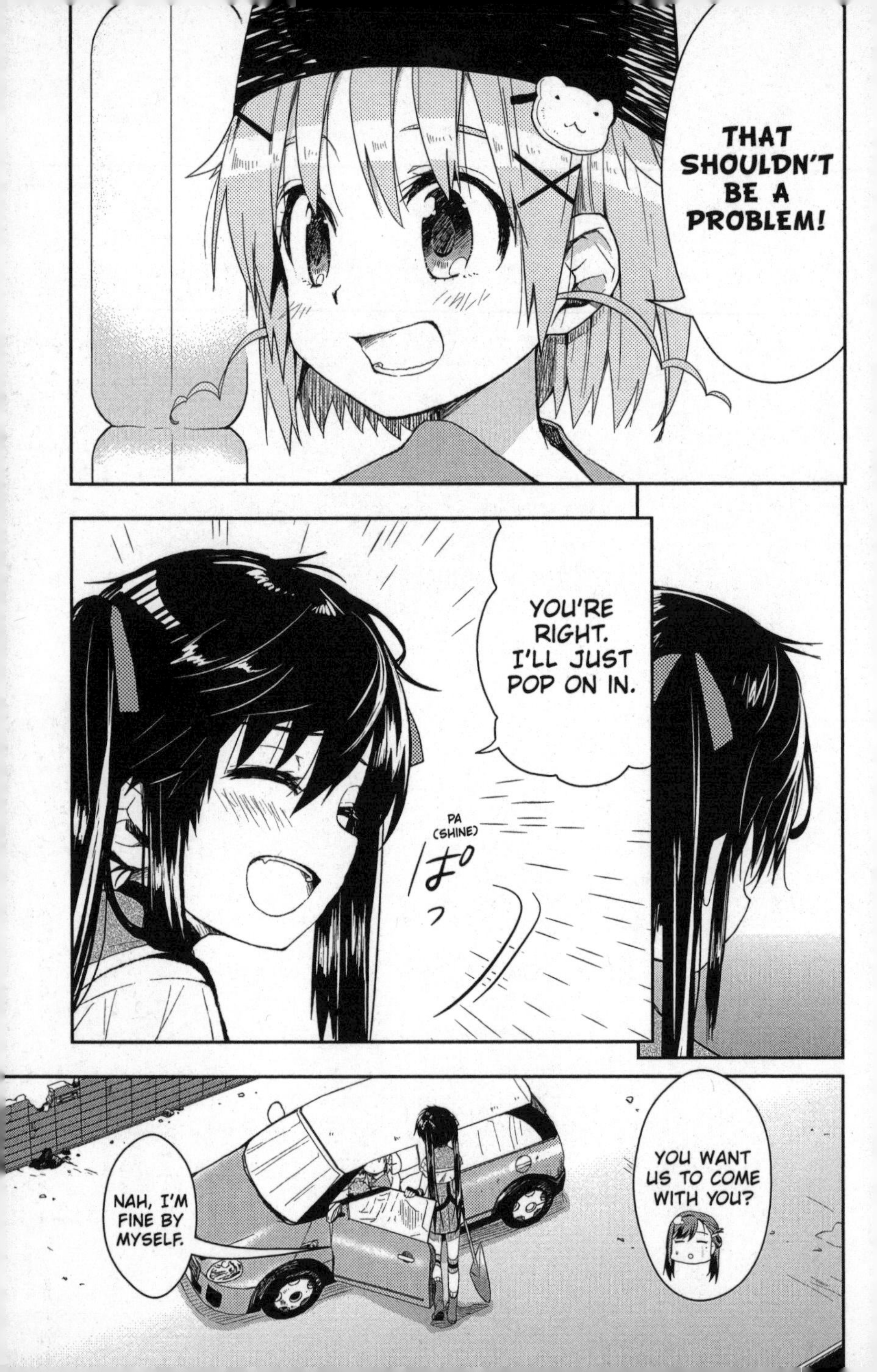
THAT SHOULDN'T BE A PROBLEM!
YOU'RE RIGHT. I'LL JUST POP ON IN.
PA (SHINE)
ぱっ
YOU WANT US TO COME WITH YOU?
NAH, I'M FINE BY MYSELF.

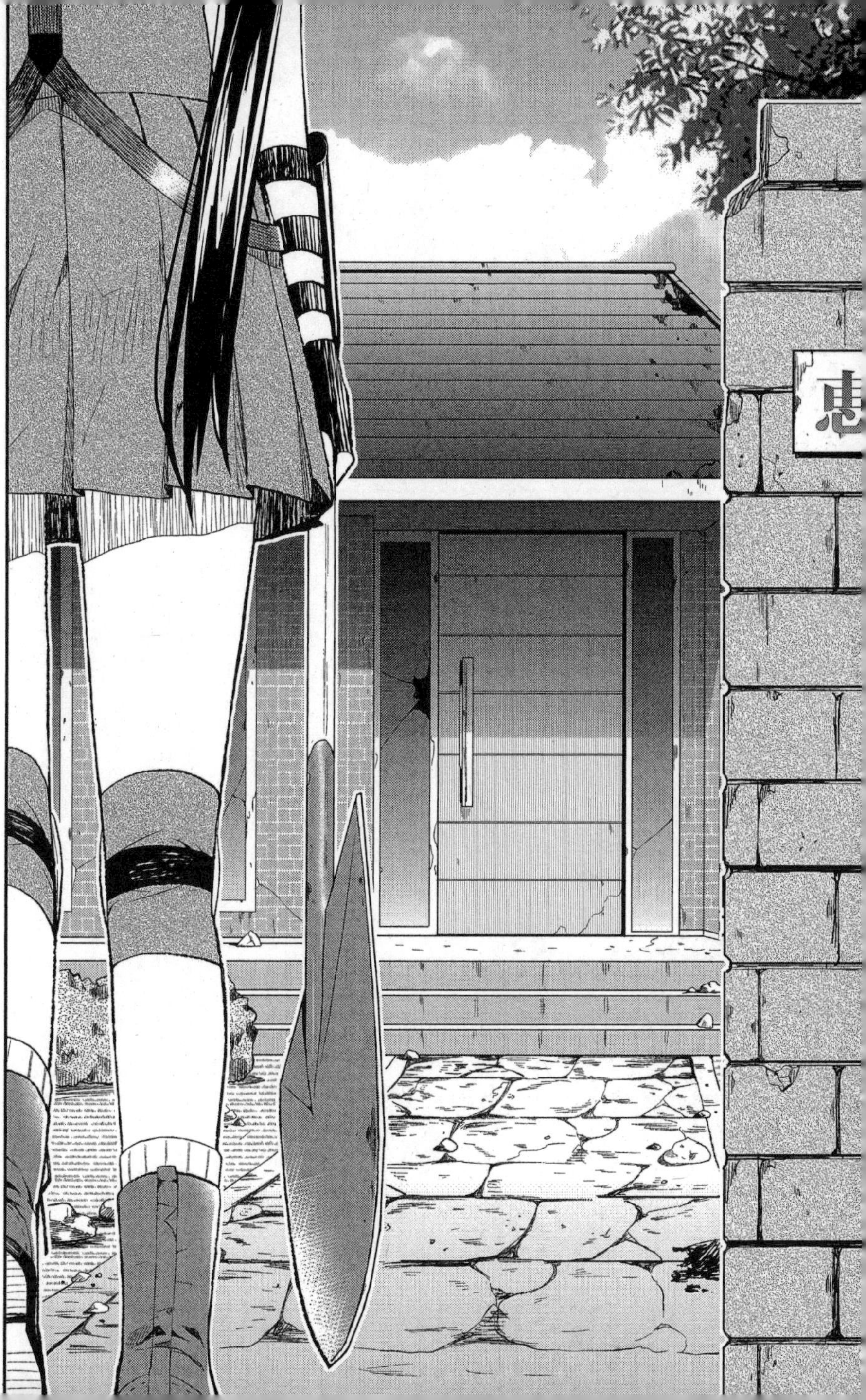

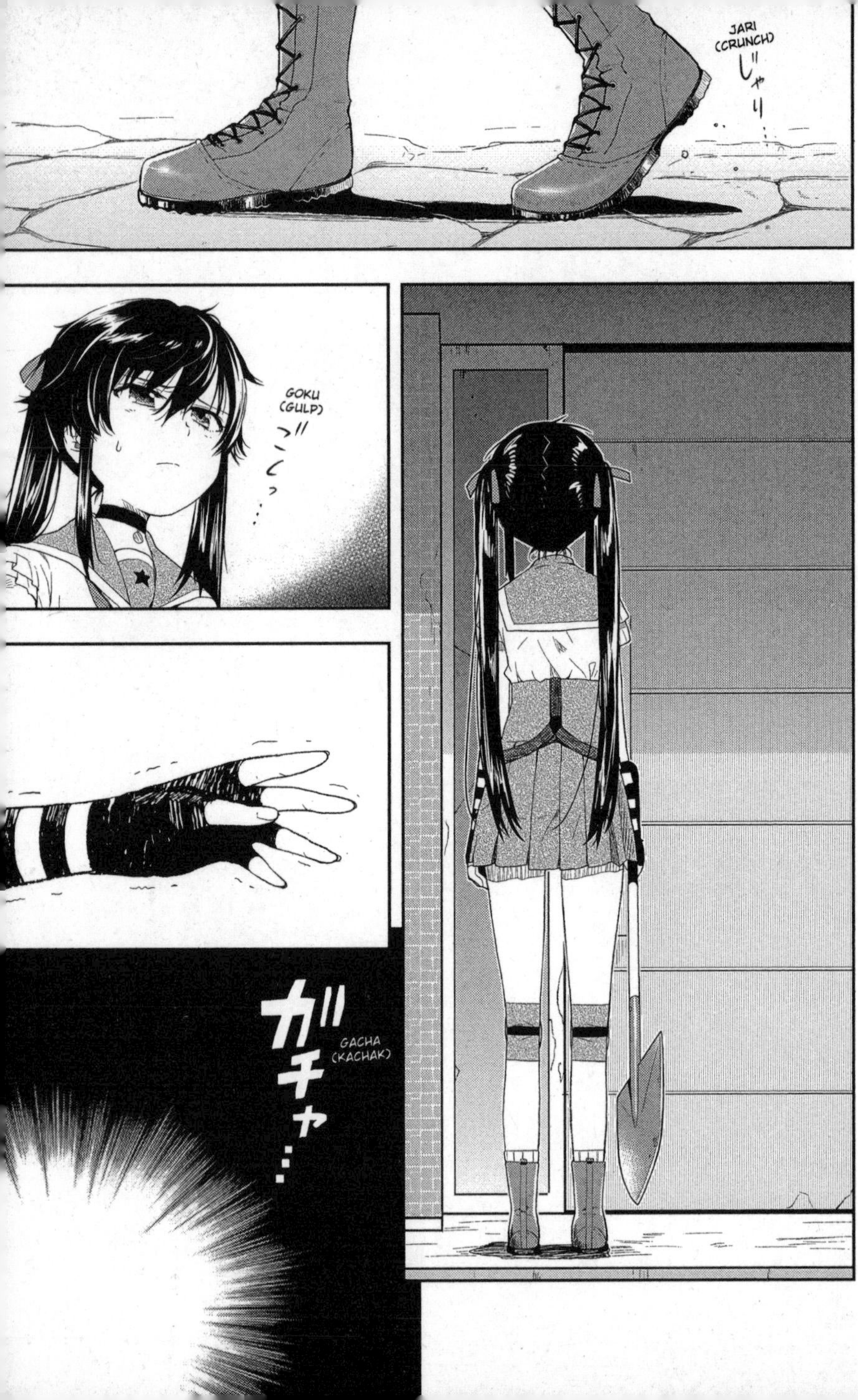
JARI (CRUNCH)
じゃり
GOKU (GULP)
ごくっ…
GACHA (KACHAK)
ガチャ…

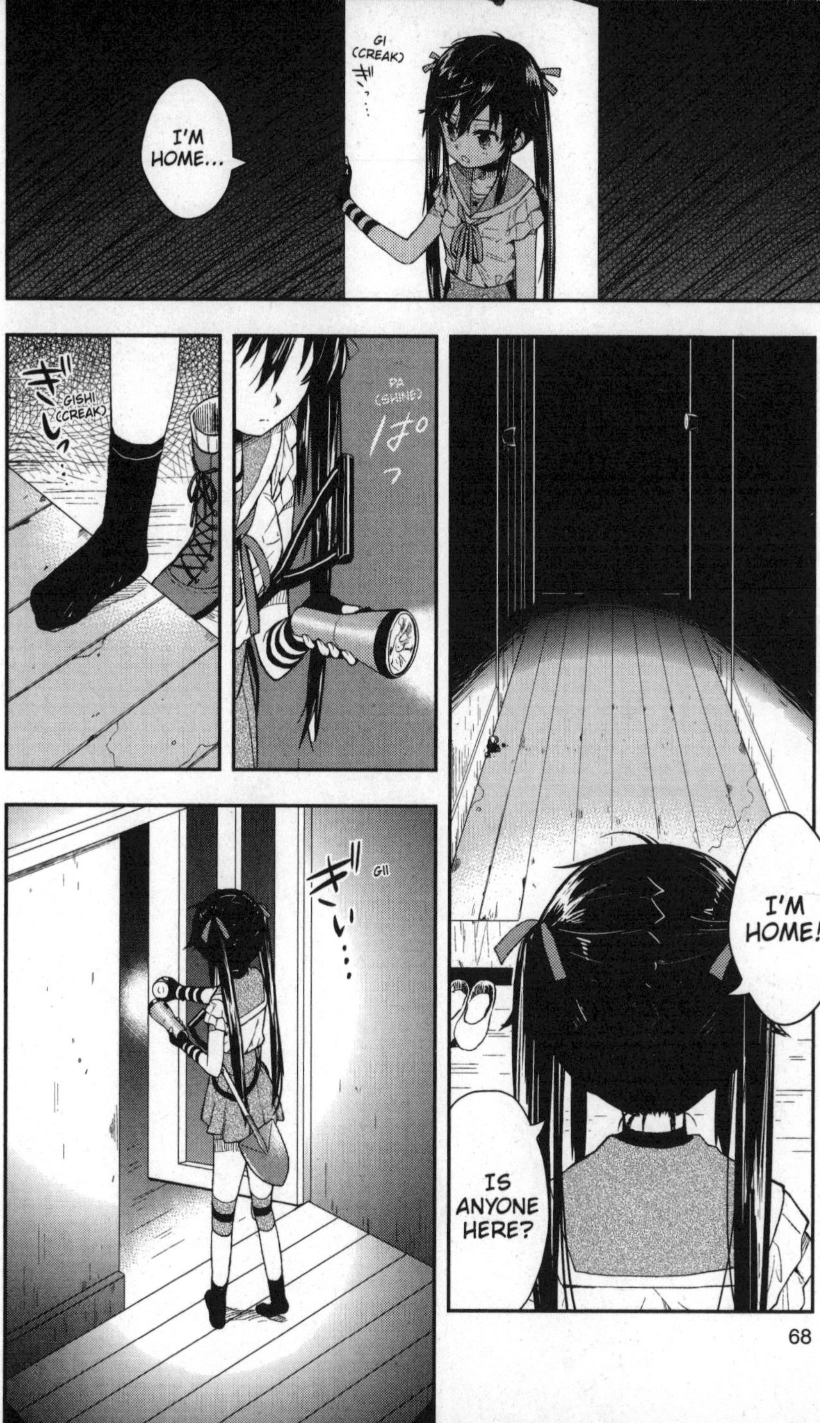
GI (CREAK)
ぎっ…
I'M HOME…
I'M HOME!
IS ANYONE HERE?
PA (SHINE)
ぱっ
GISHI (CREAK)
ぎしっ…
GII
ぎぃ…

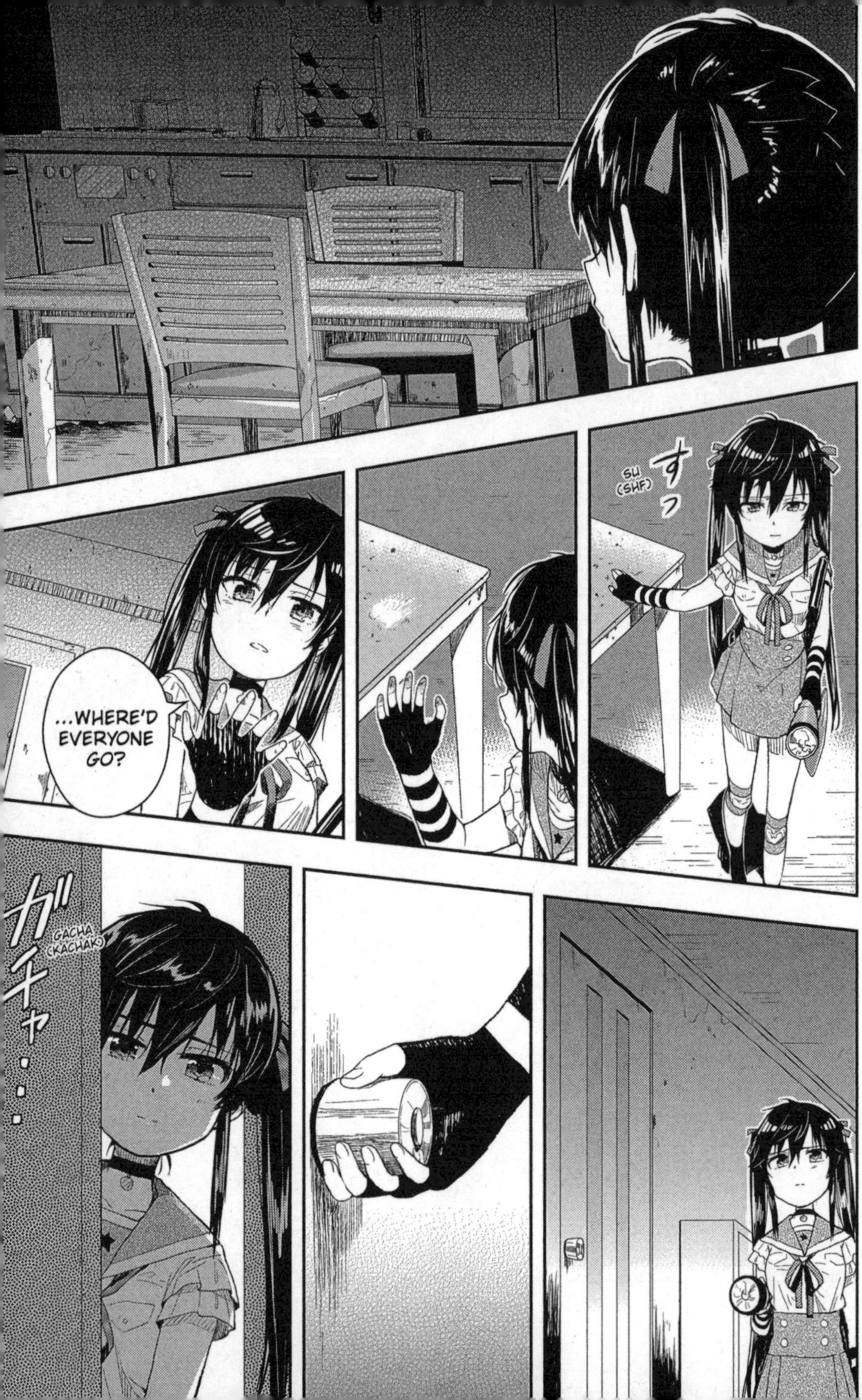
すっ
SU (SHF)
...WHERE'D EVERYONE GO?
ガチャ...
GACHA (KACHAK)

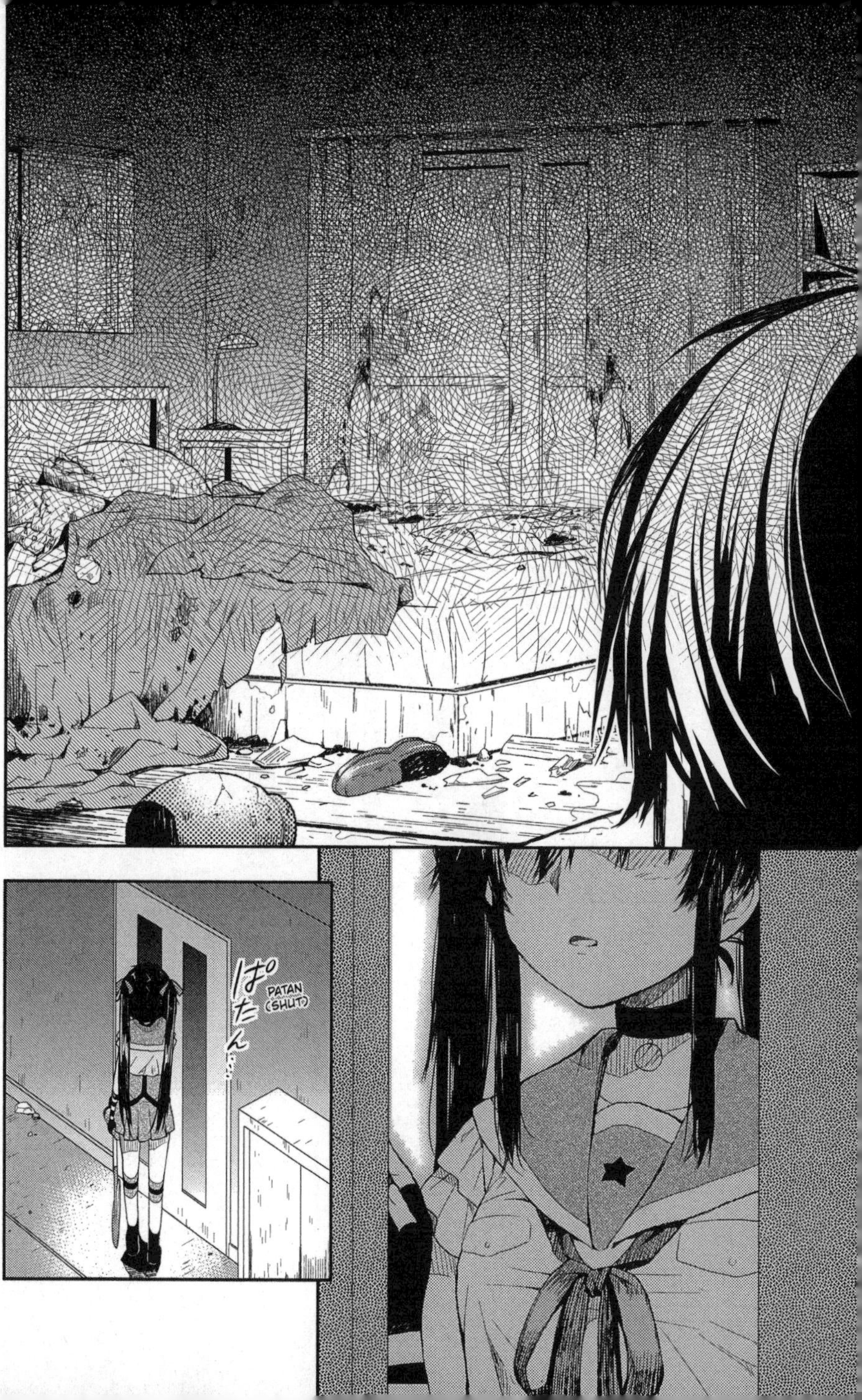
ぱたん…
PATAN (SHUT)

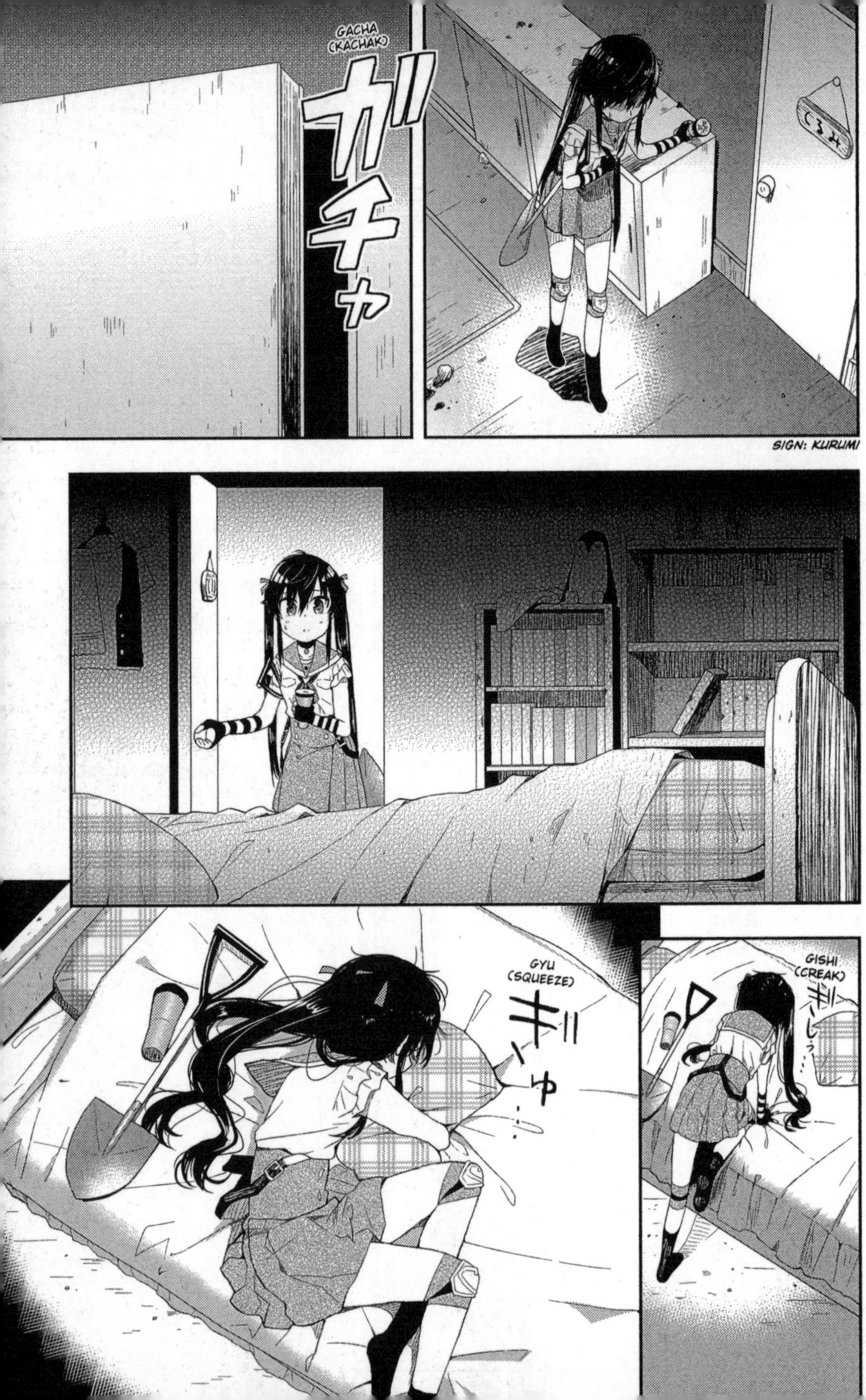
くるみ
SIGN: KURUMI
GACHA (KACHAK)
ガチャ
GISHI (CREAK)
ぎしぃ…
GYU (SQUEEZE)
ぎゅ…

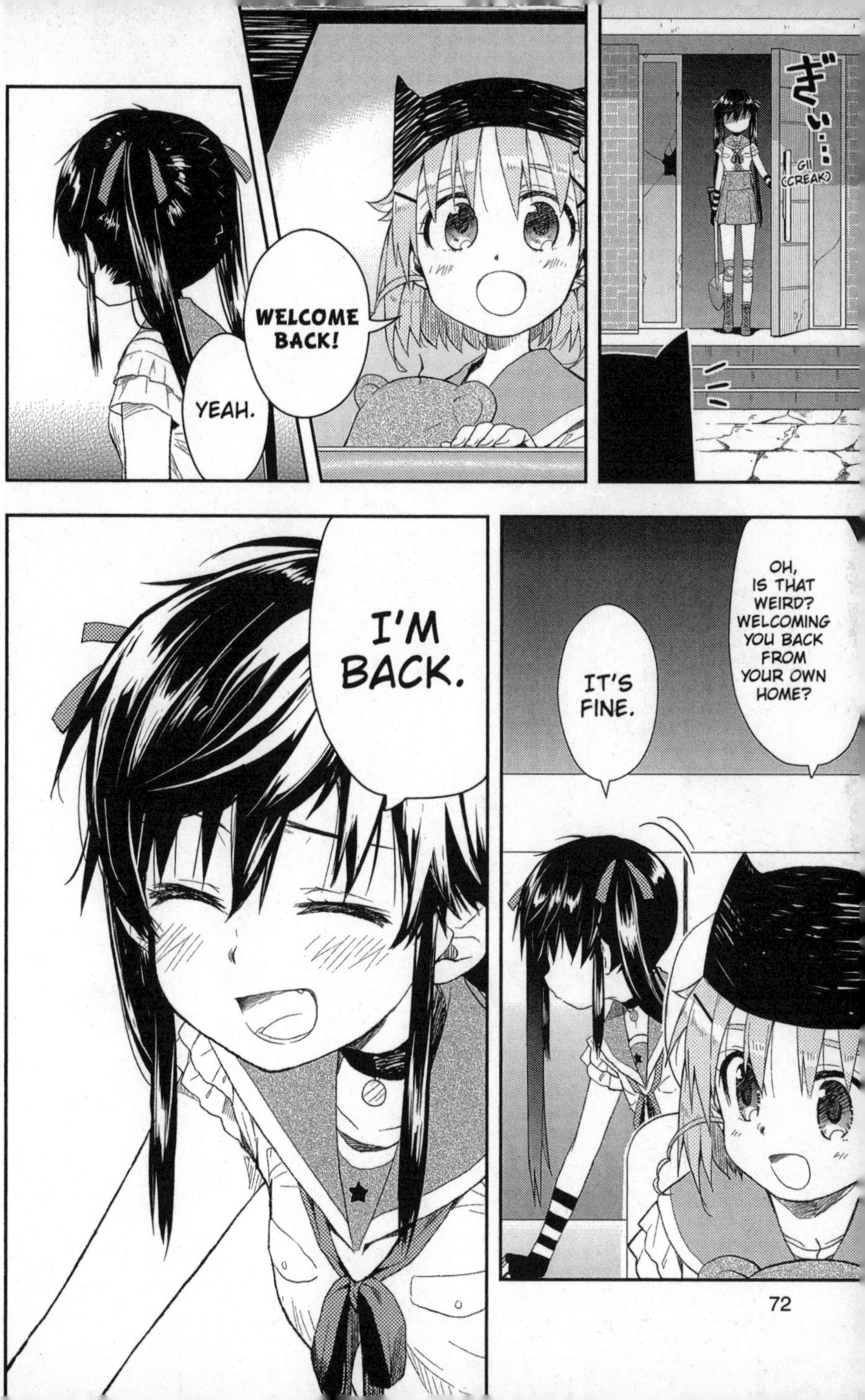
ぎい…
GII (CREAK)
WELCOME BACK!
YEAH.
OH, IS THAT WEIRD? WELCOMING YOU BACK FROM YOUR OWN HOME?
IT'S FINE.
I'M BACK.

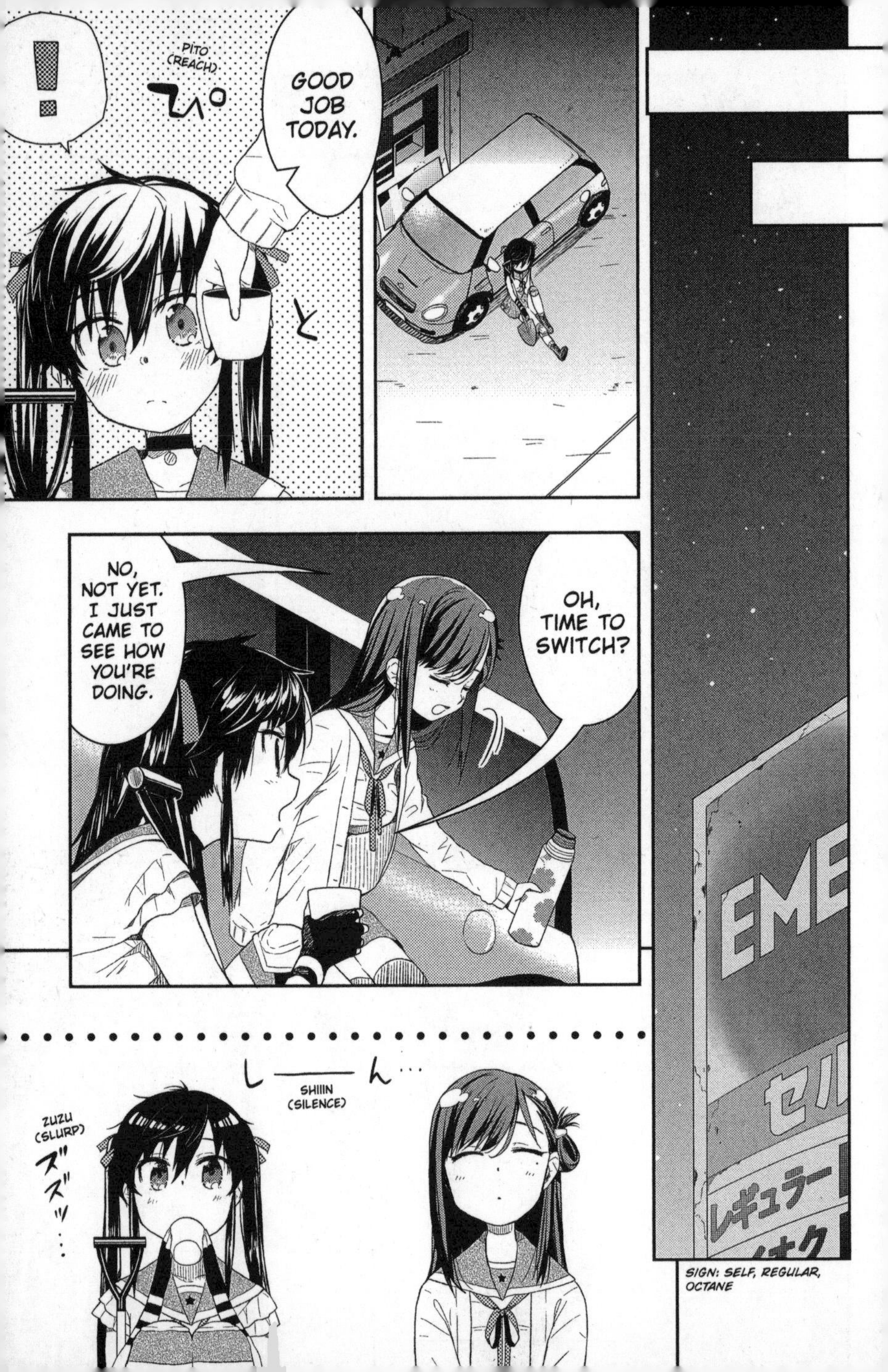
EME
レギュラー
SIGN: SELF, REGULAR, OCTANE
GOOD JOB TODAY.
PITO (REACH)
!
OH, TIME TO SWITCH?
NO, NOT YET. I JUST CAME TO SEE HOW YOU'RE DOING.
しーん…
SHIIIN (SILENCE)
ズズッ…
ZUZU (SLURP)

BUILDING: MOTORS

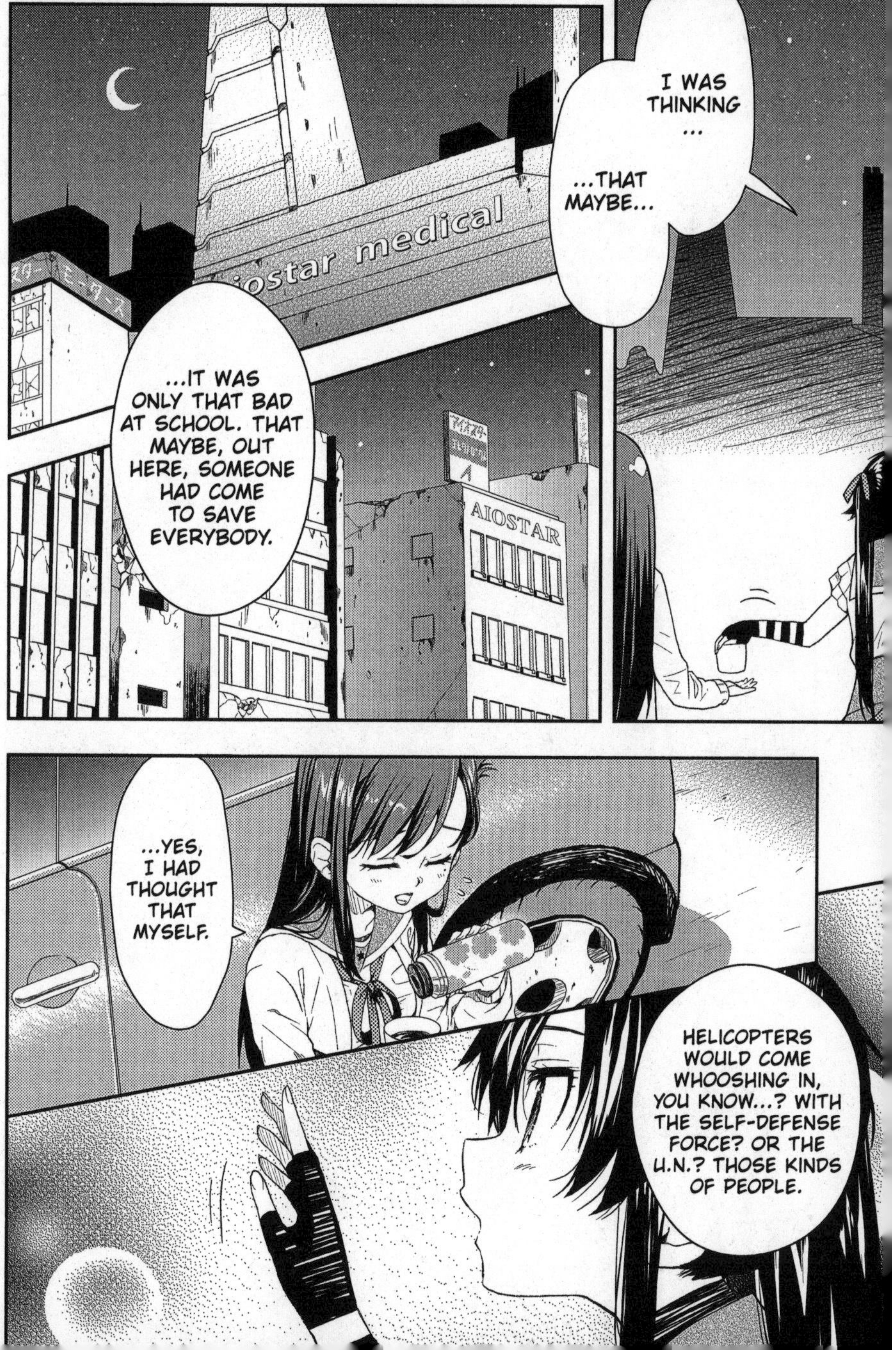
I WAS THINKING ...
...THAT MAYBE...
...IT WAS ONLY THAT BAD AT SCHOOL. THAT MAYBE, OUT HERE, SOMEONE HAD COME TO SAVE EVERYBODY.
AIOSTAR
...YES, I HAD THOUGHT THAT MYSELF.
HELICOPTERS WOULD COME WHOOSHING IN, YOU KNOW...? WITH THE SELF-DEFENSE FORCE? OR THE U.N.? THOSE KINDS OF PEOPLE.

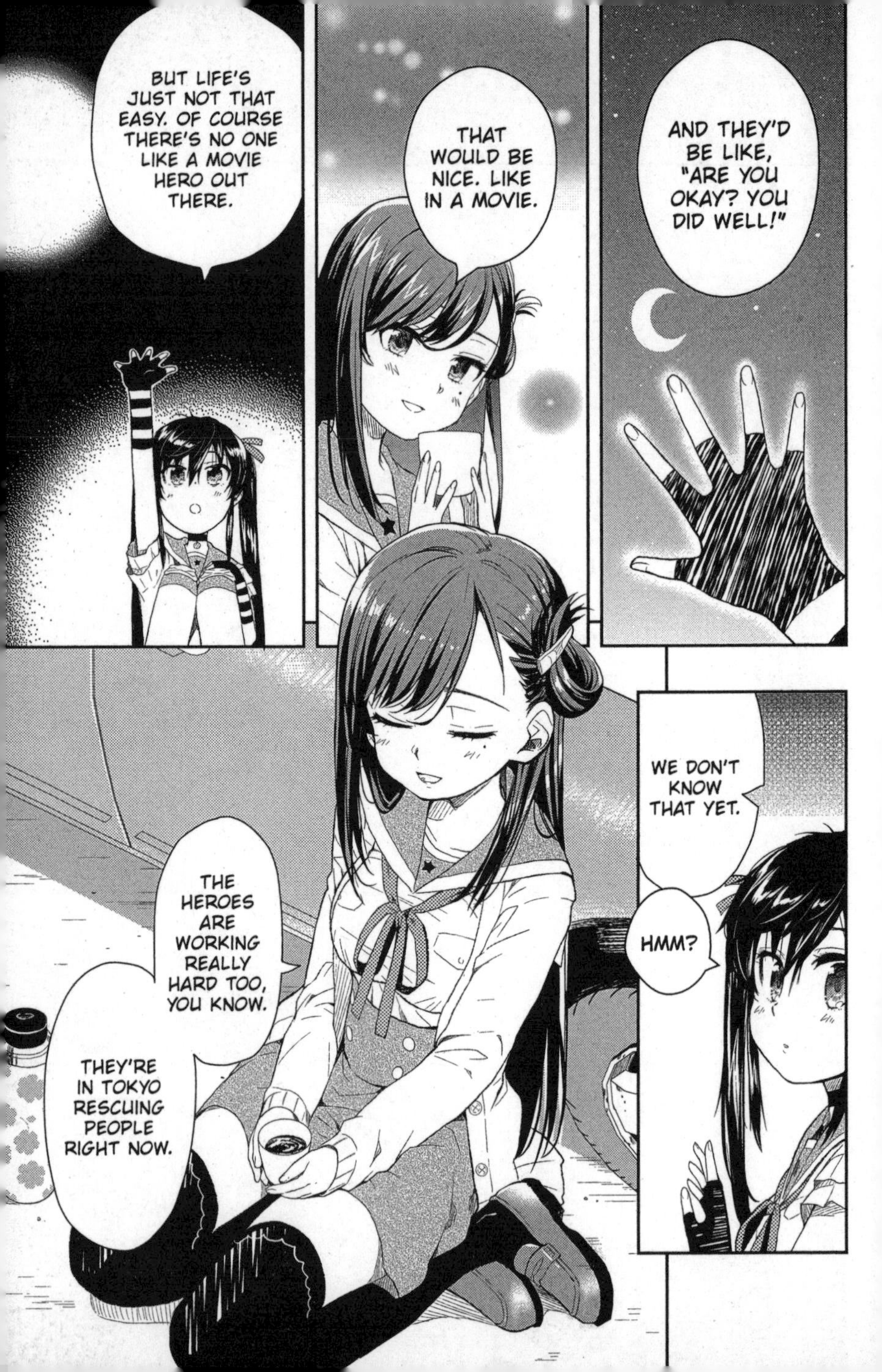
AND THEY'D BE LIKE, "ARE YOU OKAY? YOU DID WELL!"
THAT WOULD BE NICE. LIKE IN A MOVIE.
BUT LIFE'S JUST NOT THAT EASY. OF COURSE THERE'S NO ONE LIKE A MOVIE HERO OUT THERE.
WE DON'T KNOW THAT YET.
HMM?
THE HEROES ARE WORKING REALLY HARD TOO, YOU KNOW.
THEY'RE IN TOKYO RESCUING PEOPLE RIGHT NOW.

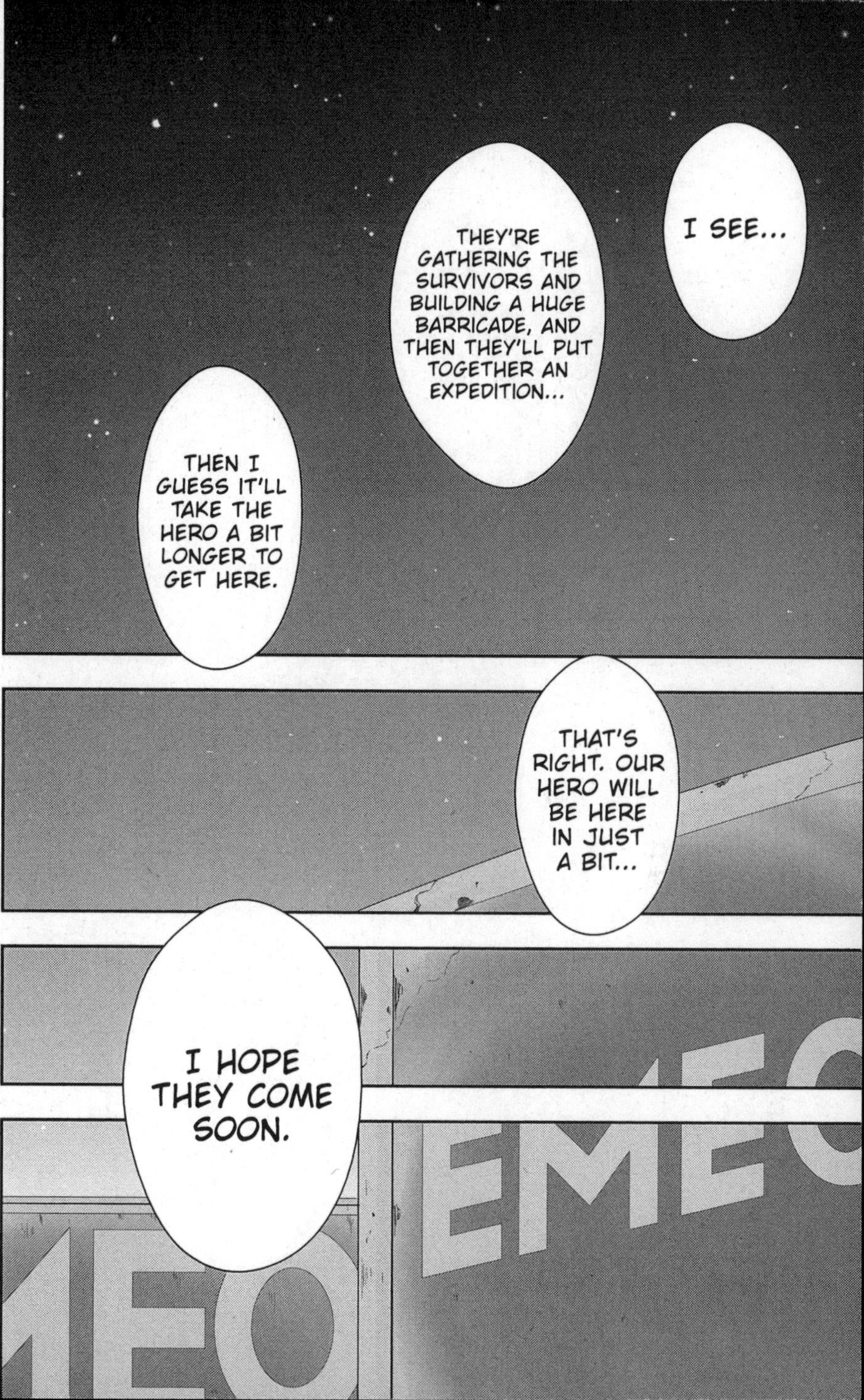
I SEE...
THEY'RE GATHERING THE SURVIVORS AND BUILDING A HUGE BARRICADE, AND THEN THEY'LL PUT TOGETHER AN EXPEDITION...
THEN I GUESS IT'LL TAKE THE HERO A BIT LONGER TO GET HERE.
THAT'S RIGHT. OUR HERO WILL BE HERE IN JUST A BIT...
I HOPE THEY COME SOON.

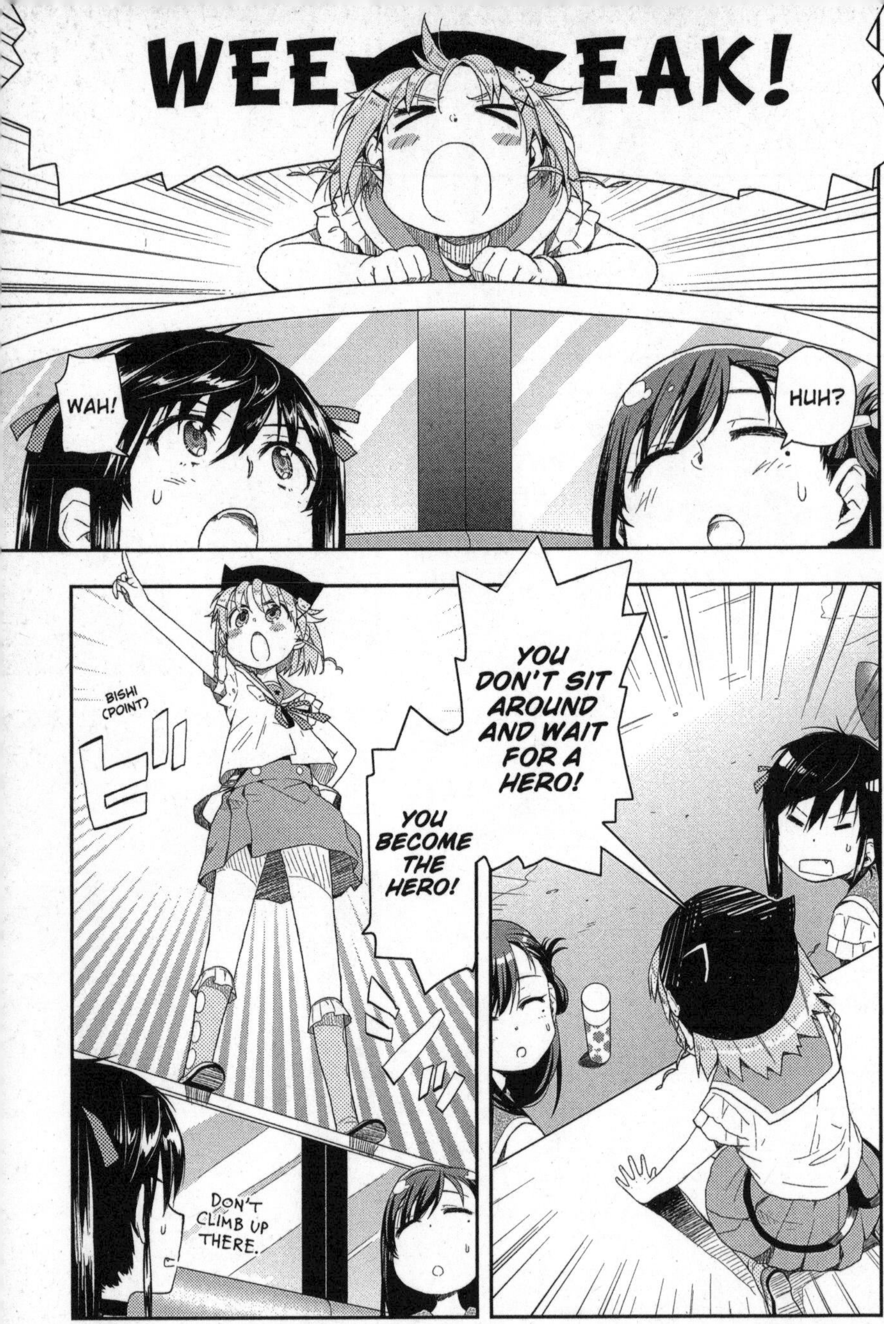
WEEEEAK!
HUH?
WAH!
YOU DON'T SIT AROUND AND WAIT FOR A HERO!
YOU BECOME THE HERO!
BISHI (POINT)
DON'T CLIMB UP THERE.

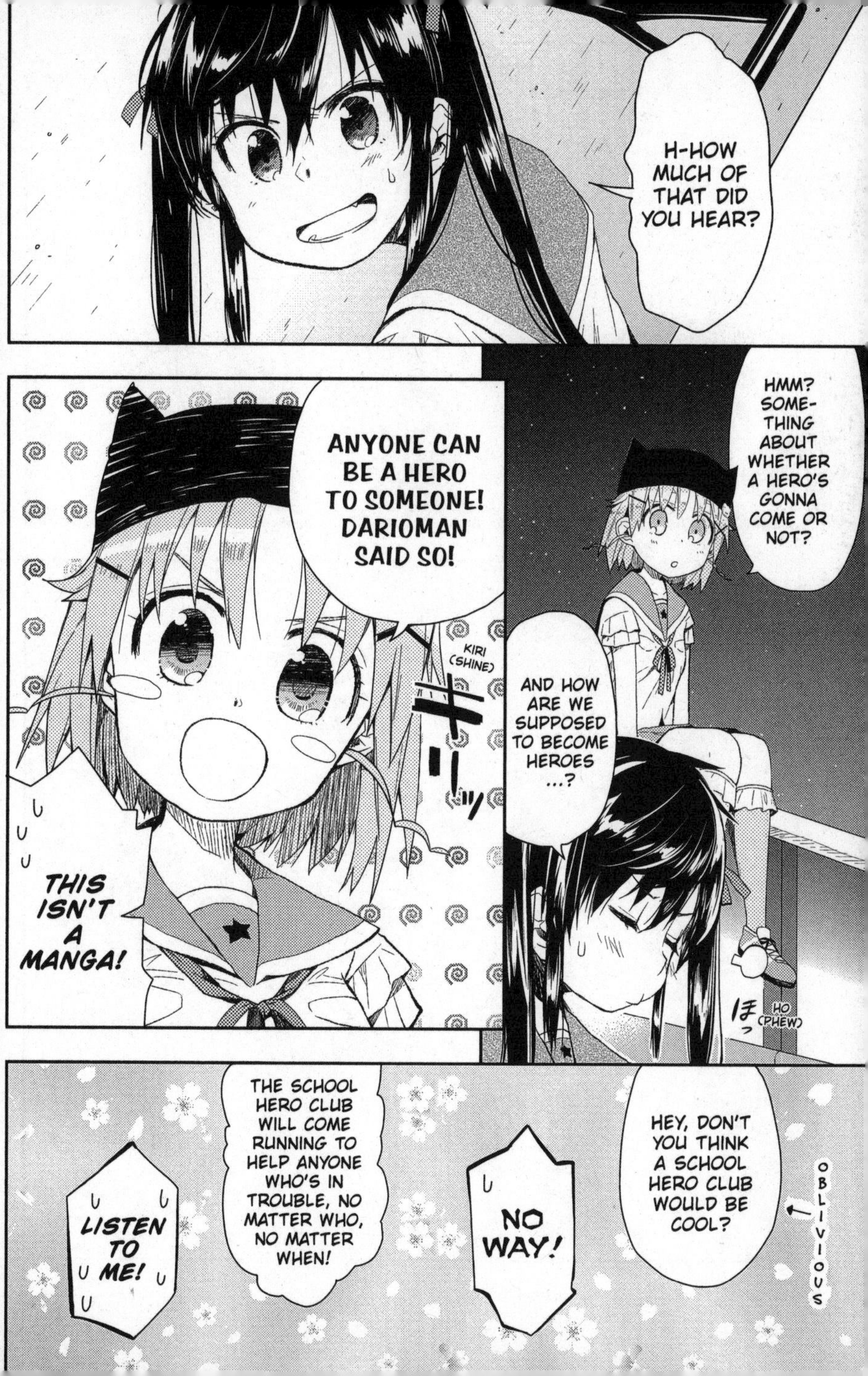
H-HOW MUCH OF THAT DID YOU HEAR?
HMM? SOMETHING ABOUT WHETHER A HERO'S GONNA COME OR NOT?
AND HOW ARE WE SUPPOSED TO BECOME HEROES ...?
HO (PHEW)
ANYONE CAN BE A HERO TO SOMEONE! DARIOMAN SAID SO!
KIRI (SHINE)
THIS ISN'T A MANGA!
OBLIVIOUS
HEY, DON'T YOU THINK A SCHOOL HERO CLUB WOULD BE COOL?
NO WAY!
THE SCHOOL HERO CLUB WILL COME RUNNING TO HELP ANYONE WHO'S IN TROUBLE, NO MATTER WHO, NO MATTER WHEN!
LISTEN TO ME!

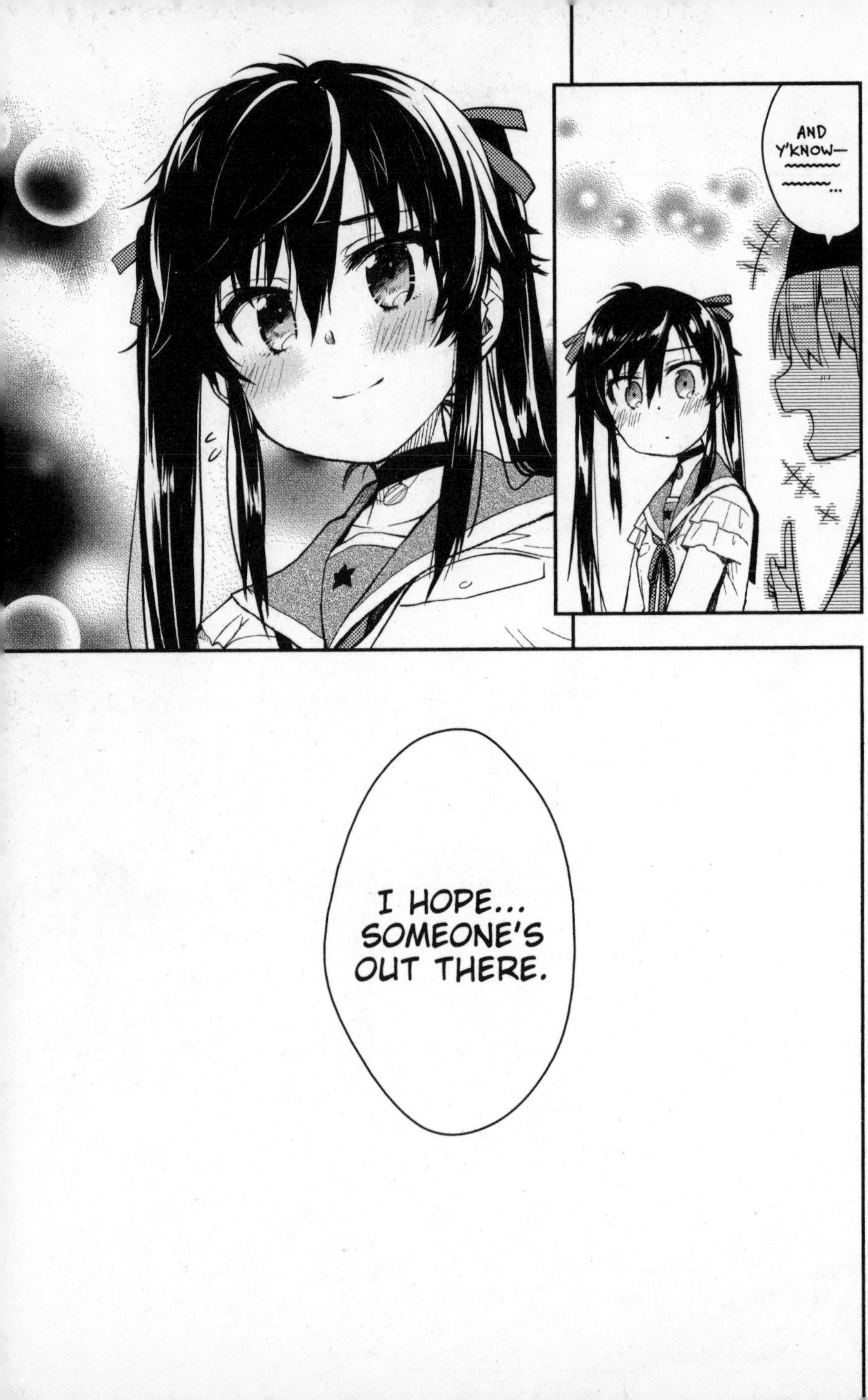AND Y'KNOW—~~~~~...
I HOPE... SOMEONE'S OUT THERE.

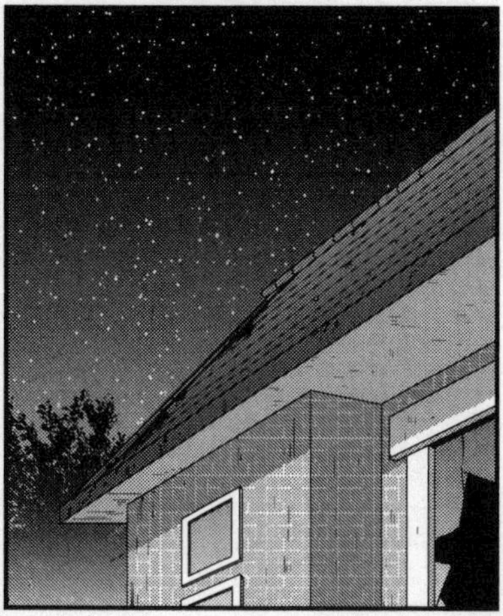

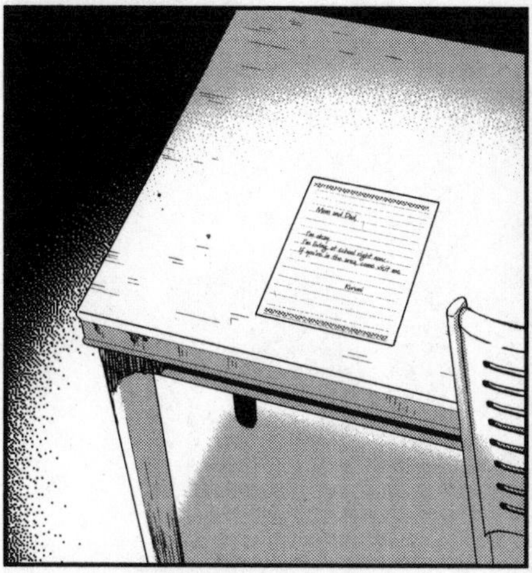

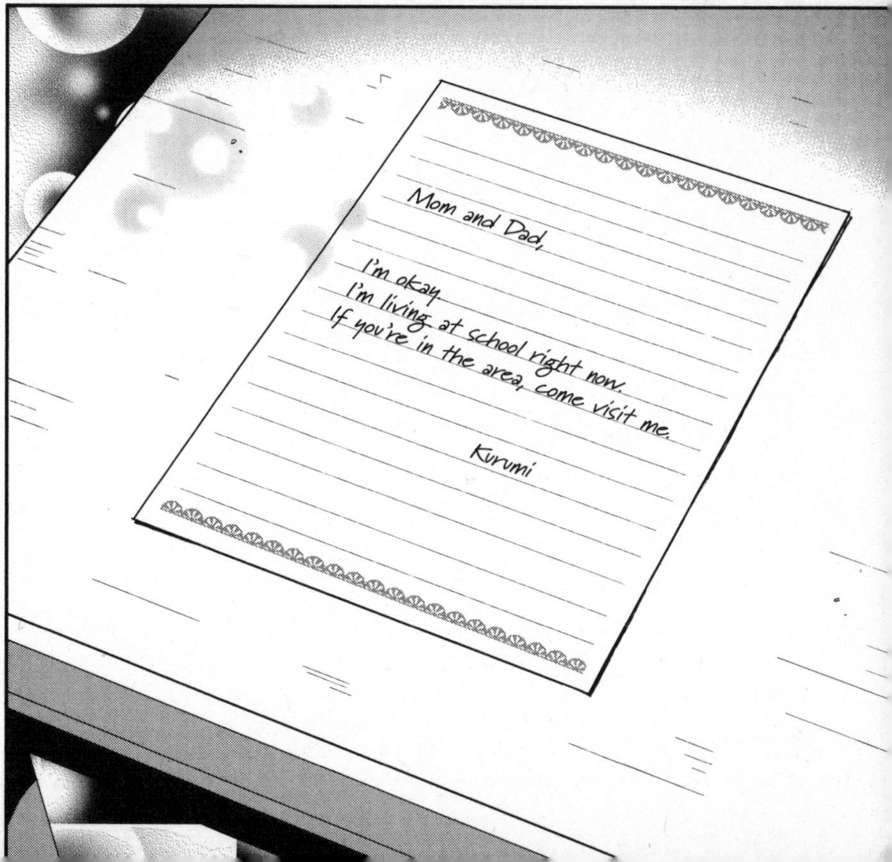
Mom and Dad,
I'm okay.
I'm living at school right now.
If you're in the area, come visit me.
Kurumi

SCHOOL-LIVE!

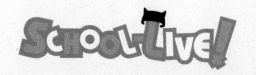

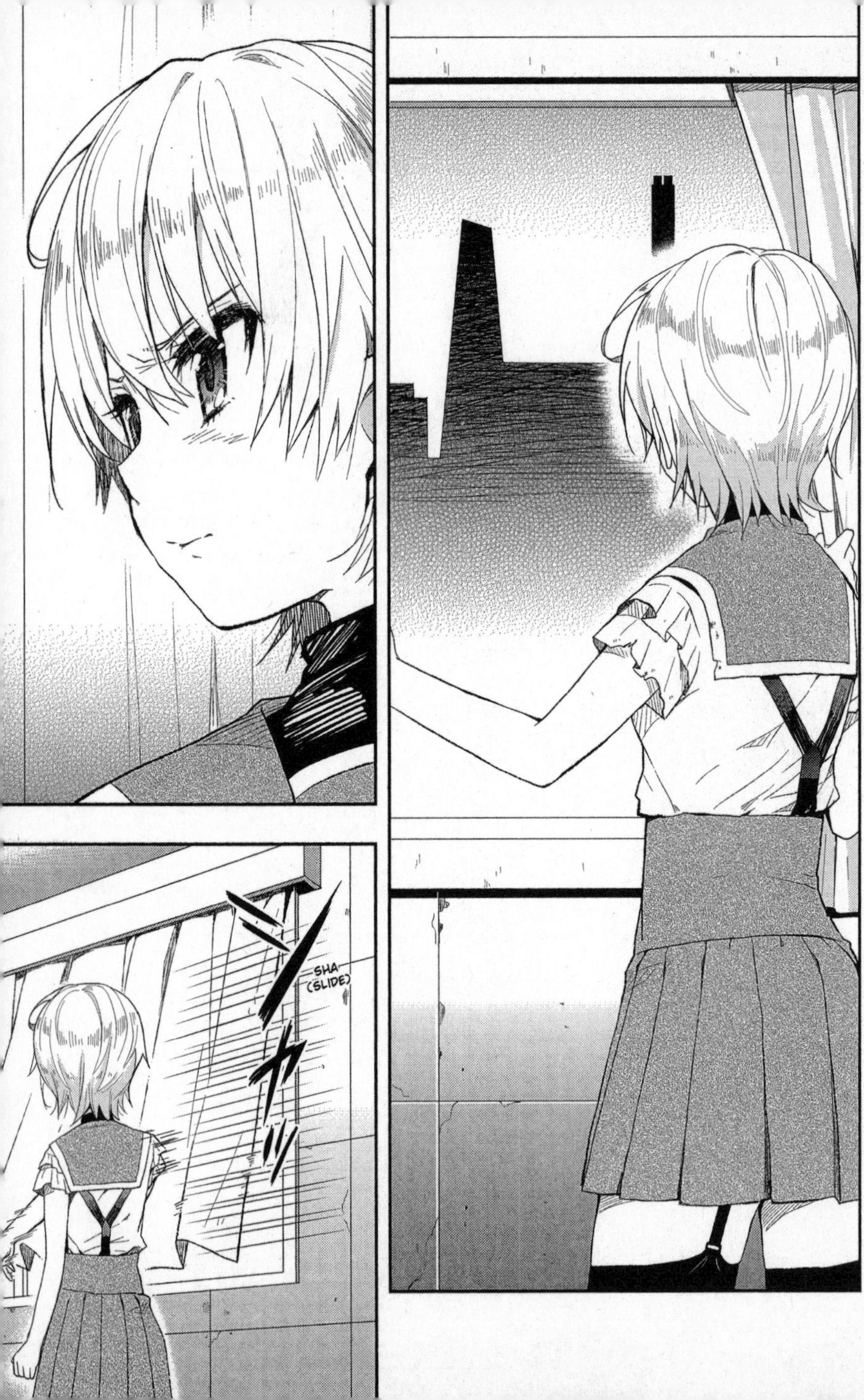
SHA
(SLIDE)

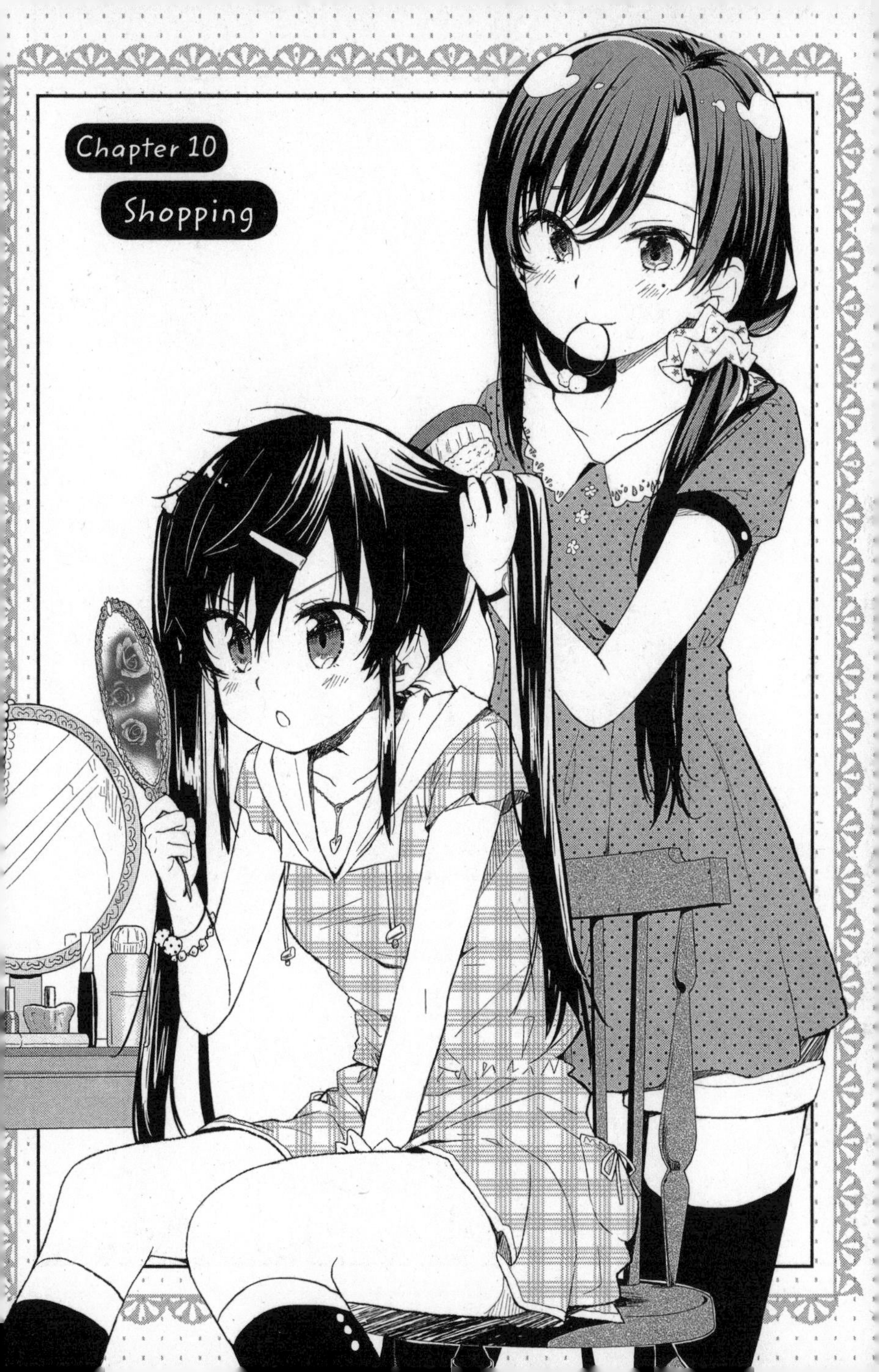
Chapter 10
Shopping

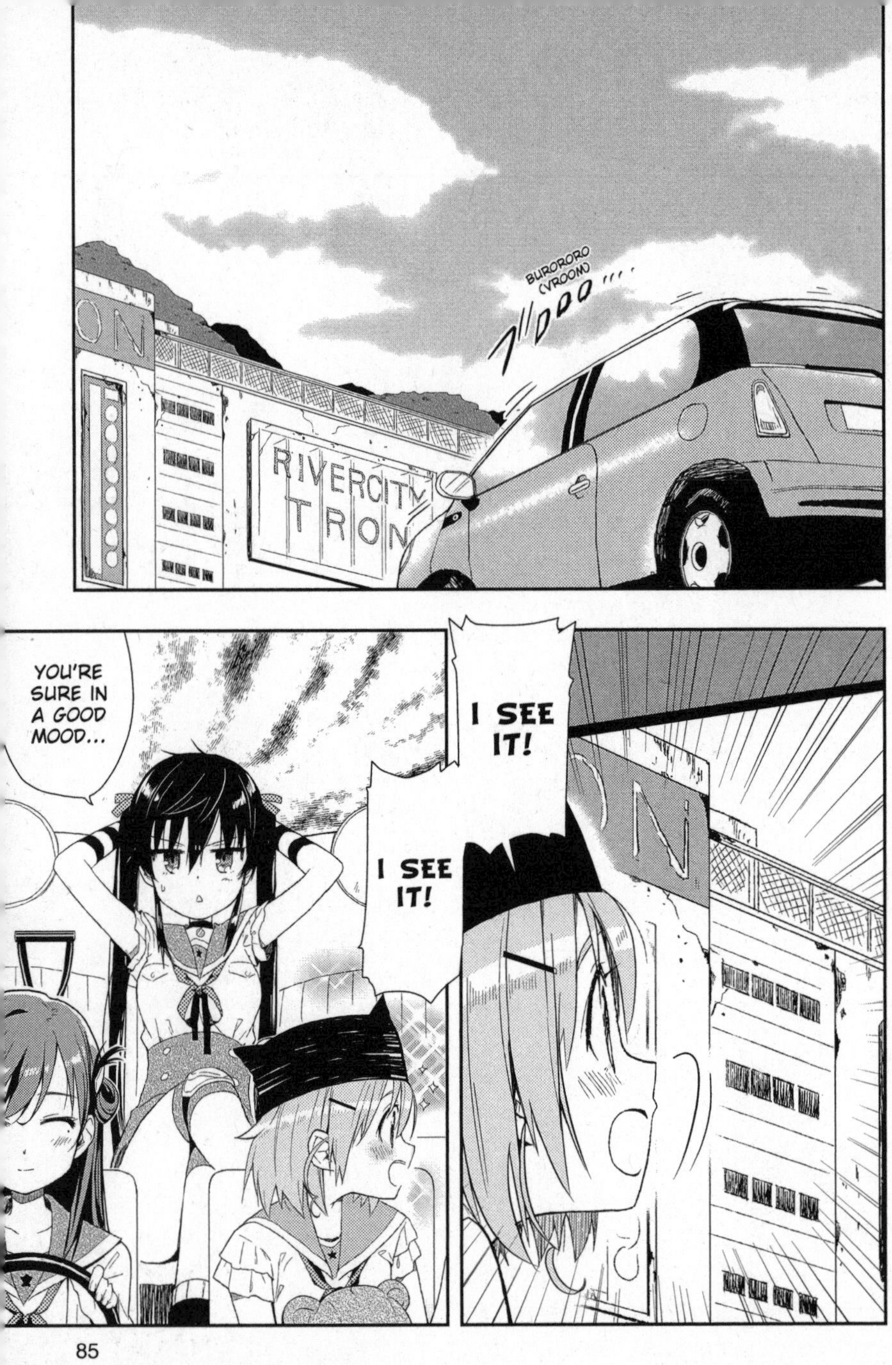
BURORORO (VROOM)
I SEE IT!
I SEE IT!
YOU'RE SURE IN A GOOD MOOD...

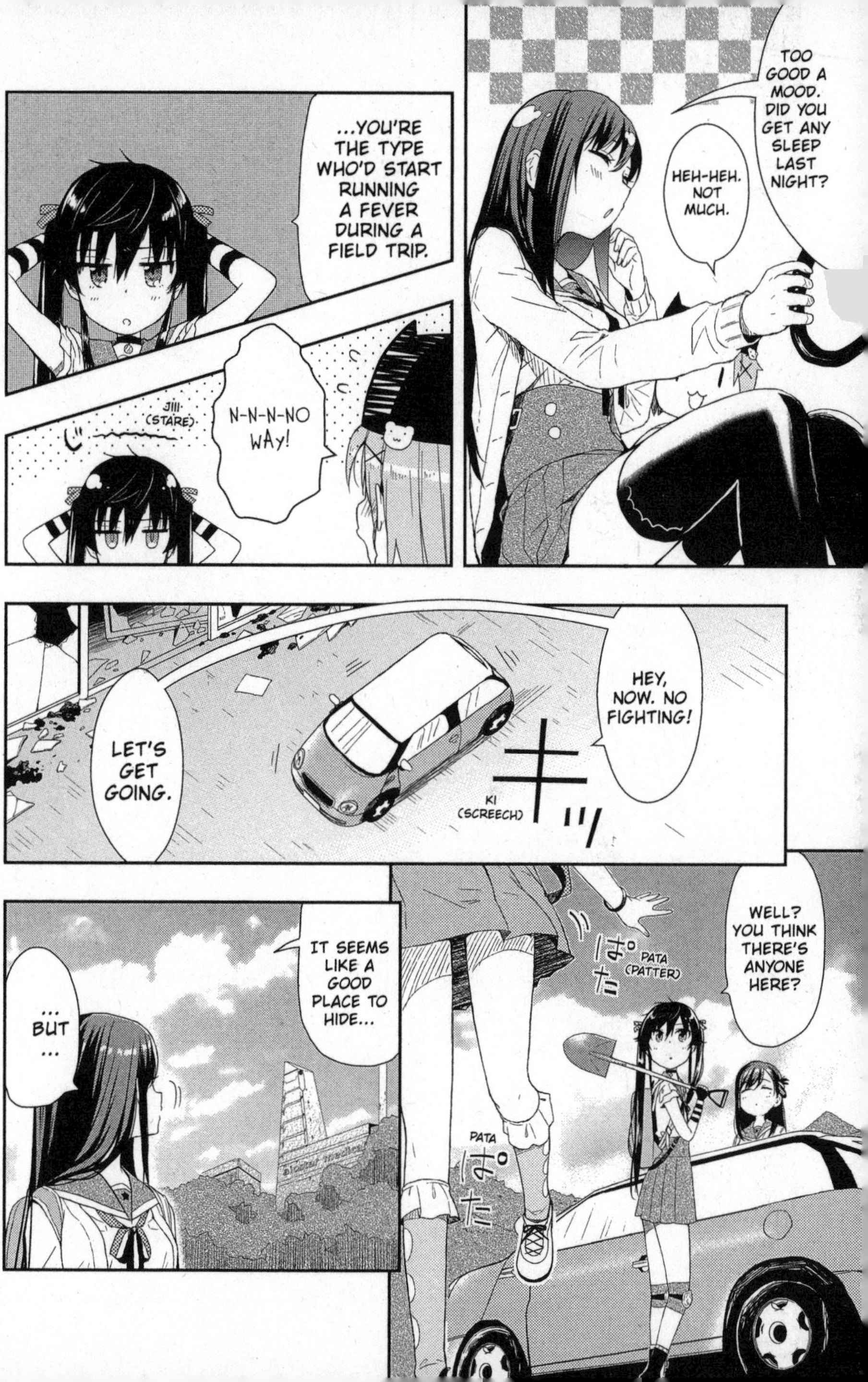
TOO GOOD A MOOD. DID YOU GET ANY SLEEP LAST NIGHT?
HEH-HEH. NOT MUCH.
...YOU'RE THE TYPE WHO'D START RUNNING A FEVER DURING A FIELD TRIP.
N-N-N-NO WAy!
JIII (STARE)
HEY, NOW. NO FIGHTING!
KI (SCREECH)
LET'S GET GOING.
WELL? YOU THINK THERE'S ANYONE HERE?
PATA (PATTER)
PATA
IT SEEMS LIKE A GOOD PLACE TO HIDE...
... BUT ...

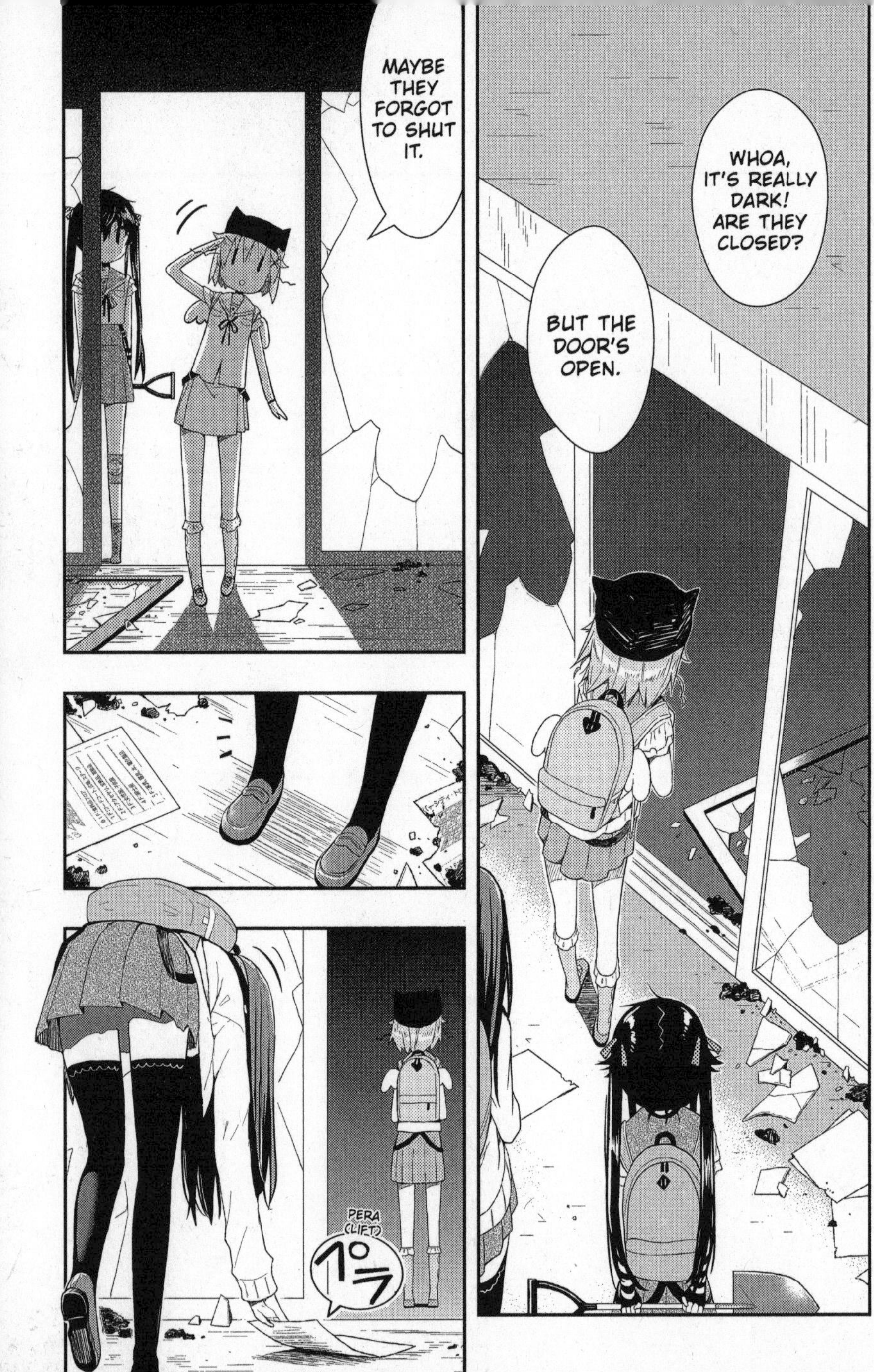
WHOA, IT'S REALLY DARK! ARE THEY CLOSED?
BUT THE DOOR'S OPEN.
MAYBE THEY FORGOT TO SHUT IT.
PERA (LIFT)
ペラ

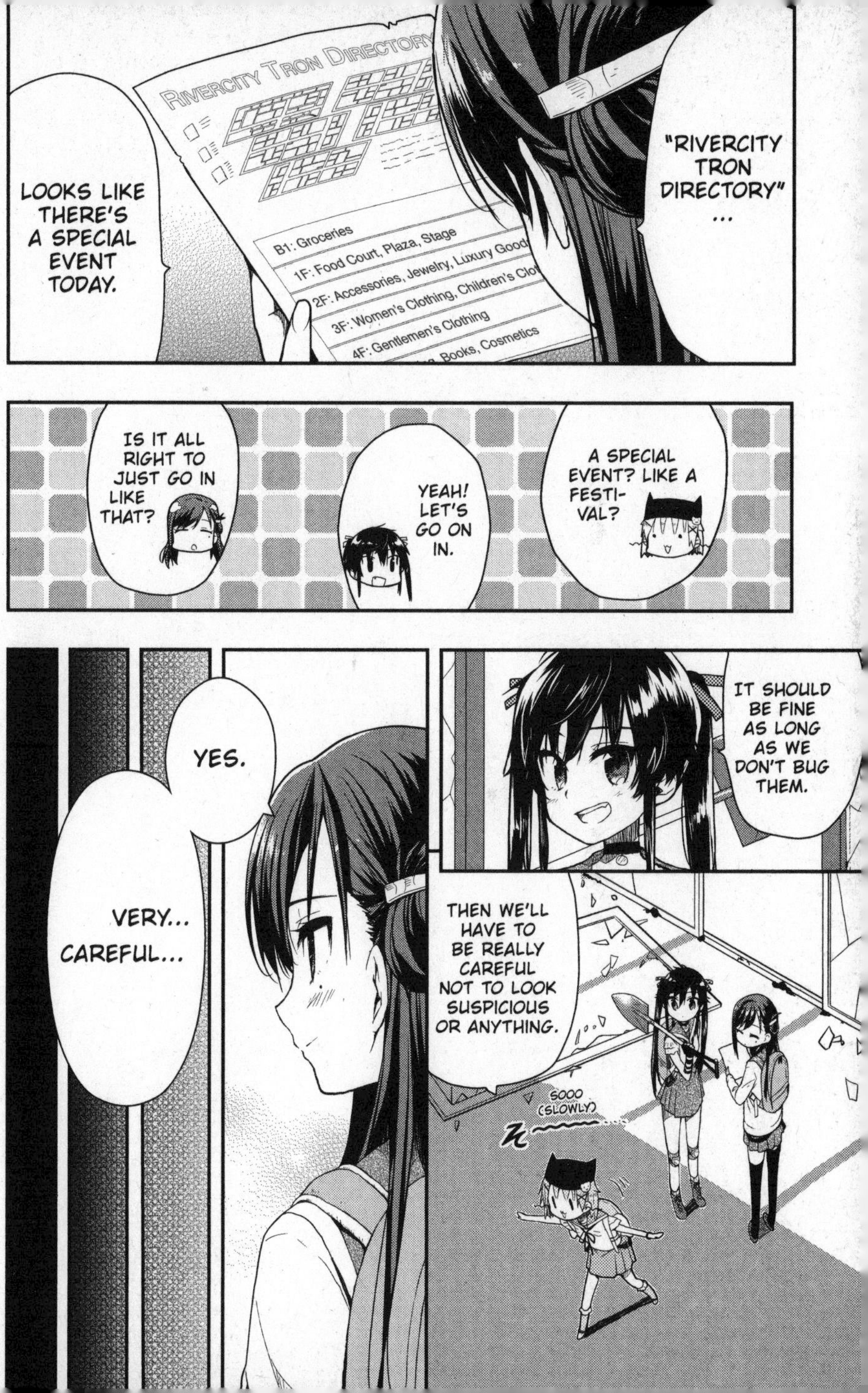
"RIVERCITY TRON DIRECTORY" ...
RIVERCITY TRON DIRECTORY
B1: Groceries
1F: Food Court, Plaza, Stage
2F: Accessories, Jewelry, Luxury
3F: Women's Clothing, Children's
4F: Gentlemen's Clothing
Books, Cosmetics
LOOKS LIKE THERE'S A SPECIAL EVENT TODAY.
A SPECIAL EVENT? LIKE A FESTIVAL?
YEAH! LET'S GO ON IN.
IS IT ALL RIGHT TO JUST GO IN LIKE THAT?
IT SHOULD BE FINE AS LONG AS WE DON'T BUG THEM.
THEN WE'LL HAVE TO BE REALLY CAREFUL NOT TO LOOK SUSPICIOUS OR ANYTHING.
SOOO (SLOWLY)
YES.
VERY... CAREFUL...

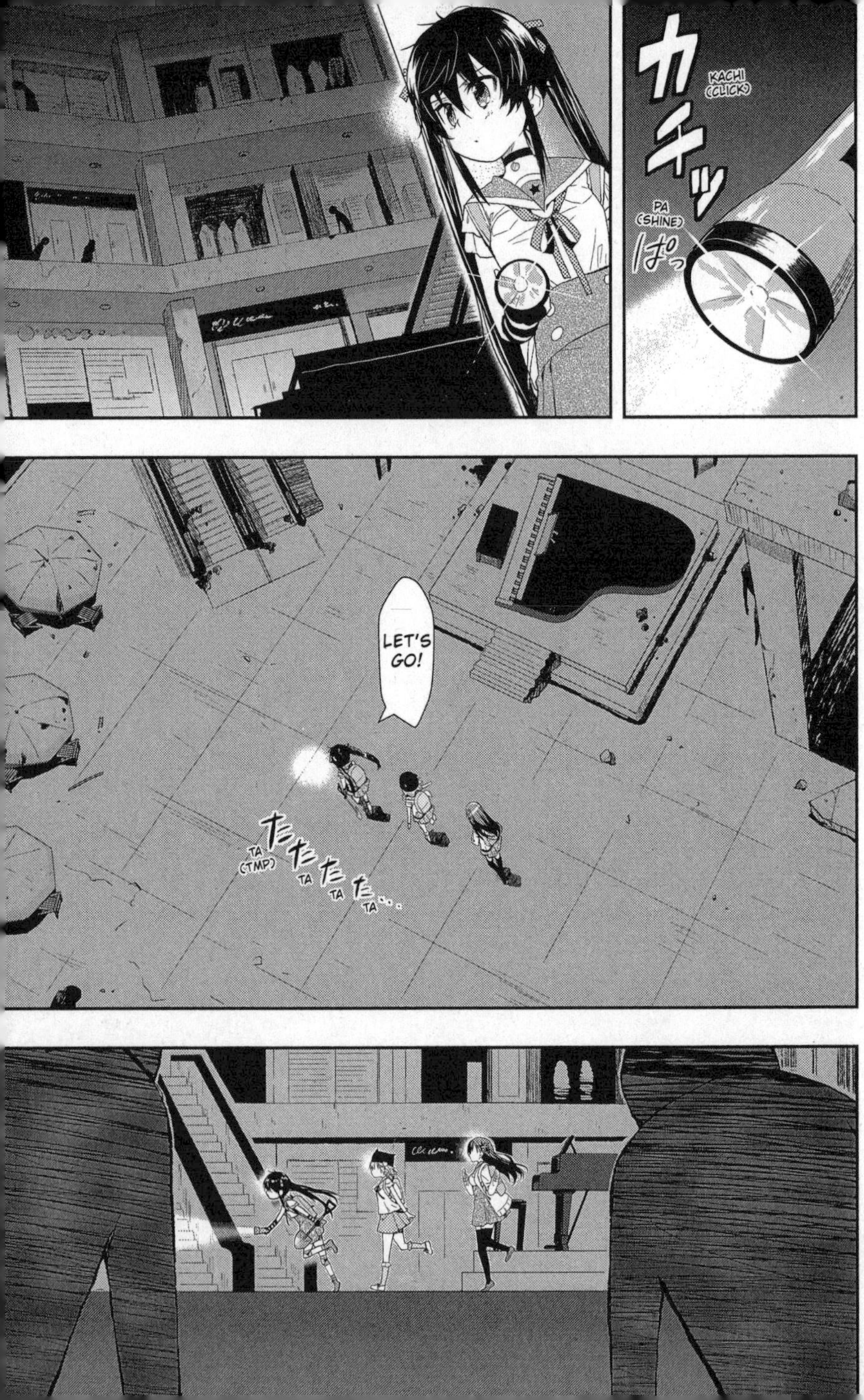
カチッ
KACHI (CLICK)
PA (SHINE)
ぱっ
LET'S GO!
たたたた
TA (TMP) TA TA TA...

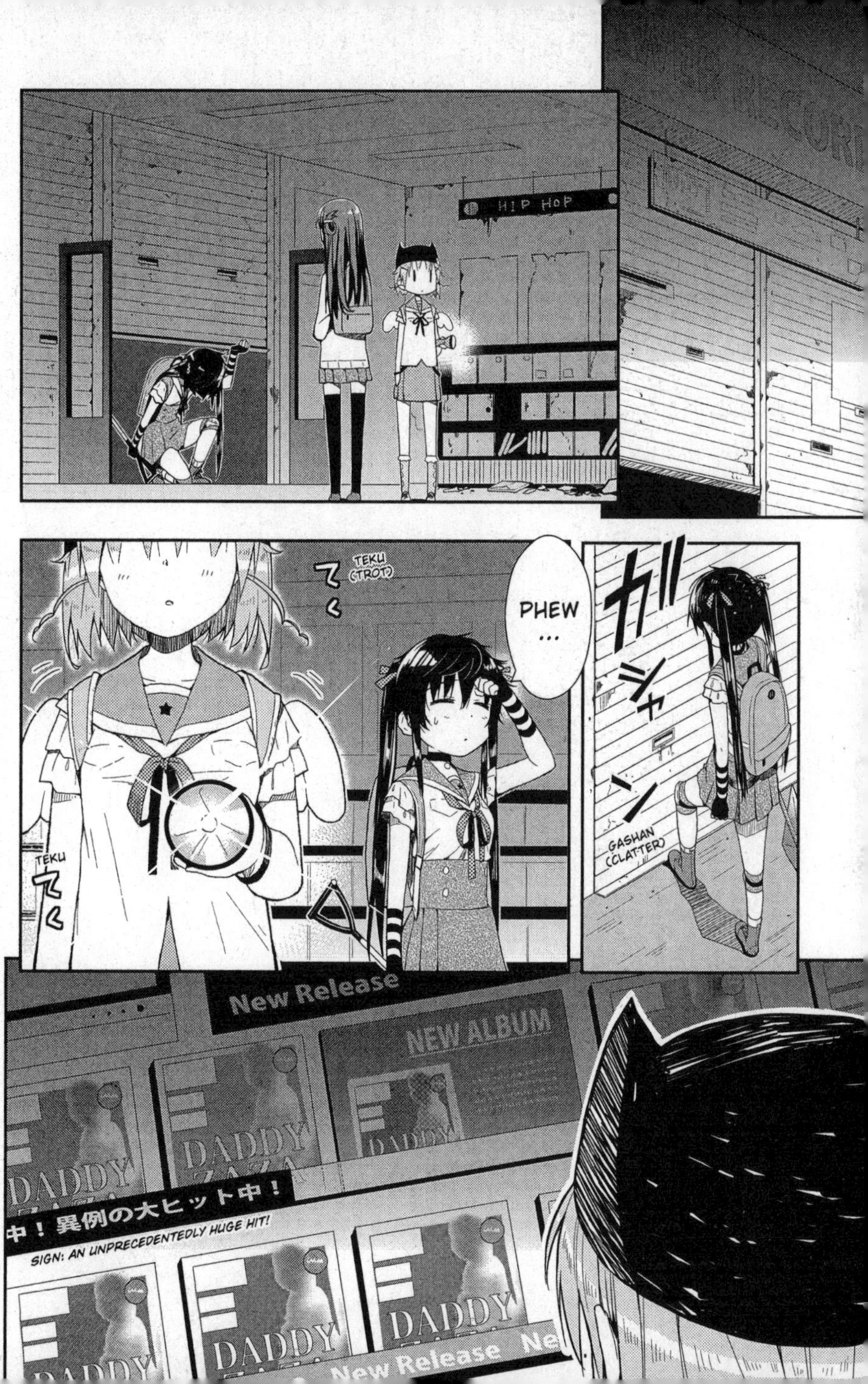

HIP HOP
ガシャン
GASHAN (CLATTER)
PHEW ...
てく
TEKU (TROT)
TEKU
てく
New Release
NEW ALBUM
DADDY
DADDY ZAZA
異例の大ヒット中！
中！異例の大ヒット中！
SIGN: AN UNPRECEDENTEDLY HUGE HIT!
DADDY
New Release

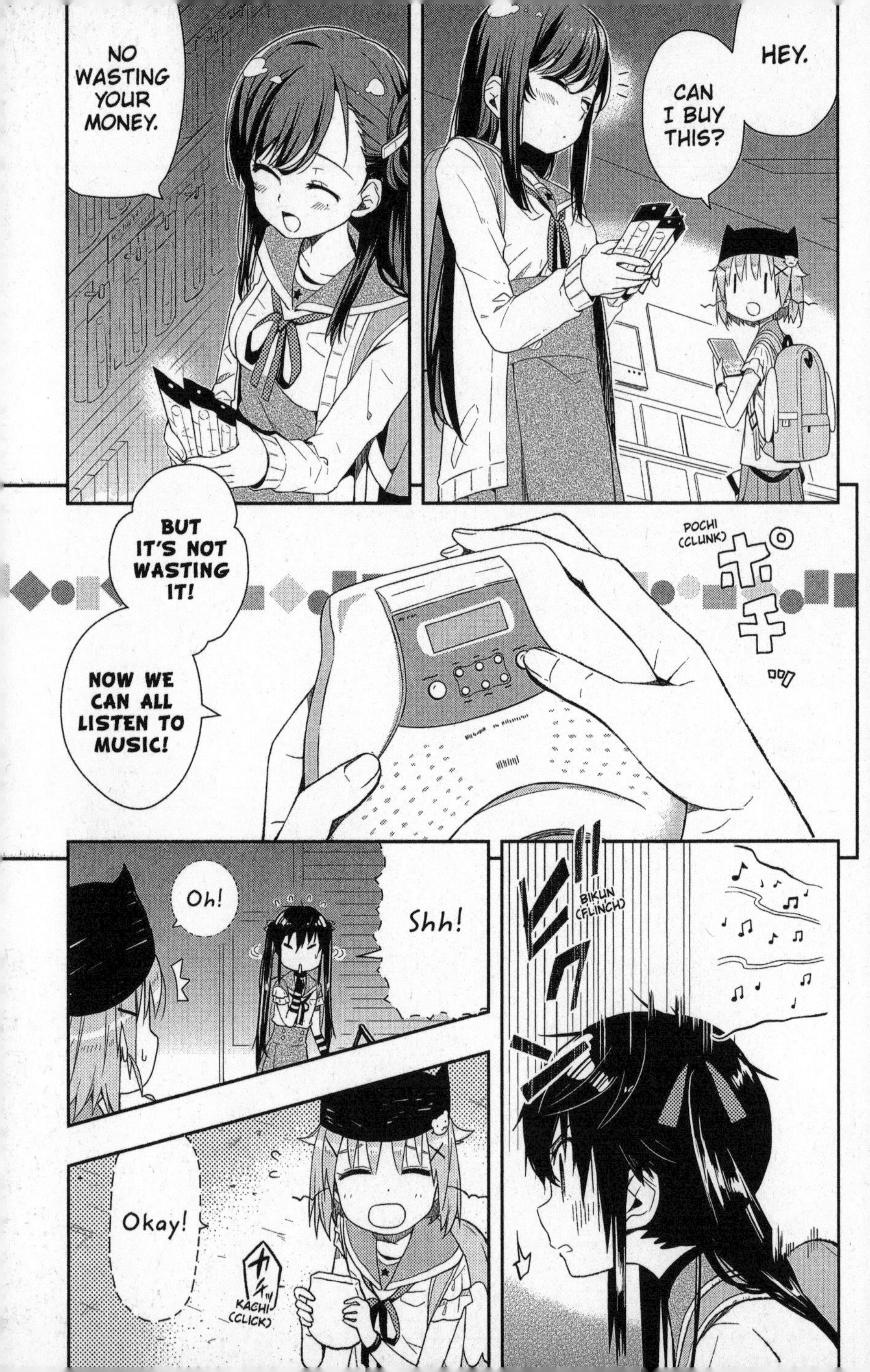
HEY.
CAN I BUY THIS?
NO WASTING YOUR MONEY.
POCHI (CLUNK)
BUT IT'S NOT WASTING IT!
NOW WE CAN ALL LISTEN TO MUSIC!
BIKUN (FLINCH)
Shh!
Oh!
Okay!
KACHI (CLICK)

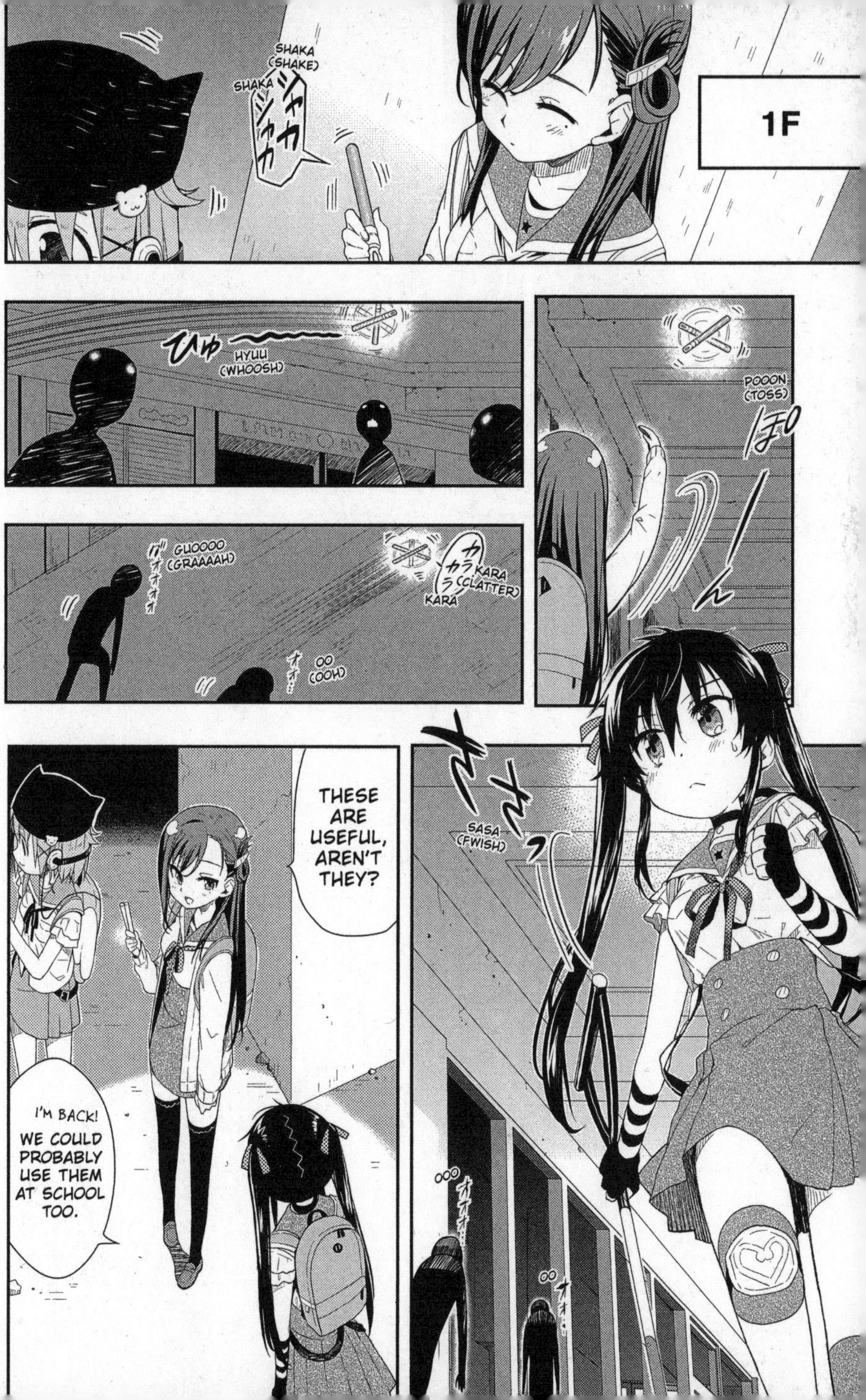

1F
シャカシャカ
SHAKA (SHAKE) SHAKA
ぽーん
POOON (TOSS)
ひゅ〜
HYUU (WHOOSH)
ゴォオオオ
GUOOOO (GRAAAAH)
カラカラ
KARA KARA (CLATTER)
オオ…
OO (OOH)
ささっ
SASA (FWISH)
オオオ…
OOO
オオ…
OO
THESE ARE USEFUL, AREN'T THEY?
I'M BACK! WE COULD PROBABLY USE THEM AT SCHOOL TOO.

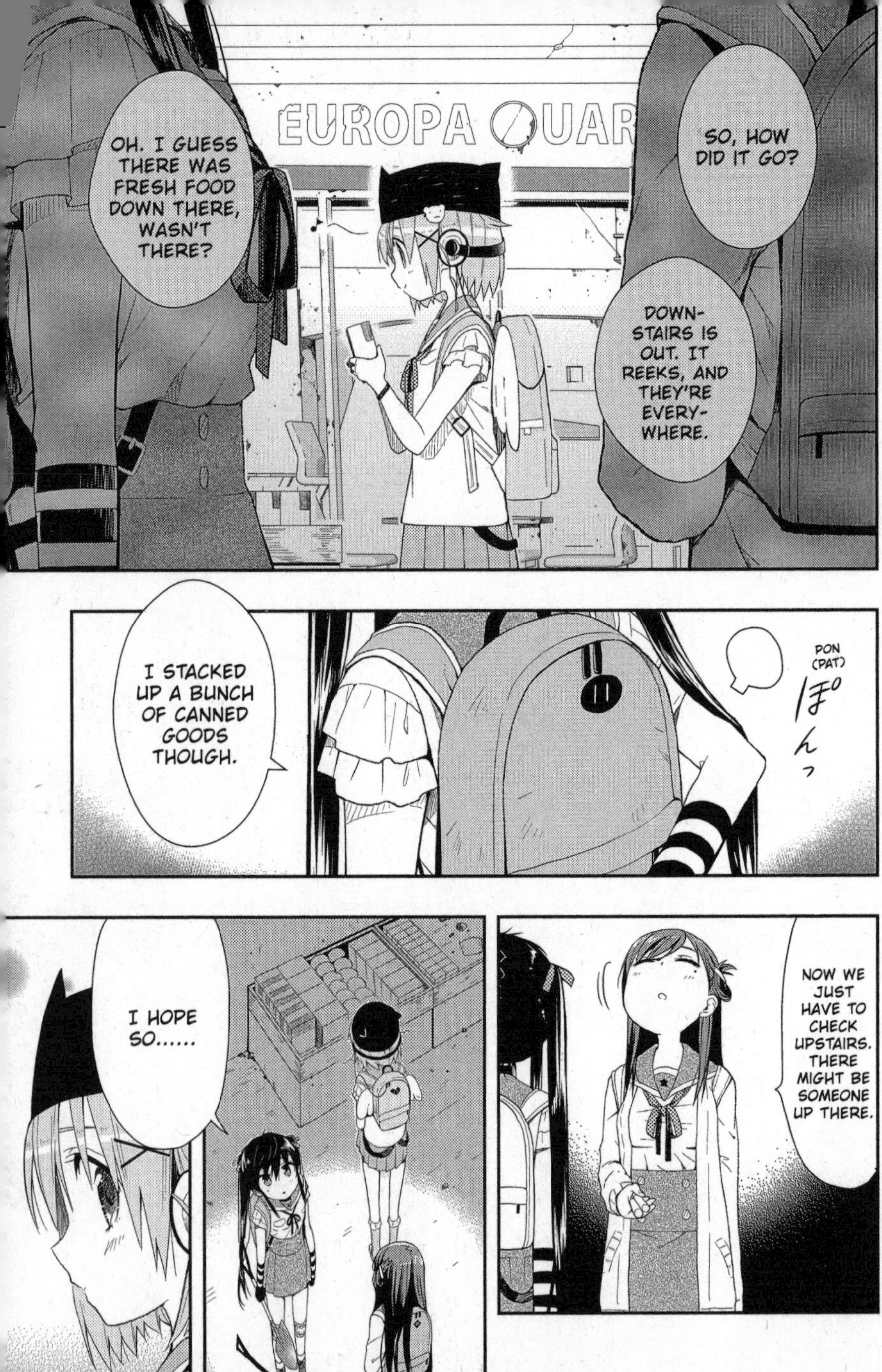
EUROPA UAR
SO, HOW DID IT GO?
DOWN-STAIRS IS OUT. IT REEKS, AND THEY'RE EVERY-WHERE.
OH. I GUESS THERE WAS FRESH FOOD DOWN THERE, WASN'T THERE?
PON (PAT)
ぽんっ
I STACKED UP A BUNCH OF CANNED GOODS THOUGH.
NOW WE JUST HAVE TO CHECK UPSTAIRS. THERE MIGHT BE SOMEONE UP THERE.
I HOPE SO......

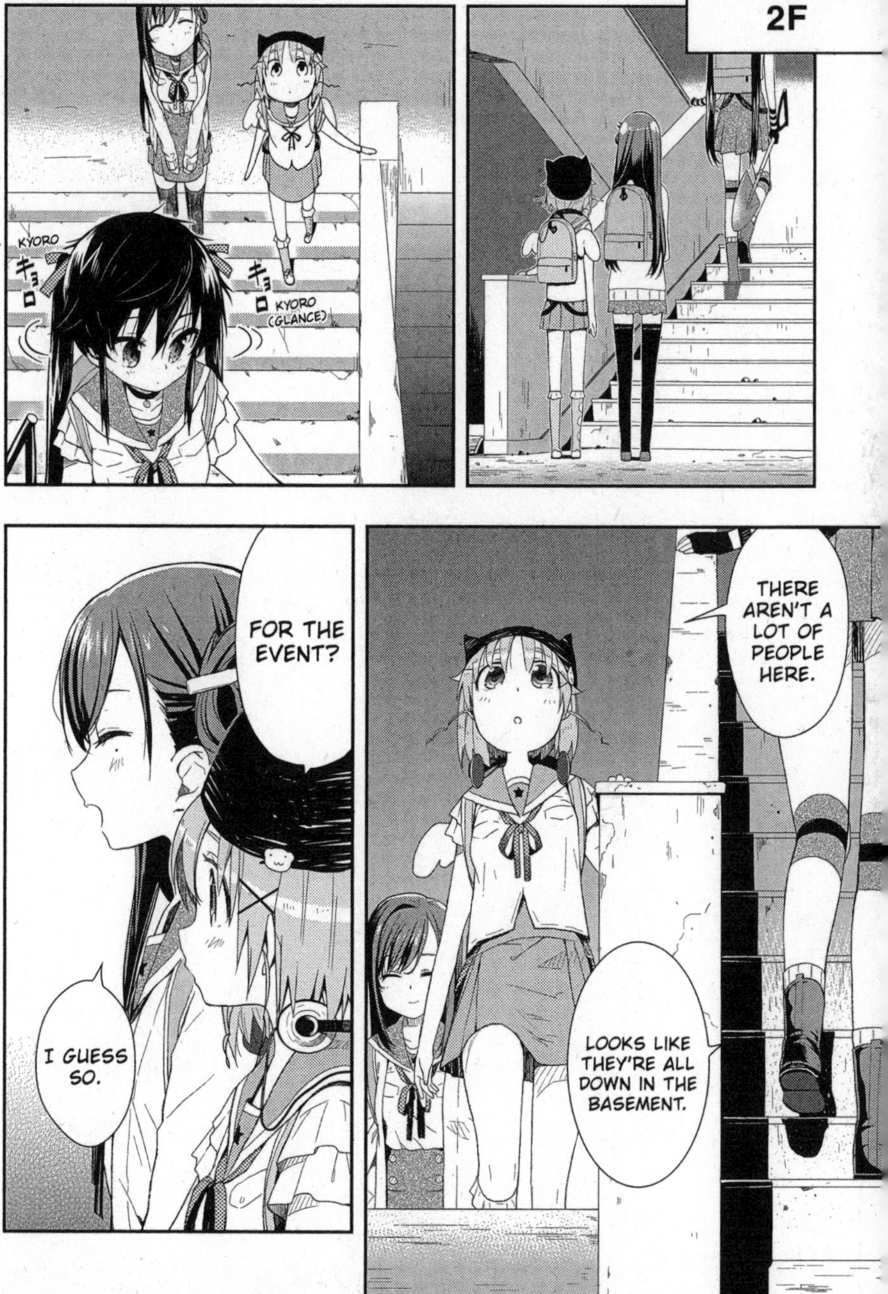
2F
キョロ
KYORO (GLANCE)
KYORO
キョロ
THERE AREN'T A LOT OF PEOPLE HERE.
LOOKS LIKE THEY'RE ALL DOWN IN THE BASEMENT.
FOR THE EVENT?
I GUESS SO.

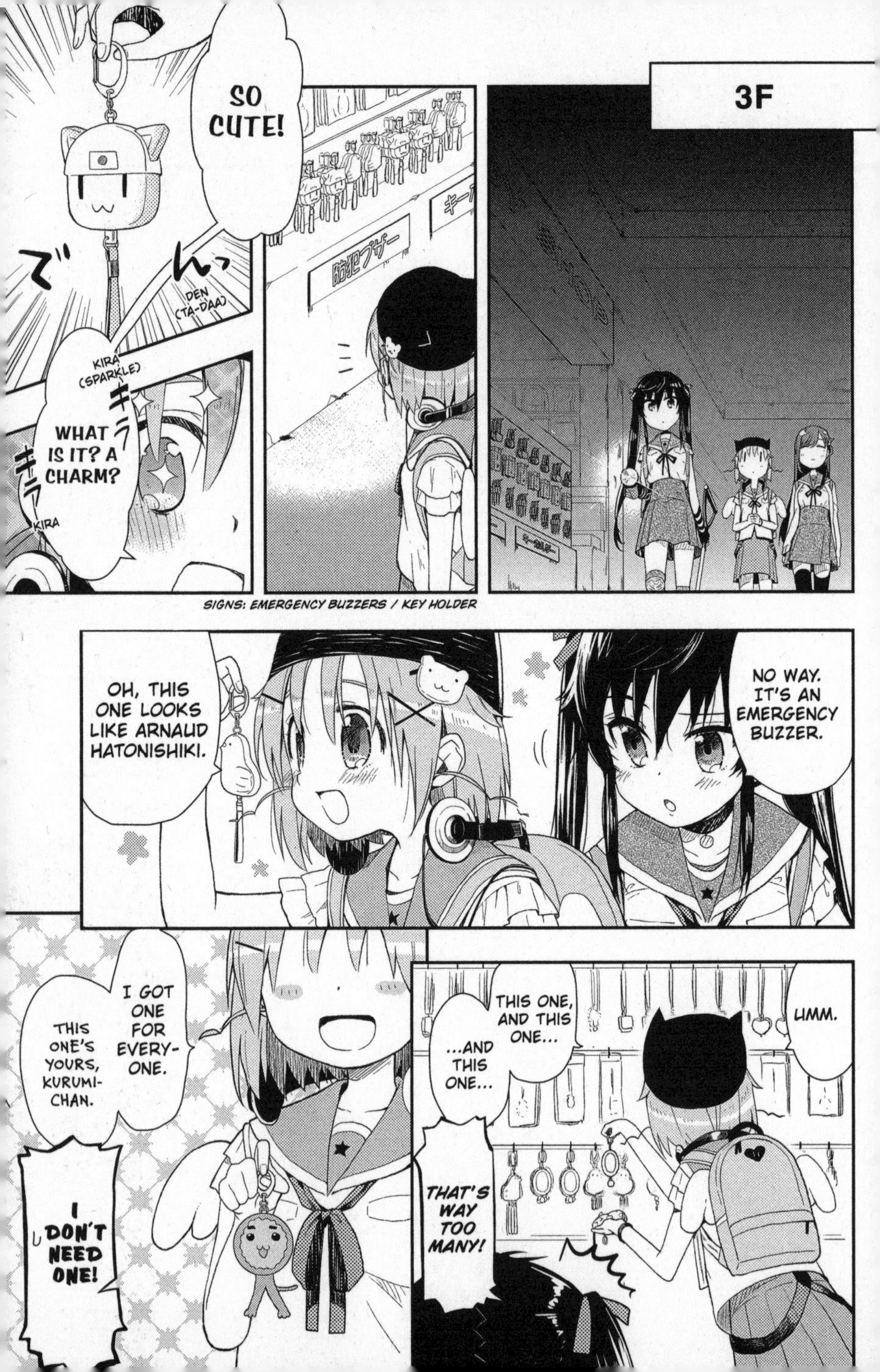
3F
防犯ブザー
SO CUTE!
でんっ
DEN (TA-DAA)
KIRA (SPARKLE)
キラ
WHAT IS IT? A CHARM?
キラ
KIRA
SIGNS: EMERGENCY BUZZERS / KEY HOLDER
NO WAY. IT'S AN EMERGENCY BUZZER.
OH, THIS ONE LOOKS LIKE ARNAUD HATONISHIKI.
UMM.
THIS ONE, AND THIS ONE...
...AND THIS ONE...
THAT'S WAY TOO MANY!
I GOT ONE FOR EVERY-ONE.
THIS ONE'S YOURS, KURUMI-CHAN.
I DON'T NEED ONE!

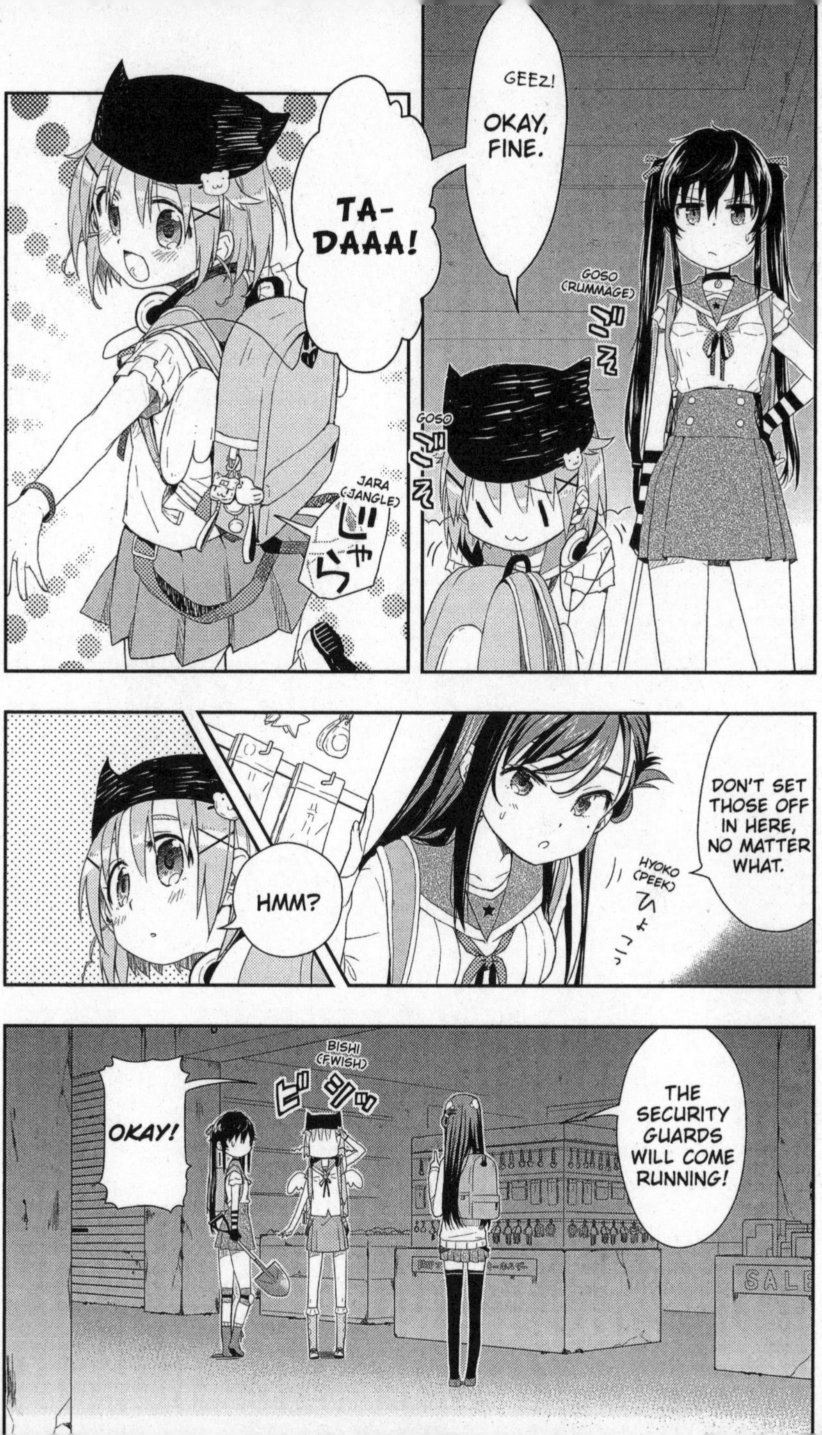
GEEZ!
OKAY, FINE.
GOSO (RUMMAGE)
ゴソ
GOSO
ゴソ
TA-DAAA!
JARA (JANGLE)
じゃら
DON'T SET THOSE OFF IN HERE, NO MATTER WHAT.
HYOKO (PEEK)
ひょこっ
HMM?
THE SECURITY GUARDS WILL COME RUNNING!
BISHI (FWISH)
ビシッ
OKAY!
SALE

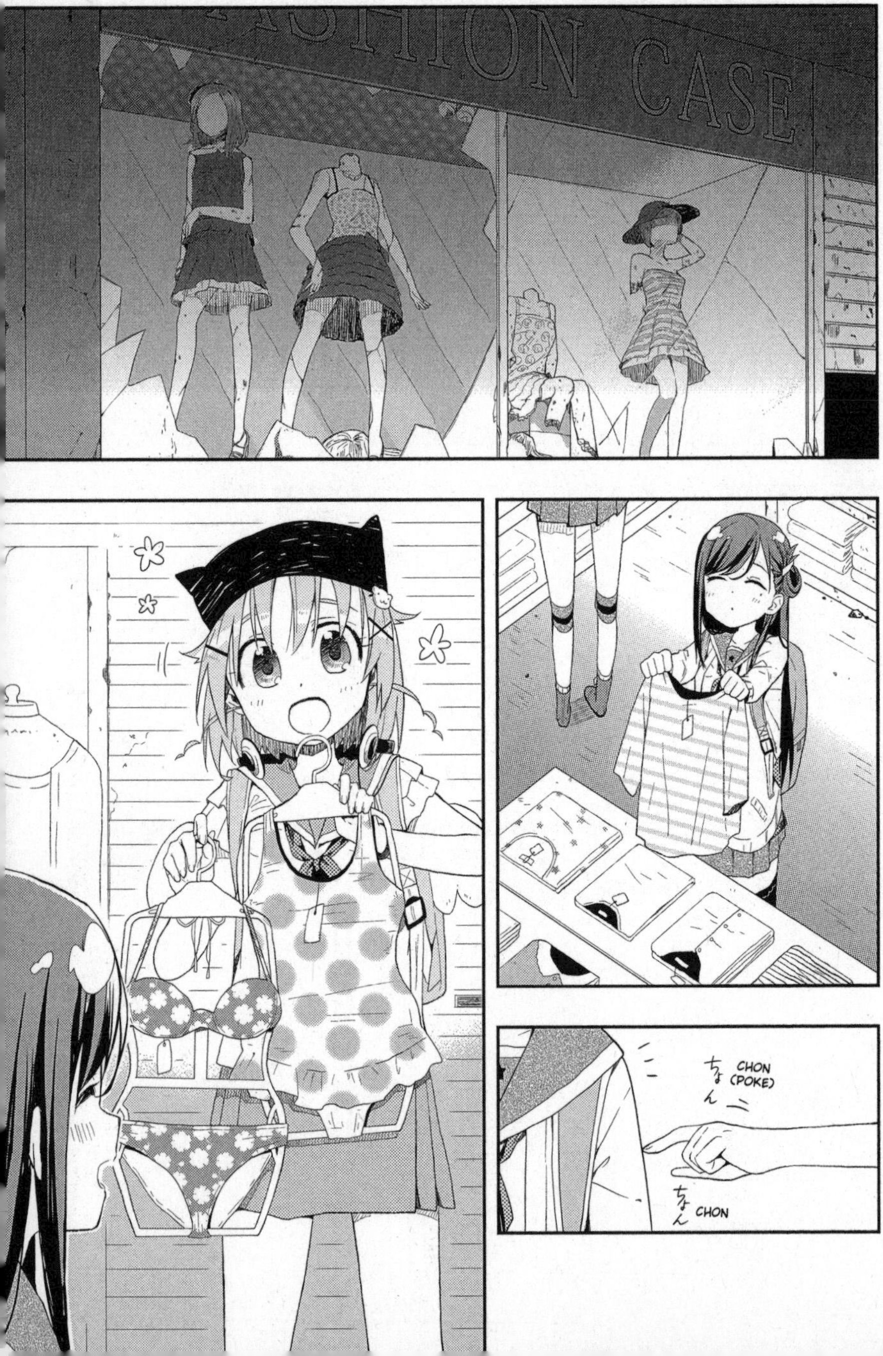
ASHION CASE
ちょん
CHON (POKE)
ちょん
CHON

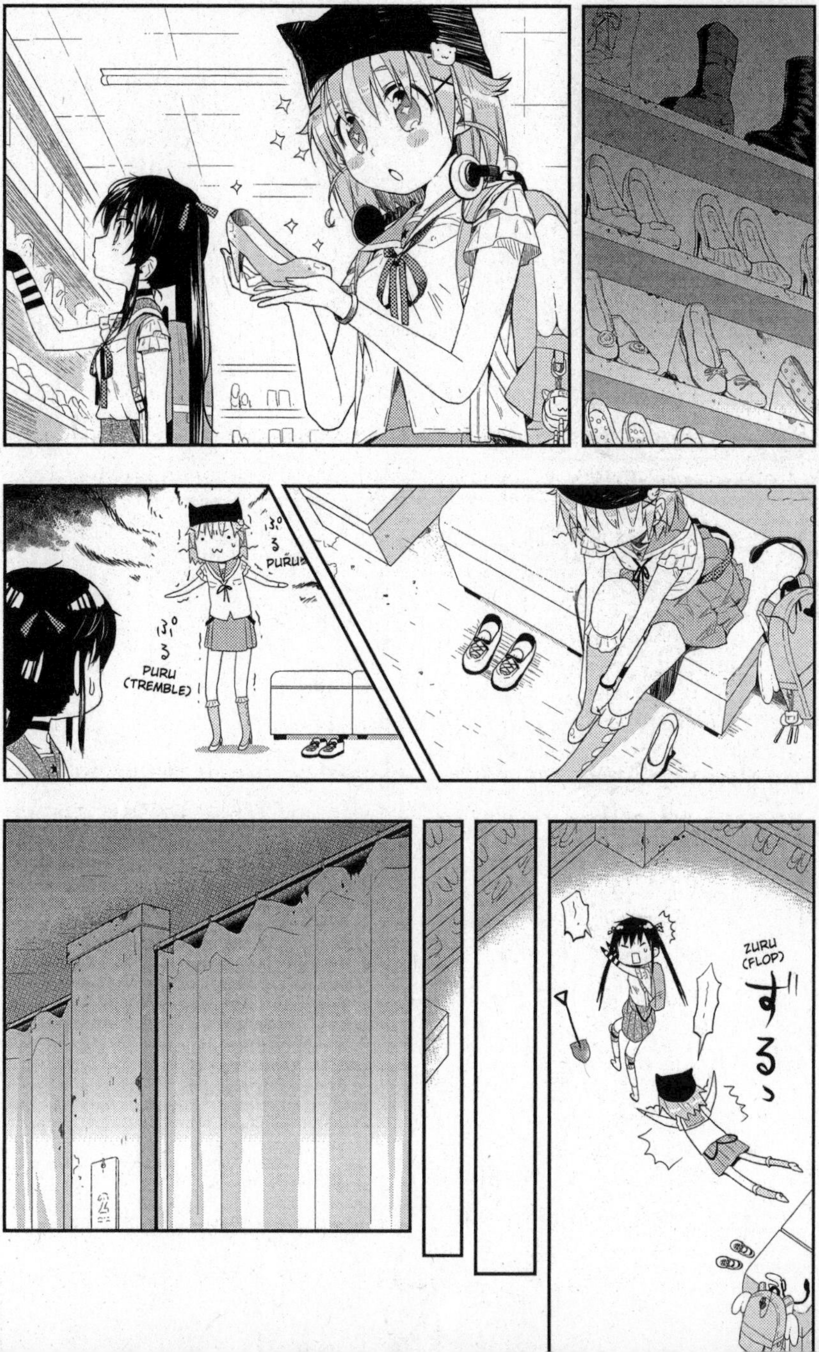
ぷる
PURU
ぷる
PURU (TREMBLE)
ずるっ
ZURU (FLOP)

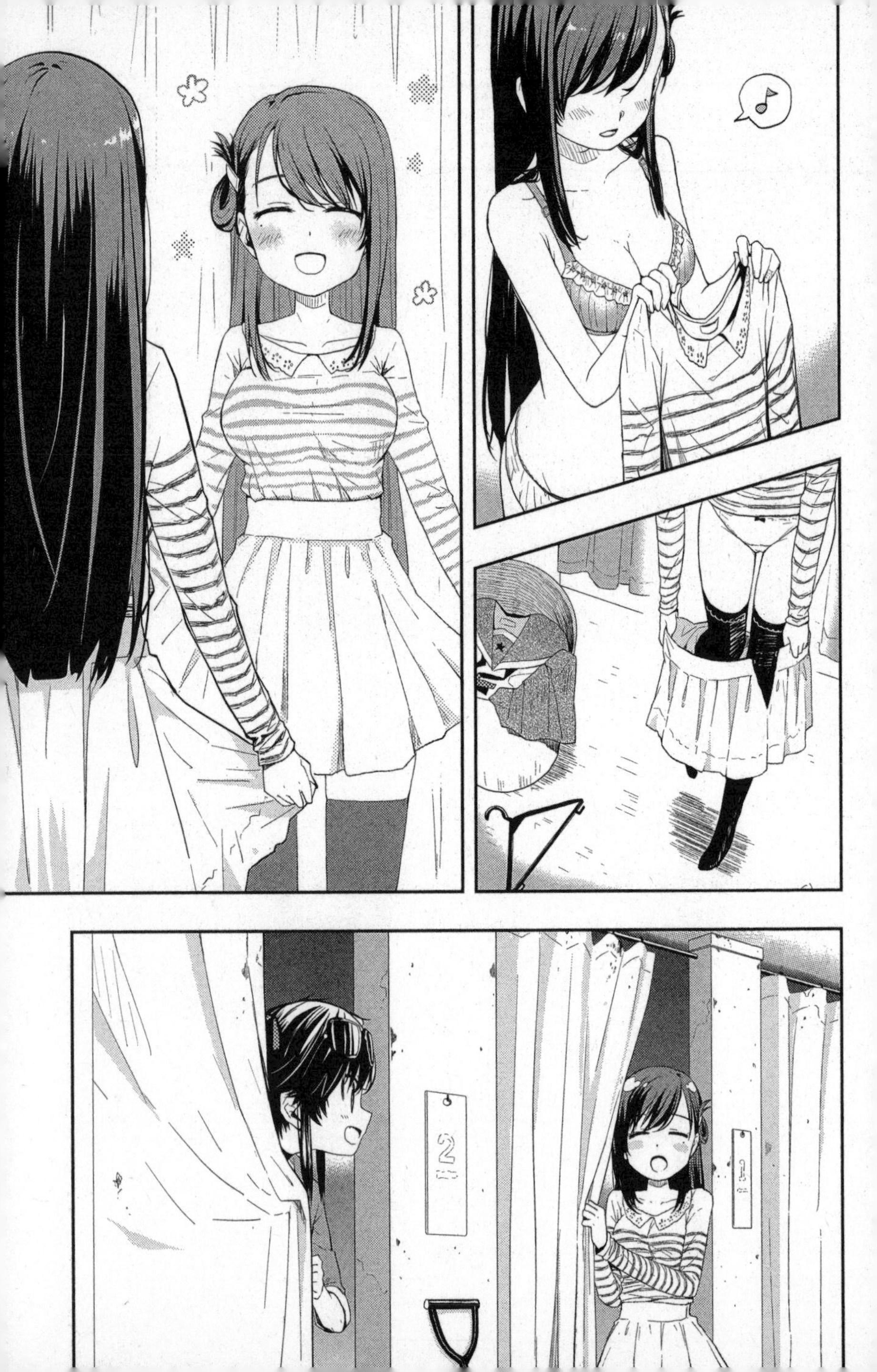
2

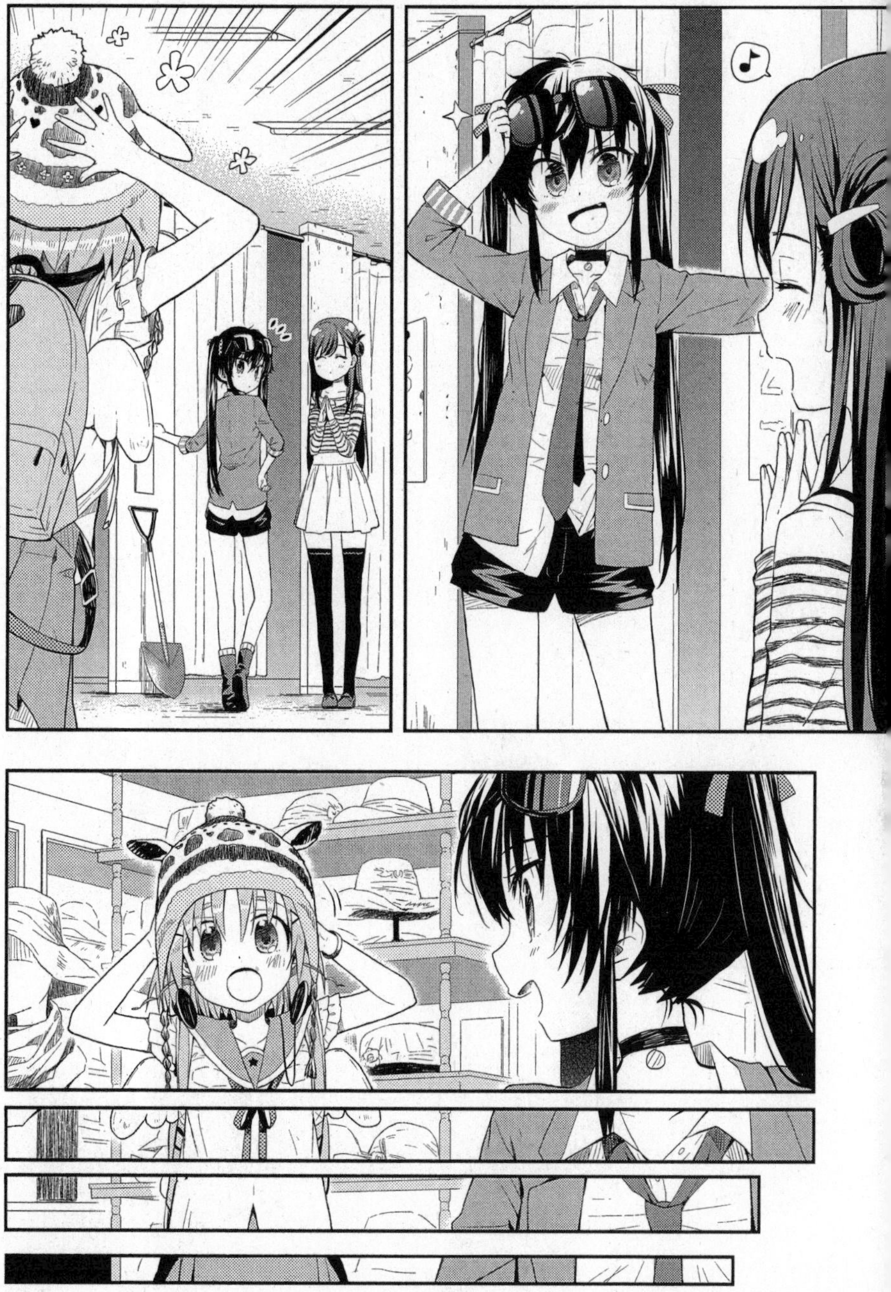

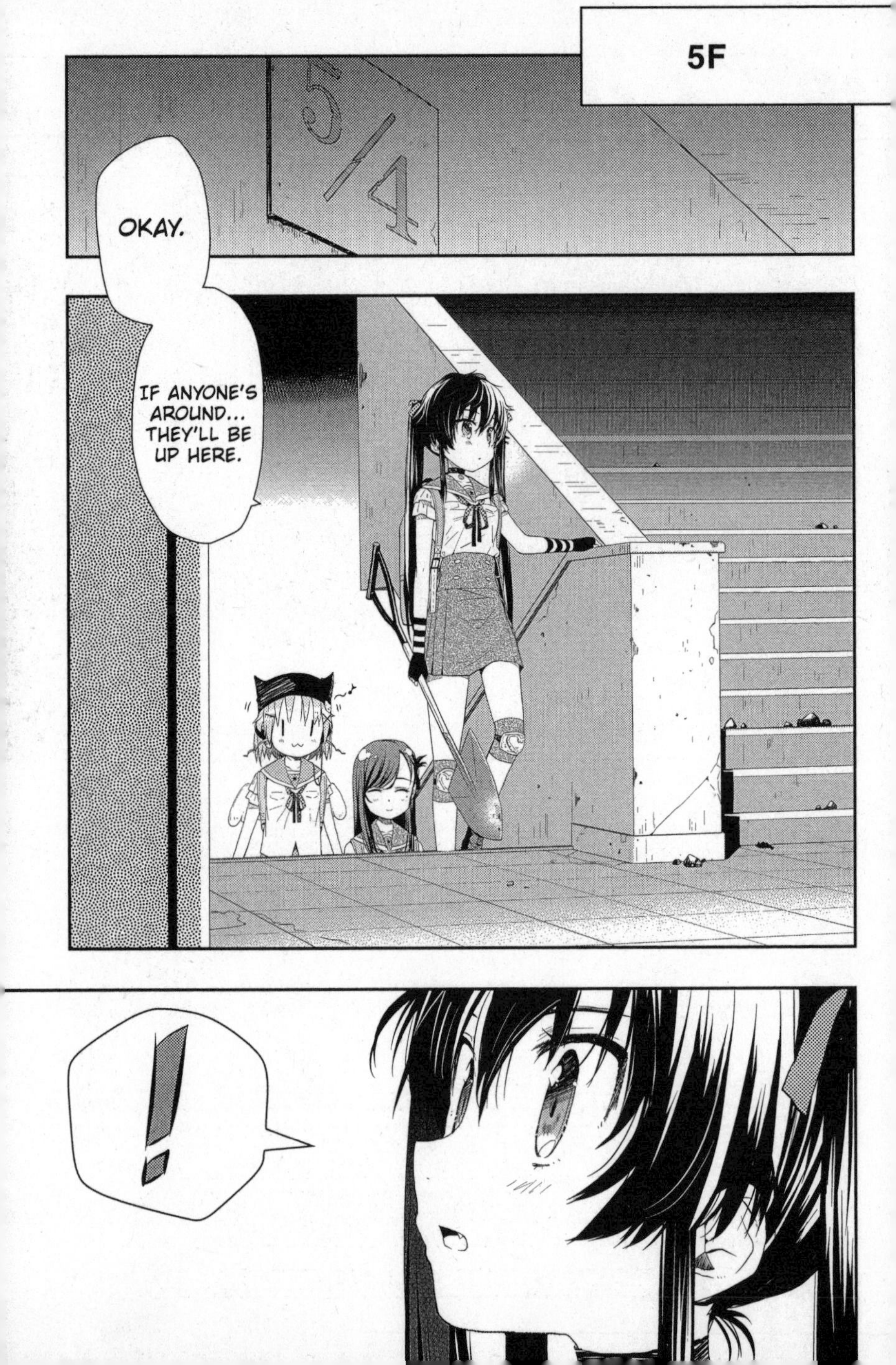
5F
5/4
OKAY.
IF ANYONE'S AROUND... THEY'LL BE UP HERE.
!

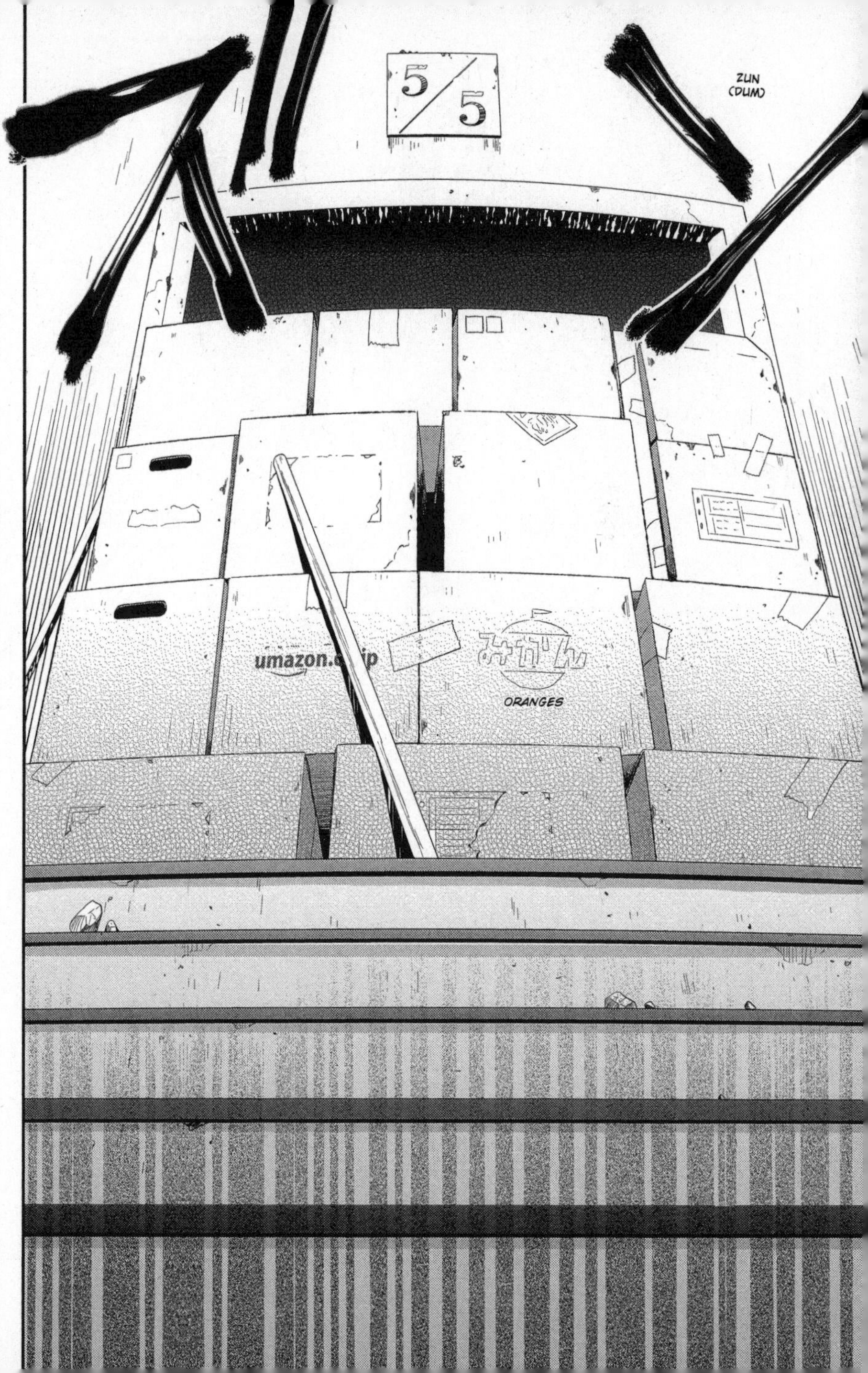
5/5
ZUN
(DUM)
umazon.co.jp
みかん
ORANGES

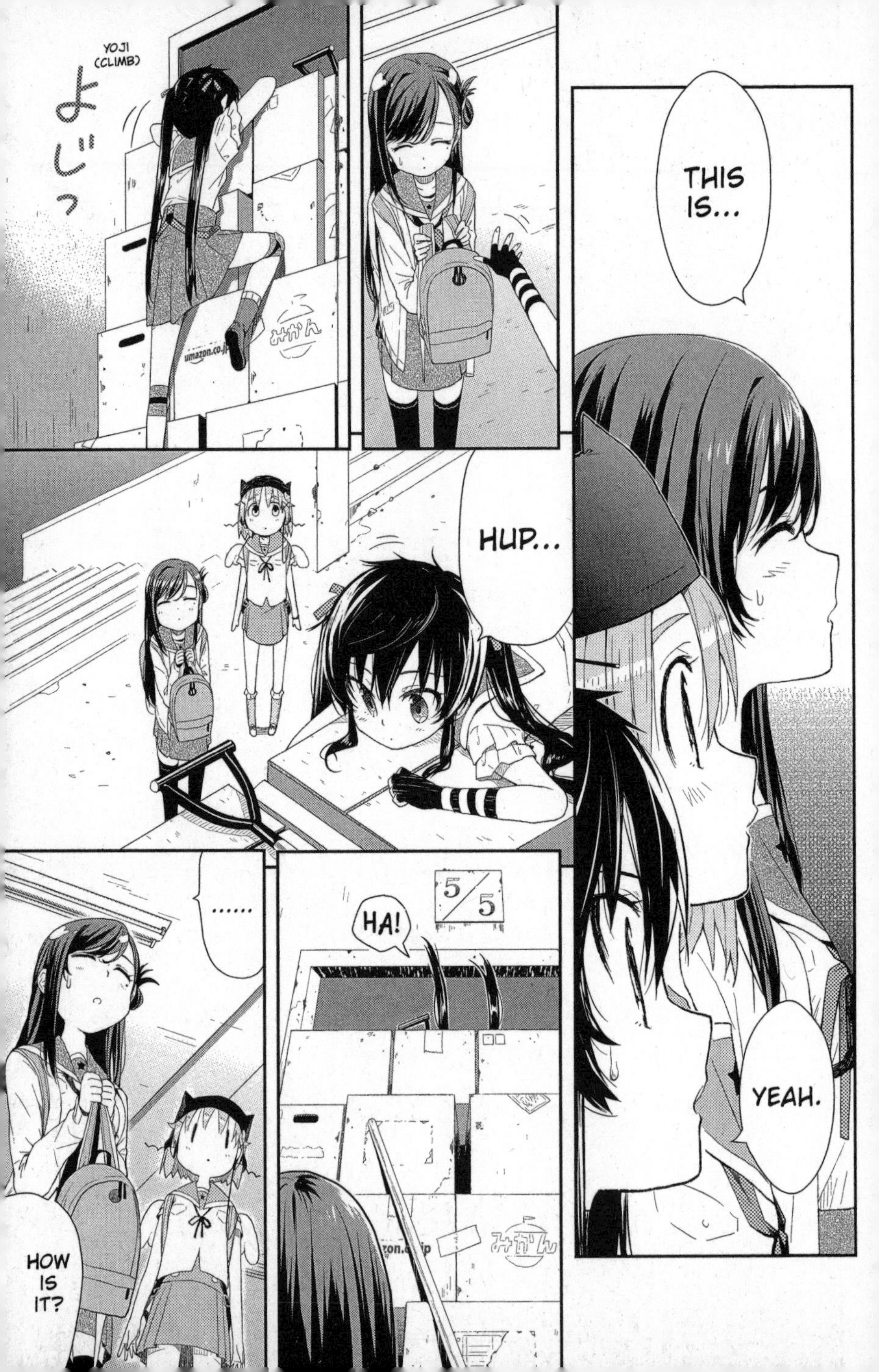

THIS IS...
YEAH.
YOJI (CLIMB)
よじっ
HUP...
HA!
......
HOW IS IT?

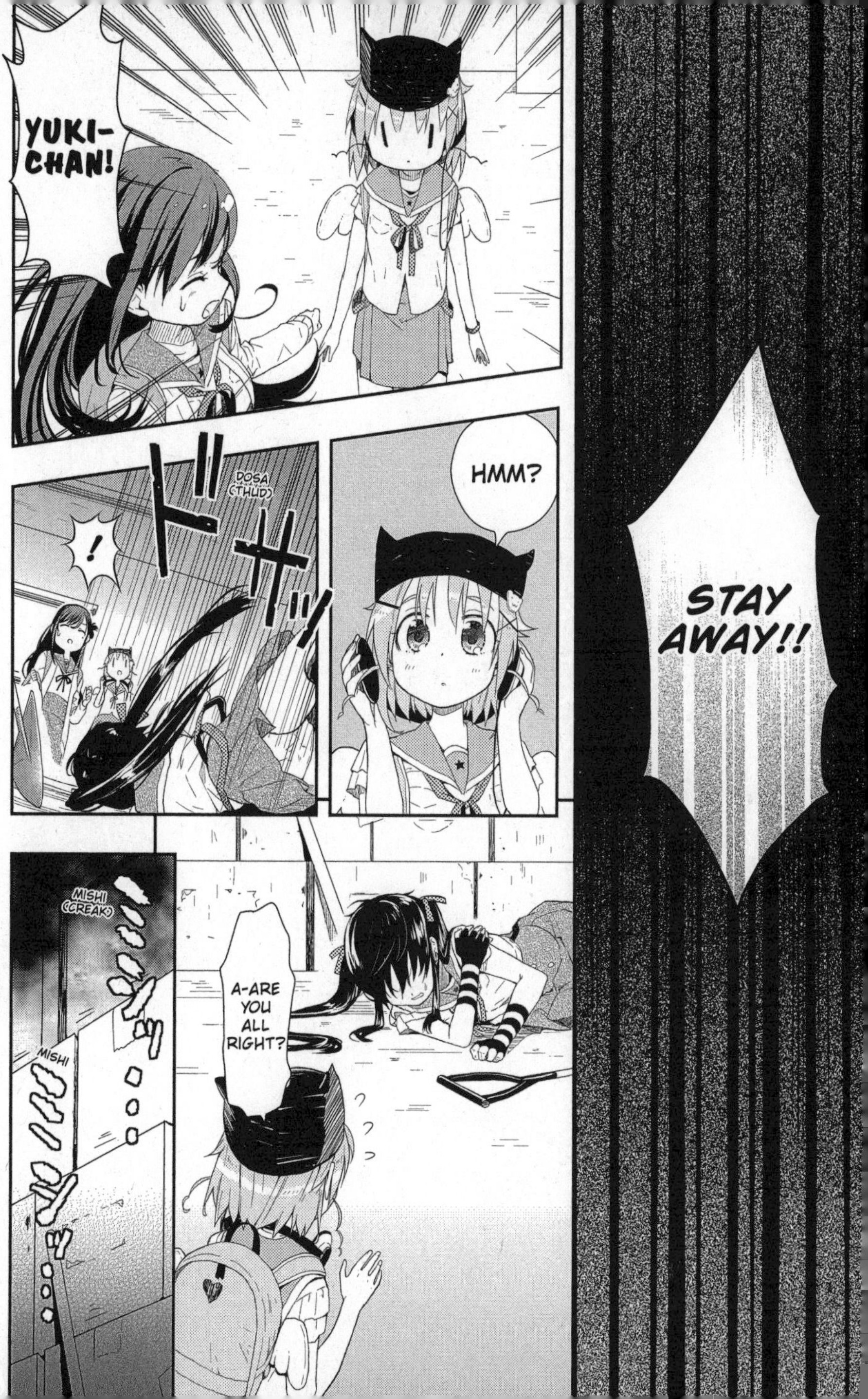

STAY AWAY!!
YUKI-CHAN!
HMM?
DOSA (THUD)
!
A-ARE YOU ALL RIGHT?
MISHI (CREAK)
MISHI

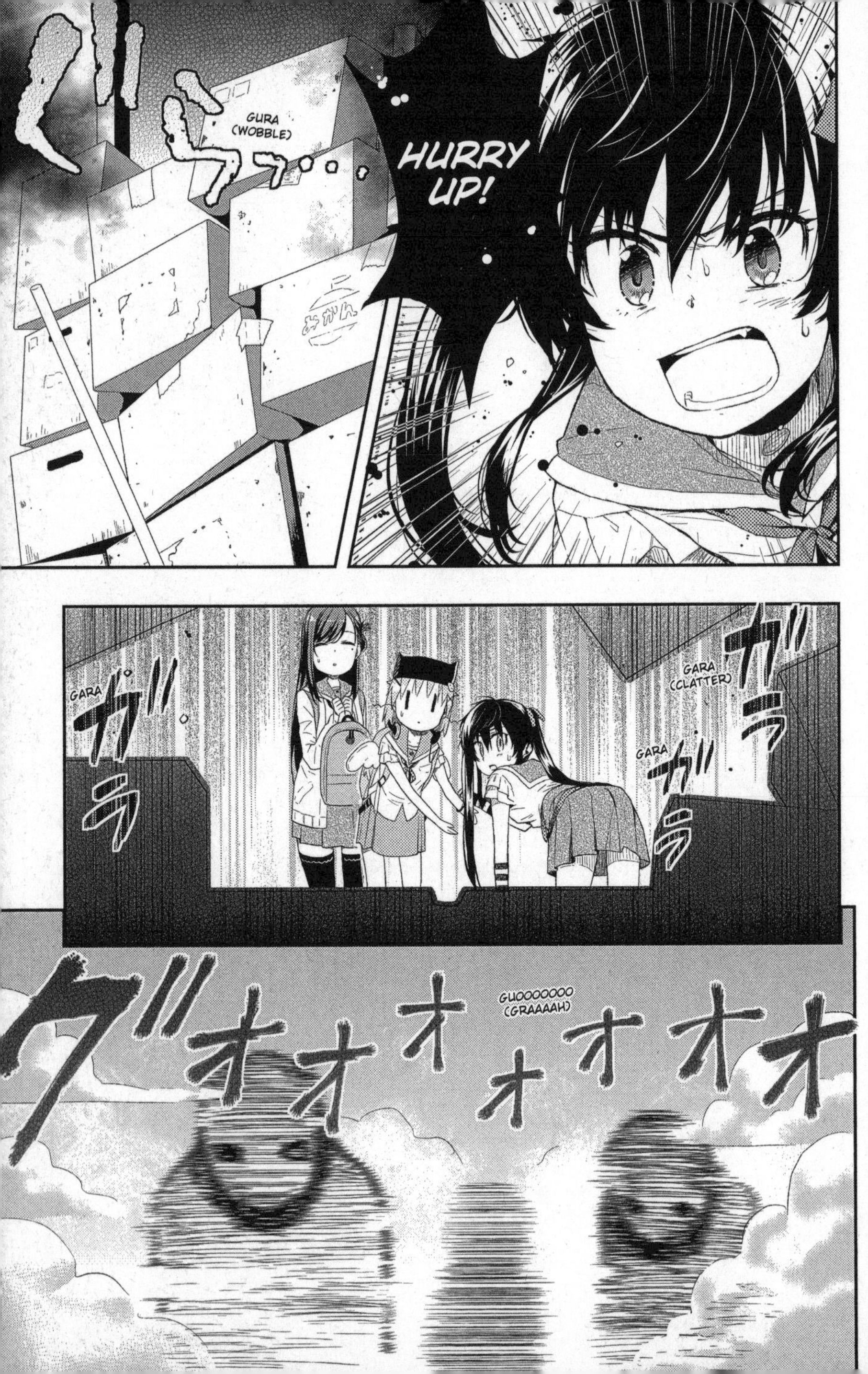
HURRY UP!
GURA (WOBBLE)
みかん
GARA (CLATTER)
GARA
GARA
GUOOOOOOO (GRAAAAH)

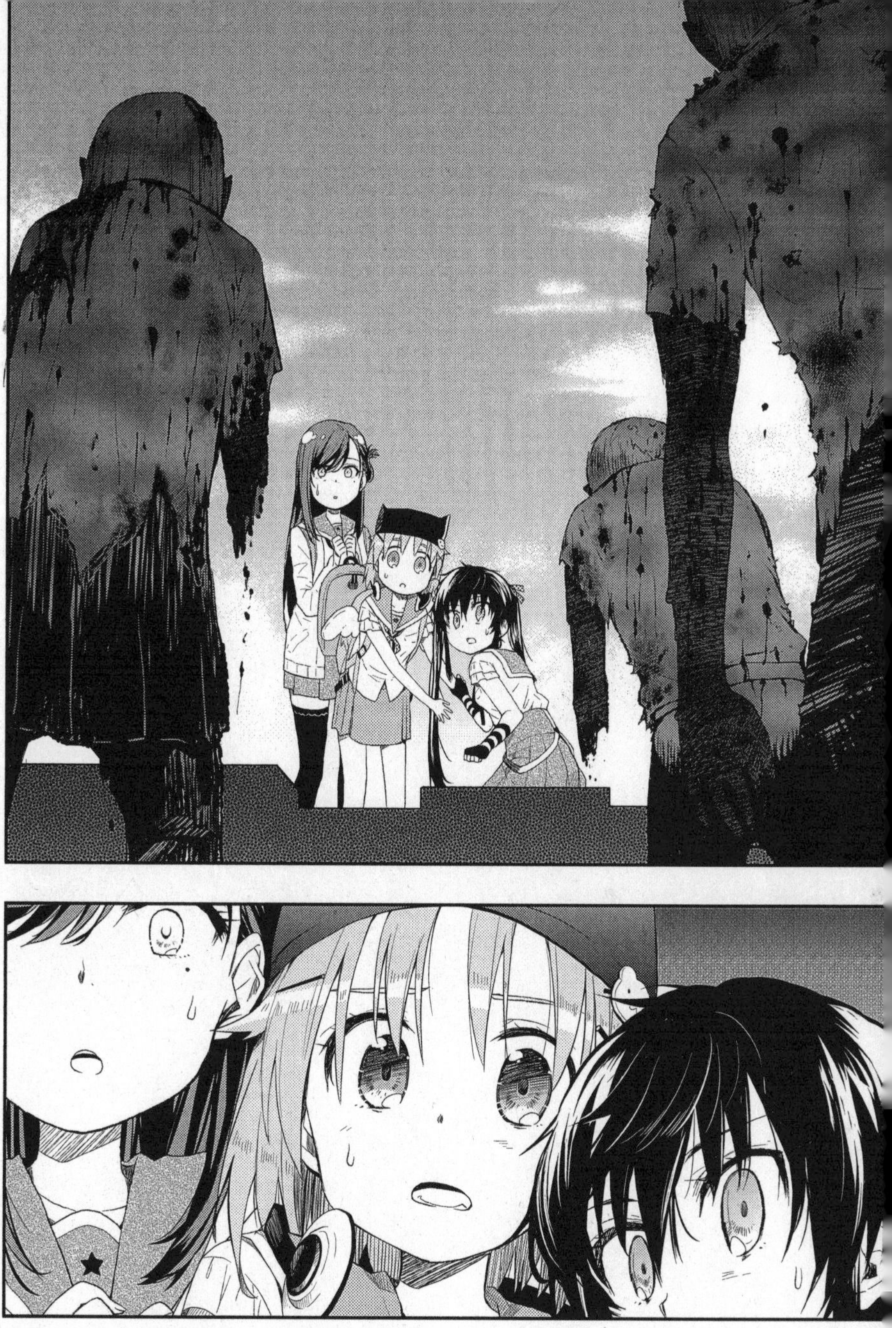

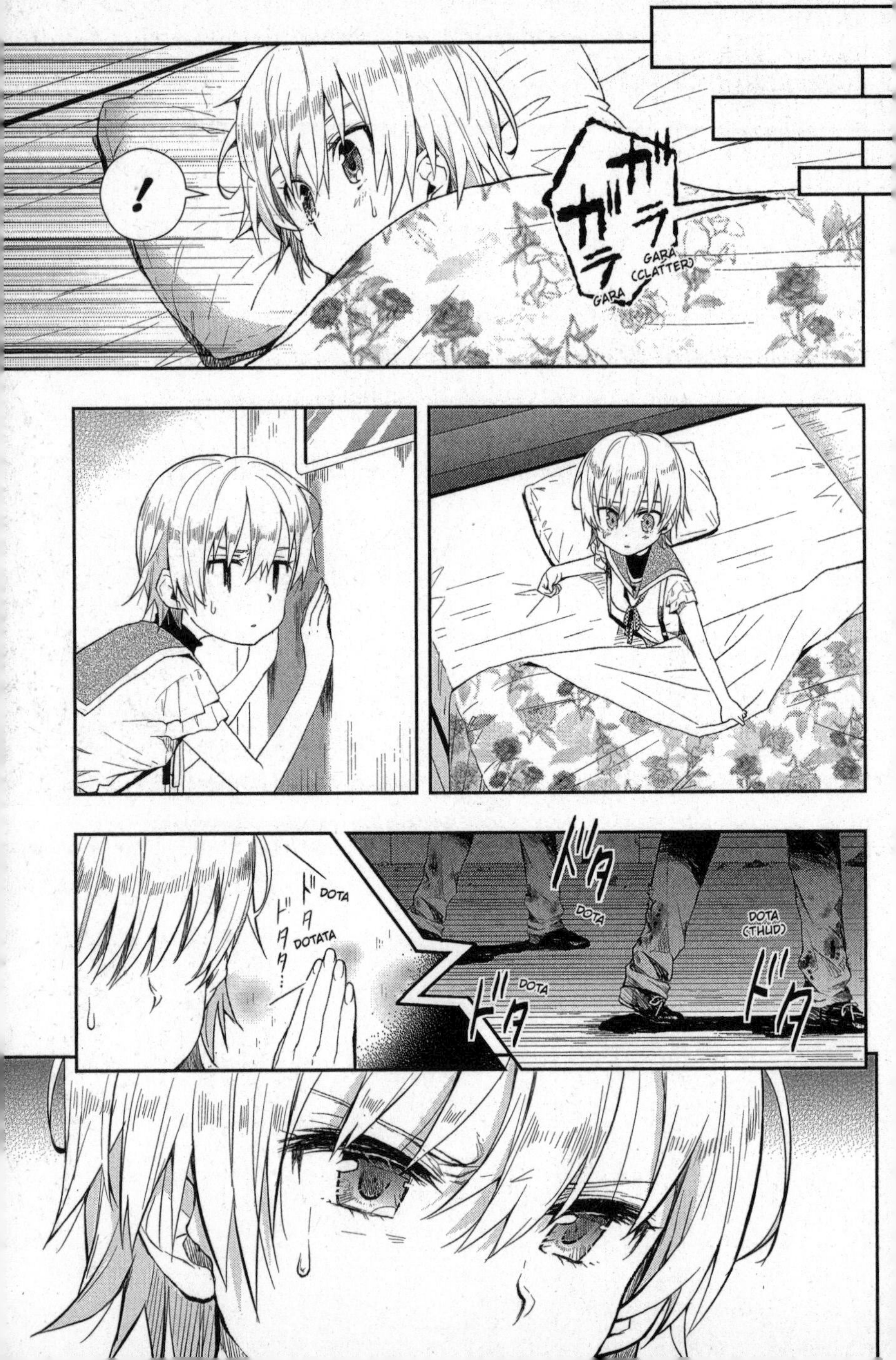
ガラガラ
GARA GARA (CLATTER)
!
ドタ
DOTA
DOTA (THUD)
ドタ
ドタ
DOTA
ドタドタ…
DOTA DOTATA

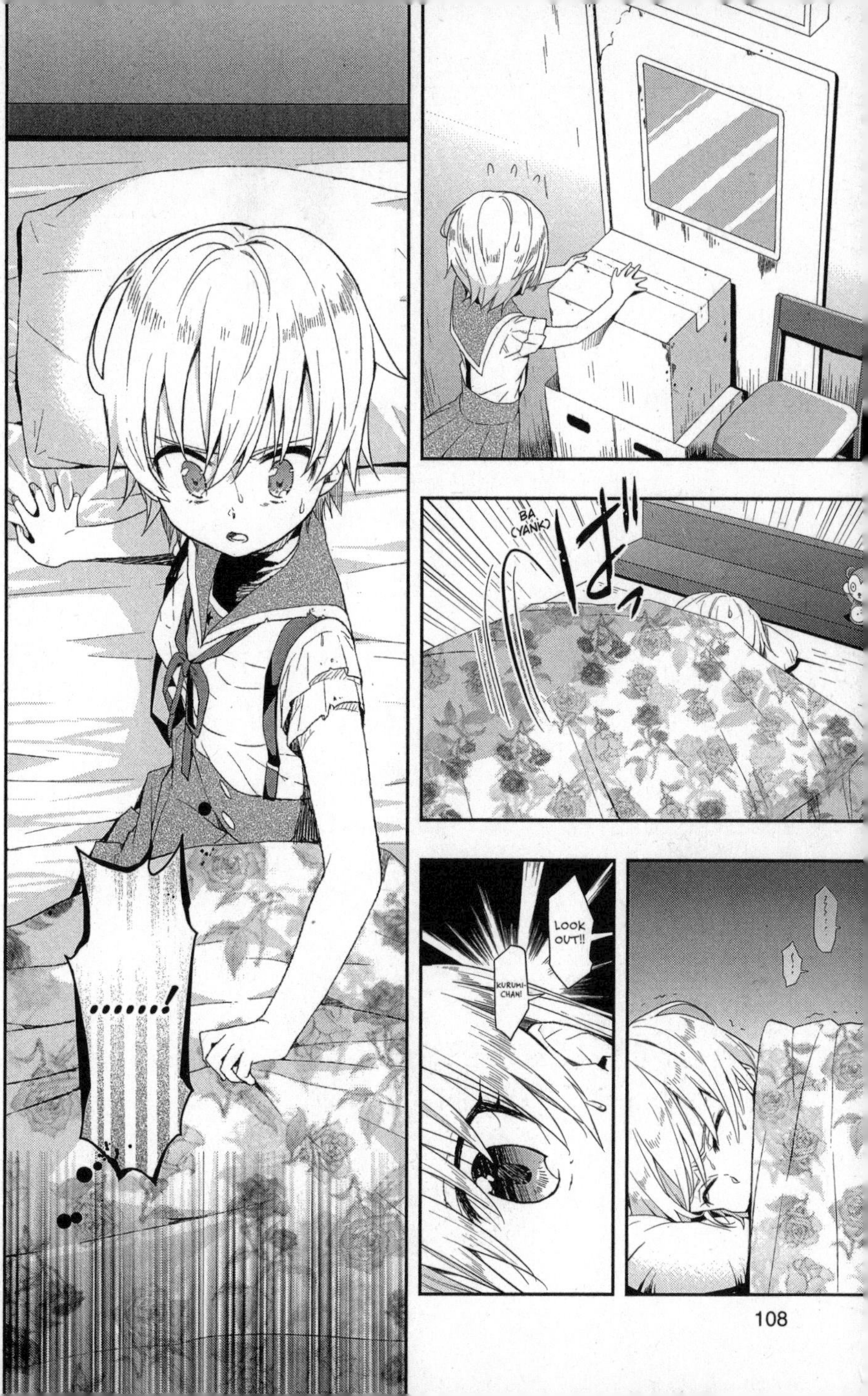
BA (YANK)
LOOK OUT!!
KURUMI-CHAN!
......!

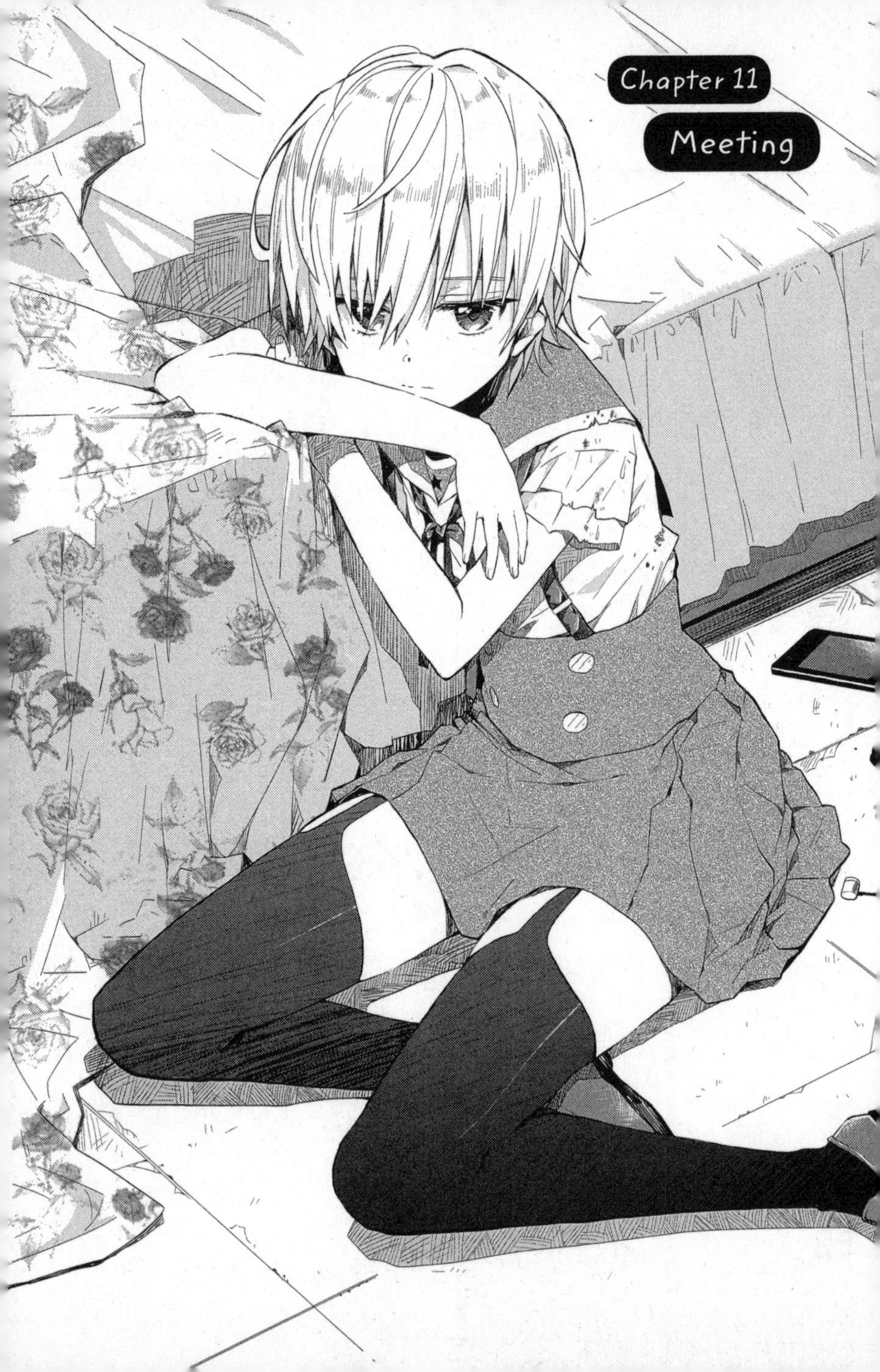
Chapter 11
Meeting

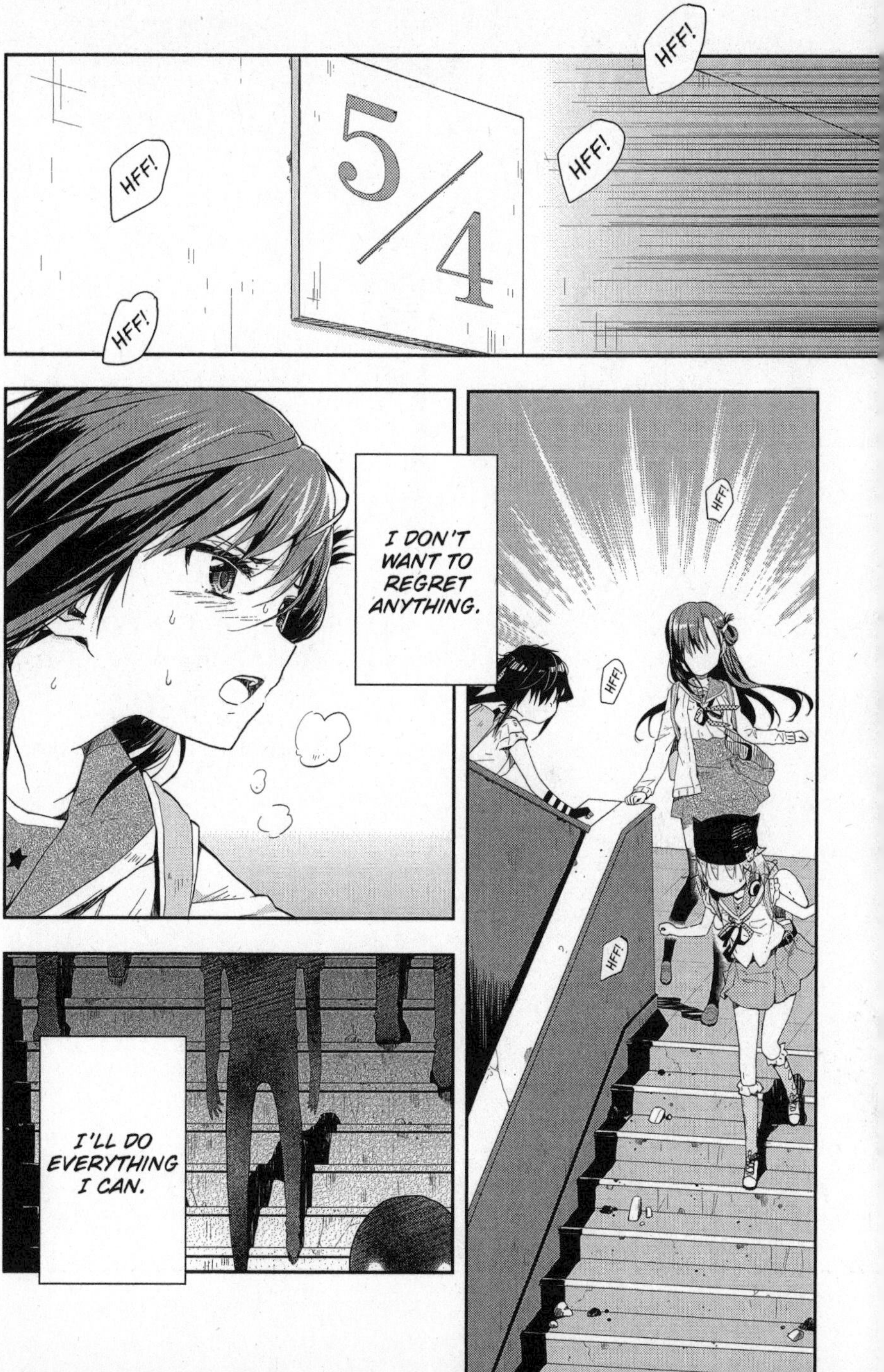
HFF!
HFF!
HFF!
HFF!
HFF!
HFF!
HFF!
I DON'T WANT TO REGRET ANYTHING.
I'LL DO EVERYTHING I CAN.

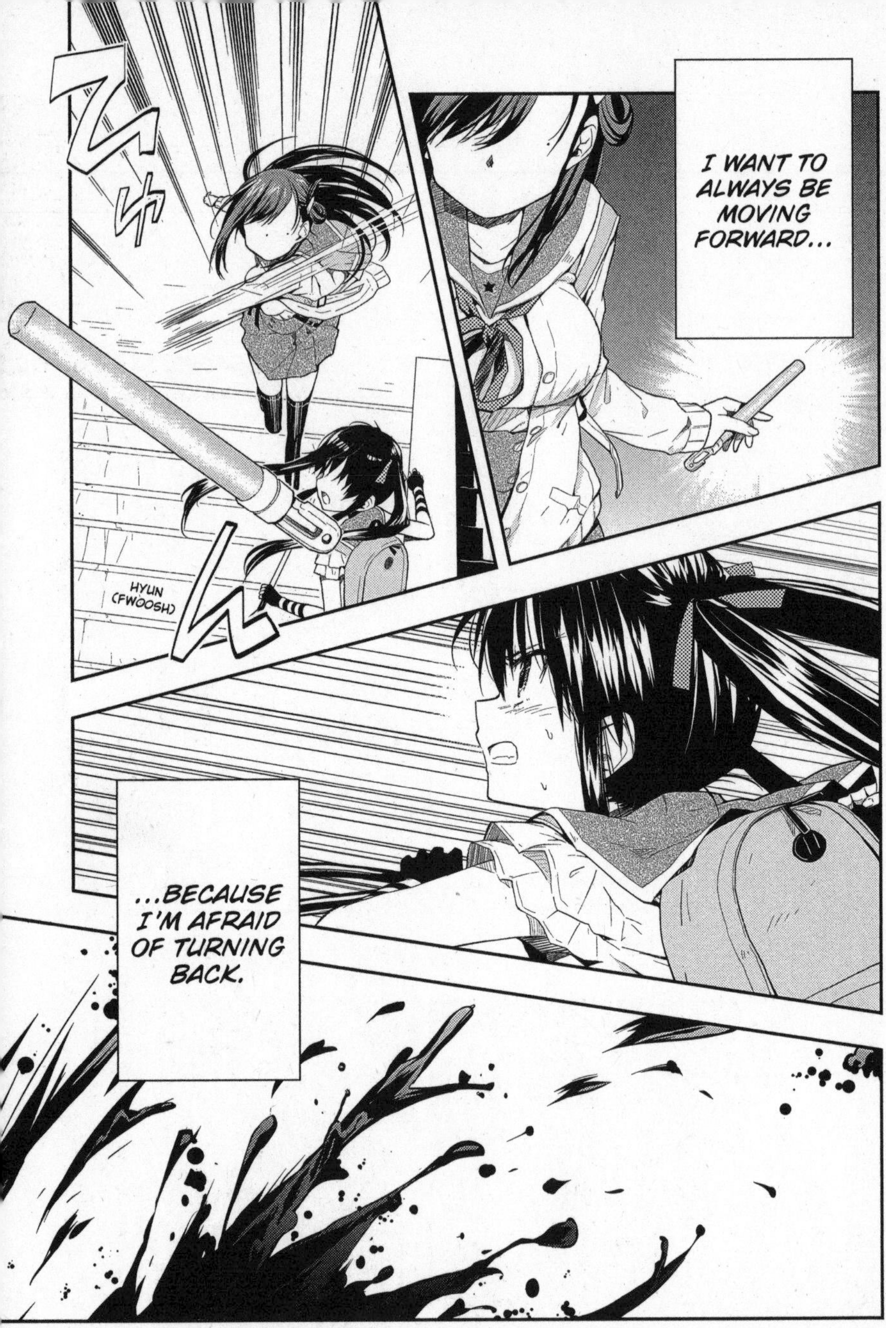

I WANT TO ALWAYS BE MOVING FORWARD...
ひゅん
HYUN (FWOOSH)
...BECAUSE I'M AFRAID OF TURNING BACK.

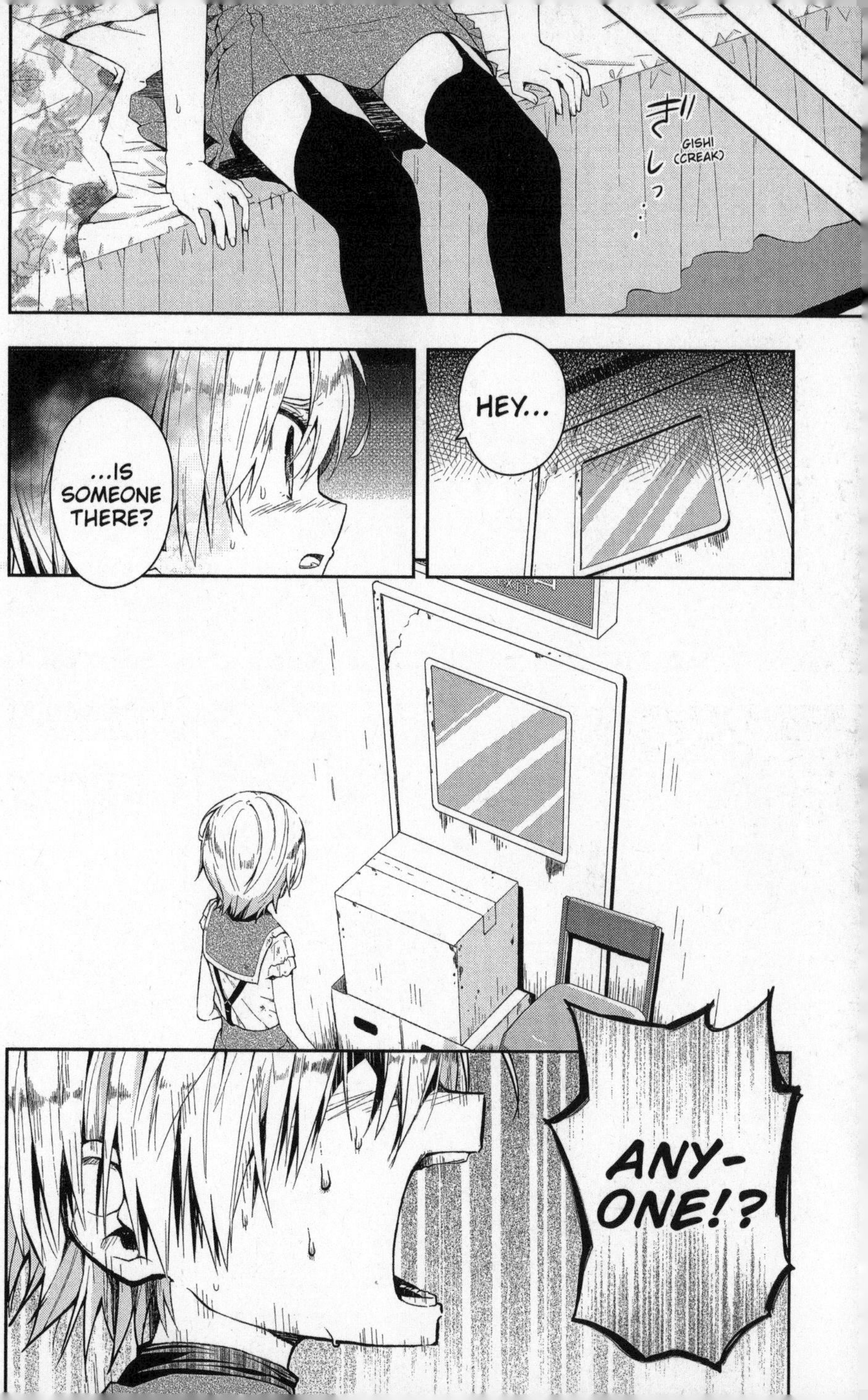
ぎしっ・・・
GISHI (CREAK)
HEY...
...IS SOMEONE THERE?
ANY-ONE!?

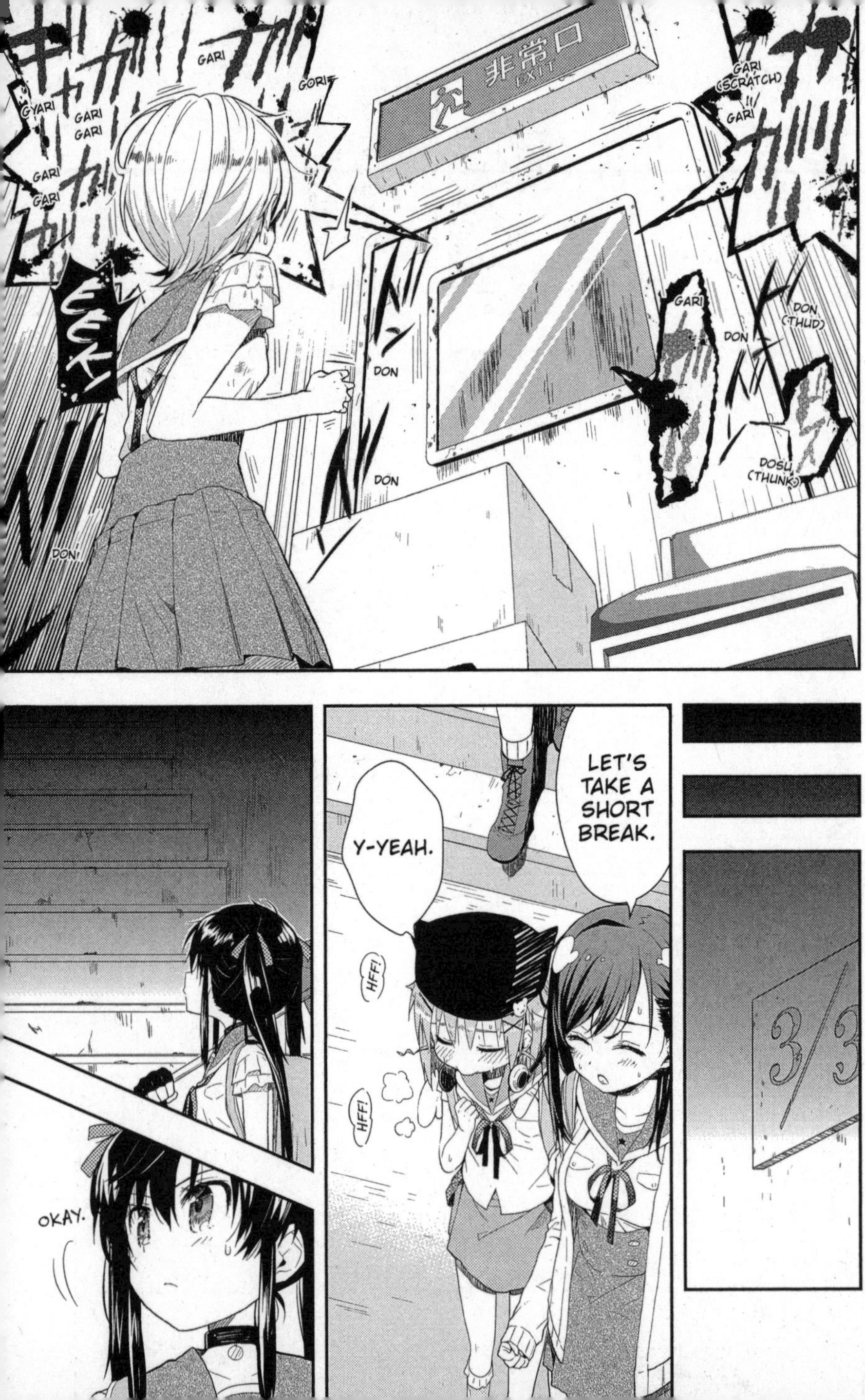
GARI (SCRATCH)
GARI
GARI
DON (THUD)
DON
DOSU (THUNK)
GARI
GORI
GYARI
GARI
GARI
GARI
GARI
EEK!
DON
DON
DON
3/3
LET'S TAKE A SHORT BREAK.
Y-YEAH.
HFF!
HFF!
OKAY.

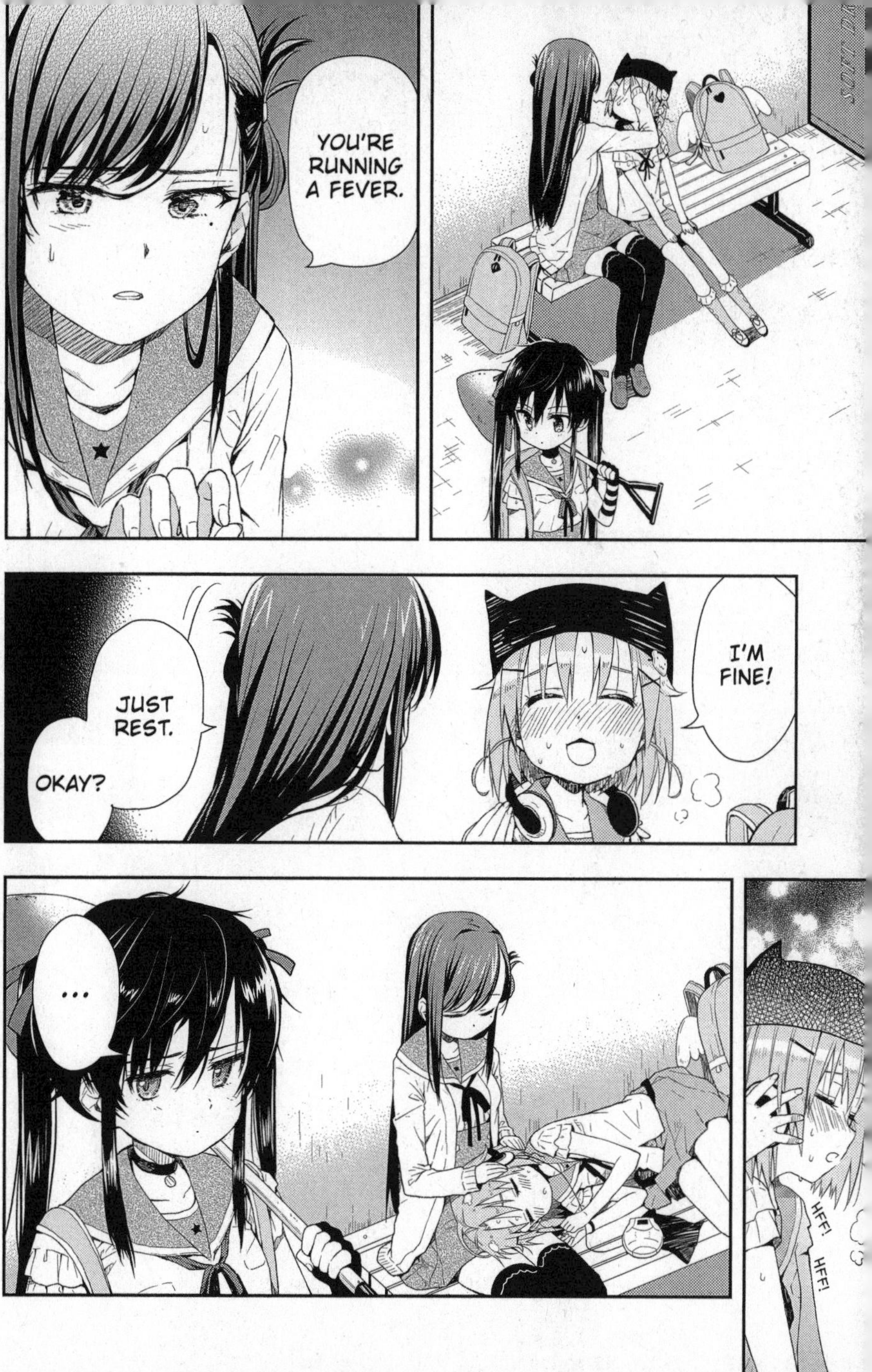
YOU'RE RUNNING A FEVER.
I'M FINE!
JUST REST.
OKAY?
HFF! HFF!
...

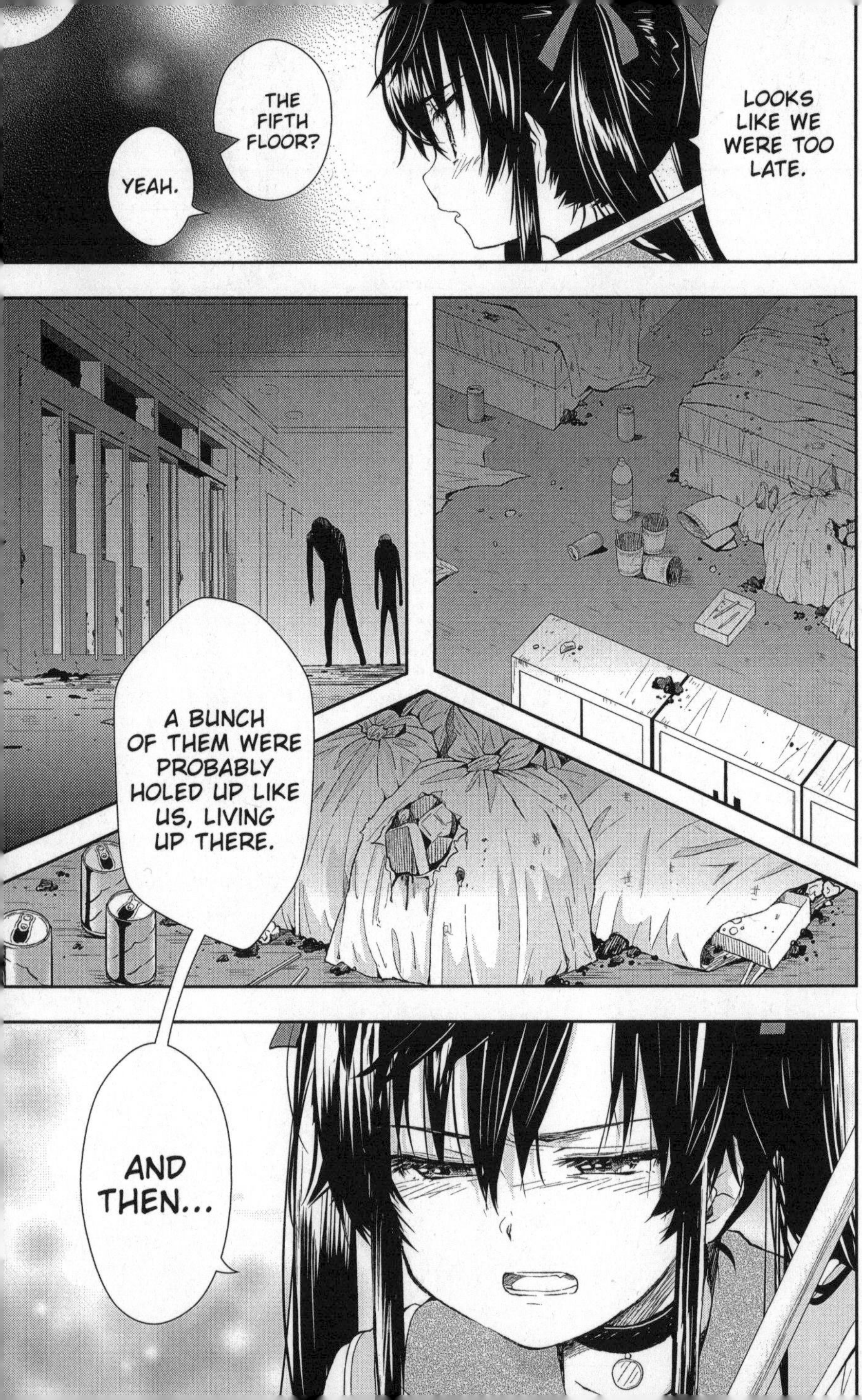
LOOKS LIKE WE WERE TOO LATE.
THE FIFTH FLOOR?
YEAH.
A BUNCH OF THEM WERE PROBABLY HOLED UP LIKE US, LIVING UP THERE.
AND THEN...

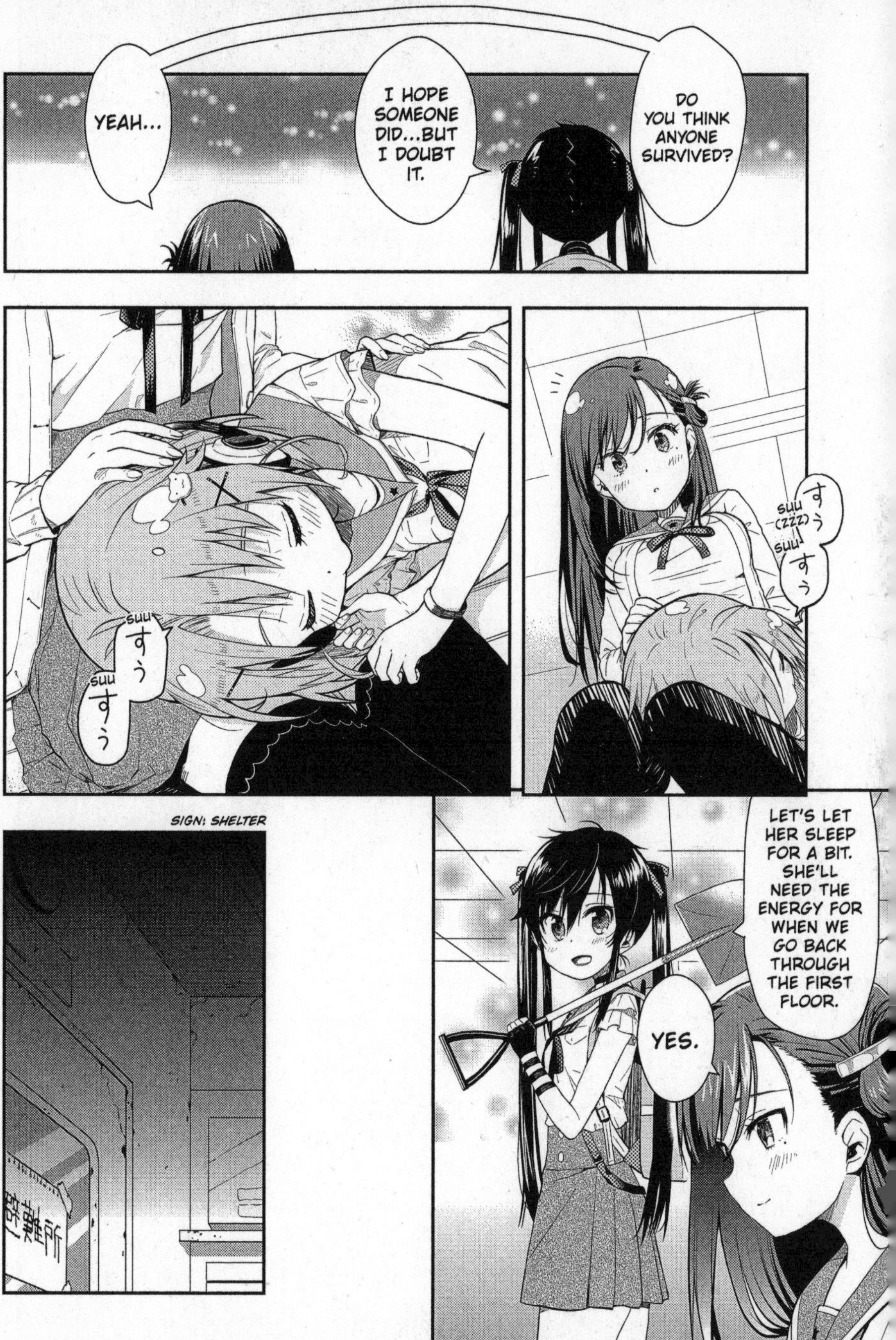
DO YOU THINK ANYONE SURVIVED?
I HOPE SOMEONE DID...BUT I DOUBT IT.
YEAH...
すう
SUU (ZZZ)
すう
SUU
すう
SUU
すう
SUU
LET'S LET HER SLEEP FOR A BIT. SHE'LL NEED THE ENERGY FOR WHEN WE GO BACK THROUGH THE FIRST FLOOR.
YES.
SIGN: SHELTER
避難所

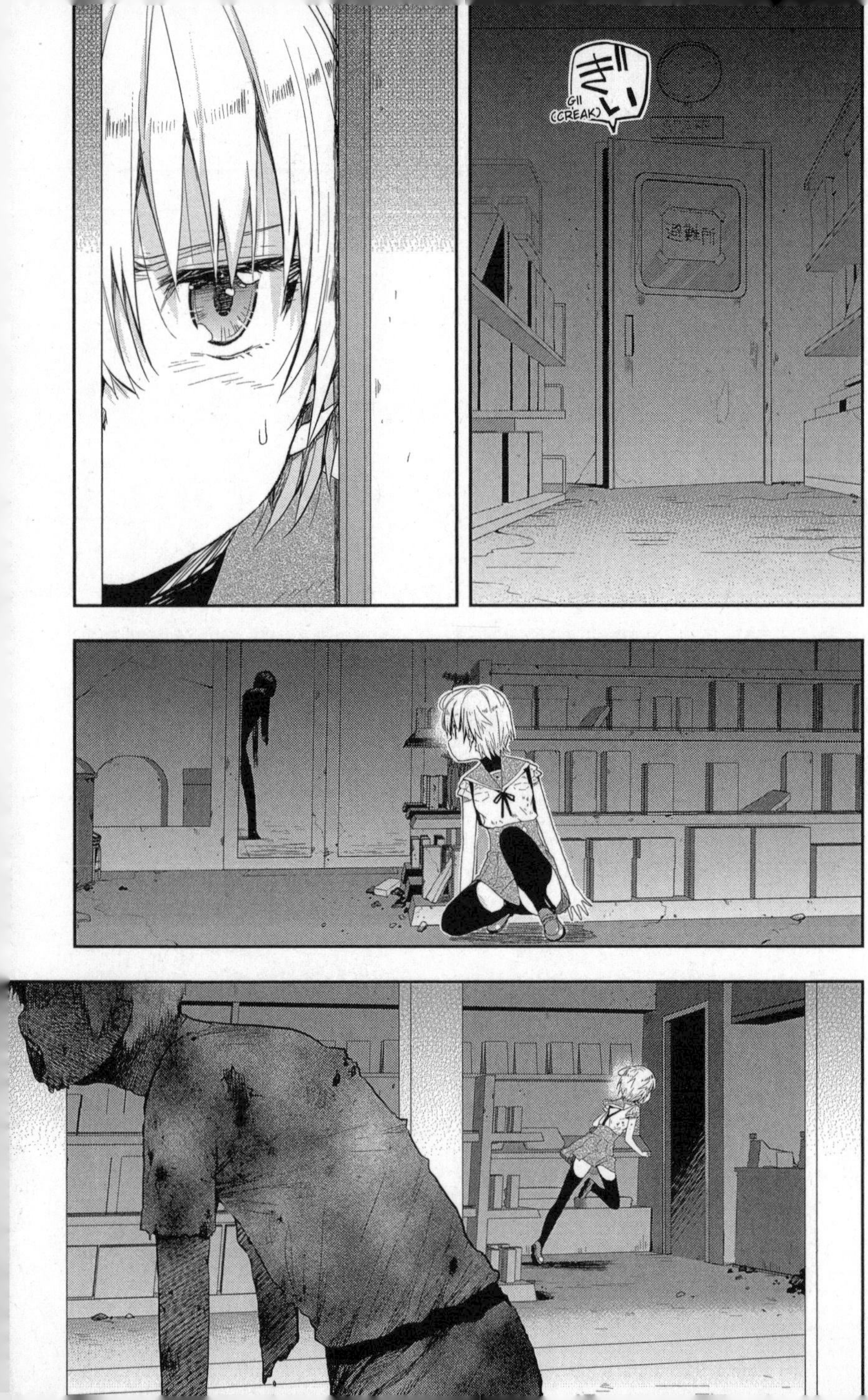
ぎぃ
GII
(CREAK)

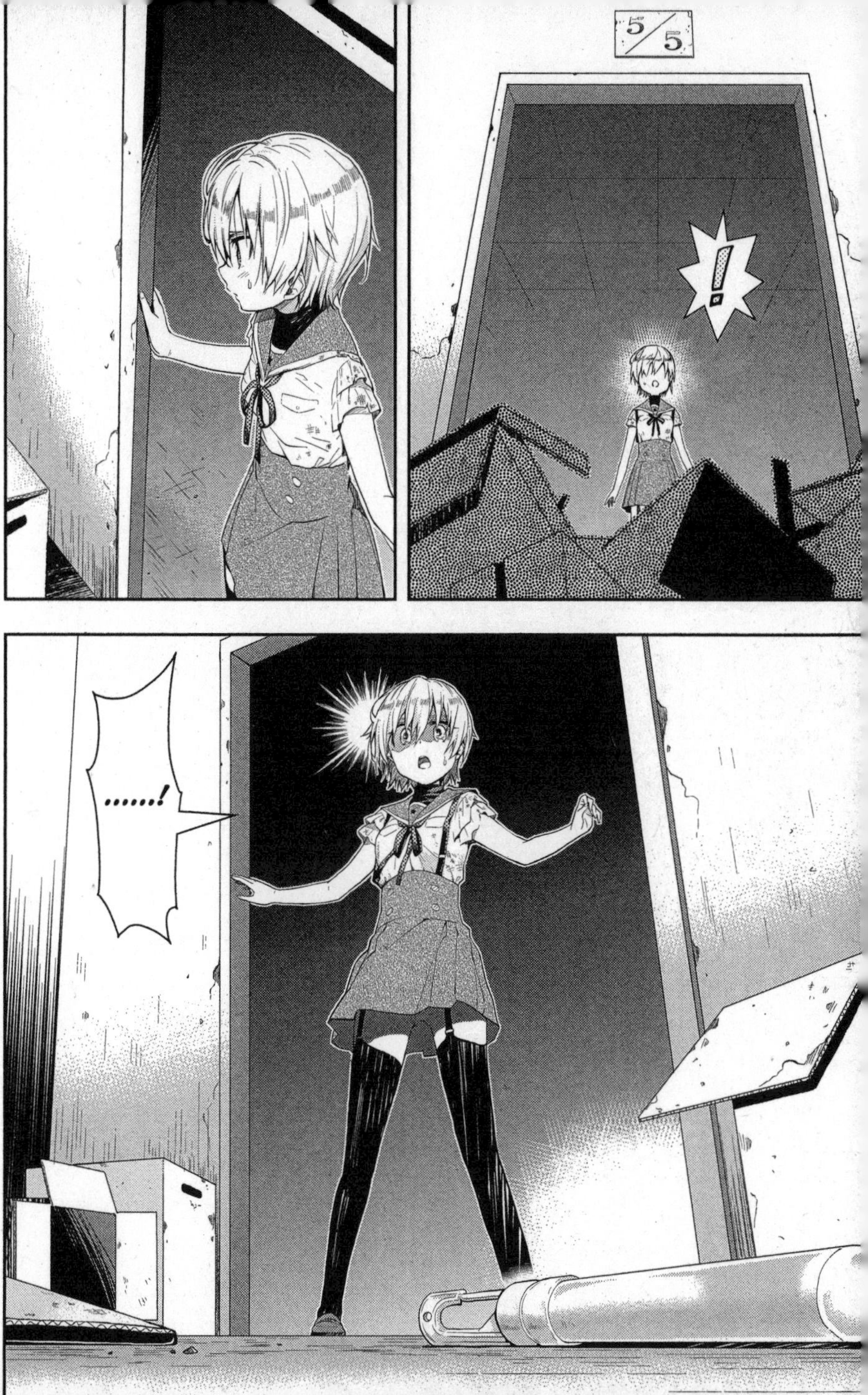
5/5
!
......!

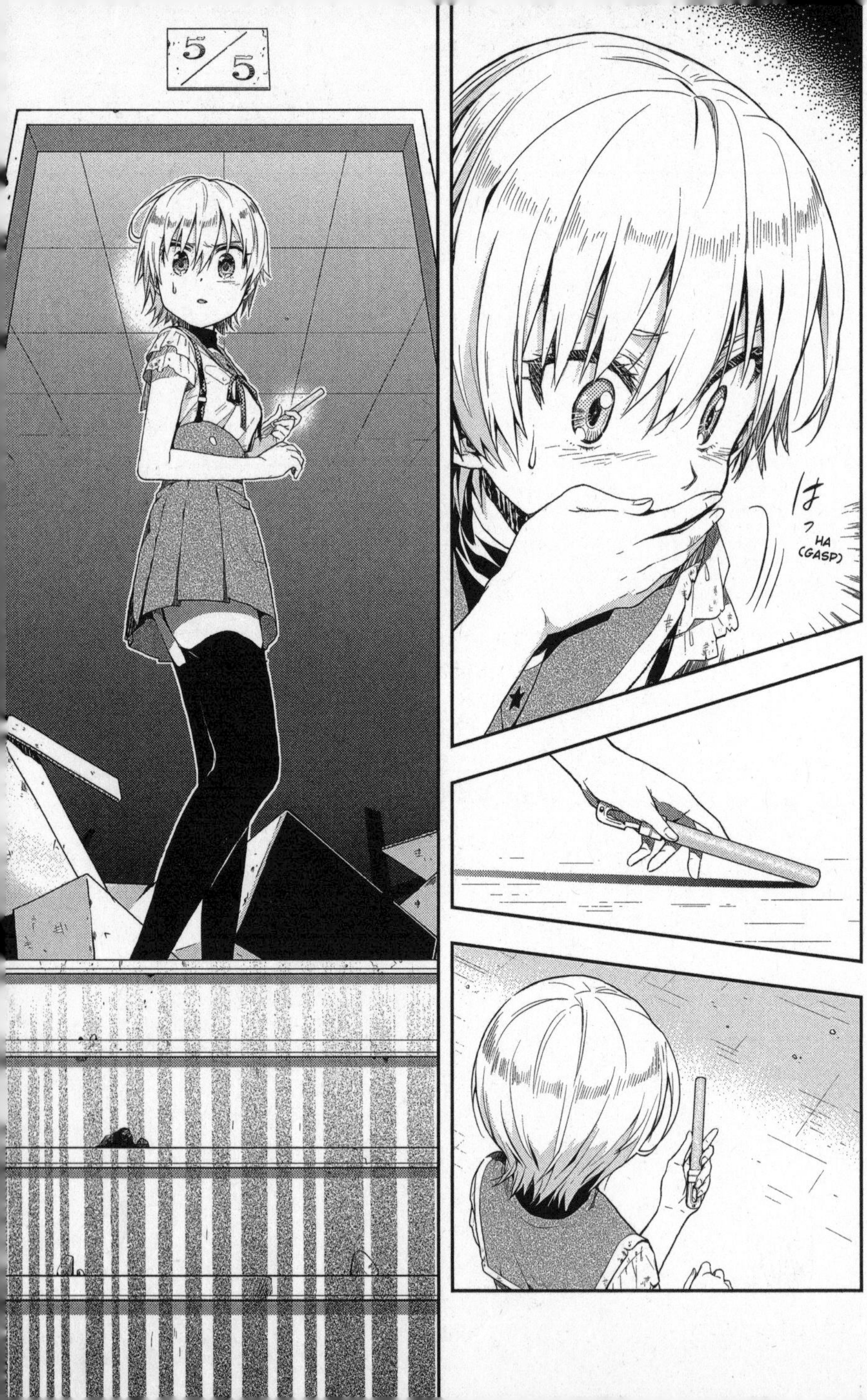
はっ
HA
(GASP)
5/5

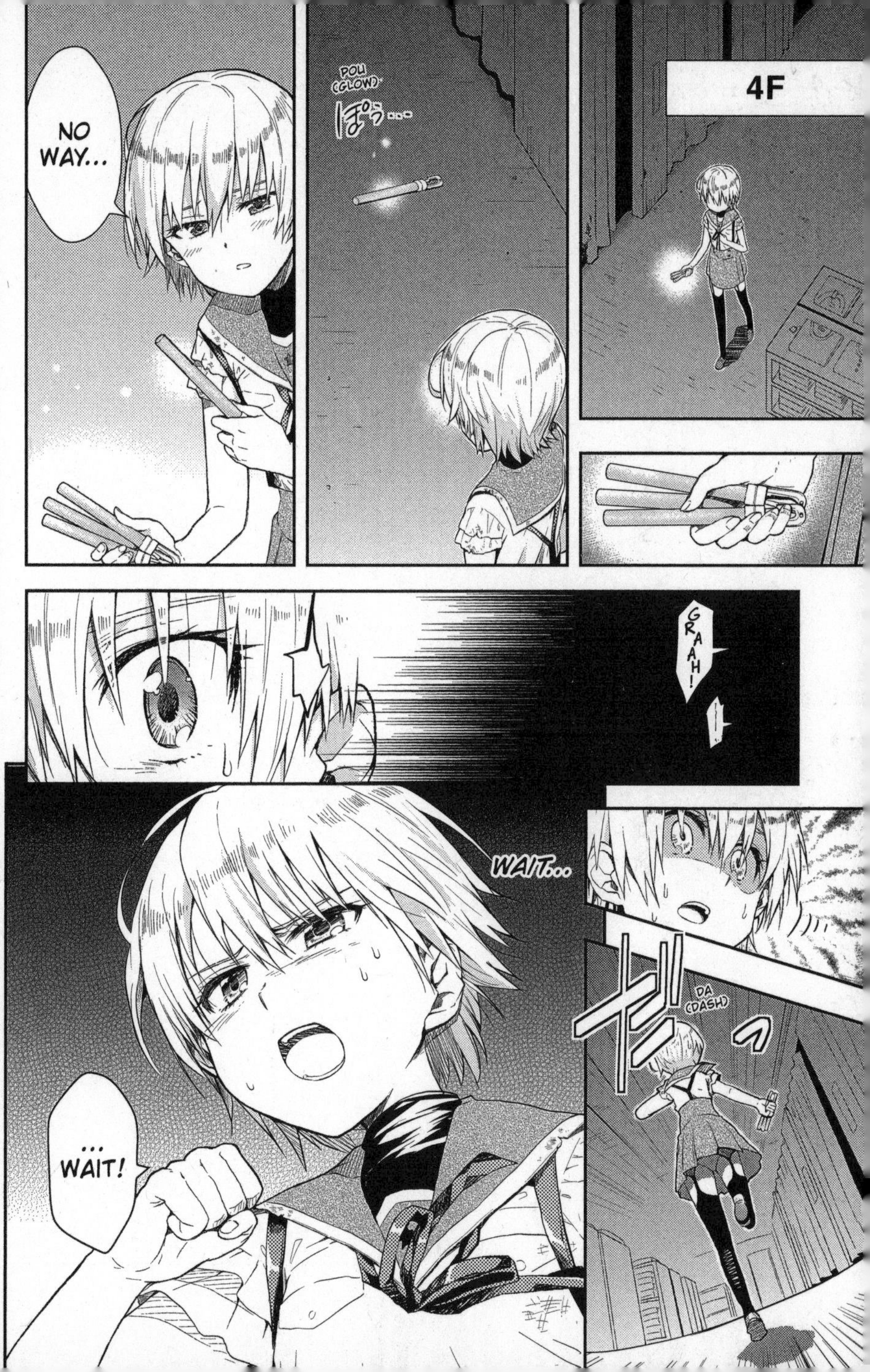
4F
POU (GLOW)
ぽぅ…
NO WAY...
GRAAH!
ダッ
DA (DASH)
WAIT...
...WAIT!

WAIT!!

HUH?

LET'S GO. THERE'S ALWAYS NEXT TIME.

HEY...

KURU (TURN)

YES, LET'S GO.

...DID YOU GUYS HEAR THAT?

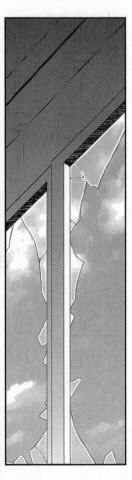

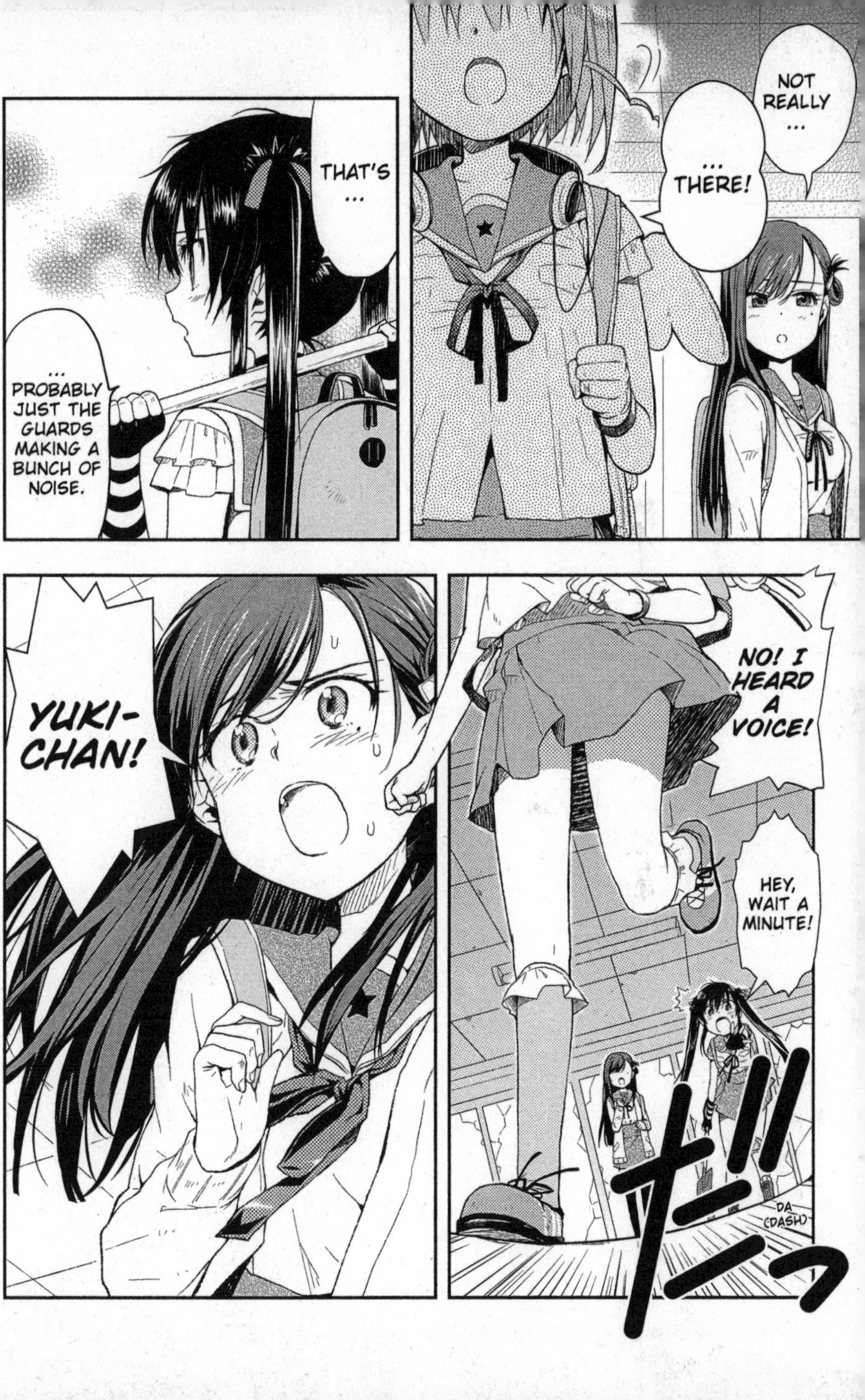
NOT REALLY ...
... THERE!
THAT'S ...
... PROBABLY JUST THE GUARDS MAKING A BUNCH OF NOISE.
NO! I HEARD A VOICE!
HEY, WAIT A MINUTE!
DA (DASH)
YUKI-CHAN!

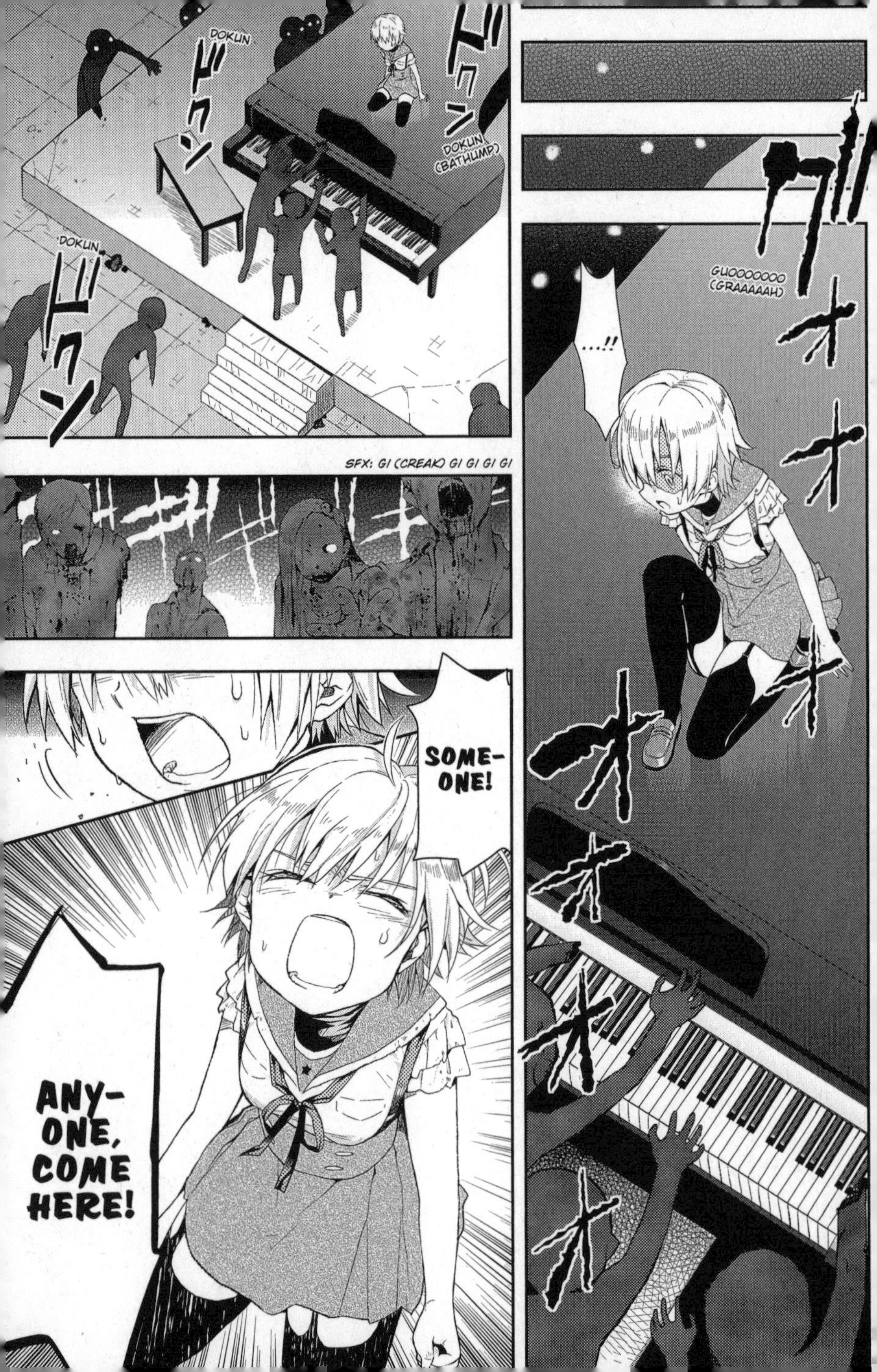

GUOOOOOOO (GRAAAAAAH)
...!!
DOKUN
DOKUN (BATHUMP)
DOKUN
SFX: GI (CREAK) GI GI GI GI
SOME-ONE!
ANY-ONE, COME HERE!

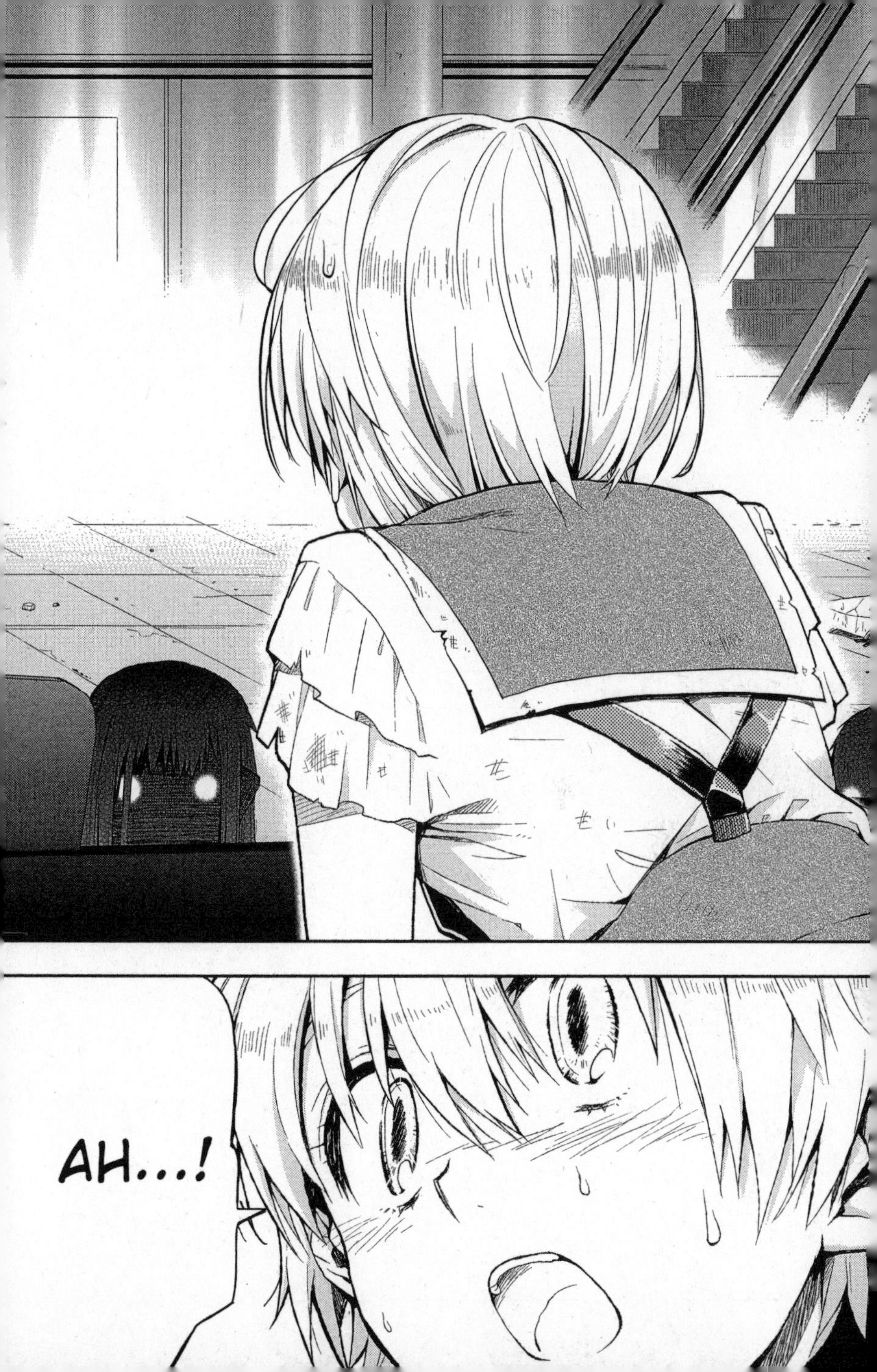
AH...!

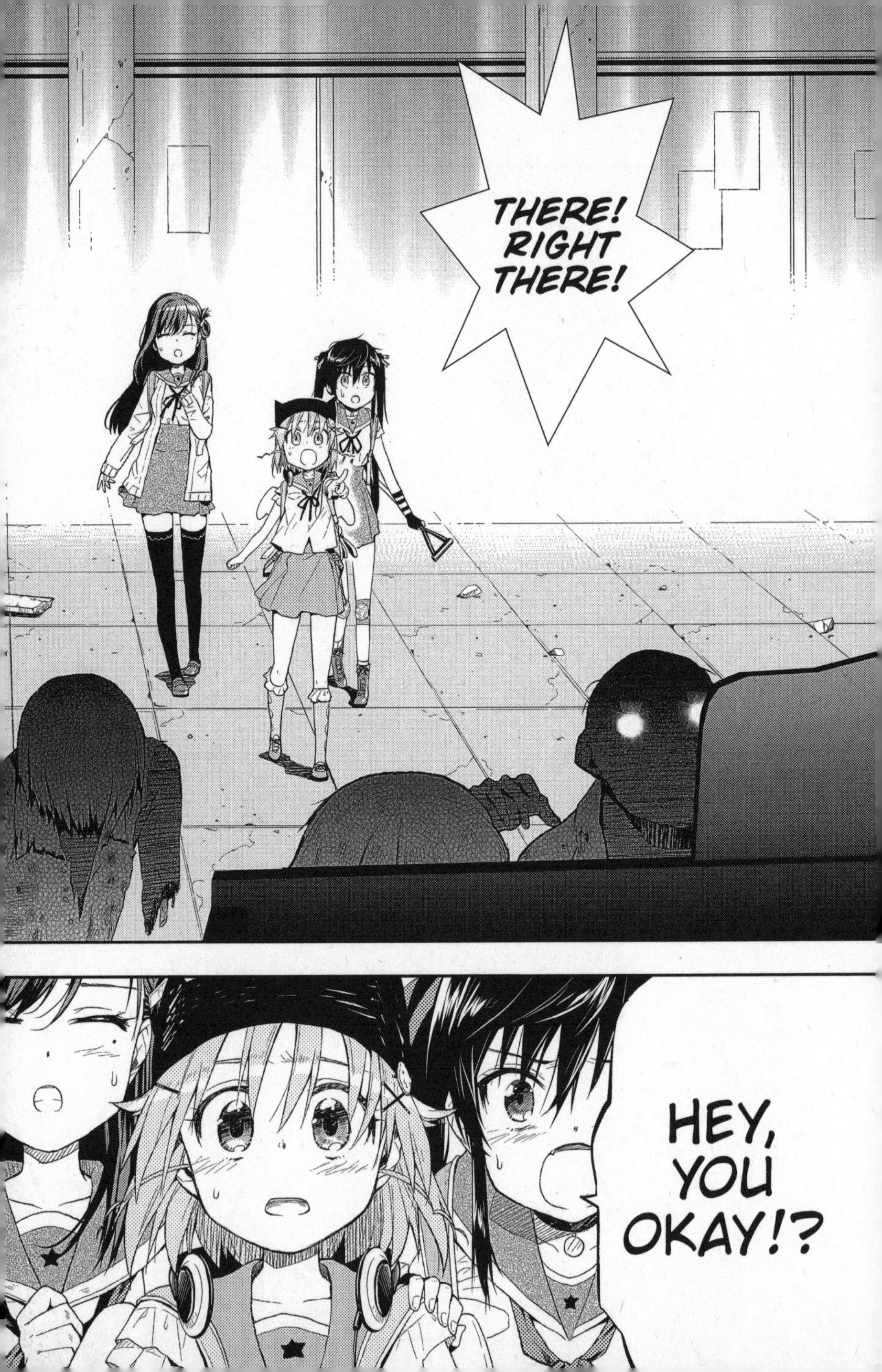
THERE! RIGHT THERE!
HEY, YOU OKAY!?

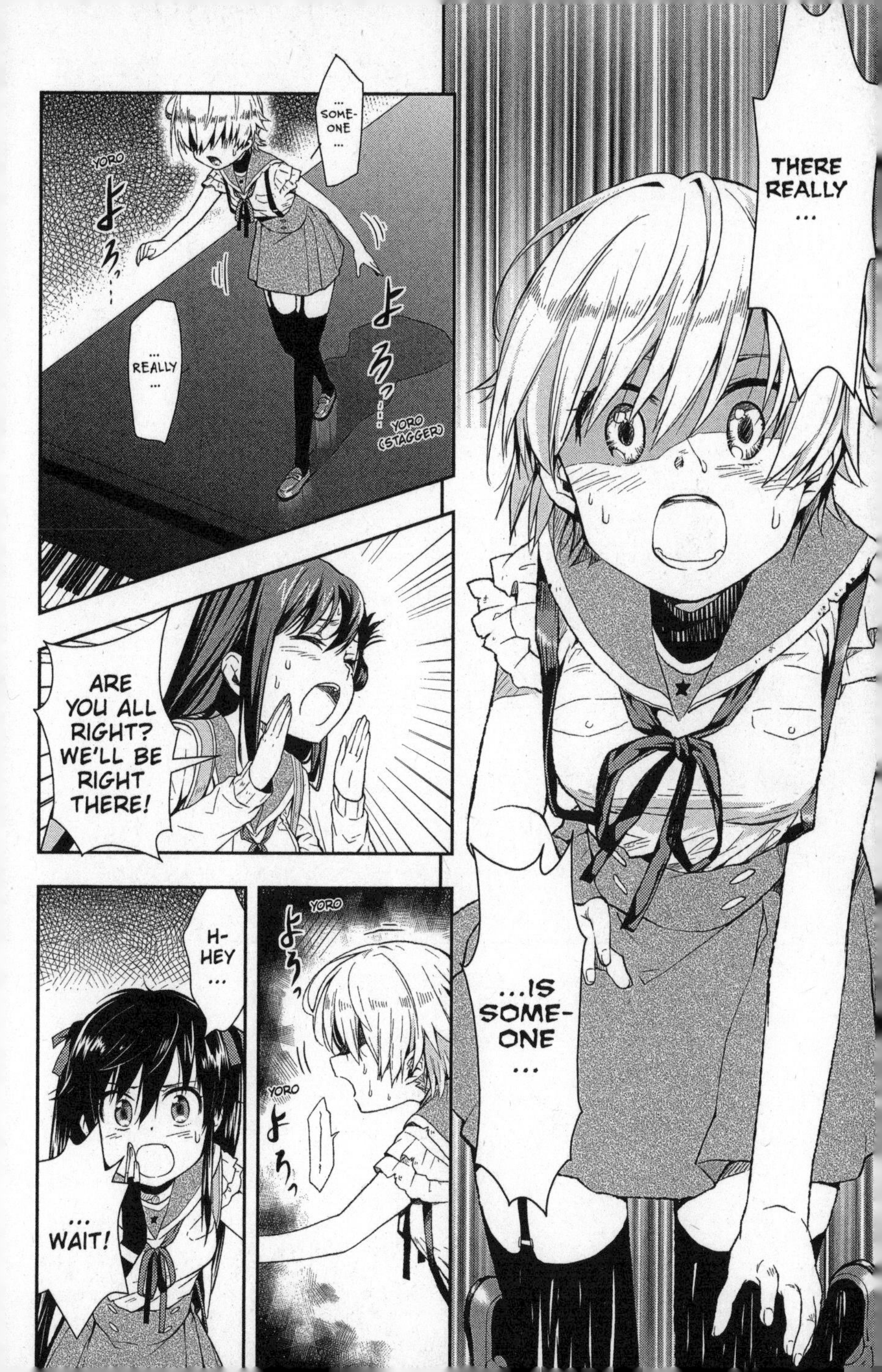
THERE REALLY ...
...IS SOME-ONE ...
... SOME-ONE ...
YORO
よろっ
... REALLY ...
よろっ
YORO (STAGGER)
ARE YOU ALL RIGHT? WE'LL BE RIGHT THERE!
YORO
よろっ
YORO
よろっ
!
H-HEY ...
... WAIT!

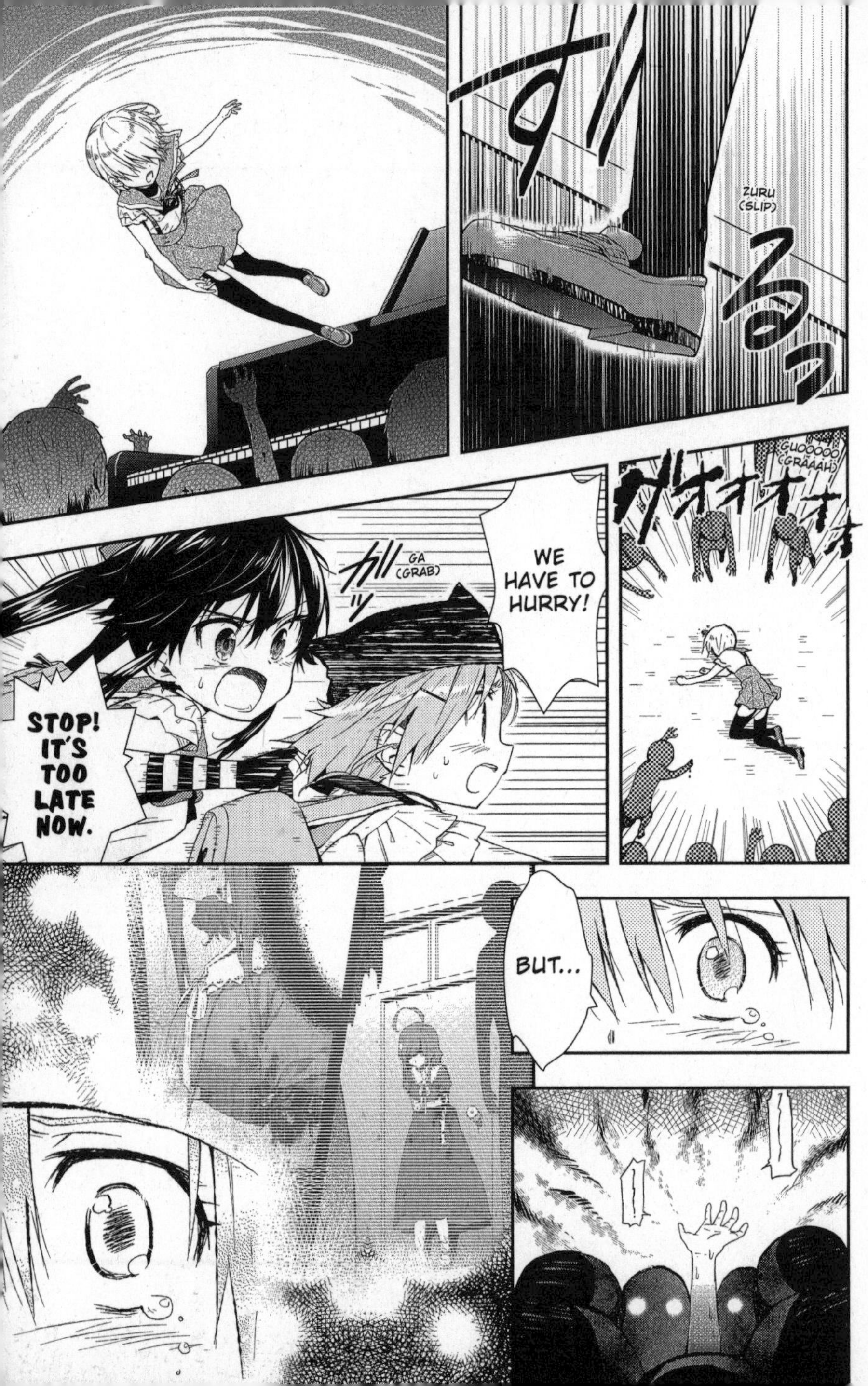
ZURU
(SLIP)
GUOOOOO
(GRAAAH)
WE HAVE TO HURRY!
GA
(GRAB)
STOP! IT'S TOO LATE NOW.
BUT...

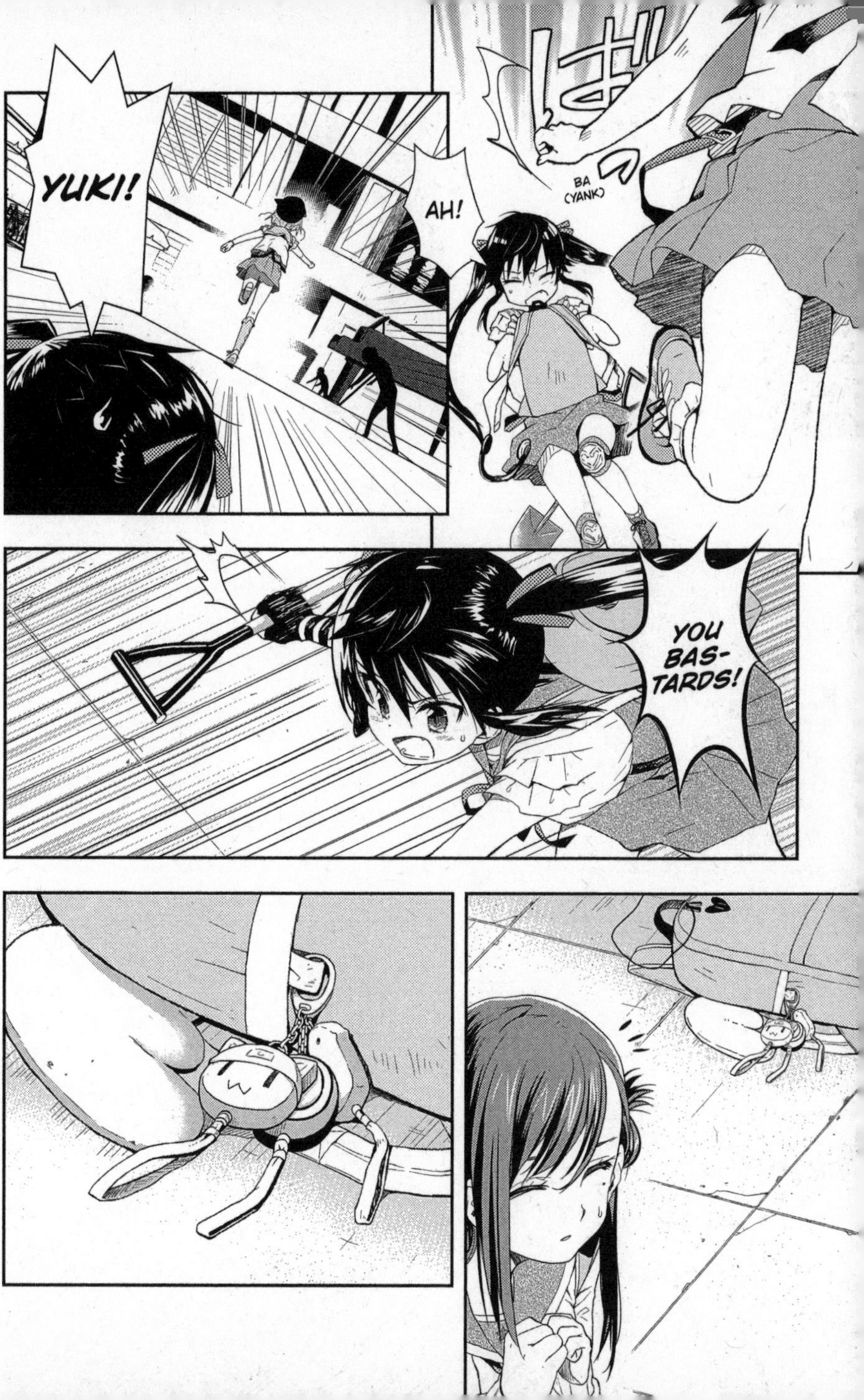
BA (YANK)
AH!
YUKI!
YOU BAS- TARDS!

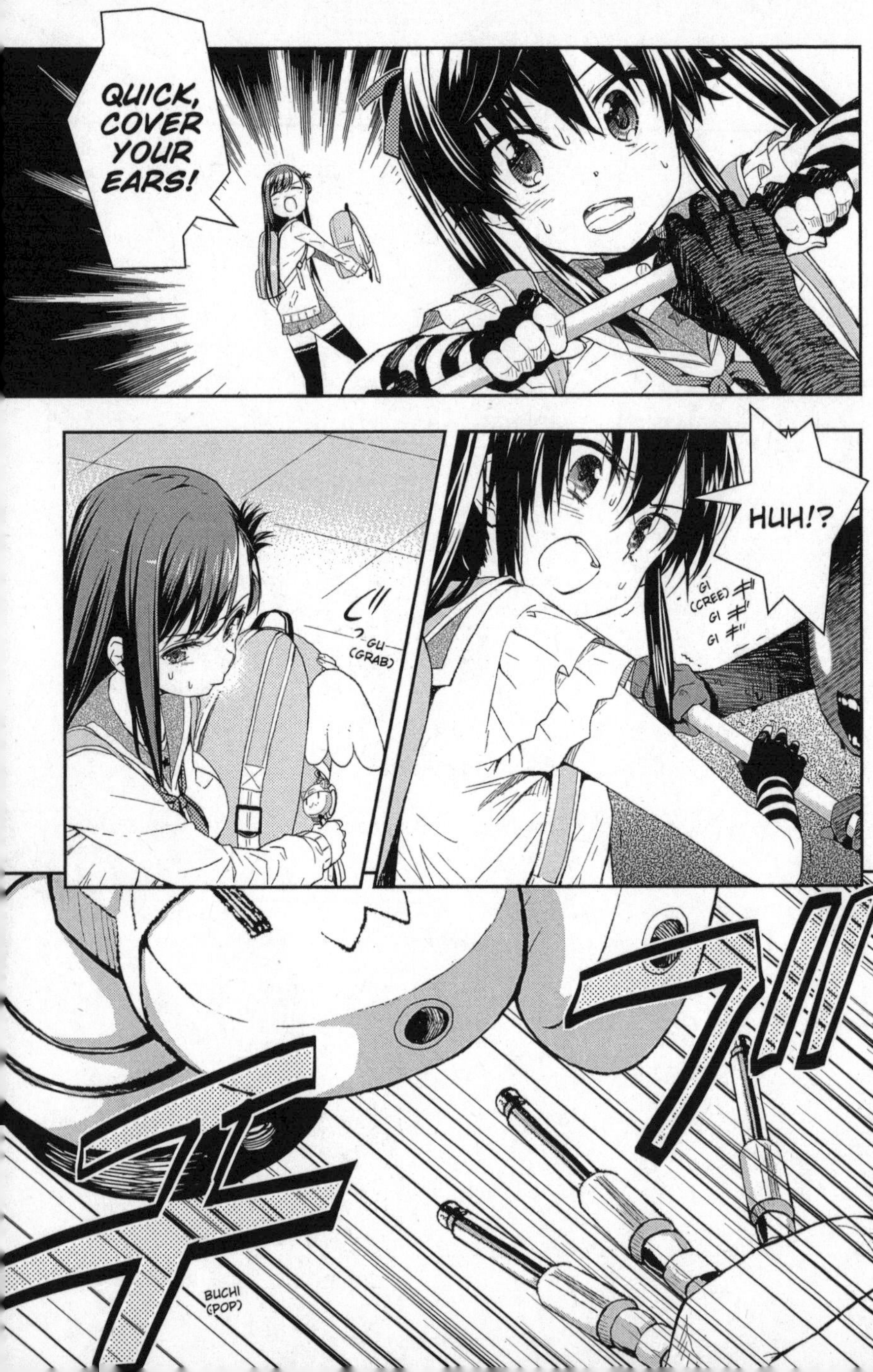
QUICK, COVER YOUR EARS!
HUH!?
GI (CREE) GI GI
GU (GRAB)
BUCHI (POP)

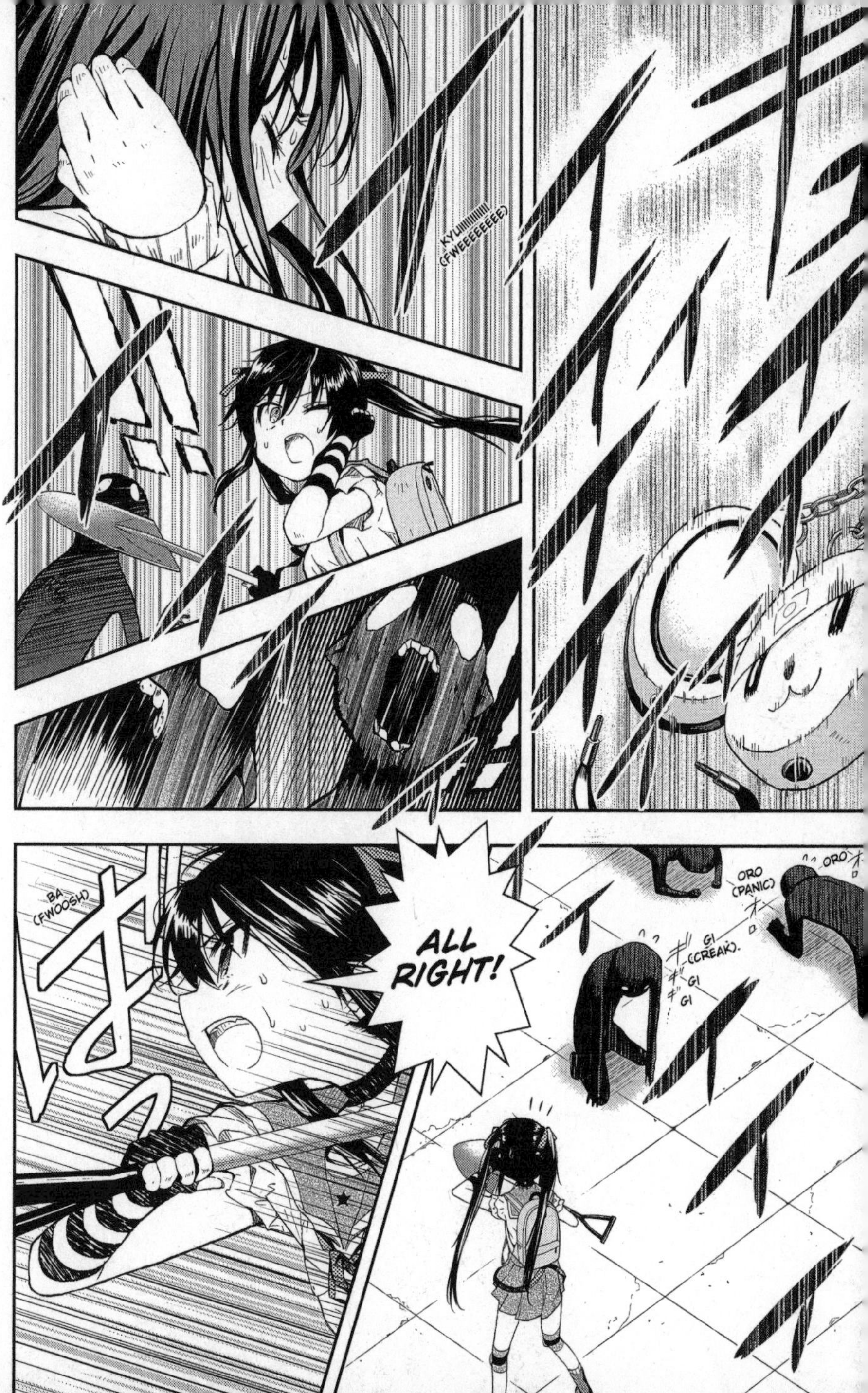
KYUIIIIIIIII
(FWEEEEEEEEE)
ORO
ORO
(PANIC)
GI
(CREAK)
GI
GI
ALL RIGHT!
BA
(FWOOSH)

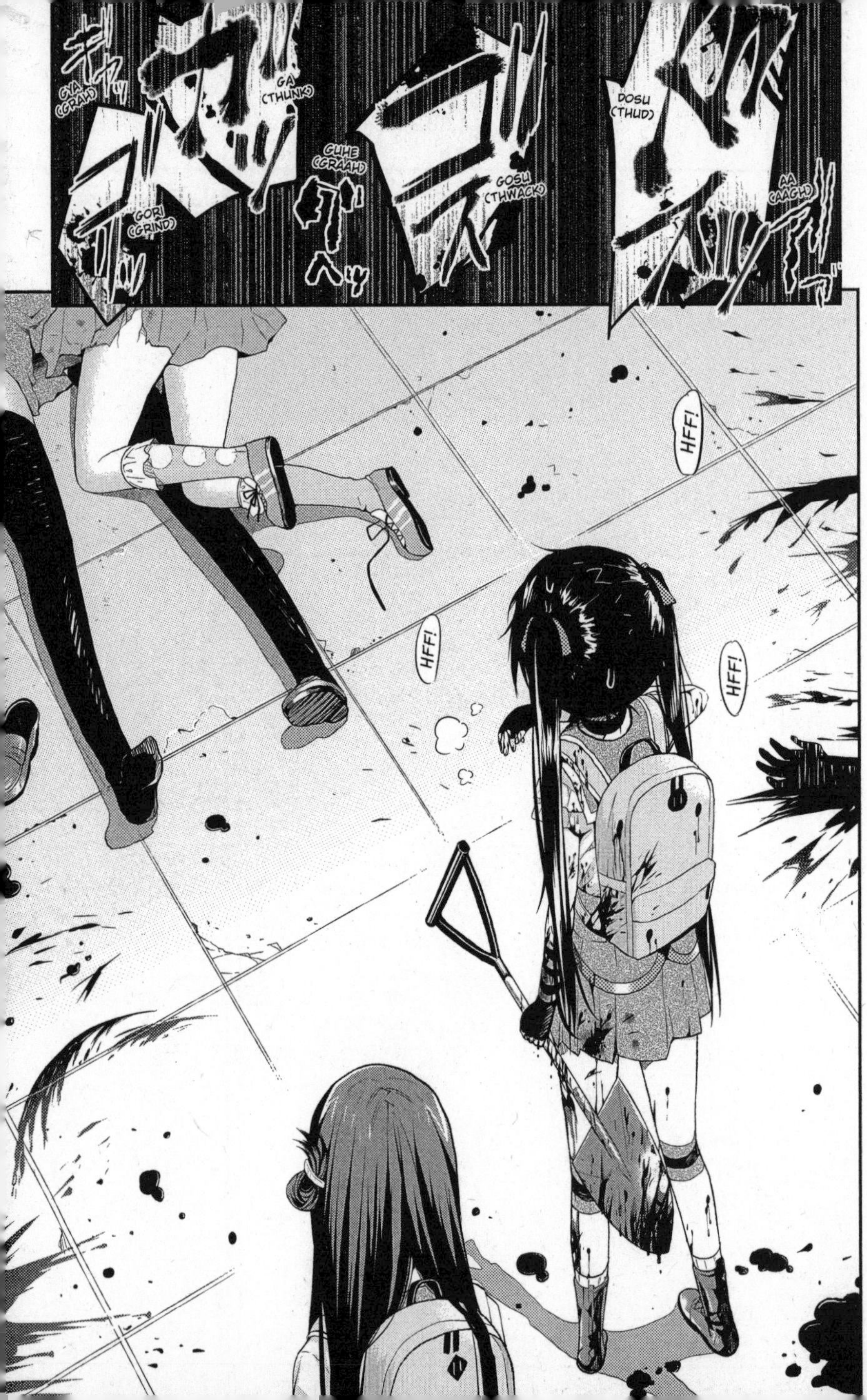
DOSU (THUD)
AA (AAGH)
GOSU (THWACK)
GA (THUNK)
GUHE (GRAAH)
GYA (GRAAH)
GORI (GRIND)
HFF!
HFF!
HFF!

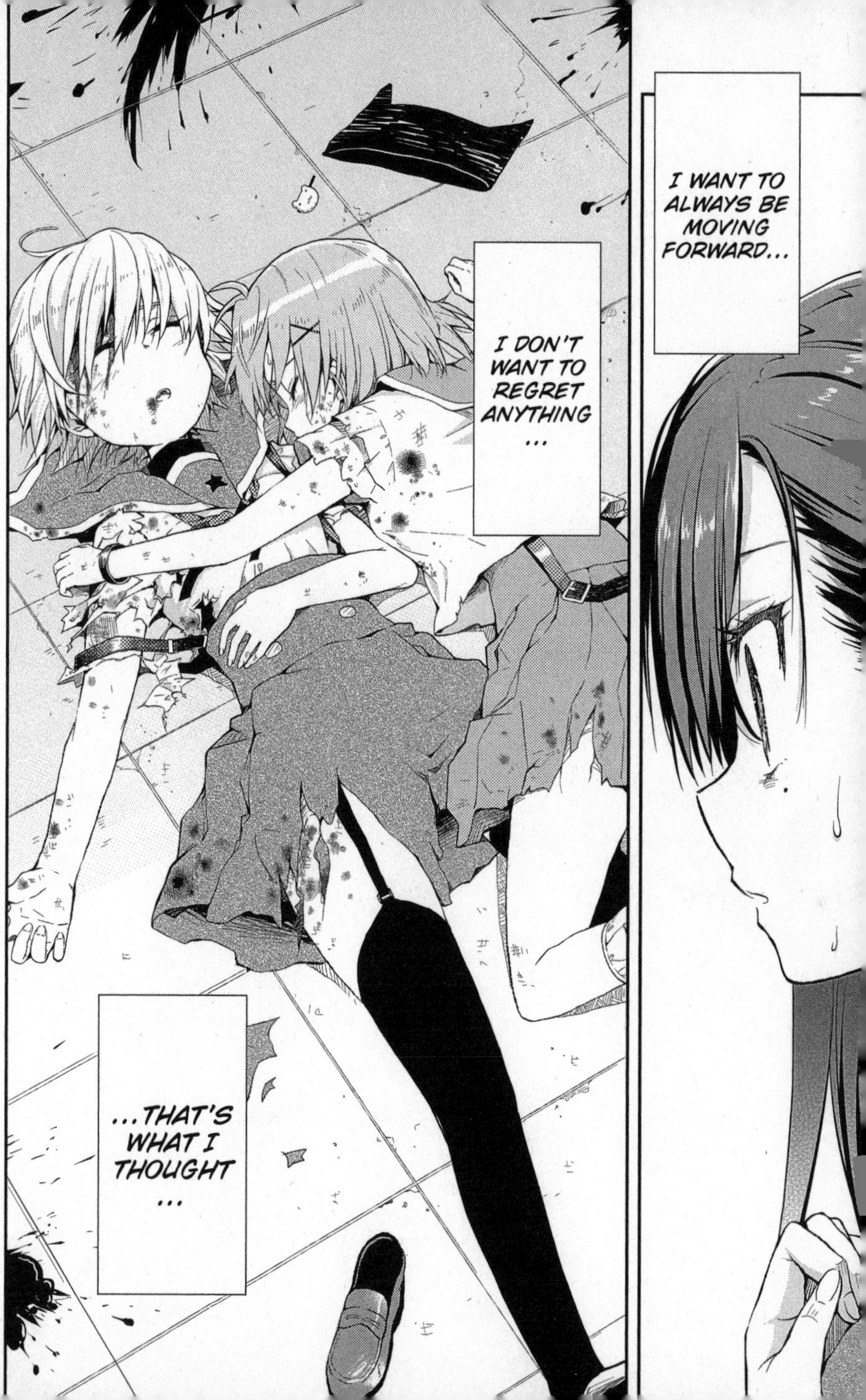
I WANT TO ALWAYS BE MOVING FORWARD...
I DON'T WANT TO REGRET ANYTHING...
...THAT'S WHAT I THOUGHT...

SCHOOL-LIVE!

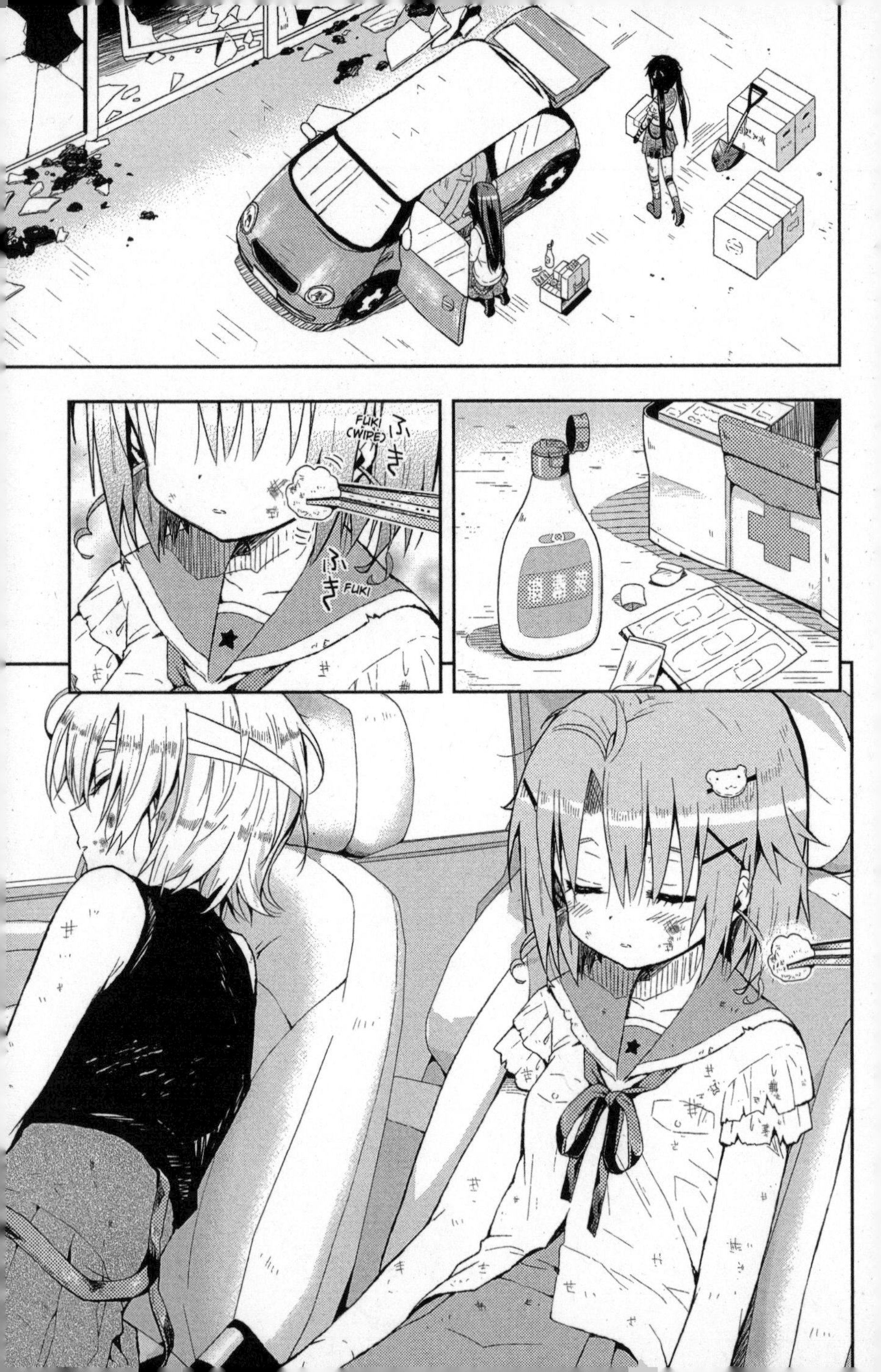
ふき
FUKI (WIPE)
ふき
FUKI

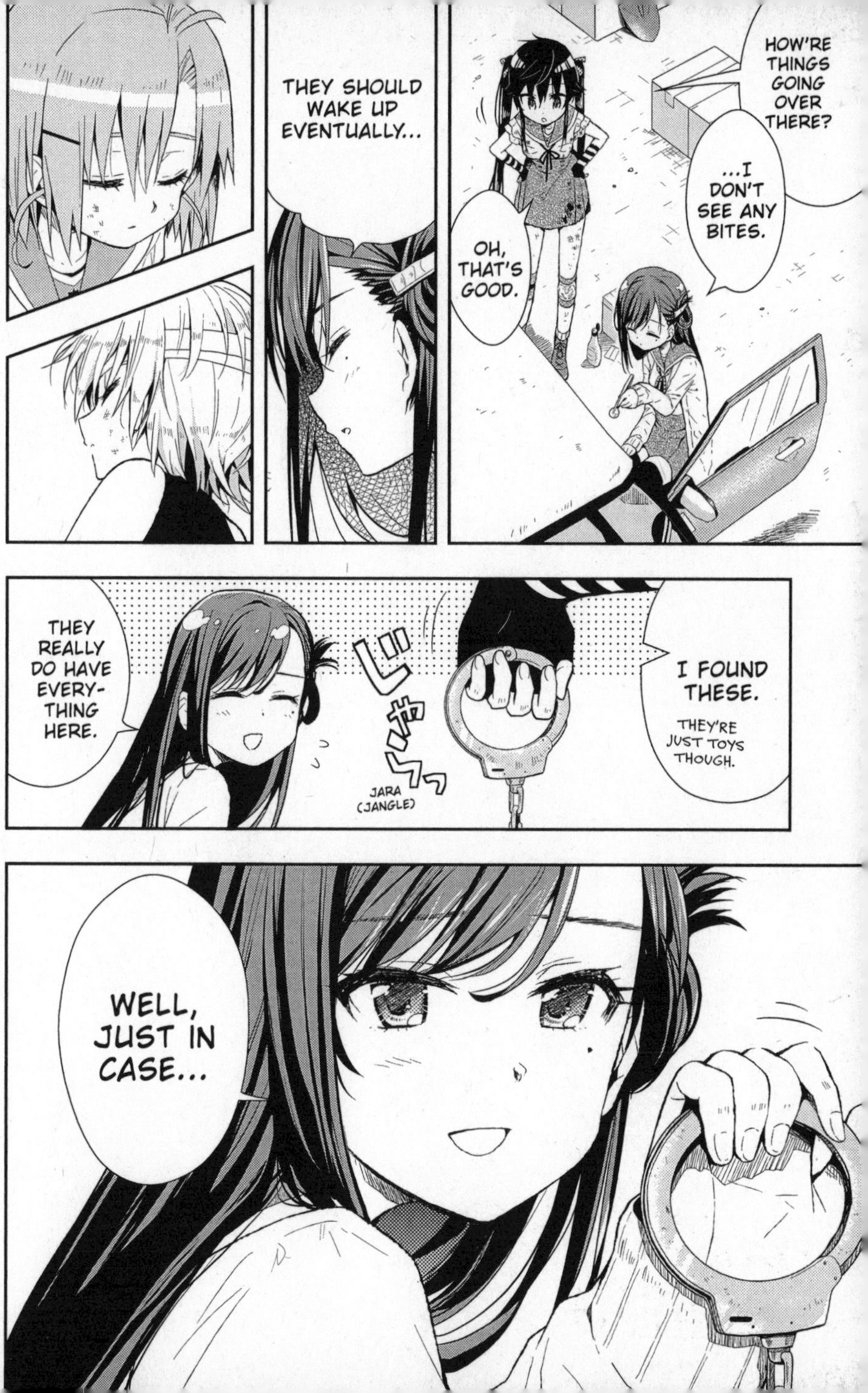
HOW'RE THINGS GOING OVER THERE?
...I DON'T SEE ANY BITES.
OH, THAT'S GOOD.
THEY SHOULD WAKE UP EVENTUALLY...
I FOUND THESE.
THEY'RE JUST TOYS THOUGH.
THEY REALLY DO HAVE EVERY-THING HERE.
JARA (JANGLE)
WELL, JUST IN CASE...

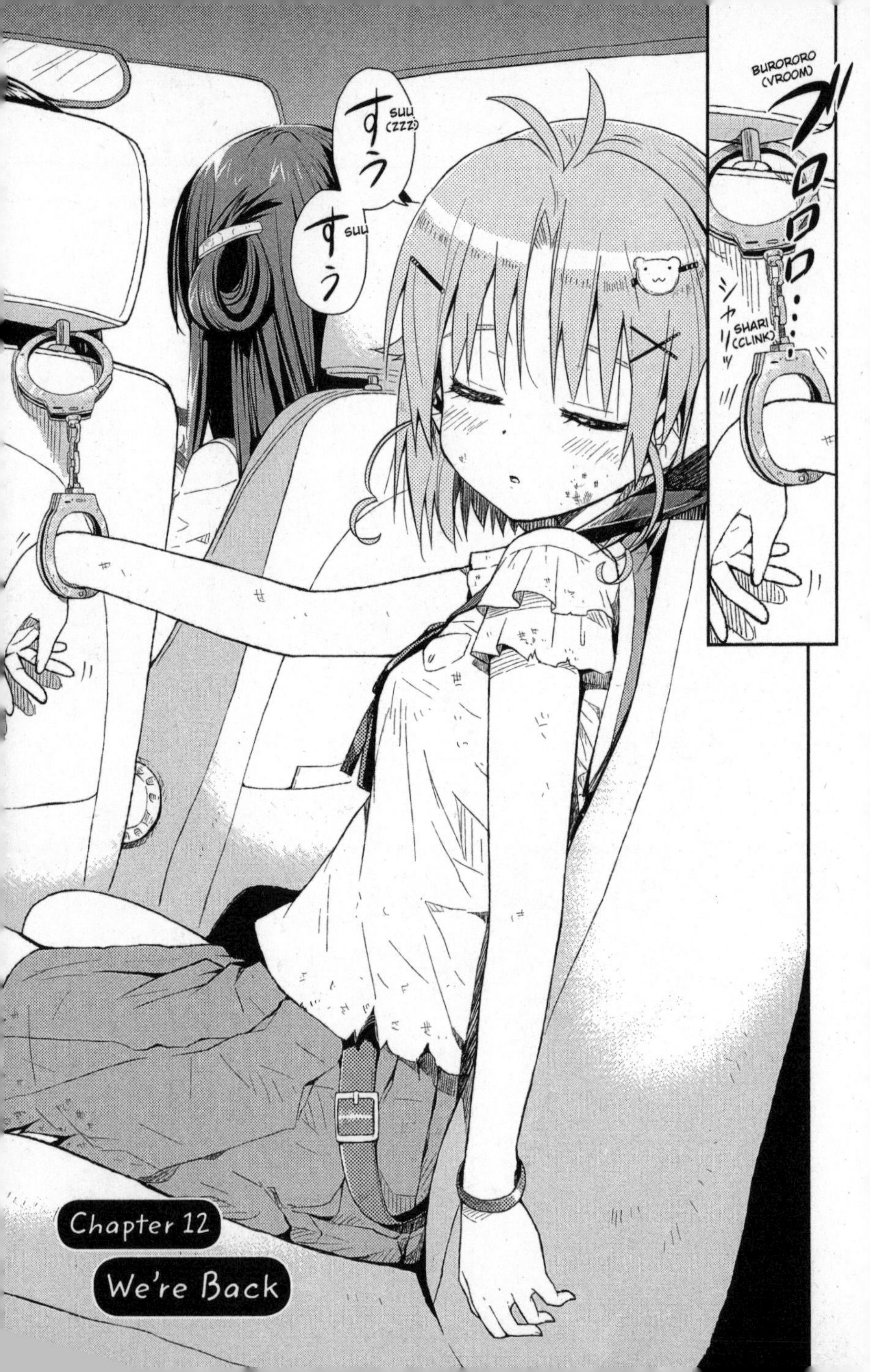
ブロロロ…
BURORORO (VROOM)
シャリッ
SHARI (CLINK)
すう
SUU (ZZZ)
すう
SUU

Chapter 12
We're Back

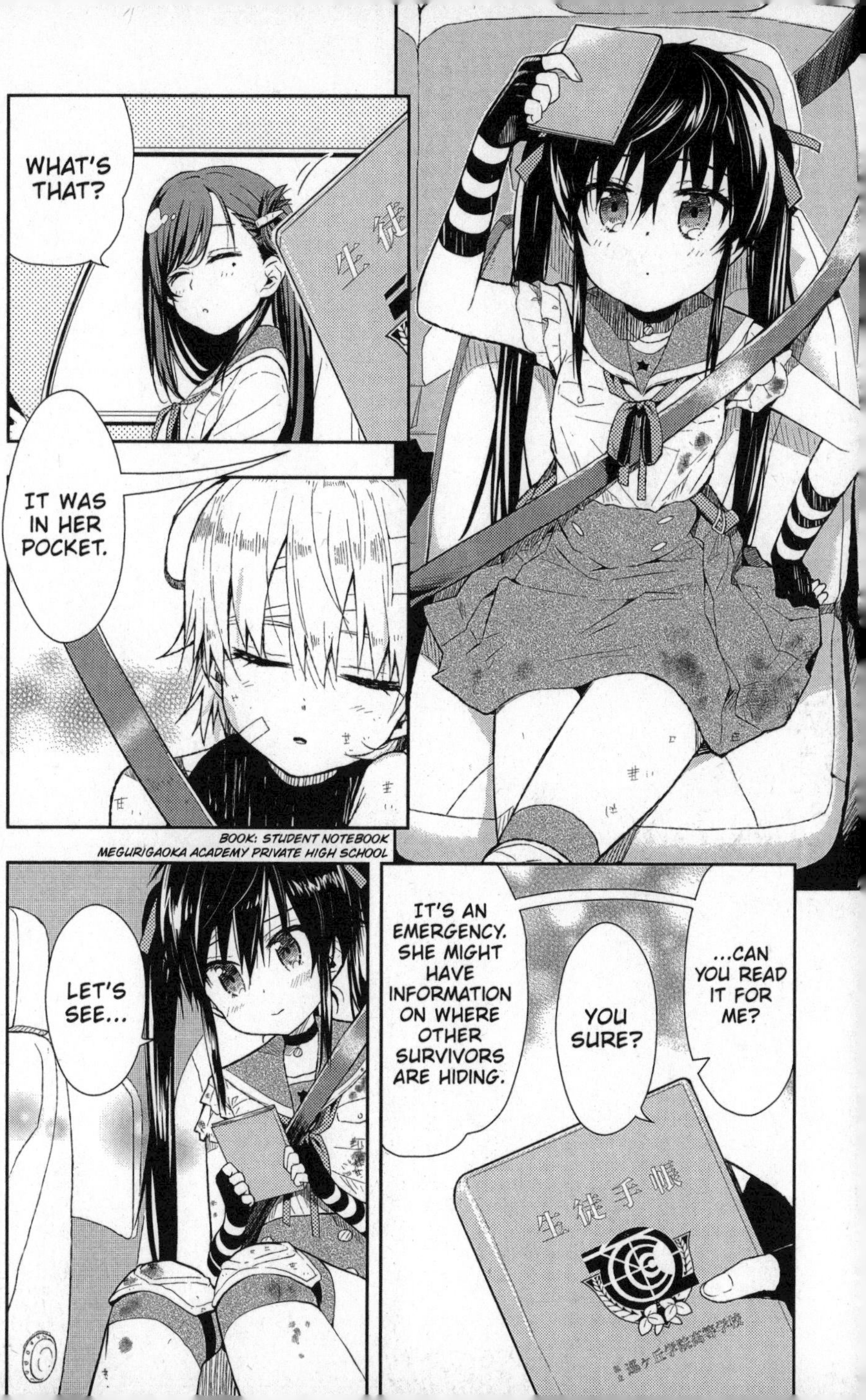
WHAT'S THAT?
IT WAS IN HER POCKET.
BOOK: STUDENT NOTEBOOK
MEGURIGAOKA ACADEMY PRIVATE HIGH SCHOOL
...CAN YOU READ IT FOR ME?
YOU SURE?
IT'S AN EMERGENCY. SHE MIGHT HAVE INFORMATION ON WHERE OTHER SURVIVORS ARE HIDING.
生徒手帳
LET'S SEE...

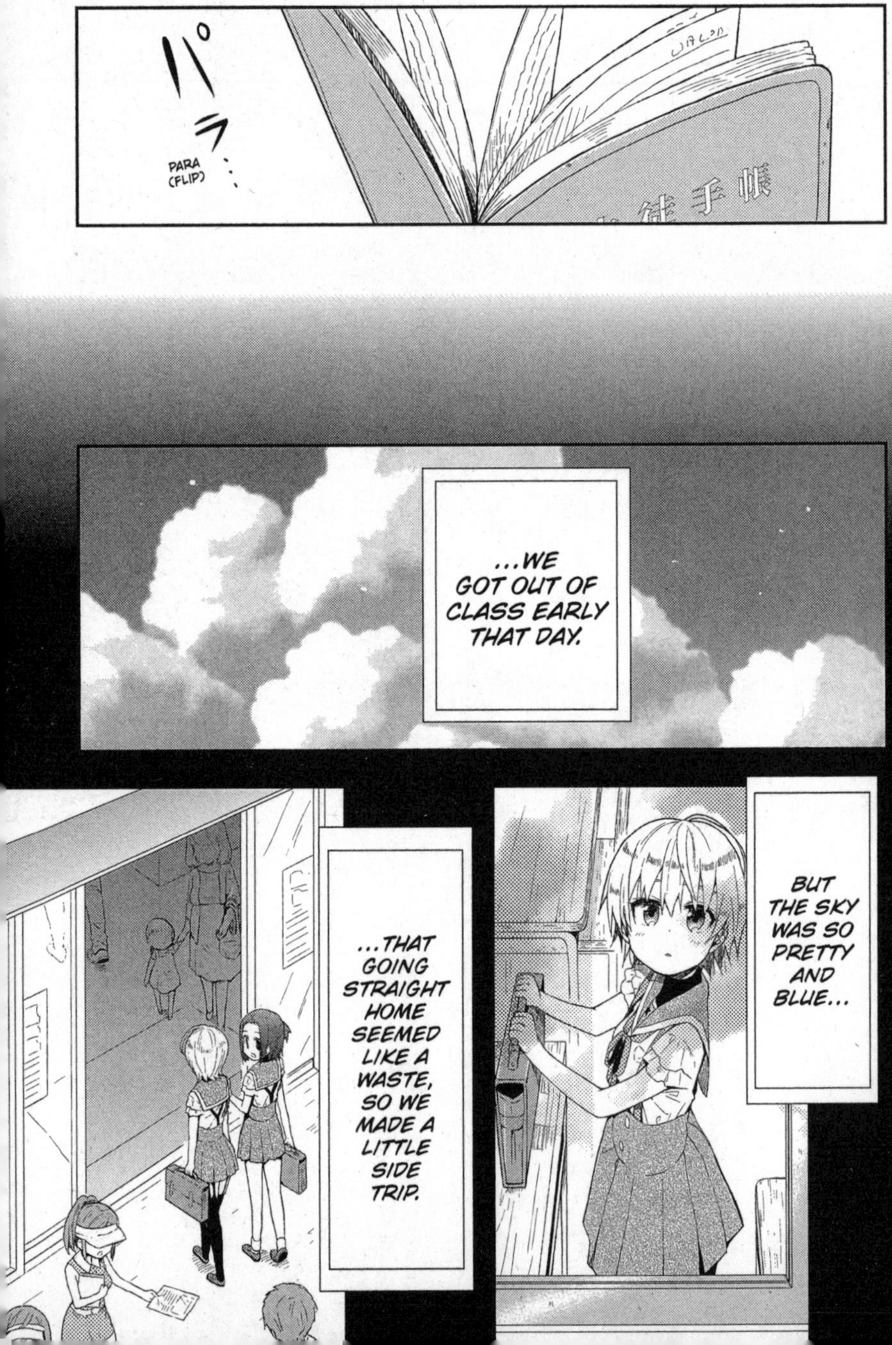
パラ…
PARA (FLIP)
...WE GOT OUT OF CLASS EARLY THAT DAY.
BUT THE SKY WAS SO PRETTY AND BLUE...
...THAT GOING STRAIGHT HOME SEEMED LIKE A WASTE, SO WE MADE A LITTLE SIDE TRIP.

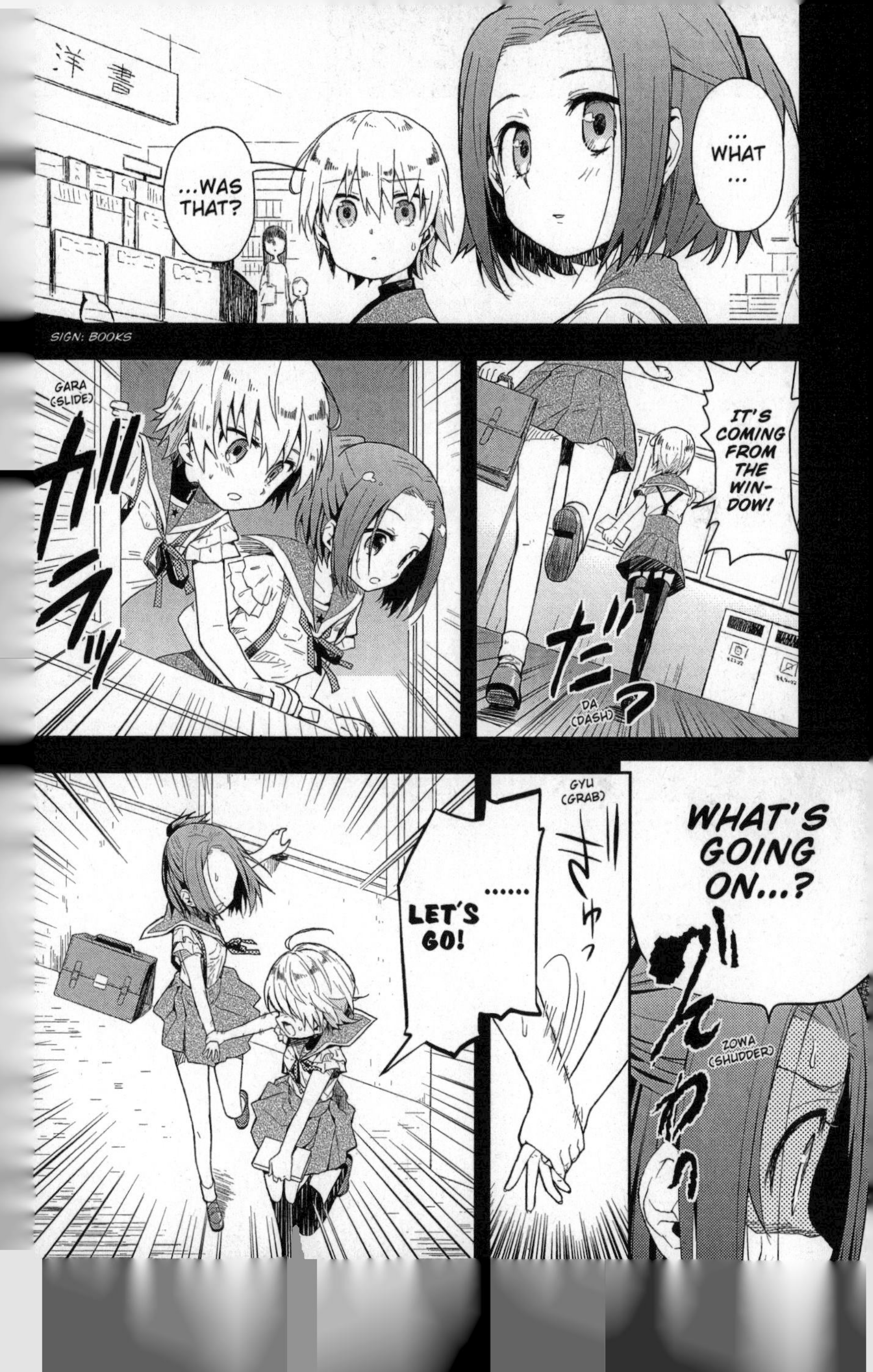
... WHAT ...
...WAS THAT?
SIGN: BOOKS
IT'S COMING FROM THE WIN-DOW!
DA (DASH)
GARA (SLIDE)
WHAT'S GOING ON...?
ZOWA (SHUDDER)
GYU (GRAB)
...... LET'S GO!

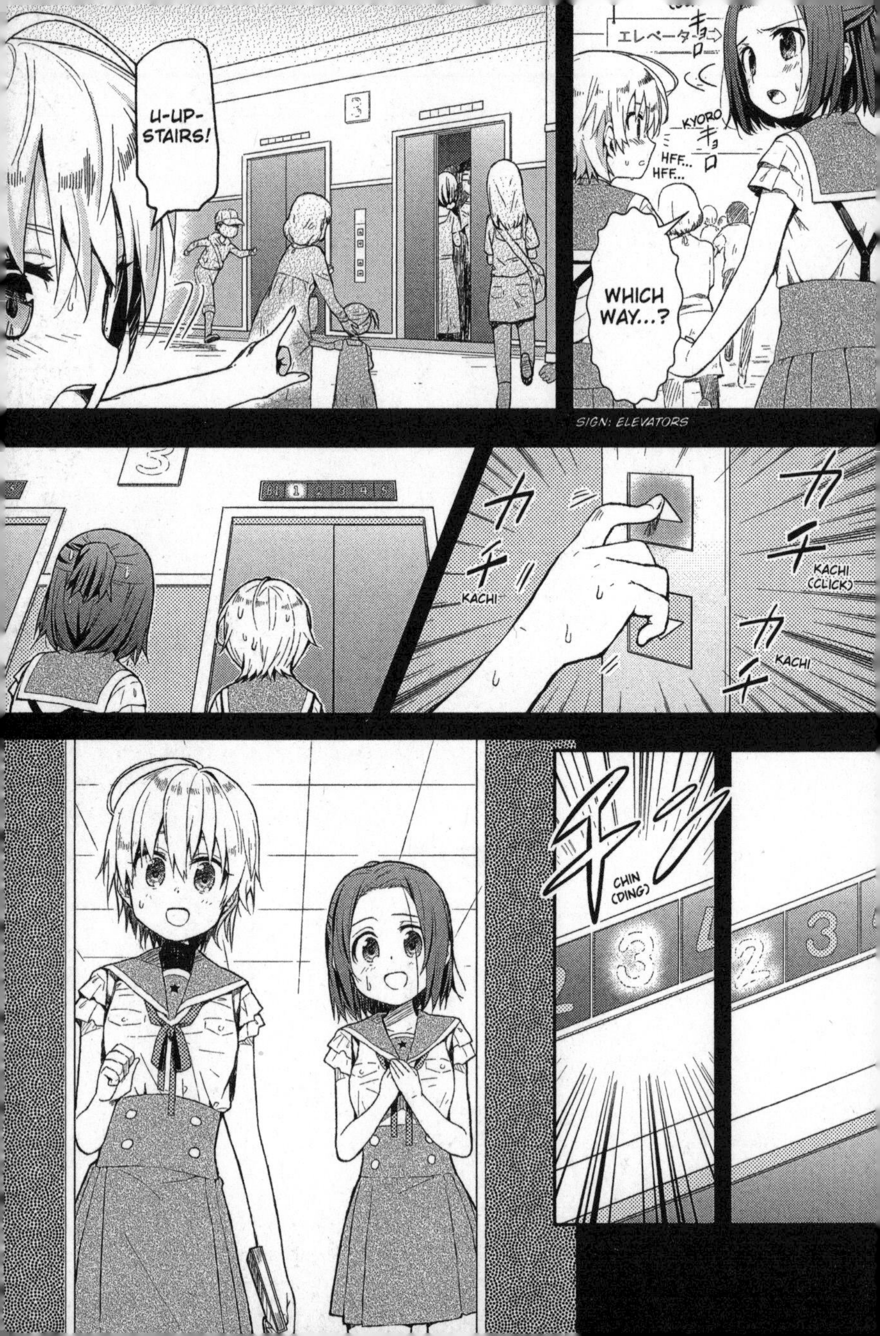
エレベーター
キョロ
KYORO
キョロ
HFF... HFF...
WHICH WAY...?
SIGN: ELEVATORS
U-UP-STAIRS!
カチ
KACHI (CLICK)
カチ
KACHI
カチ
KACHI
B1 1 2 3 4 5
チン
CHIN (DING)

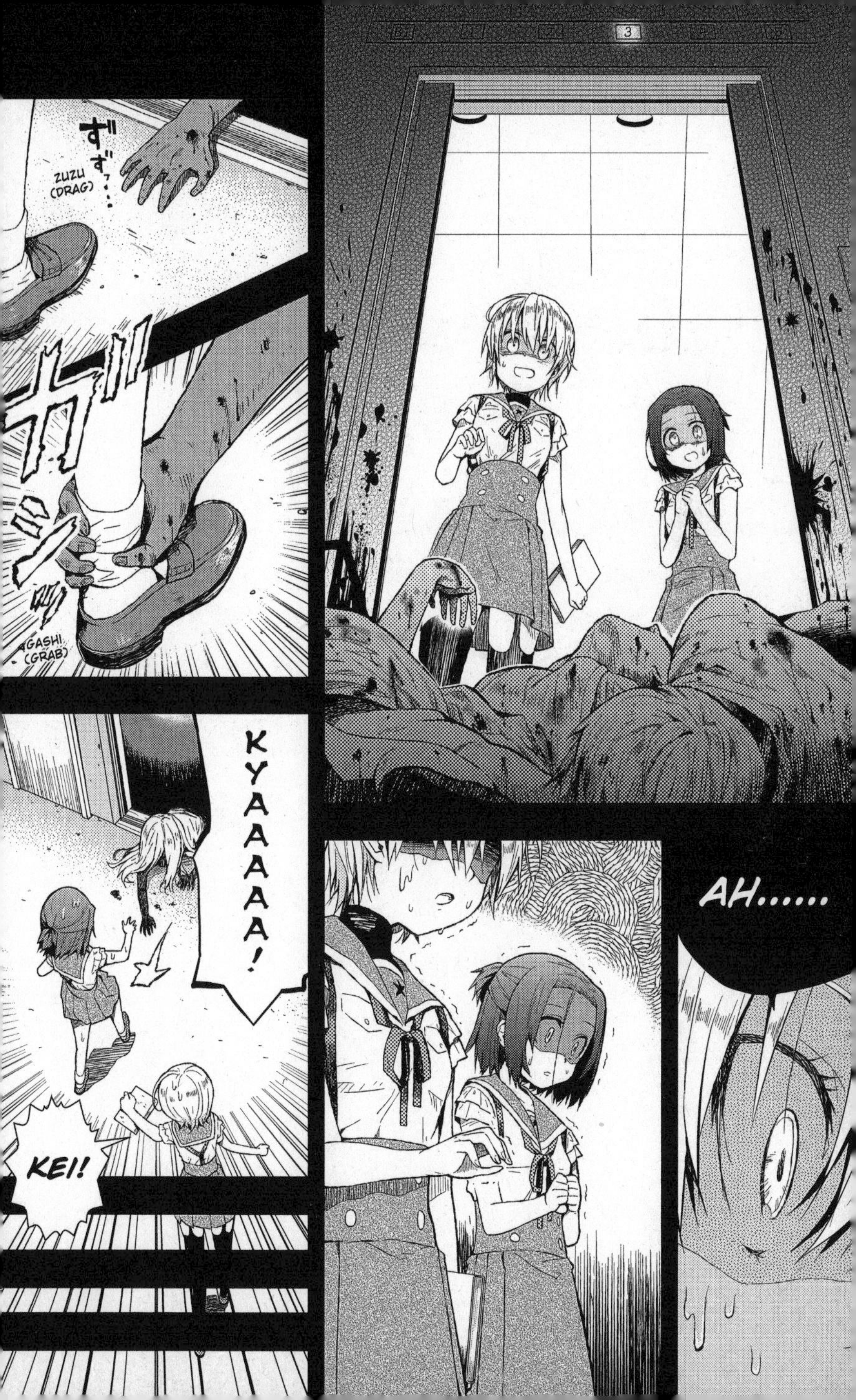

ずず…
ZUZU (DRAG)
ガシッ
GASHI (GRAB)
AH......
KYAAAAA!
KEI!

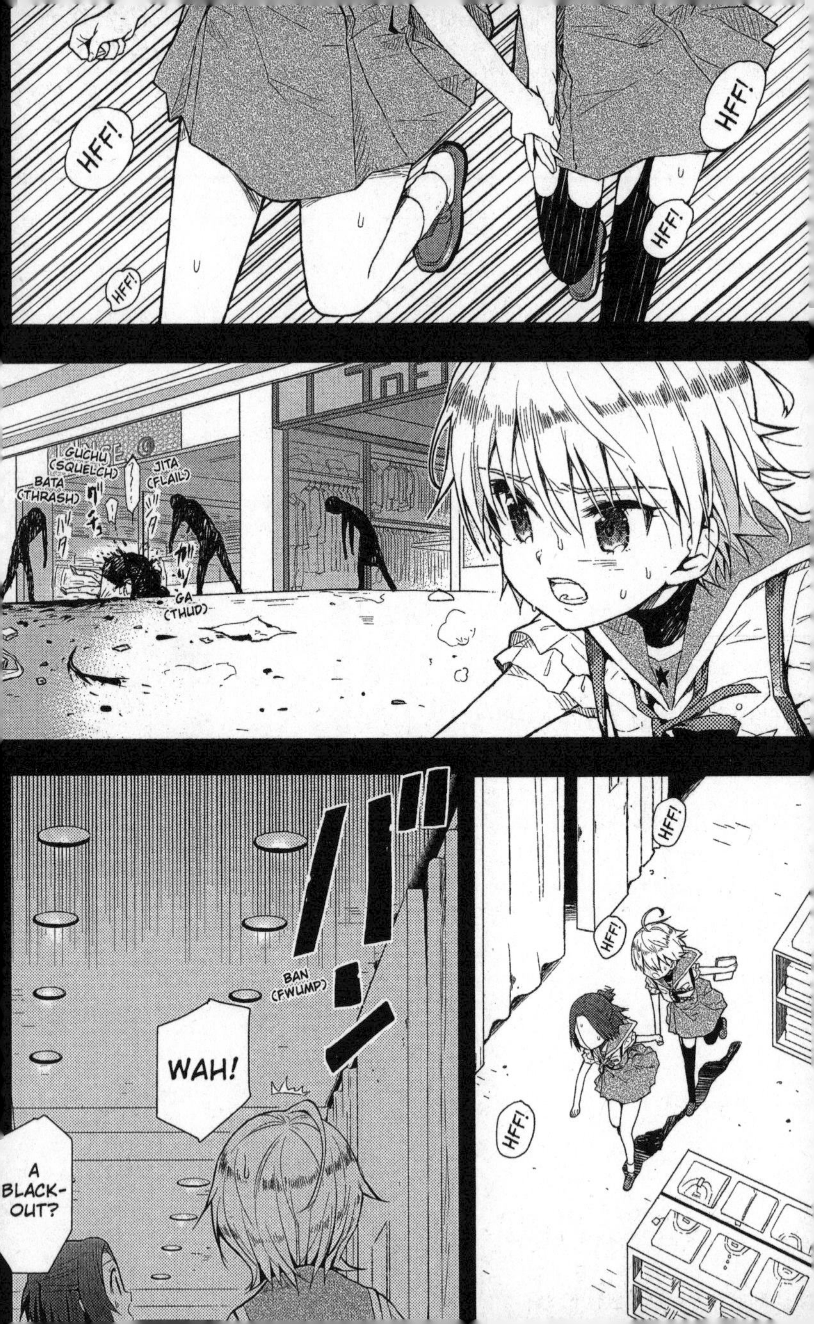
HFF!
HFF!
HFF!
HFF!
JITA (FLAIL)
GUCHU (SQUELCH)
BATA (THRASH)
GA (THUD)
HFF!
HFF!
HFF!
BAN (FWUMP)
WAH!
A BLACK-OUT?

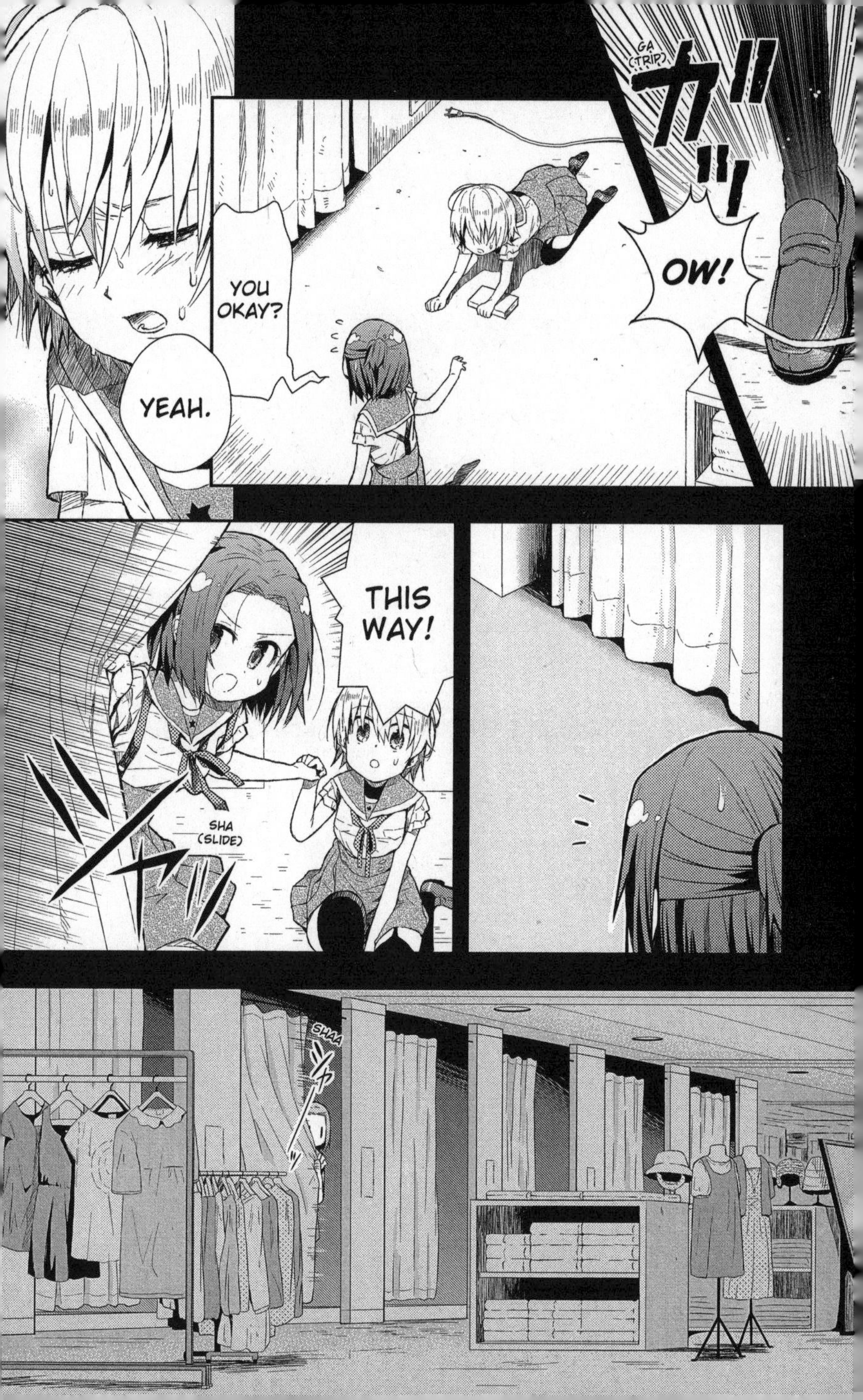
GA (TRIP)
OW!
YOU OKAY?
YEAH.
THIS WAY!
SHA (SLIDE)
SHAA

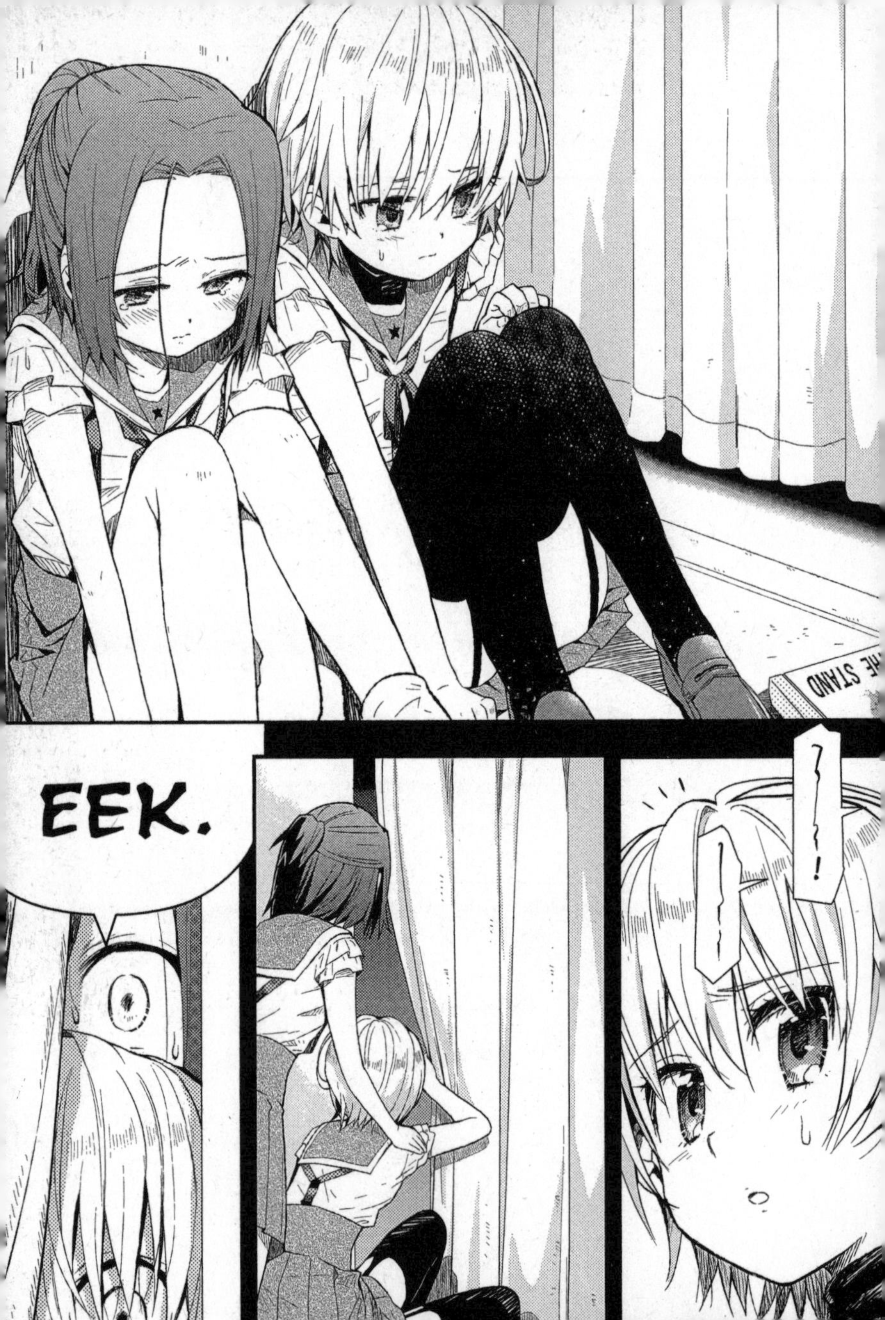
EEK.

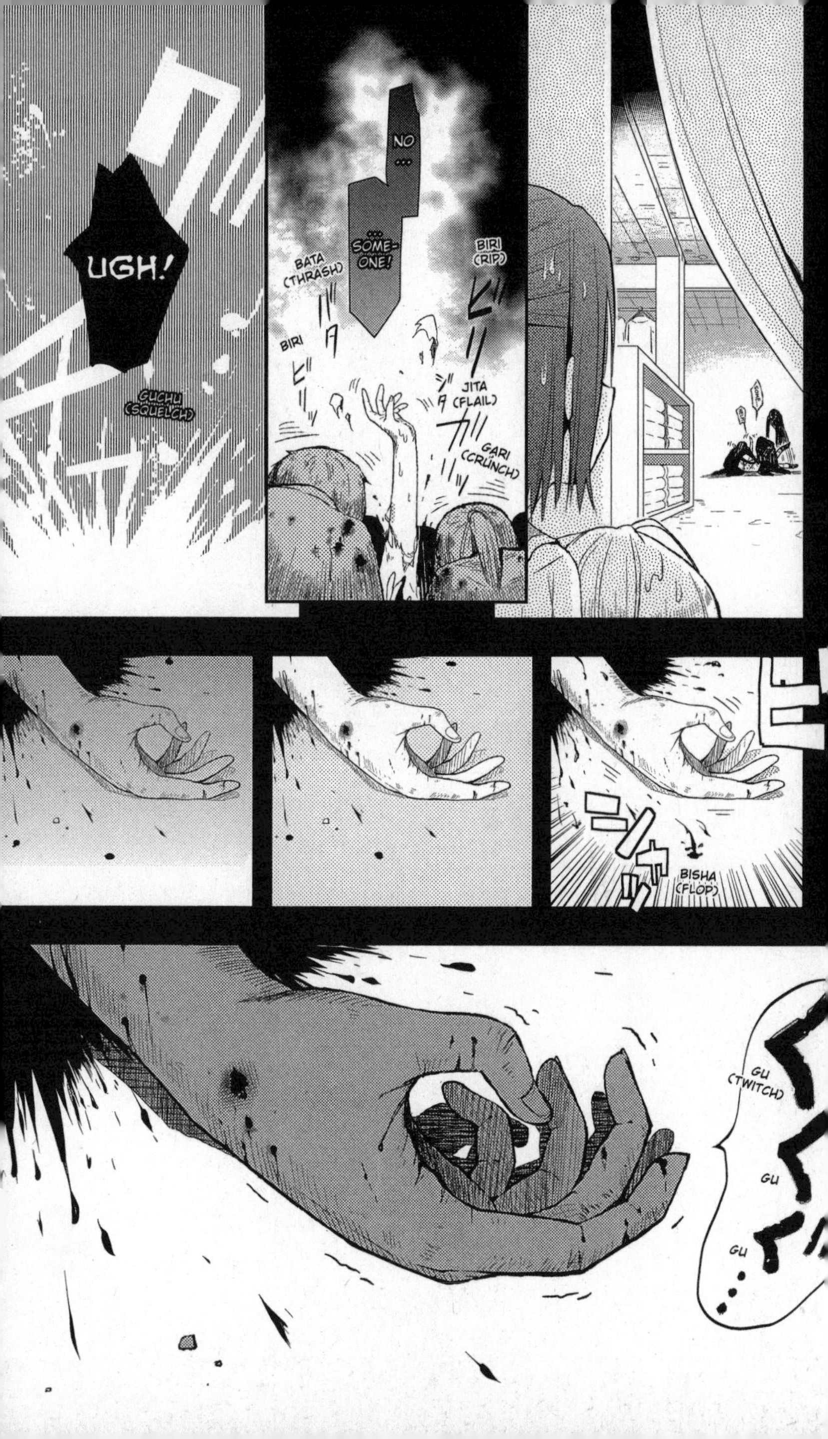
BIRI (RIP)
NO ... ... SOME-ONE!
BATA (THRASH)
BIRI
JITA (FLAIL)
GARI (CRUNCH)
UGH!
GUCHU (SQUELCH)
BISHA (FLOP)
GU (TWITCH)
GU
GU

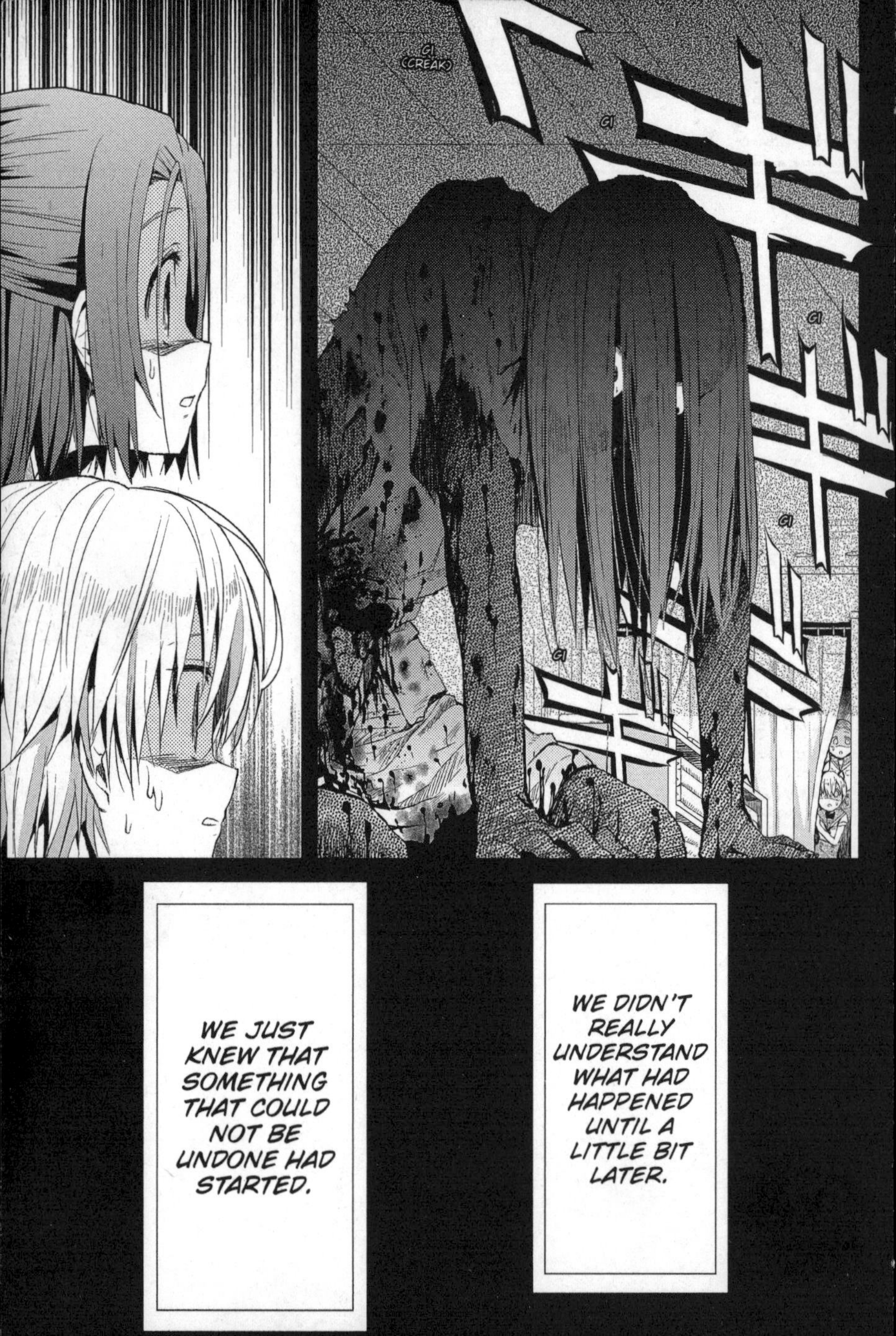
GI (CREAK)
GI
GI
GI
GI
WE DIDN'T REALLY UNDERSTAND WHAT HAD HAPPENED UNTIL A LITTLE BIT LATER.
WE JUST KNEW THAT SOMETHING THAT COULD NOT BE UNDONE HAD STARTED.

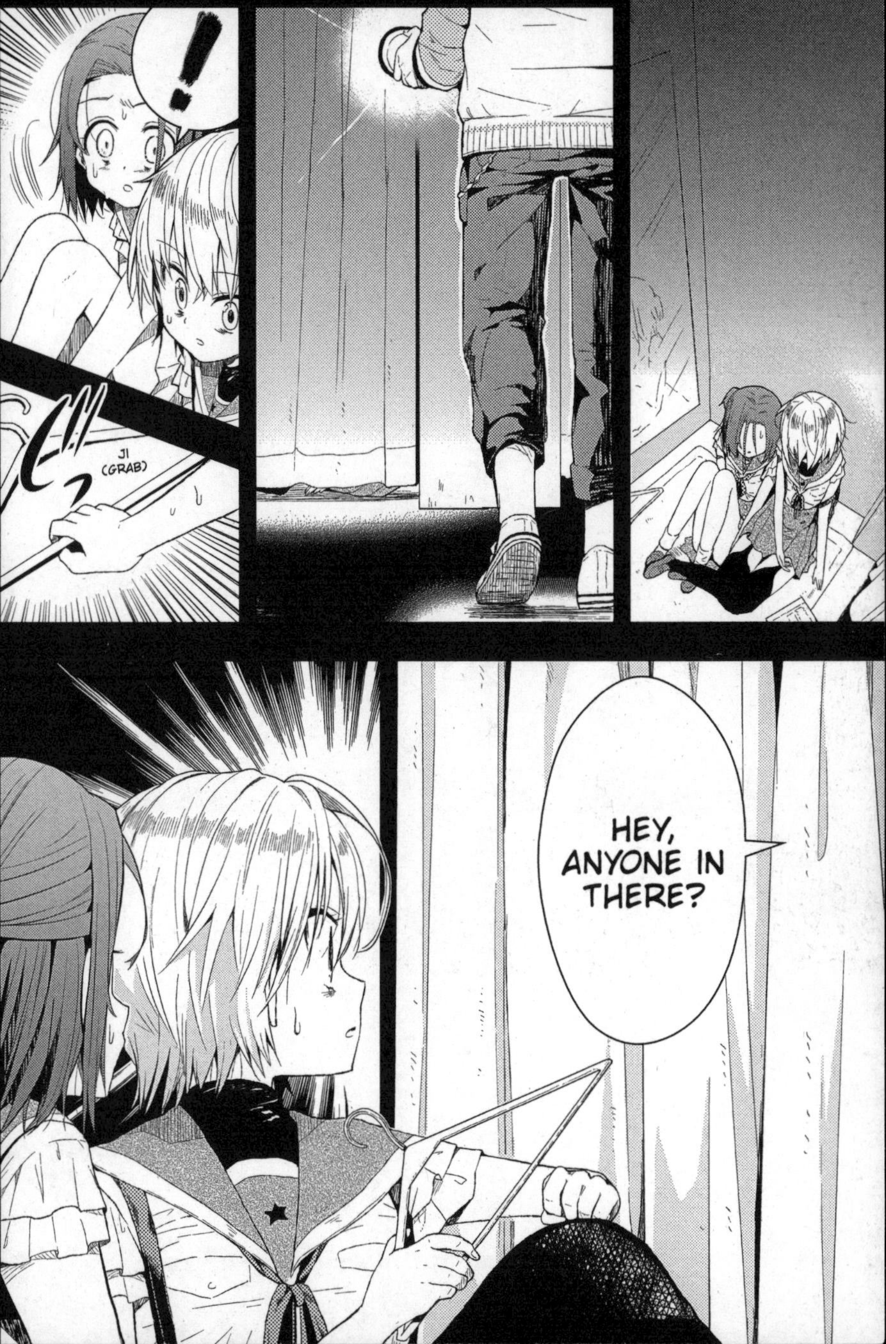
!
JI
(GRAB)
HEY, ANYONE IN THERE?

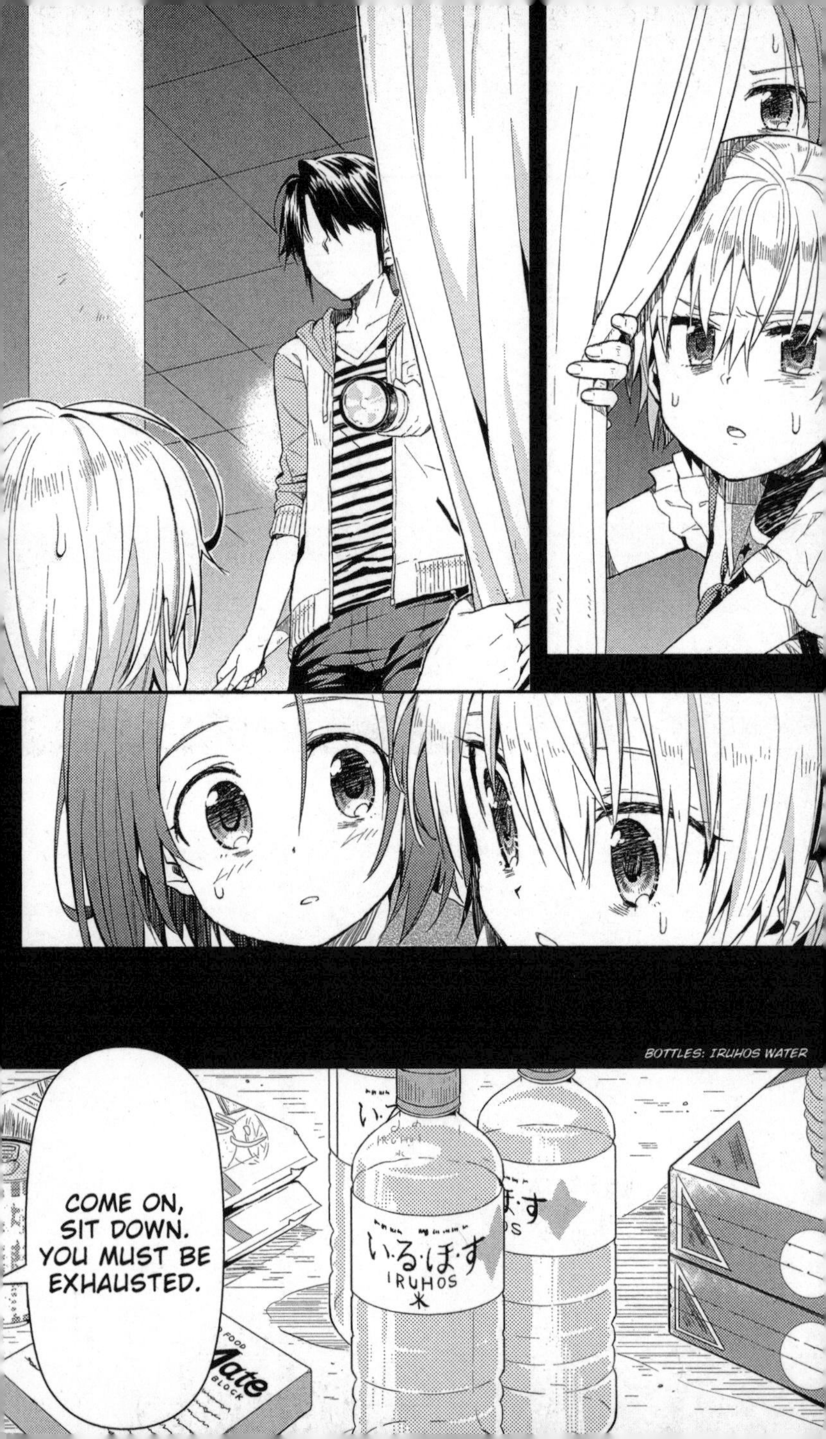
BOTTLES: IRUHOS WATER
COME ON, SIT DOWN. YOU MUST BE EXHAUSTED.
いる・ほ・す
IRUHOS
水

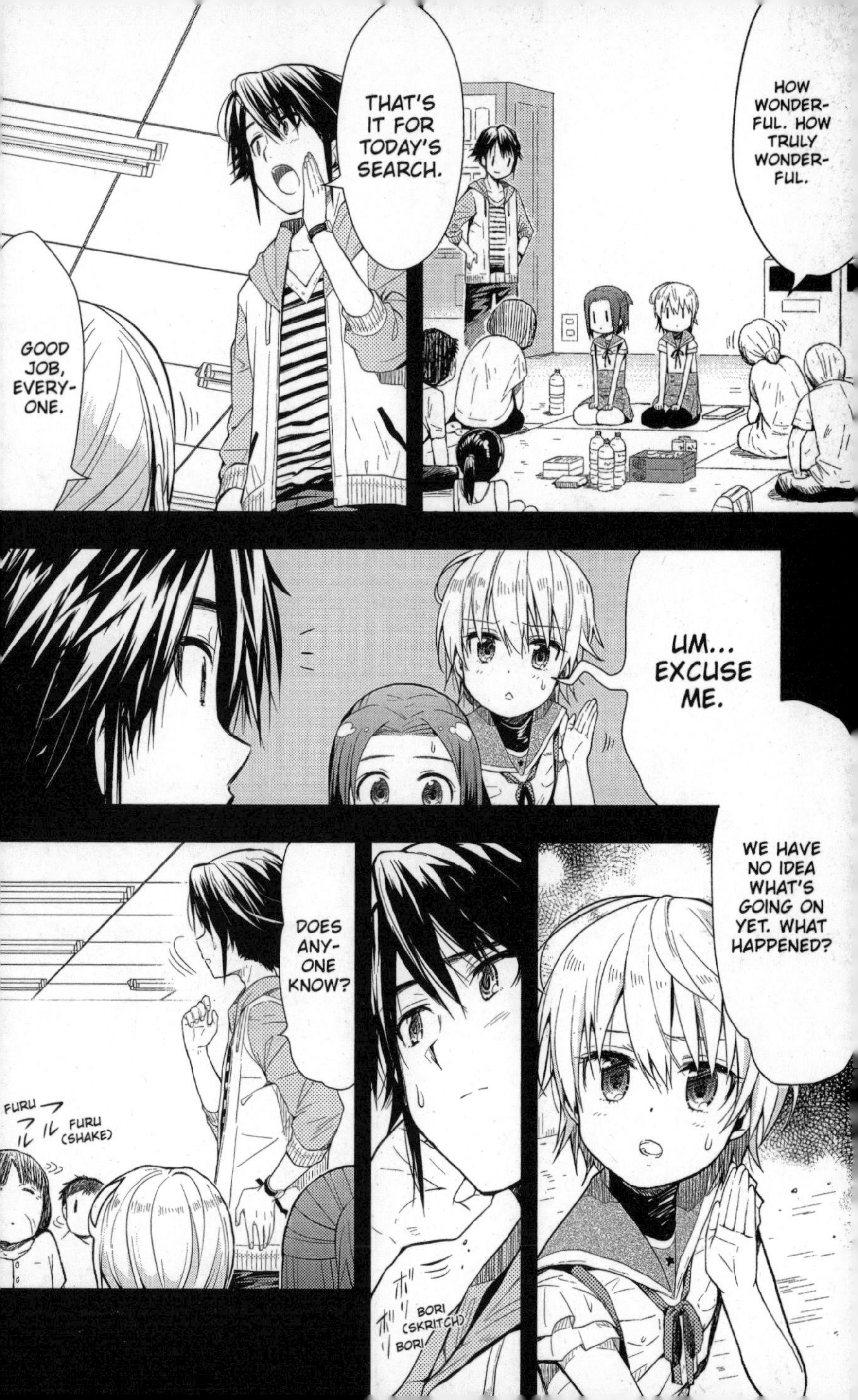
HOW WONDERFUL. HOW TRULY WONDERFUL.
THAT'S IT FOR TODAY'S SEARCH.
GOOD JOB, EVERYONE.
UM... EXCUSE ME.
WE HAVE NO IDEA WHAT'S GOING ON YET. WHAT HAPPENED?
DOES ANYONE KNOW?
BORI BORI (SKRITCH)
FURU FURU (SHAKE)

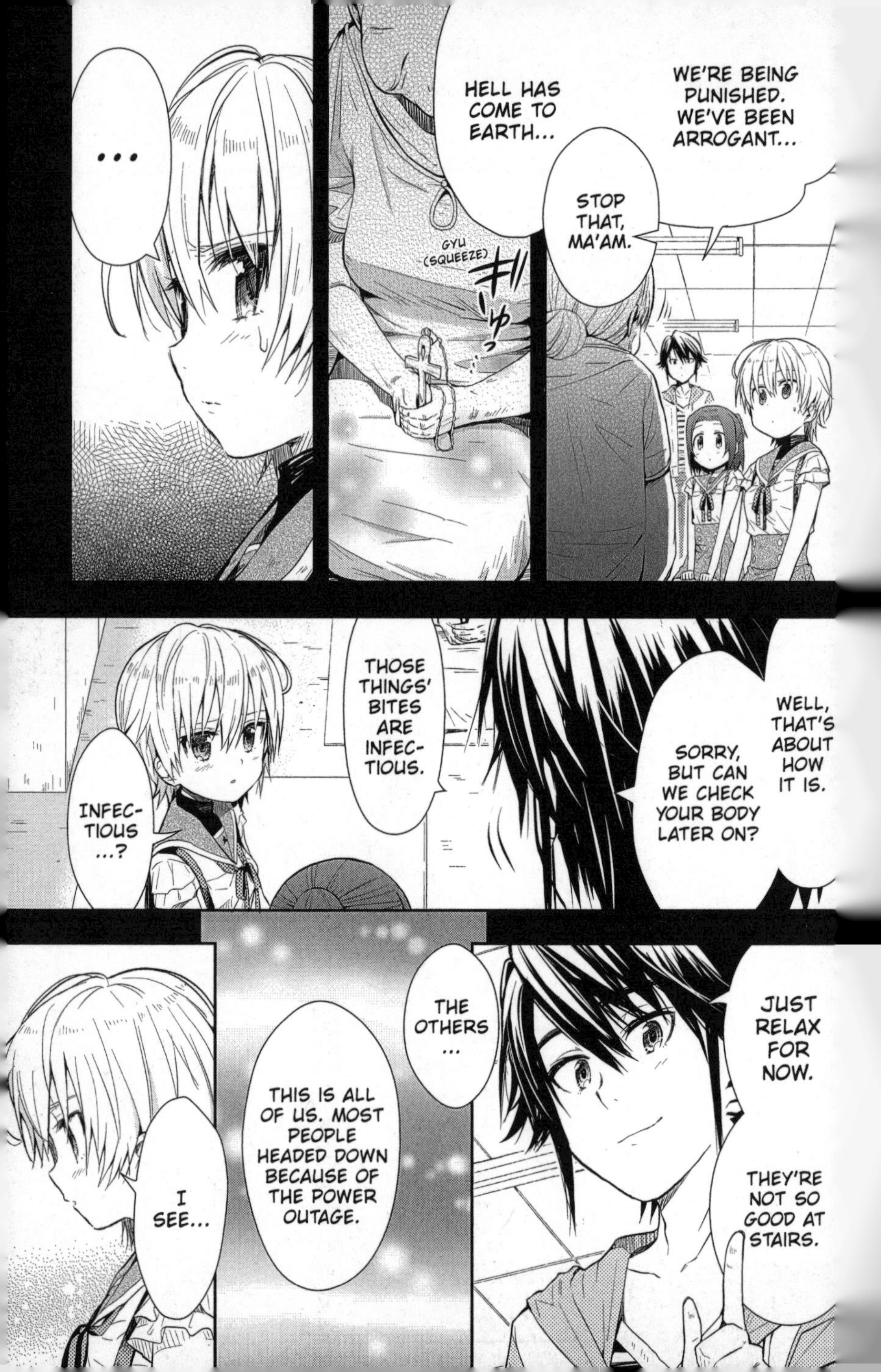
WE'RE BEING PUNISHED. WE'VE BEEN ARROGANT...
STOP THAT, MA'AM.
HELL HAS COME TO EARTH...
GYU (SQUEEZE)
...
WELL, THAT'S ABOUT HOW IT IS.
SORRY, BUT CAN WE CHECK YOUR BODY LATER ON?
THOSE THINGS' BITES ARE INFECTIOUS.
INFECTIOUS...?
THE OTHERS...
THIS IS ALL OF US. MOST PEOPLE HEADED DOWN BECAUSE OF THE POWER OUTAGE.
JUST RELAX FOR NOW.
THEY'RE NOT SO GOOD AT STAIRS.
I SEE...

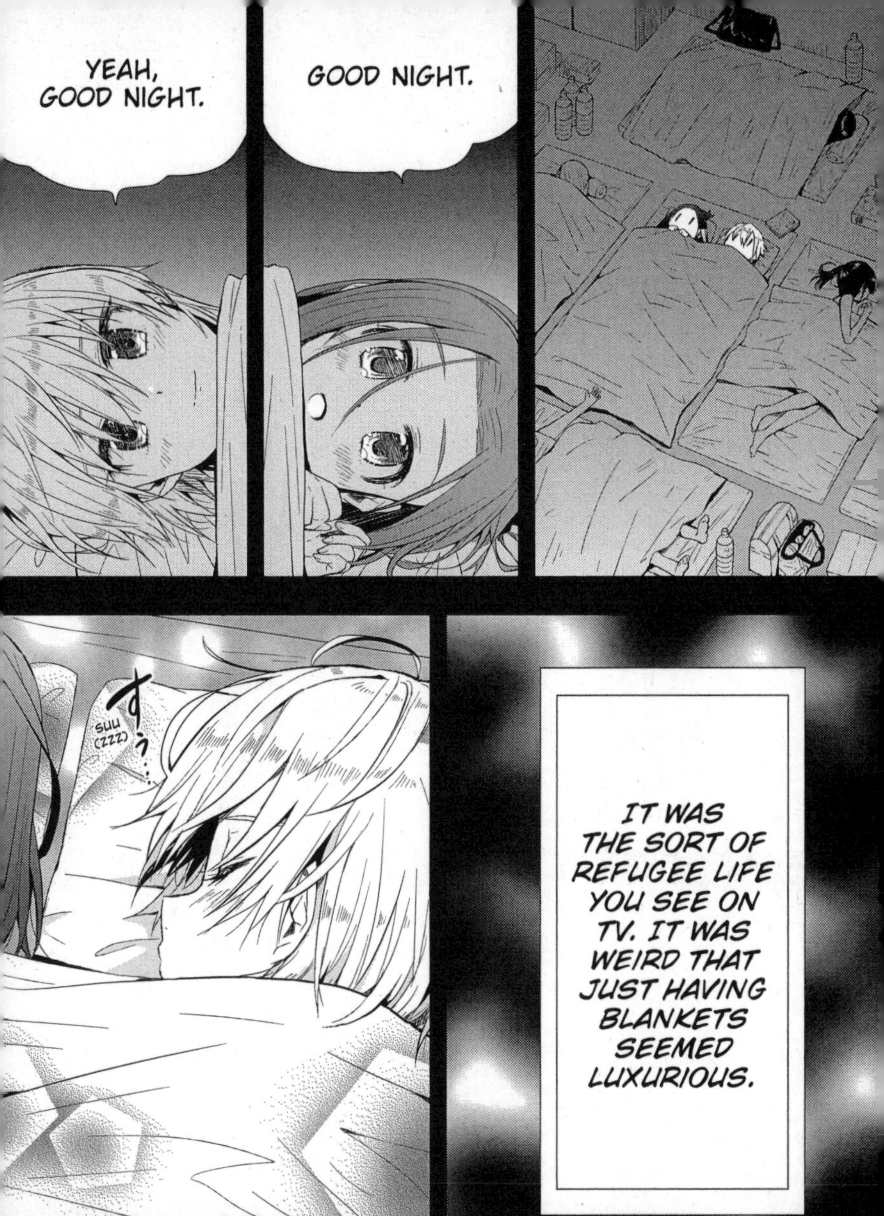
GOOD NIGHT.
YEAH, GOOD NIGHT.
IT WAS THE SORT OF REFUGEE LIFE YOU SEE ON TV. IT WAS WEIRD THAT JUST HAVING BLANKETS SEEMED LUXURIOUS.
すぅ…
SUU (ZZZ)

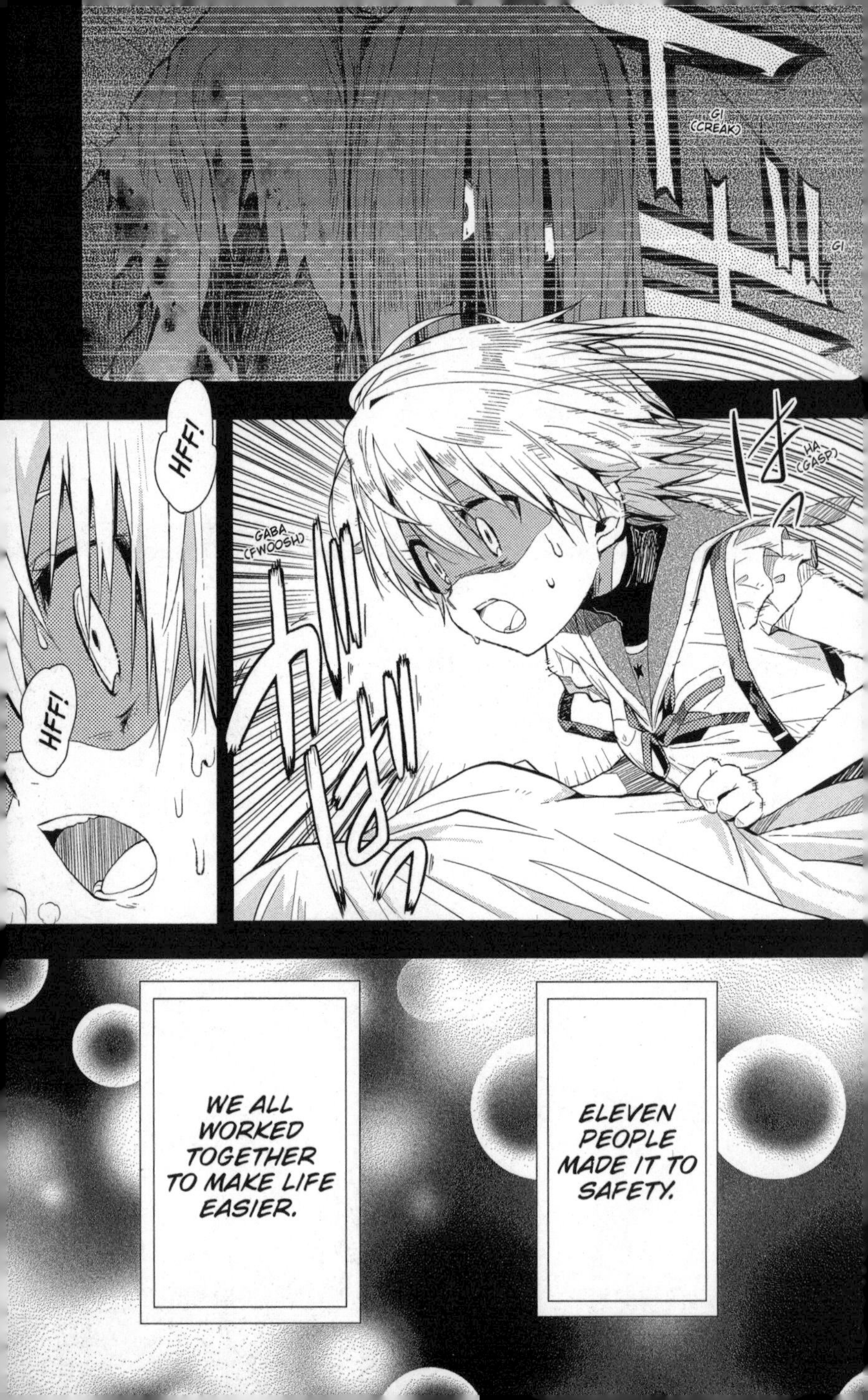
GI
(CREAK)
GI
HA
(GASP)
GABA
(FWOOSH)
HFF!
HFF!
ELEVEN PEOPLE MADE IT TO SAFETY.
WE ALL WORKED TOGETHER TO MAKE LIFE EASIER.

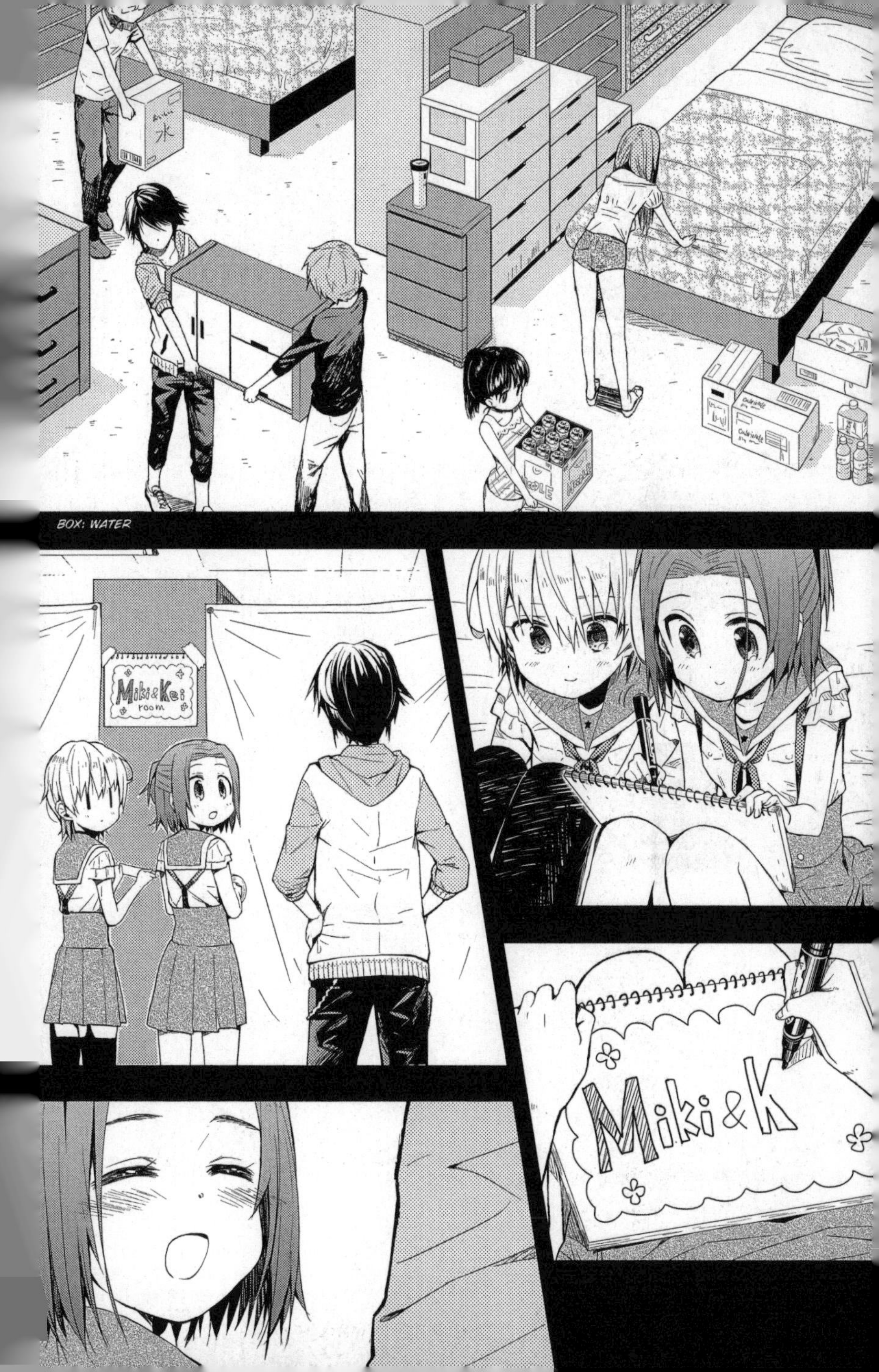
水
BOX: WATER
Miki&K
Miki&Kei
room

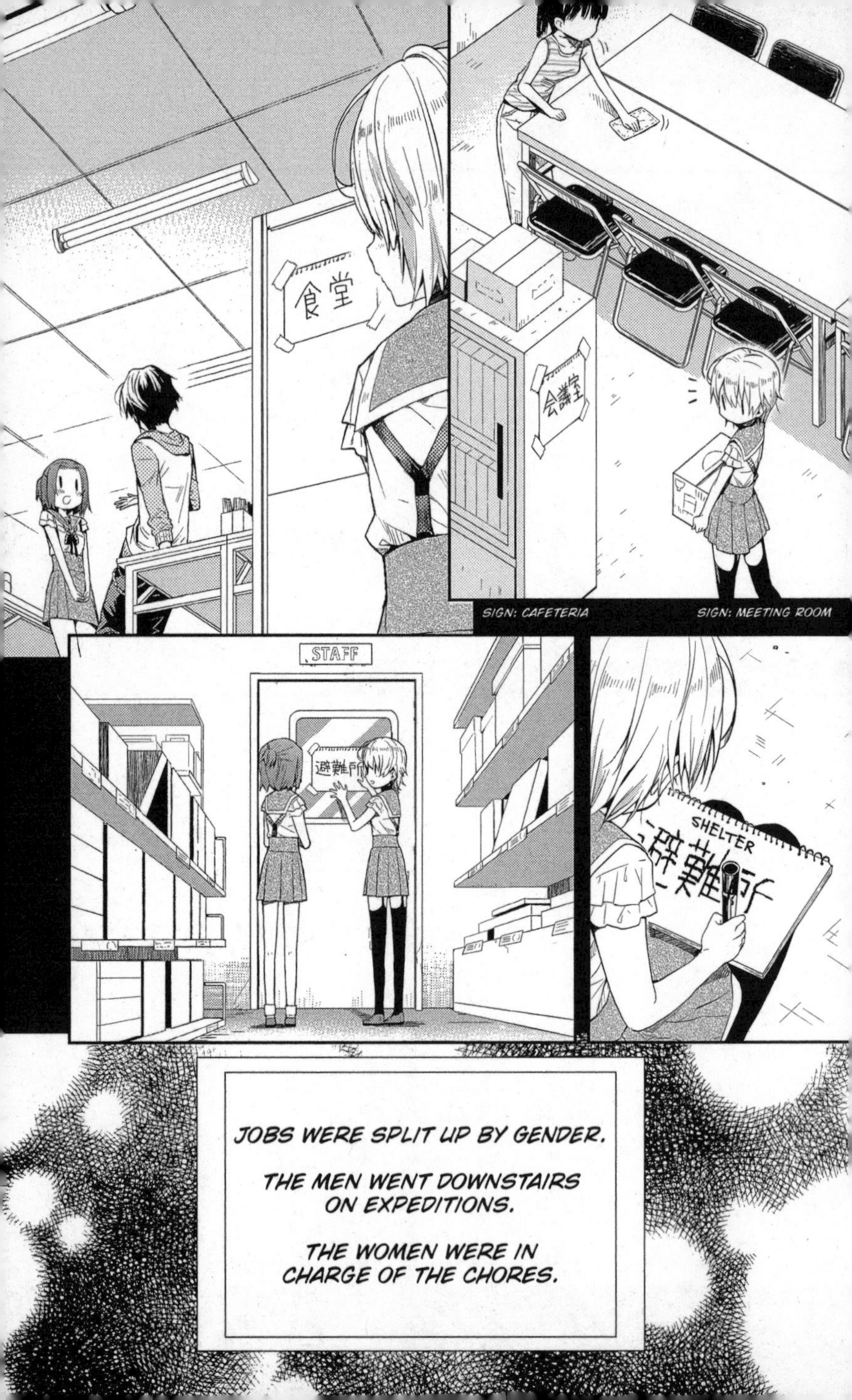
会議室
食堂
SIGN: CAFETERIA
SIGN: MEETING ROOM
SHELTER
避難所
STAFF
避難所
JOBS WERE SPLIT UP BY GENDER.
THE MEN WENT DOWNSTAIRS ON EXPEDITIONS.
THE WOMEN WERE IN CHARGE OF THE CHORES.

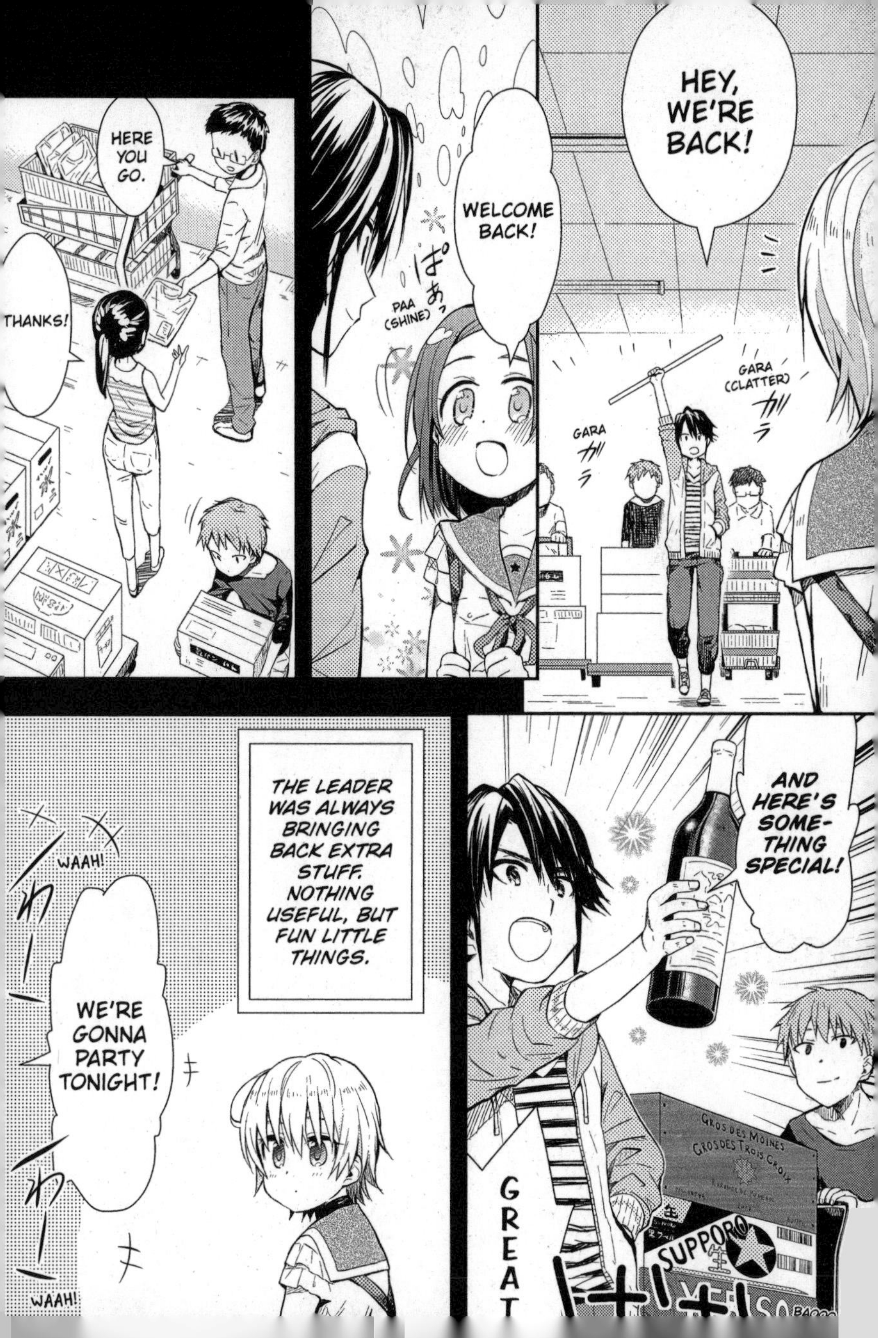
HEY, WE'RE BACK!
GARA (CLATTER)
GARA
WELCOME BACK!
PAA (SHINE)
HERE YOU GO.
THANKS!
AND HERE'S SOMETHING SPECIAL!
GREAT
SUPPORO
THE LEADER WAS ALWAYS BRINGING BACK EXTRA STUFF. NOTHING USEFUL, BUT FUN LITTLE THINGS.
WAAH!
WE'RE GONNA PARTY TONIGHT!
WAAH!

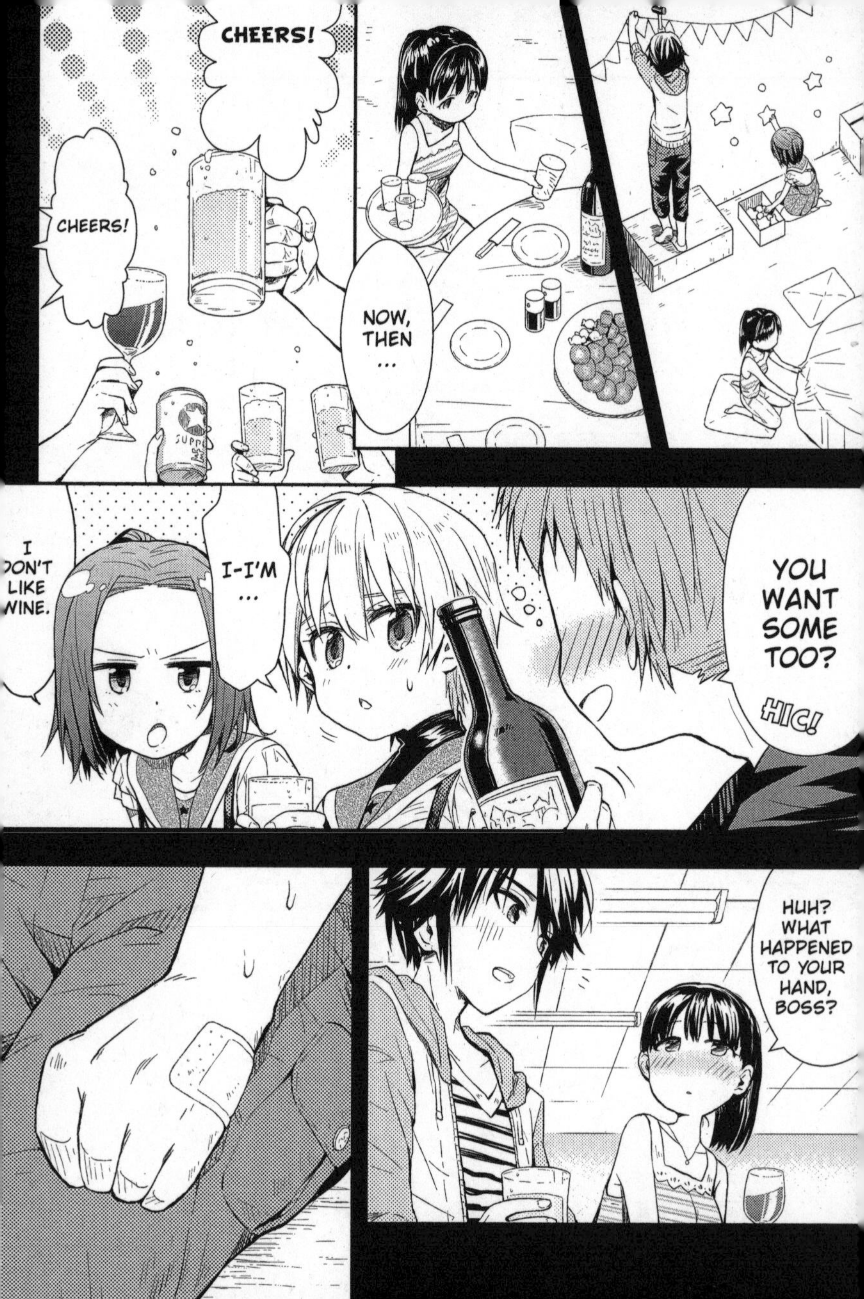
NOW, THEN ...
CHEERS!
CHEERS!
YOU WANT SOME TOO?
HIC!
I-I'M ...
I DON'T LIKE WINE.
HUH? WHAT HAPPENED TO YOUR HAND, BOSS?

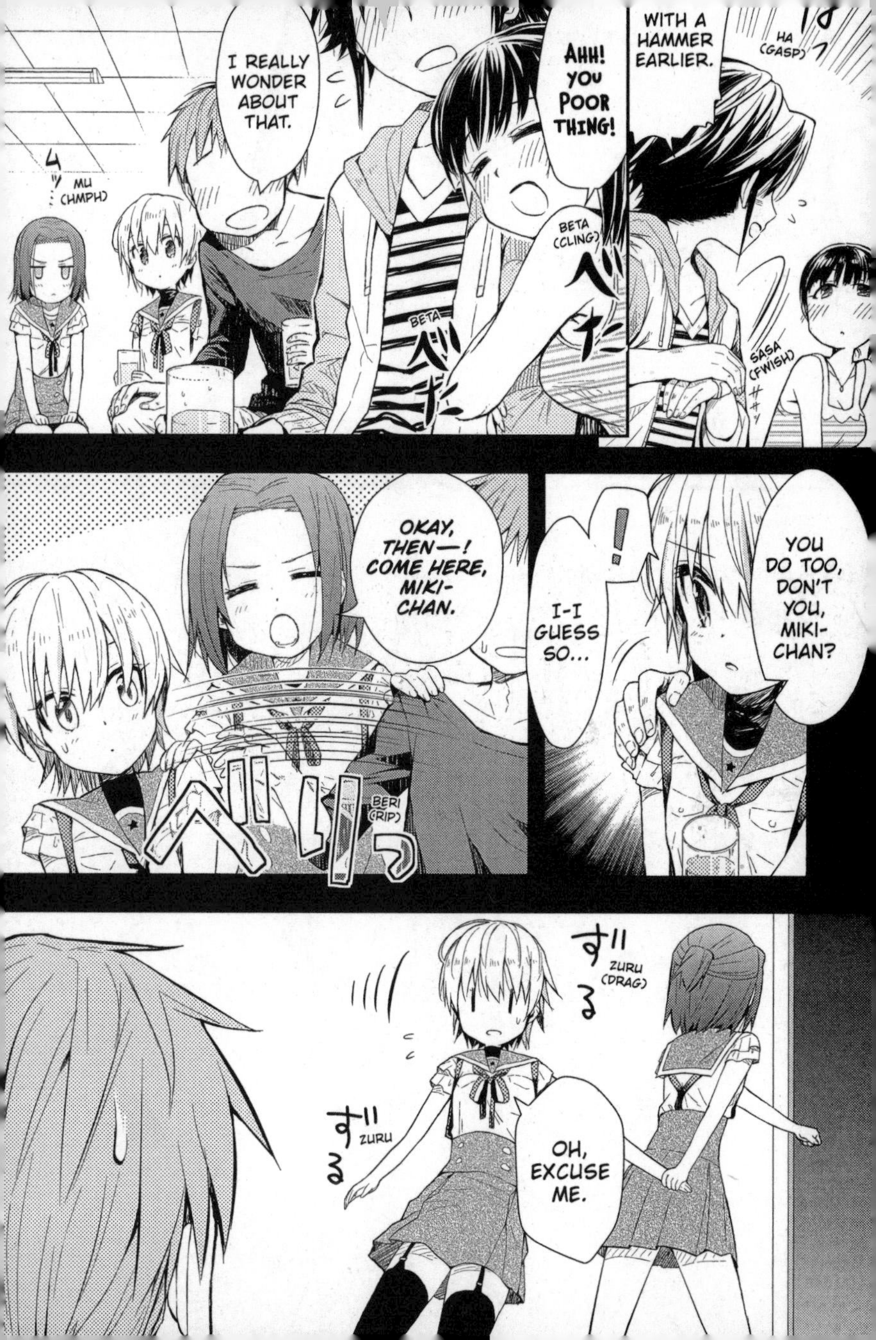
WITH A HAMMER EARLIER.
HA (GASP)
SASA (FWISH)
AHH! YOU POOR THING!
BETA (CLING)
I REALLY WONDER ABOUT THAT.
BETA
MU (HMPH)
YOU DO TOO, DON'T YOU, MIKI-CHAN?
!
I-I GUESS SO...
OKAY, THEN—! COME HERE, MIKI-CHAN.
BERI (RIP)
ZURU (DRAG)
OH, EXCUSE ME.
ZURU

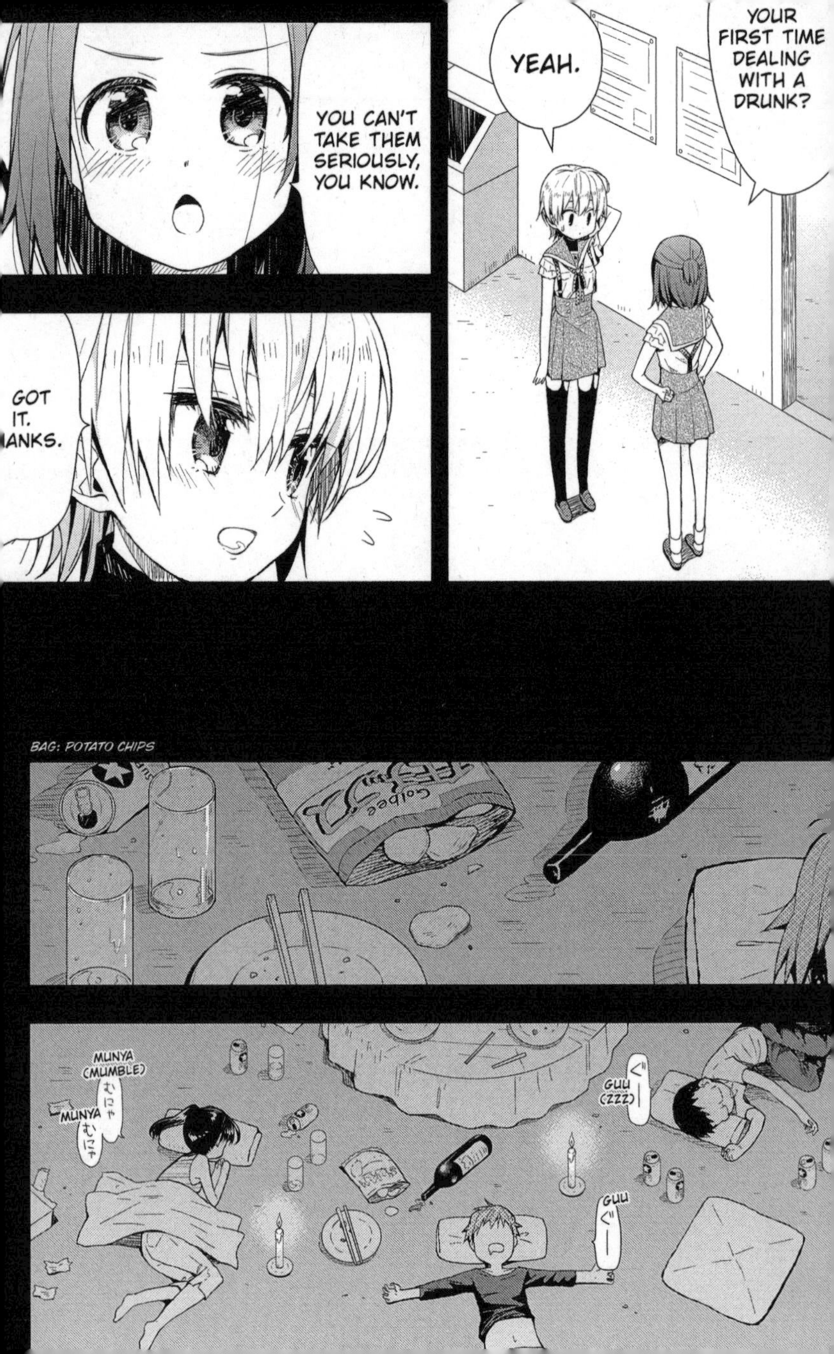
YOUR FIRST TIME DEALING WITH A DRUNK?
YEAH.
YOU CAN'T TAKE THEM SERIOUSLY, YOU KNOW.
GOT IT. ANKS.
BAG: POTATO CHIPS
GUU (ZZZ) ぐー
GUU ぐー
MUNYA (MUMBLE) むにゃ
MUNYA むにゃ

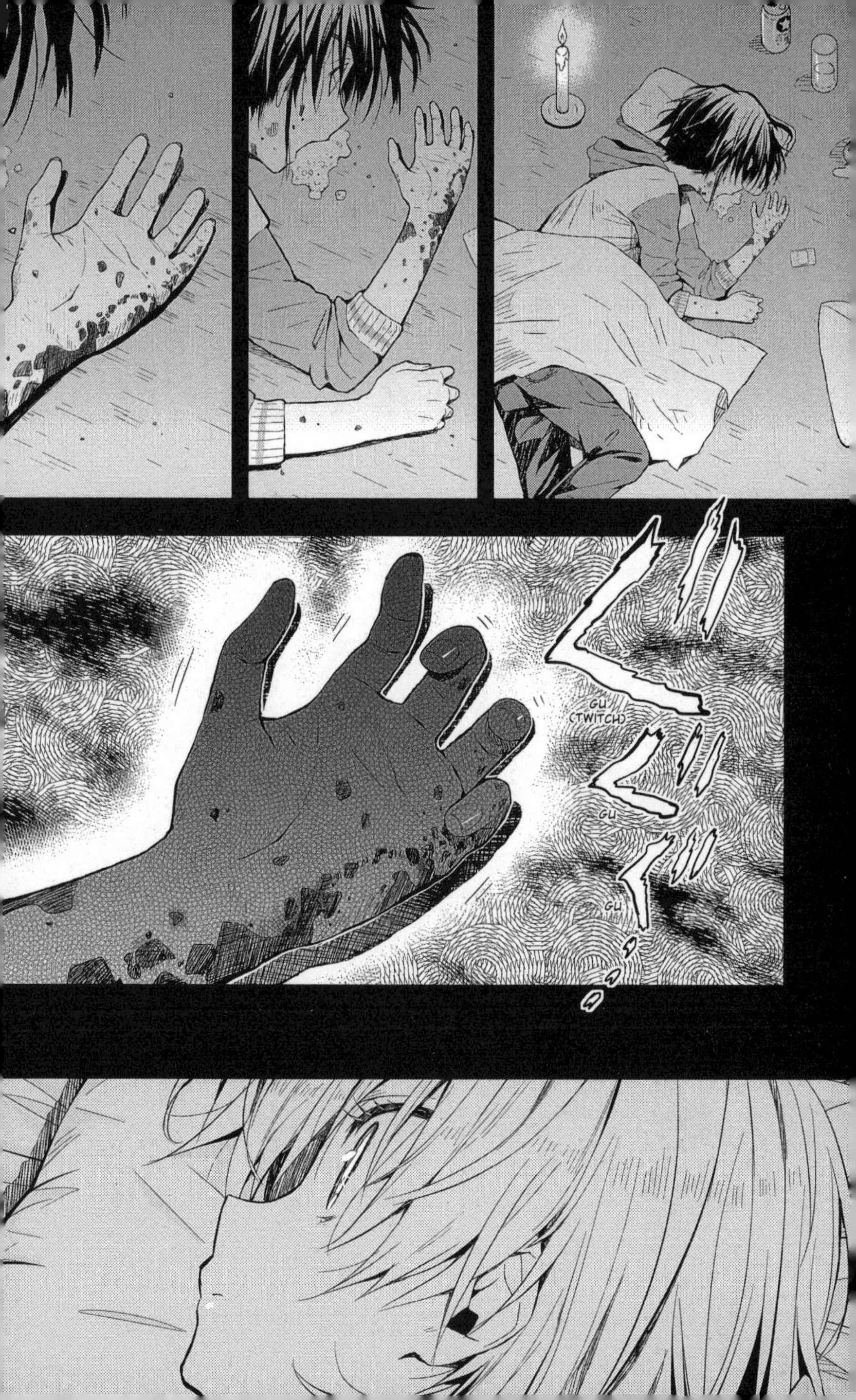
GU
(TWITCH)
GU
GU

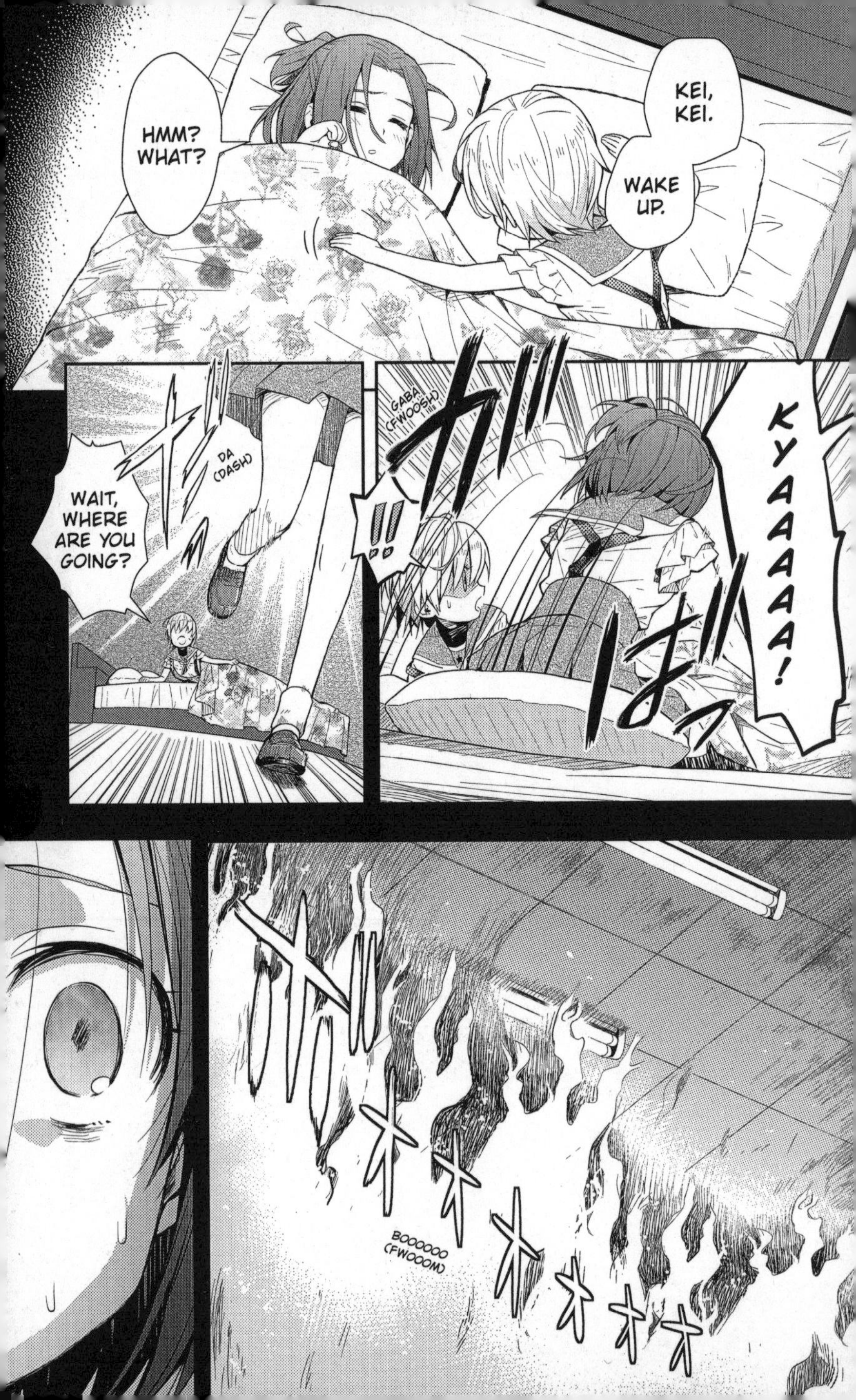
KEI, KEI.
WAKE UP.
HMM? WHAT?
KYAAAAAAA!
GABA (FWOOSH)
!!
DA (DASH)
WAIT, WHERE ARE YOU GOING?
BOOOOOO (FWOOOM)

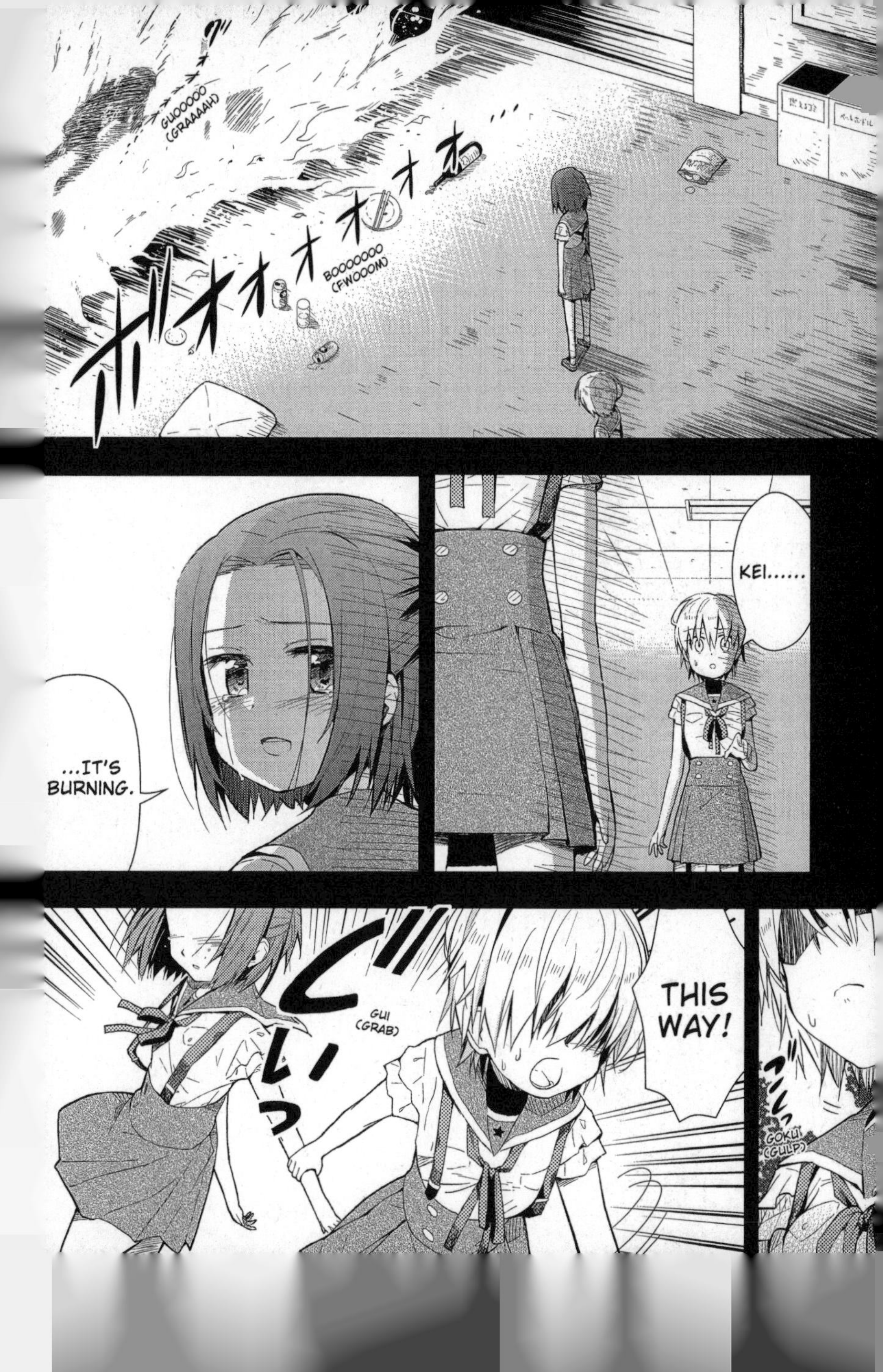
GUOOOOO (GRAAAAH)
BOOOOOOO (FWOOOM)
KEI......
...IT'S BURNING.
GOKU (GULP)
THIS WAY!
GUI (GRAB)

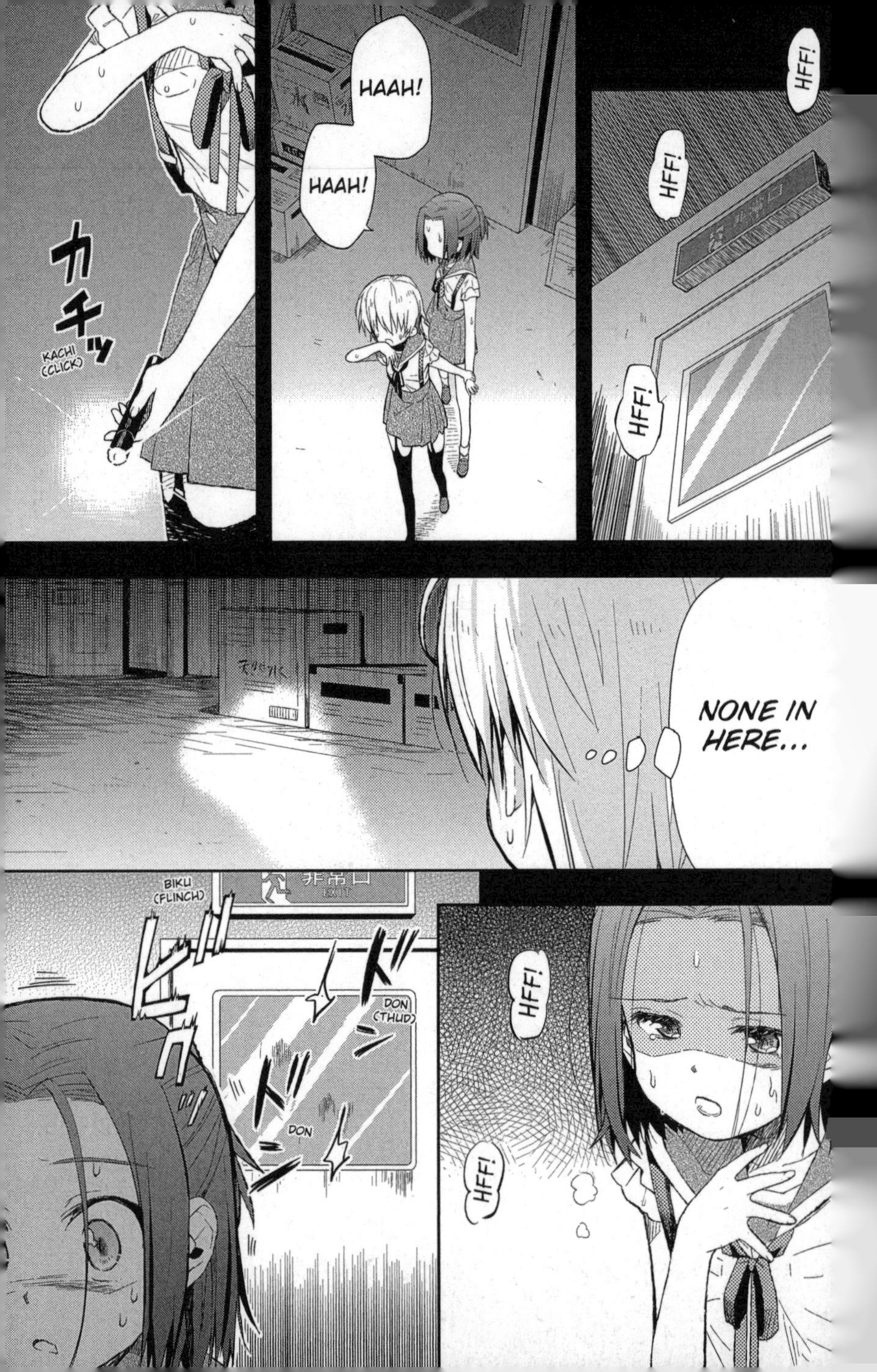
HFF!
HFF!
HFF!
HAAH!
HAAH!
カチッ
KACHI (CLICK)
NONE IN HERE...
HFF!
HFF!
非常口 EXIT
BIKU (FLINCH)
ビクッ
ド
DON (THUD)
ド
DON

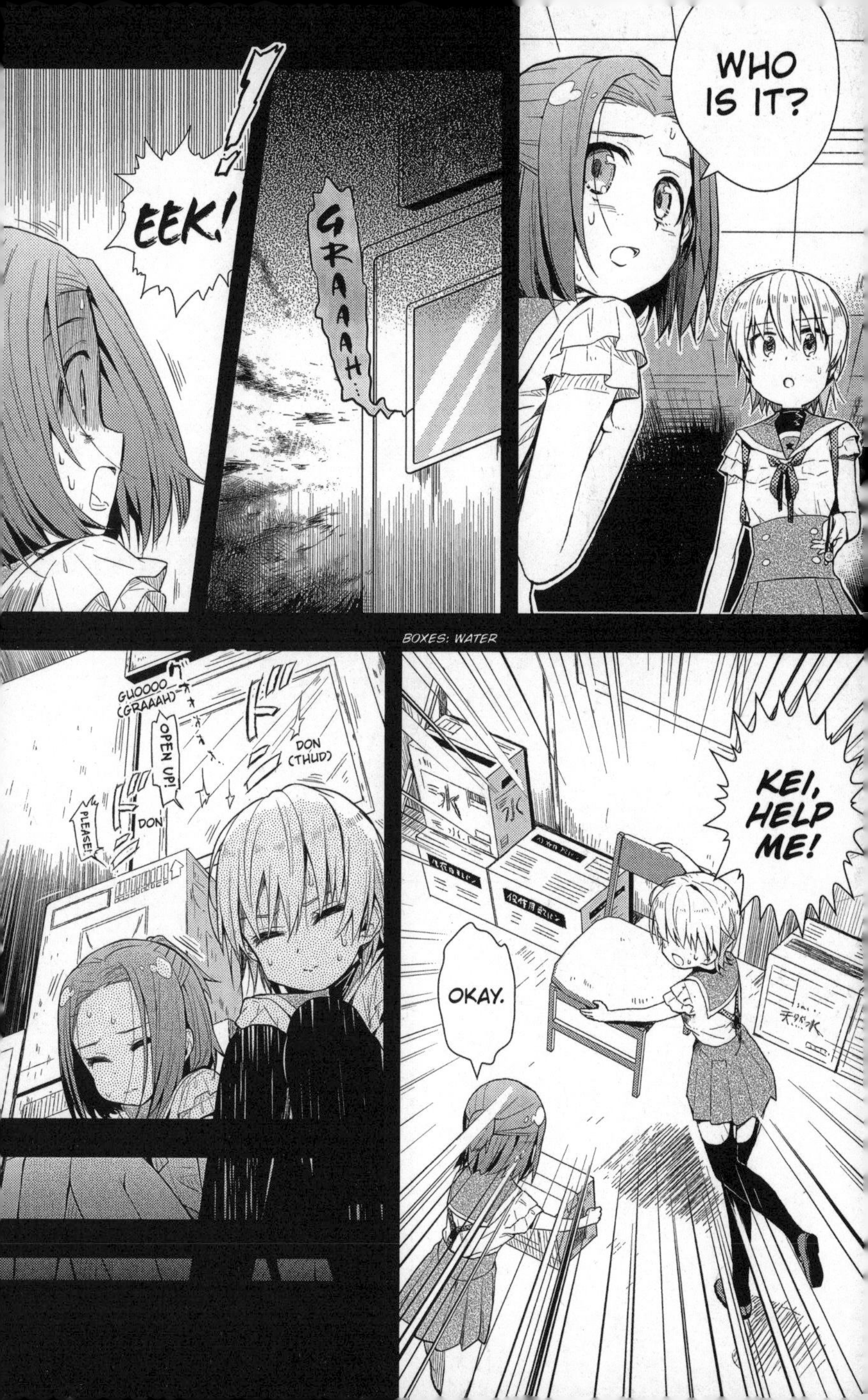
WHO IS IT?
GRAAAAH...
EEK!
BOXES: WATER
KEI, HELP ME!
OKAY.
DON (THUD)
GUOOOO (GRAAAH)
OPEN UP!
DON
PLEASE!

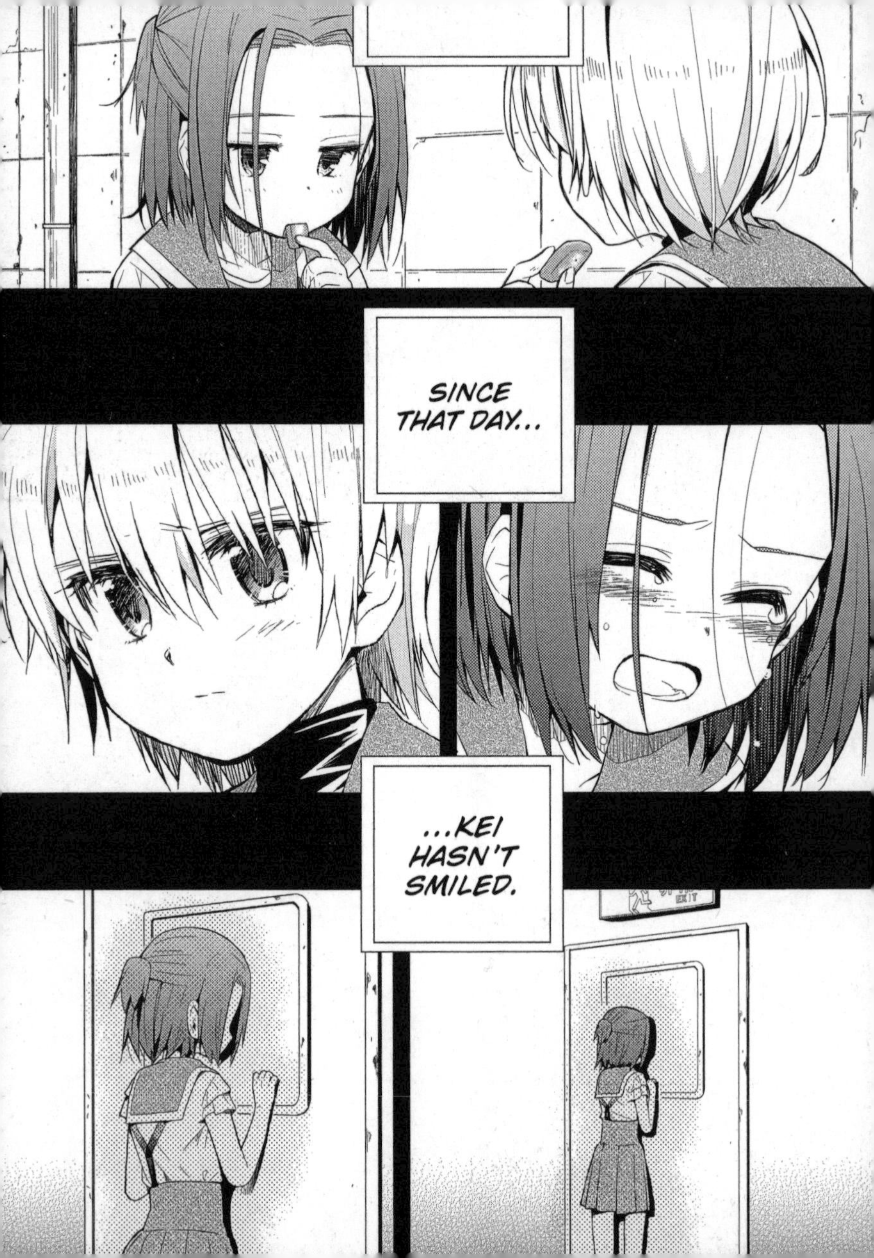
SINCE THAT DAY...
...KEI HASN'T SMILED.
EXIT

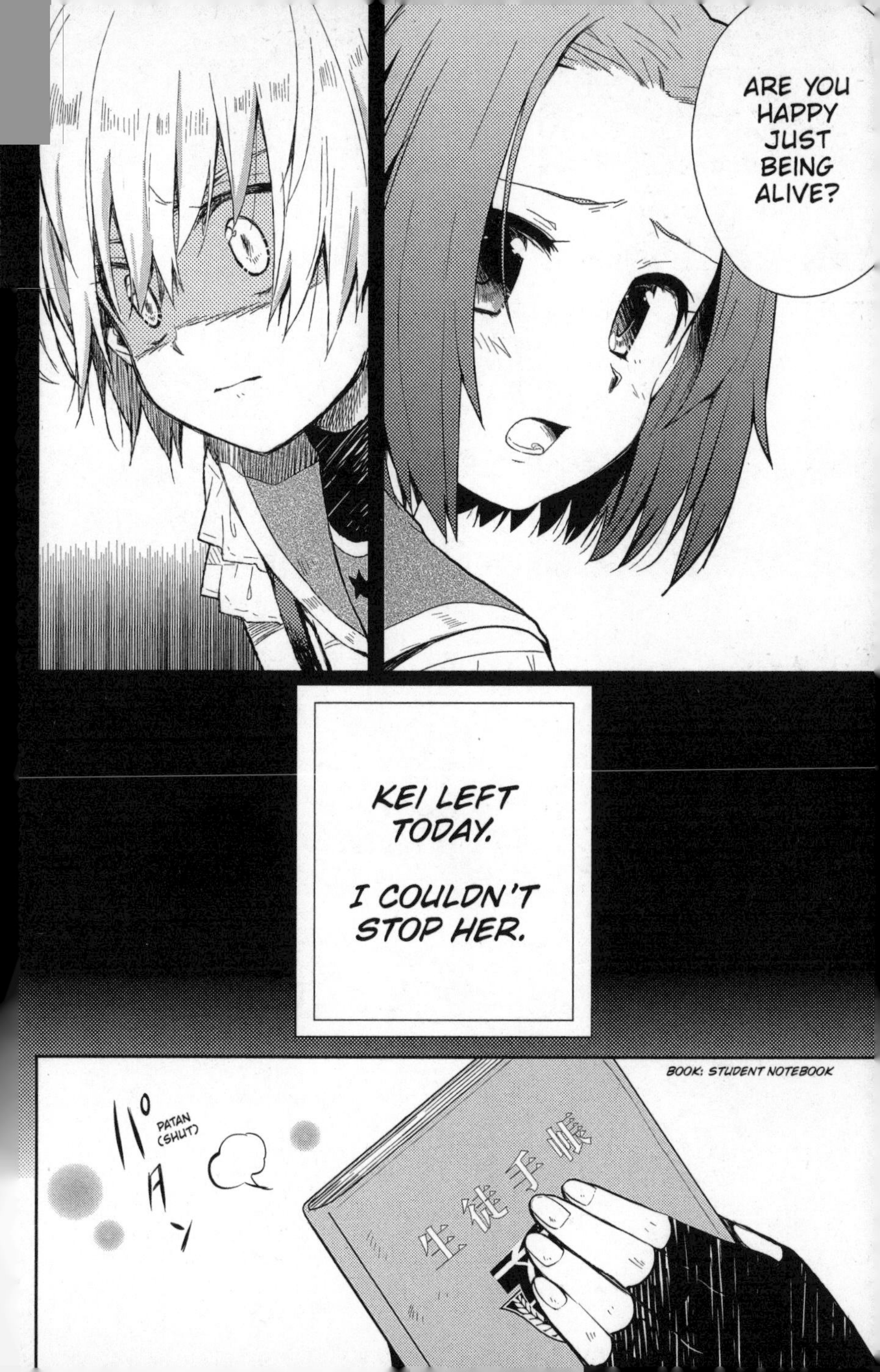
ARE YOU HAPPY JUST BEING ALIVE?
KEI LEFT TODAY.
I COULDN'T STOP HER.
BOOK: STUDENT NOTEBOOK
生徒手帳
PATAN (SHUT)

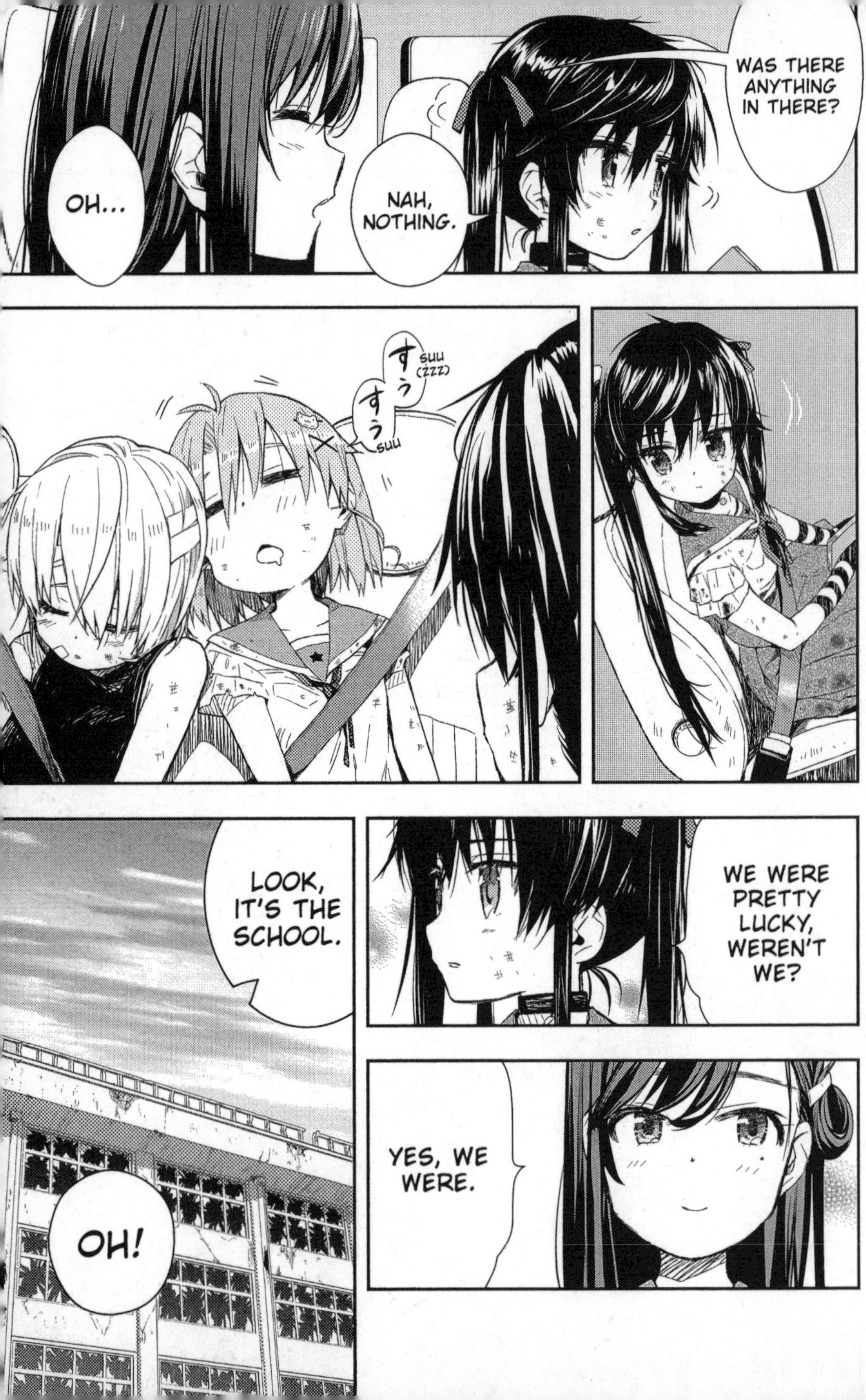
WAS THERE ANYTHING IN THERE?
NAH, NOTHING.
OH...
すう
SUU (ZZZ)
すう
SUU
WE WERE PRETTY LUCKY, WEREN'T WE?
YES, WE WERE.
LOOK, IT'S THE SCHOOL.
OH!

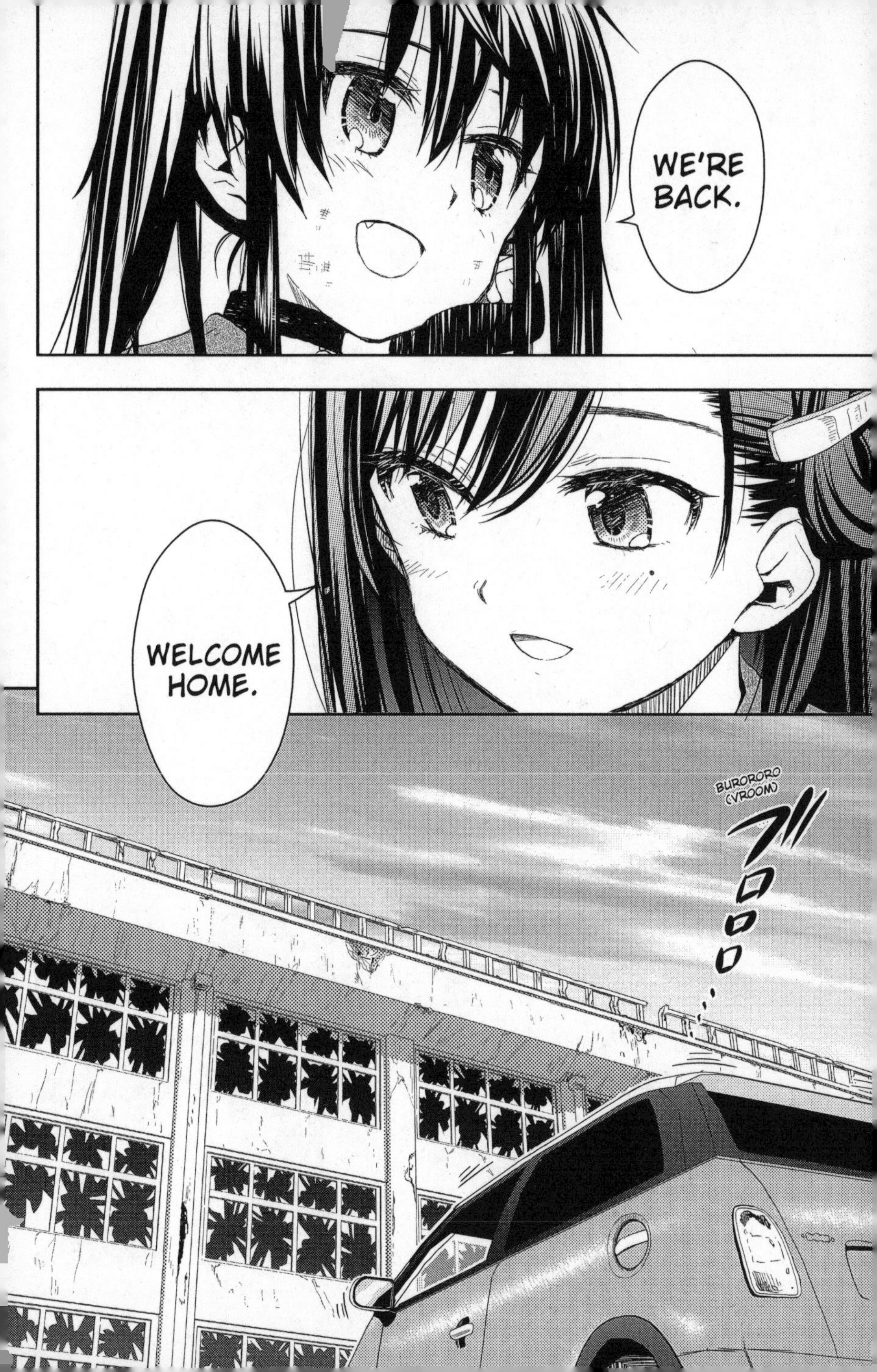
WE'RE BACK.
WELCOME HOME.
BURORORO (VROOM)
ブロロロ…

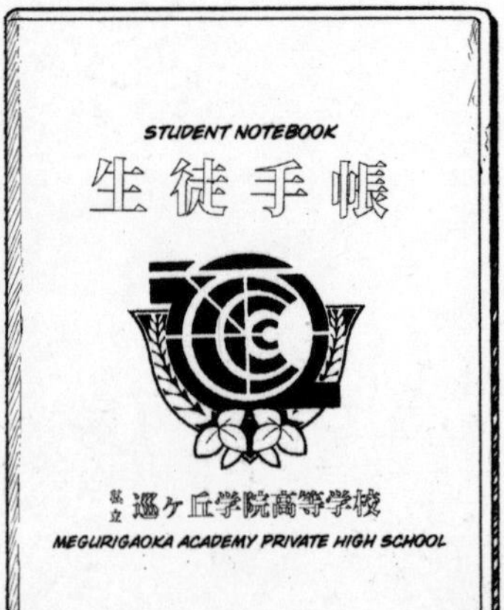
STUDENT NOTEBOOK
生徒手帳
私立 巡ヶ丘学院高等学校
MEGURIGAOKA ACADEMY PRIVATE HIGH SCHOOL

SCHOOL-LIVE!

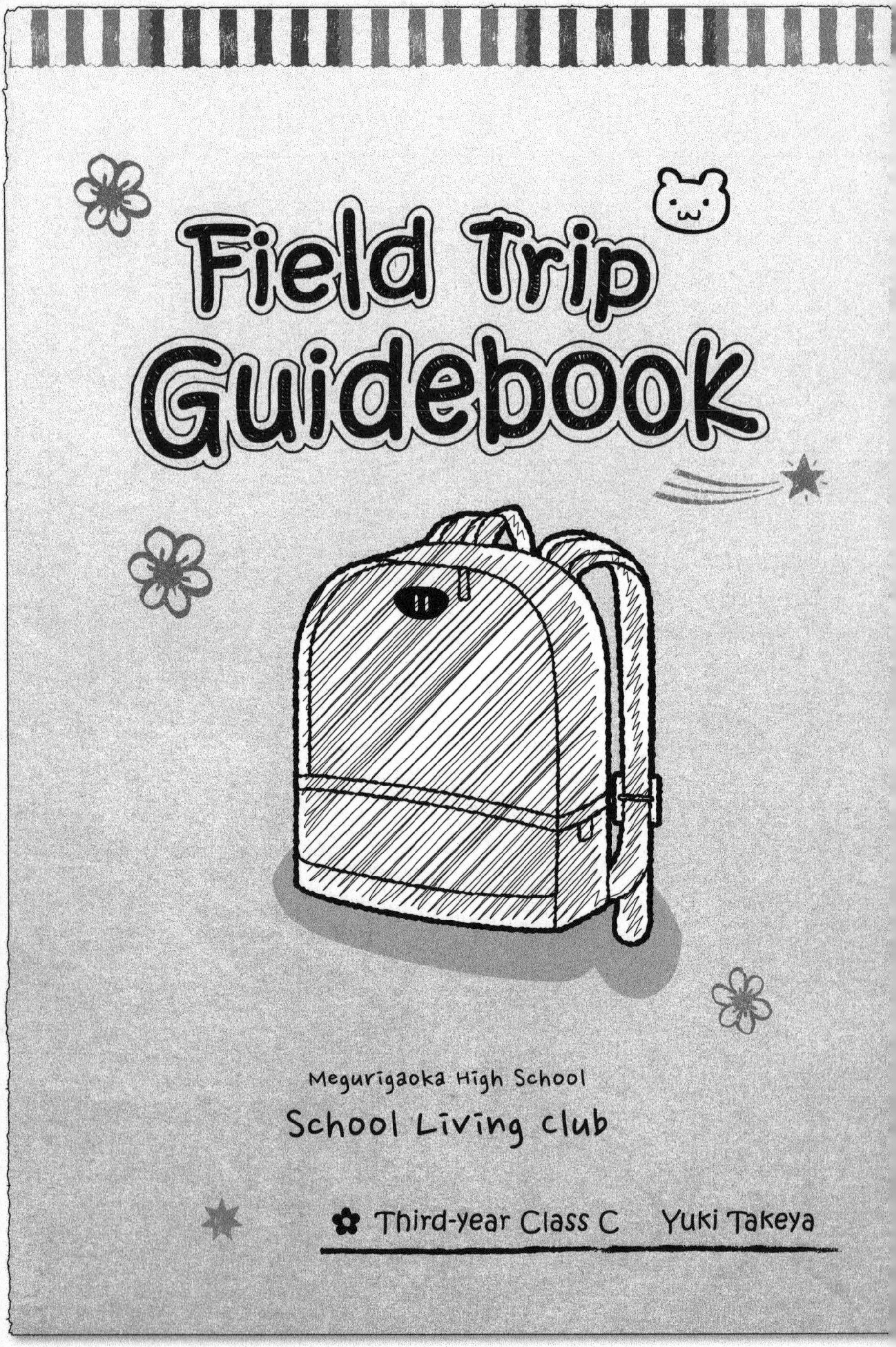
Field Trip Guidebook
Megurigaoka High School
School Living Club
Third-year Class C Yuki Takeya

School Living Club

First Exciting Field Trip!

Destination

Rivercity Tron Shopping Mall

And some other places.

Schedule

About three days

Things to Bring

▶ Snacks
▶ Lunch
▶ Towel
▶ Water

Shovel!

→ Participants

☑ Yuuri Wakasa (club president)

☑ Kurumi Ebisuzawa

☑ Yuki Takeya

Field Trip Rules

1. Everyone get along. ← No fighting!

2. This is our first activity outside.
↑ Don't get carried away! ♪

3. No getting lost!!
↑ Especially Yuki. ⇐ Awww!

4. Shopping is okay.
↑ Let's buy lots of stuff!
↑ Get big backpacks and bags ready.

5. Let's look for people in trouble.
↑ They might be future members!?
⇐ Scouting on the street corner!?

6. Let's have fun.
↑ Yeah!!

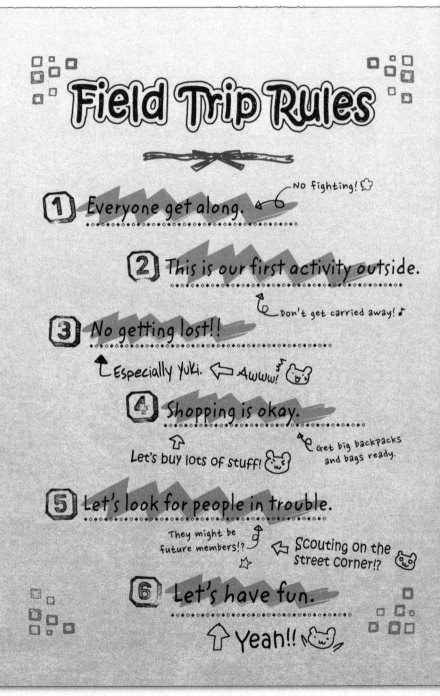

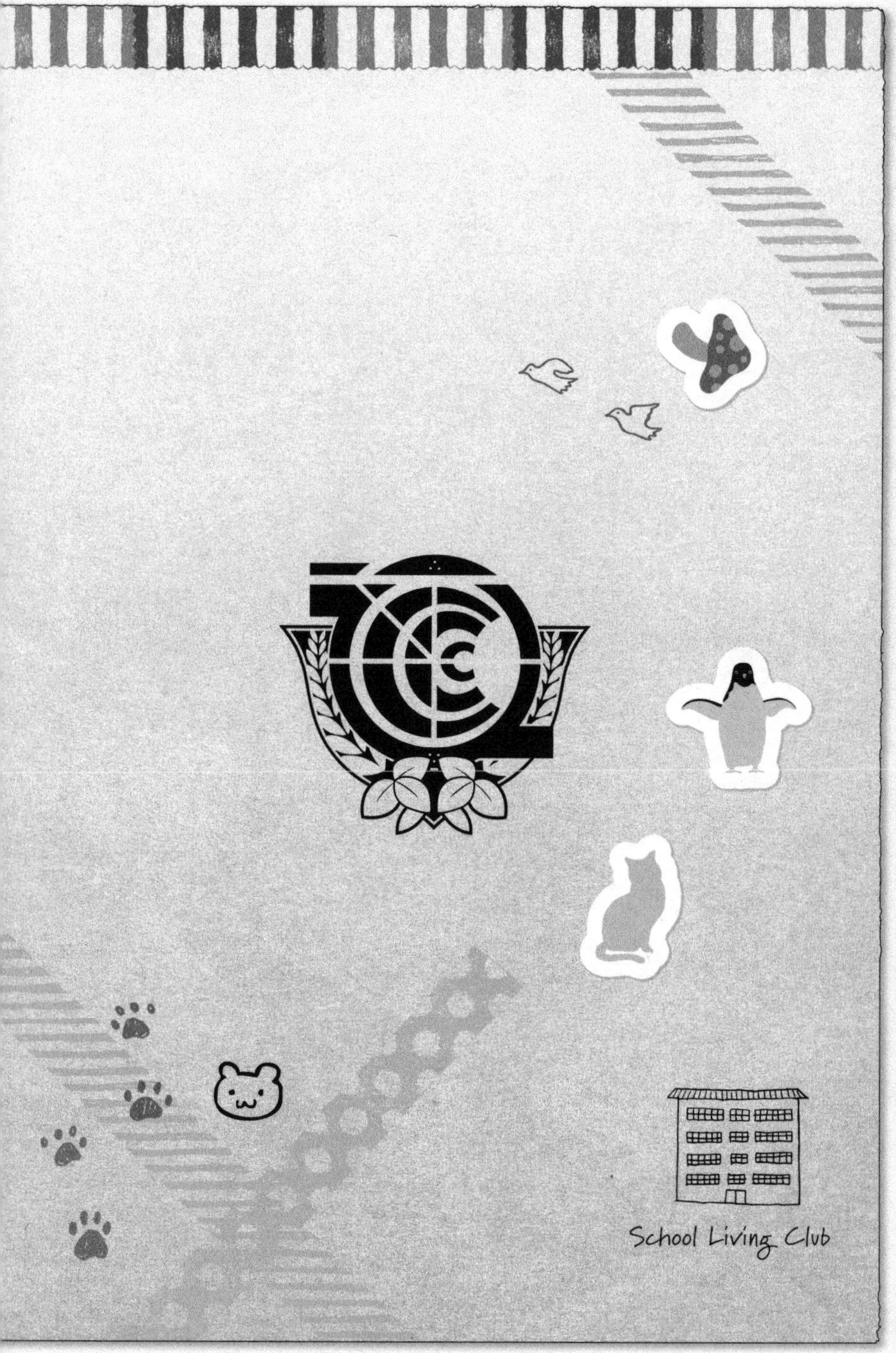
School Living Club

When I was little, I'd be walking around town in the afternoon during summer break, and sometimes I wouldn't see anyone else around for just a moment. I'd imagine that everyone had disappeared from town, and I'd think that I really wanted to have the entire town to myself, just like that.

I could stand around reading manga at the bookstore as much as I wanted. I could play as many video games as I wanted, and when I was hungry, I could go to the convenience store or the grocery store and just open snacks and cans of stuff. I could sleep wherever and whenever I wanted.

Doesn't that sound kind of nice? And if you had some like-minded friends with you, it would be the best.

So because of that (?), this time, we had a field trip. They went out to a shopping mall in this installment. Please look forward to the next volume of *School-Live!* with a new club member.

And thank you to everyone who picked up this book.

Thank you.

Norimitsu Kaihou

Look forward to next time, when Yuki becomes a senpai!

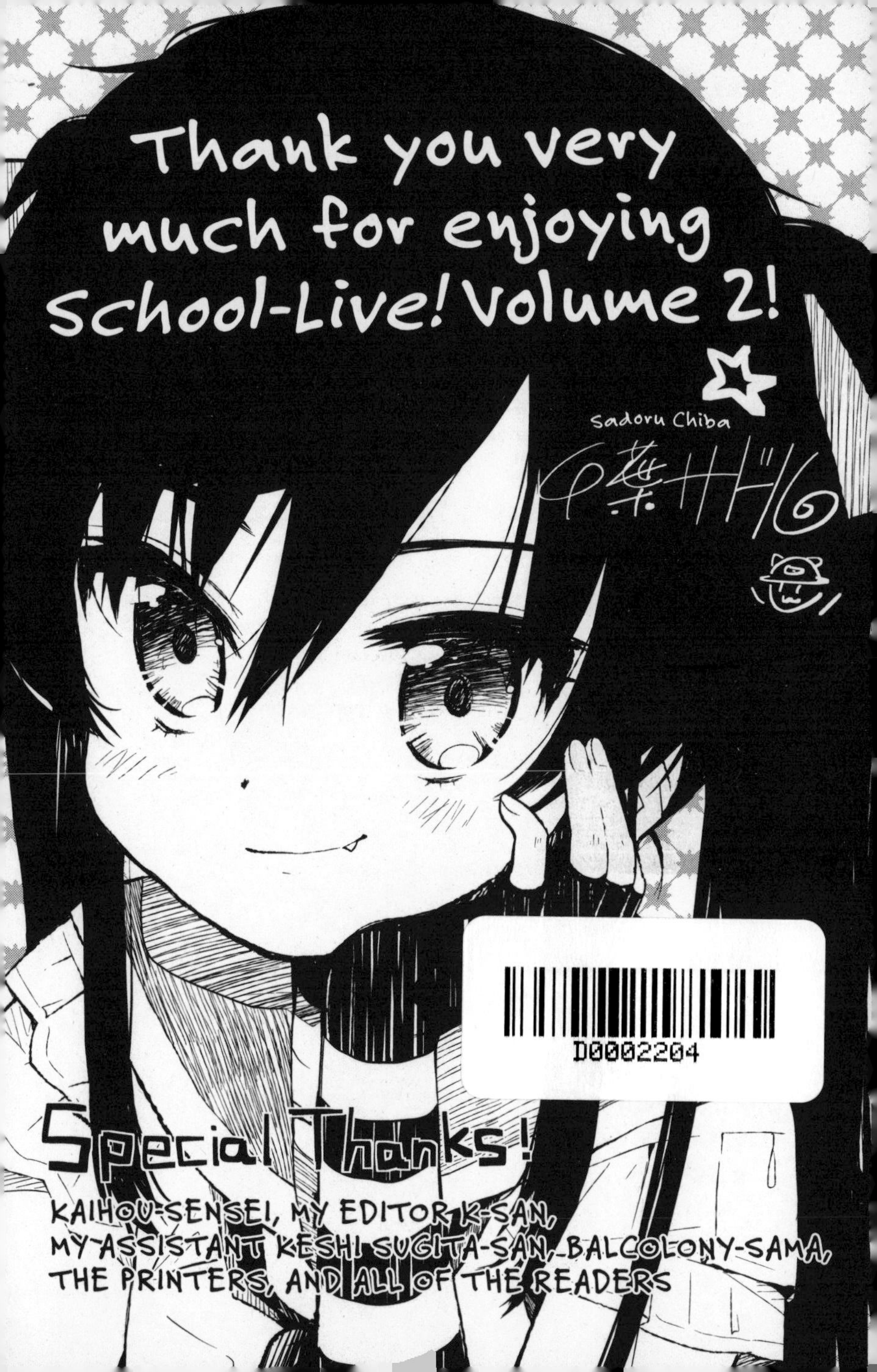
Thank you very much for enjoying School-Live! Volume 2!
Sadoru Chiba
Special Thanks!
KAIHOU-SENSEI, MY EDITOR K-SAN, MY ASSISTANT KESHI SUGITA-SAN, BALCOLONY-SAMA, THE PRINTERS, AND ALL OF THE READERS